D0338441

Codex 632

Codex 632

THE SECRET IDENTITY
OF CHRISTOPHER COLUMBUS:
A NOVEL

José Rodrigues dos Santos

TRANSLATED FROM THE PORTUGUESE
BY ALISON ENTREKIN

wm

WILLIAM MORROW
An Imprint of HarperCollins*Publishers*

Originally published in Portuguese as *O Codex 632* by Gradiva in Portugal in 2005.

HarperCollins books may be purchased for educational, business, or sales promotional use. For information please write: Special Markets Department, HarperCollins Publishers, 10 East 53rd Street, New York, NY 10022.

FIRST EDITION

Designed by Gretchen Achilles

Library of Congress Cataloging-in-Publication Data has been applied for.

ISBN 978-0-06-117318-9

08 09 10 11 12 WBC/RRD 10 9 8 7 6 5 4 3 2 1

To Florbela, Catarina, and Inês:

my three women

Columbus discovered no isle or key so lonely as himself.

RALPH WALDO EMERSON

Author's Note

All of the books, manuscripts, and documents mentioned in this novel do exist.

Including *Codex 632*.

Prologue

RIO DE JANEIRO

Four.

The old historian couldn't know that he only had four minutes left to live.

The hotel elevator seemed to wait to trap him with wide-open doors. He stepped on and pressed the button for the twelfth floor. As he ascended, he studied himself in the mirror embedded into the elevator's wall. He thought he looked every bit the haggard historian—bald on top, the only hair he had left growing behind his ears and at the back of his head. And it was turning as white as the sparse beard that hid his hollow, deeply wrinkled cheeks. Oblivious to what would soon befall him, he pulled his lips back into a forced smile and studied his crooked teeth, yellow and lusterless, except for the ivory-white false ones.

Three.

The elevator's soft *ding* told him he'd arrived at the twelfth floor. The historian walked down the corridor, turned left, and felt around in his right pocket for his key card. He pushed the card into the slot on the door and a green light came on. He turned the door handle and entered the room.

Two.

A cold, dry blast of air-conditioning stood the hair on the nape of his neck on end. The wall of air felt good after a morning spent outside in the scorching heat. He grabbed a juice from the minibar in the corner of the room and walked to the large window. Sighing, he admired the view of the tall buildings that made up Rio's skyline. Immediately facing him was a small, white, five-story building, on top of which a swimming pool glimmered turquoise under the hot early-afternoon sun. The hills around the city formed a natural barrier between the gray of the urban concrete and the surrounding lush green of the jungle. Atop the tree-covered Corcovado, the city's highest mountain, Christ the Redeemer could be seen in profile, a slender, ivory-colored figure, fragile and tiny, embracing the city from on high, balanced over the abyss. A tuft of white cloud had attached itself to the horizontal beam of the iconic crucifix.

The historian pondered the last several months of his life and the material he had uncovered—his big breakthrough. The historian thought about his next move. What he would do with all that information he had amassed would be crucial. Absolutely crucial. He had to be careful.

One.

The old man lifted the bottle to his mouth and drank. The juice slid down his throat, sweet and cool. Mango was his favorite. The sugar brought out the sweet-tartness of the tropical fruit. The juice bars in Rio squeezed the juice from fresh fruit, peeling it on the spot so it remained fibrous and invigorating. He drank it to the last drop, his eyes shut, slowly, greedily savoring it. When he was finished, he opened his eyes and gazed at the resplendent blue of the swimming pool on the next building, a satisfied look on his face. That was the last thing he saw.

Pain.

A sharpness shot through his chest. He convulsed, doubled over, seizing in an uncontrollable spasm. The pain was unbearable. He fell to the ground, stricken. His eyes rolled back until they fixed a glassy stare on the ceiling. He lay there belly up, arms and legs flung wide, his body shaking in a last contraction.

His eyes never closed. His discovery, silent once more.

Chapter 1

LISBON

Had someone told Thomas Noronha, that morning, that the next few months would take him all over the world and into the unraveling of a five-hundred-year-old conspiracy, complete with stories of seafaring adventures during the Age of Discovery, royal espionage between the first two global superpowers, and the esoteric world of Kabbalah and the Knights Templar, he wouldn't have believed it. As it turned out, he was to experience all of it.

He parked in the university garage, still semi-deserted at nine thirty. Students were gathered in the hall, engrossed in their morning chatter, and as he passed, he heard excited whispering among some of the girls—Thomas was a tall, good-looking thirty-five-year-old with sparkling green eyes, his most striking inheritance from his beautiful French great-grandmother. He opened the door of room T9, flipped a series of switches to turn on all the lights, and placed his briefcase on the desk.

Students poured in and spread through the small room in groups, sitting more or less in their habitual places next to their usual companions. Thomas took his notes out of his briefcase and sat down, waiting for the students to get settled and for the late ones to stream in. He studied their faces—almost all girls—some looking still sleepy, some caffeinated and perky.

After a few minutes, he stood and greeted the class. "Well, good morning."

"Good morning," they chorused.

"In our last meeting," Thomas began, pacing a few steps in front of the first row of desks, "we examined a stele to the god Marduk and analyzed the symbols of Akkad, Assyria, and Babylonia. We then discussed the Egyptians and the hieroglyphs, reading passages from the *Book of the Dead*, and the inscriptions in the temple of Karnak and on a series of papyri. To conclude our discussion of Egypt, today we are going to learn how the hieroglyphs were deciphered." He stopped pacing and looked around. "Does anyone have any idea?"

The students smiled, accustomed to the clumsy way their teacher invited them to participate in the lesson.

"The Rosetta stone," someone called out.

"Yes," said Thomas, "the Rosetta stone did play a role, but we can't say it was the only factor. Nor was it, if you will, the most important."

The students looked surprised. The student who had responded to the question looked dejected over not having given the perfect answer. A few others fidgeted in their seats.

"So it wasn't the Rosetta stone that provided the key to deciphering the hieroglyphics?" asked a short, chubby girl with glasses, one of the most attentive, engaged members of the class.

Thomas smiled. Depreciating the importance of the Rosetta stone had produced the desired effect. It had woken up the class.

"It helped," he said. "But there was much more than that. As you know, for centuries the hieroglyphics were a great mystery. The first ones date back to three thousand years before Christ. Hieroglyphics fell out of use at the end of the fourth century A.D. and after just one generation, nobody could read them. Does anyone know why?"

The class was silent.

"The Egyptians got amnesia?" joked one of the few young men in the class.

"Because of the Christian Church," explained Thomas with a

strained smile. "The Christians didn't let the Egyptians use their hieroglyphics. They wanted to cut them off from their pagan past, making them forget their numerous gods. It was such a drastic measure that knowledge of the ancient form of writing simply disappeared, became history in the blink of an eye. Interest in the hieroglyphics died down and was only rekindled at the end of the sixteenth century, when Pope Sixtus V, influenced by a mysterious book entitled *Hypnerotomachia Poliphili* by Francesco Colonna, had Egyptian obelisks placed on Rome's new street corners."

Thomas's lecture was interrupted by the creaking of the classroom door. A young woman walked into the room, and Thomas glanced at her distractedly. He hesitated, fixing his attention on the newcomer. He'd never seen her before. She had blond hair, clear turquoise-blue eyes, and creamy white skin. She made her way to the last row and sat down, isolated from everyone. She walked with an air of confidence that seemed to fully acknowledge her radiant beauty.

After a moment, Thomas continued. "Scholars began trying to decipher the hieroglyphics, but they got nowhere. When Napoleon invaded Egypt, he had a team of historians and scientists follow him, with the mission of mapping, registering, and measuring everything they found. This team reached Egypt in 1798, and the following year they were summoned by the soldiers stationed at Fort Julien, in the Nile Delta, to examine an object they had found in the city of Rosetta.

"The soldiers had been given the task of demolishing a wall in the fort they were occupying, and there they discovered a stone bearing three types of inscription."

Thomas concluded that the young woman was a foreigner—hair that fair was rare in Portugal.

"The French scientists looked at the stone and identified Greek characters, demotic script, and hieroglyphics. They came to the conclusion that it was the same text written in three languages and immediately realized the importance of the discovery.

"Then British troops moved into Egypt and defeated the French, and the stone, which was supposed to be sent to Paris, ended up at the

British Museum. The translation from the Greek revealed that the stone contained a decree by a council of Egyptian priests, recording the benefits that the pharaoh Ptolemy had offered the Egyptian people and the honors that the priests had granted the pharaoh in exchange.

"The English concluded that if the other two inscriptions contained the same text, it wouldn't be difficult to decipher the demotic script. But there were three problems." Thomas held up his thumb. "First of all, it was damaged. The Greek text was relatively intact, but there were important parts missing from the demotic and especially the hieroglyphic sections. Half the lines in the hieroglyphic text had disappeared, and the remaining fourteen lines were severely deteriorated."

He held up his index finger. "Then there was the problem that the two texts to be deciphered were written in Egyptian, a language believed not to have been spoken for at least eight centuries. The English were able to tell which hieroglyphics corresponded to certain Greek words, but they didn't know what those words sounded like."

He held up a third finger. "Finally, scholars had this very ingrained idea that the hieroglyphics were semagrams, each symbol representing a complete idea, instead of phonograms, wherein each symbol represents a sound, as is the case with our phonetic alphabet."

"So how did they decipher the hieroglyphics?" someone called out.

"The first crack in the mystery was made by a talented Englishman named Thomas Young. Young, by the age of fourteen, had already studied Greek, Latin, Italian, Hebrew, Chaldean, Syriac, Persian, Arabic, Ethiopian, Turkish, and . . . um . . . and . . . let me see . . ."

"Chinish?" offered the class jester.

There was laughter all around.

"Samaritan," remembered Thomas.

"Ah, then if he knew Samaritan, he must have been a nice guy," insisted the jester, encouraged by his success. "A good Samaritan."

More laughter. Thomas ignored him and continued.

"Well, Young took a copy of the three Rosetta stone inscriptions with him on his summer holiday in 1814. He began to study them in detail, and something caught his attention. It was a set of hieroglyphics in a cartouche, a kind of ring. He assumed that the purpose of the cartouche was to highlight something of great importance. Now, from the Greek text he knew that the section was about the pharaoh Ptolemy, and he put two and two together and came to the conclusion that the cartouche contained the name Ptolemy and was a way of underlining the pharaoh's importance. Then he did something revolutionary.

"Instead of working from the assumption that the writing was solely ideographic, he thought that the word might be written phonetically and began to make conjectures about the sound of each hieroglyph within the cartouche." Thomas hurried over to the whiteboard and drew a square. "He presumed that this symbol, the first in the cartouche, corresponded to the first sound in the pharaoh's name, which was *p*."

Next to it Thomas drew a half-circle with the flat side facing down. "He figured that this symbol, the second in the cartouche, was a *t*."

He drew a lion lying in profile. "He thought that this little lion represented an *l*." Now Thomas sketched a new symbol on the whiteboard, this one composed of two parallel horizontal lines joined at the left. "Here he believed he had found an *m*." He drew two vertical knives side by side. "He thought these knives were an *i*." Finally, an upside-down hook. "And this symbol, he thought was *os*." He turned to look at the class.

"Do you see?" He pointed at the sketches on the whiteboard, spelling them out. "*P, t, l, m, i, os*. Ptlmios. Ptolemy." He turned to the students and smiled at the looks of fascination spreading over their fresh faces.

"We now know that he was right about most of the sounds," Thomas continued, moving away from the board and over to the first row. "And this, my dear friends, is where the role of the Rosetta stone ended." He allowed the idea to sink in. "It was a very important first step, true, but there was still much to be done. Having accomplished the first reading of a hieroglyph, Thomas Young went looking for confirmations. He discovered another cartouche in the temple of Karnak, in Thebes, and deduced that it was the name of a Ptolemaic queen, Berenice. He was also right about the sounds here. The problem was that Young believed that these phonetic transcriptions only applied to foreign names, as was the case with the Ptolemaic dynasty, descended from a general of Alexander the Great, and did not carry through with this line of thought. As a result, the code was not cracked, just scratched."

"What made him think only foreign names were written phonetically?"

Thomas hesitated, considering the best way to answer.

"Well, it's like Chinese," he said finally. "Does anyone here speak Chinese?"

Silence.

"That's okay." He smiled. "Chinese writing is ideographic. The problem with this kind of writing is that every time a new word appears, a new character must be invented. Eventually, they'd end up with thousands and thousands of characters, which would be impossible to memorize. Faced with this problem, what did they do?"

"They took ginkgo biloba!" suggested the joker.

"They phoneticized their writing," said Thomas, ignoring him. "Or actually, they kept the old ideographic symbols, but when new works appeared they used the existing symbols phonetically." He looked around and saw that the idea had been absorbed. "This was what Young thought had happened with the Egyptians."

"So, it was Young who sorted out the whole thing."

"Actually, no," said Thomas. "It was the Frenchman Jean-François Champollion."

Thomas looked at the blonde sitting at the back of the classroom and wondered what she was doing there. She looked German, or perhaps Dutch. She appeared rapt with attention, her posture as inquisitive as the steely look in her eyes.

"Our friend Champollion used Young's approach on other cartouches containing the names Ptolemy and Cleopatra, with good results. He also deciphered a reference to Alexander the Great. The problem was that they were all names with foreign origins, which served to cement his conviction that this phonetic reading applied only to words that were not in the traditional Egyptian lexicon. Everything changed in September 1822."

He paused for dramatic effect.

"Around 1822, Champollion gained access to reliefs in the temple in Abu Simbel, with cartouches dating back to before the Greco-Roman period, which meant that none of the names in them could be of foreign origin. After scrutinizing all of the hieroglyphs, he decided to concentrate on a particular cartouche."

Thomas went to the whiteboard and drew four hieroglyphs inside a cartouche. "The first two hieroglyphs in this cartouche were unknown, but the last two could be found in two others that he had already come across: the one containing 'Ptlmios' and the one containing 'Alksentr,' or Alexander." He pointed at the last hieroglyph. "In these, this symbol corresponded to *s*. Champollion thus assumed he had deciphered the last two sounds of the Abu Simbel cartouche." Thomas wrote the corresponding sounds from the Latin alphabet on the whiteboard, leaving two question marks in the place of the first two hieroglyphs. The white surface showed an enigmatic *?-?-s-s*. He turned back to the class, pointing at the two question marks on the board.

"The first two hieroglyphs were still missing. What might they be? What did they sound like?" He pointed at the first one. "Looking carefully at this round hieroglyph, with a dot in the middle, Champollion thought it looked like the sun. Working from this hypothesis, he tried to imagine the corresponding sound. He remembered that in Coptic, *sun* is pronounced 'ra,' and decided to put *ra* in the place of the first question mark." He rubbed out the first question mark and wrote *ra* in its place, leaving *ra-?-s-s* on the whiteboard.

"Now what? How to fill the second question mark? Champollion mulled it over and came to the conclusion that it should be something very simple. Whatever the word was, the fact that it was in a cartouche was a strong indication that he was dealing with a pharaoh's name. Now, what pharaoh had a name starting with *ra* and ending with double *s*?"

The question hung in the silent classroom.

"It was at this point that an idea popped into his head—a bold, extraordinary, decisive idea." One last pause to feed his students' expectations. "Why not an *m*?"

Thomas returned to the board, erased the question mark, and wrote *m* in its place.

"Ramses. And just like that, with a breakthrough in scholarship, the course of our understanding our own global history was altered."

Chapter 2

The room burst into a clamor of voices when Thomas dismissed the class. Chairs were pushed back, notebooks closed, and students stood around chatting or headed for the door. As usual, some converged on him as he gathered up his materials.

"Professor, I have a part-time job and wasn't able to make it to the last few classes. Has the final exam been set?"

"Yes, it will be given during the last class."

"What day is that?"

"I don't know off the top of my head. Check your syllabus."

"And what will it be like?"

"It'll be a practical exam." Thomas went back to organizing his briefcase. "You'll have to analyze documents and decipher ancient texts."

"Hieroglyphics?"

"Yes, but there'll be other things too. You might have to analyze Sumerian tablets with cuneiform script, Greek inscriptions, Hebrew and Aramaic texts, or much simpler things, like medieval and sixteenth-century manuscripts."

The student's mouth dropped open.

"Just kidding," said Thomas, laughing. "Just a few bits and pieces—"

"But I don't know this stuff," she whined, looking panicked.

Thomas looked at her. "That's why you're taking this course, isn't it?" he said, raising his eyebrows. "To learn."

He realized that the blonde had come to the front of the room and was waiting her turn to speak with him. The student handed him a piece of paper. "It's for you to sign," she finally said.

Thomas signed it absentmindedly, distracted by the blonde. "What is this, exactly?" he suddenly asked, realizing he had no idea what he'd just signed.

"I have to take this to work to show that I had to miss a shift to come to class."

He nodded and watched her leave, befuddled over what the world had come to.

Only two students remained in front of him, a young woman with black curly hair and the blonde. He addressed the dark-haired student first, so he'd have more time to speak with the newcomer.

"Hi, Professor. When did the Egyptian scribes use rebuses?"

"It depends on the context," answered Thomas. "The Egyptian scribes had flexible rules. They used rebuses to contract words or achieve double meanings."

"Thanks, Professor."

"See you next week."

Finally he would be able to talk to her, without anyone else in the room. She must be used to this from men, he thought. He felt unbalanced by her beauty and her height—she was almost as tall as he was—but didn't allow himself to feel intimidated. He smiled and she smiled back. "Hi," he said.

"Good morning, Professor." She had an exotic accent. "I'm new here."

Thomas chuckled to himself. "That I'd already noticed. What's your name?"

"Lena Lindholm."

"Lena?" He feigned surprise, as if he'd only just noticed that there was something different about her. "That's the diminutive of Helena in Portuguese. . . ."

She giggled discreetly. "Yes, but I'm Swedish."

"Aaaahh!" he exclaimed. "Of course." He hesitated, searching for words. "Let me see . . . um . . . *hej, trevligt att träffas!*"

Lena's eyes widened. "I beg your pardon?" she answered, looking pleasantly surprised. *"Talar du svenska?"*

Thomas shook his head. *"Jag talar inte svenska,"* he said, smiling. "That's all the Swedish I know." He shrugged, as if to beg forgiveness. *"Förlat."*

She looked at him in admiration. "Not bad, not bad. Your accent needs a few tweaks. It should be more singsong—otherwise you'll sound Danish. Where did you learn?"

"When I was a student I spent four days in Malmö. I picked up a thing or two. I know how to ask, *Var är toaletten?*"

She laughed. *"Hur mycket kostar det?"*

"Äppelkaka med vaniljsås."

This last phrase made her groan. "Professor, don't remind me about *äppelkaka.*"

"Why not?"

She ran her tongue across her fleshy pink lips. "It's delicious. I miss it so much. . . ."

He laughed, trying to hide the reaction she provoked in him. "I'm sorry, *kaka* is an odd word for dessert. *Caca* means 'crap' in Portuguese."

"It's called *kaka,* it's true, but the apple's so sweet." Lena closed her eyes and looked as though she were remembering the first time she'd eaten the dessert.

Thomas was intrigued by her. He was accustomed to being around beautiful young students—he was a married man and had not strayed. Yet, for a brief moment, he imagined himself pulling her toward him, kissing her, and he had to make an effort to squelch the sexual appetite she awoke in him. He cleared his throat with a raspy *hmm-hmm.*

"Tell me, what's your name again?"

"Lena."

"Ah, Lena." He hesitated. "Tell me, Lena. Where did you learn to speak Portuguese so well?"

"My dad was ambassador to Angola, and I lived there for five years."

Thomas closed his briefcase and straightened up. "I see. Did you like it?"

"Loved it. We had a house in Miramar and spent the weekends in Mussulo. It was a dream of a life."

"What part of Angola was that in?"

She looked at him in surprise, as if it was odd to find someone from Portugal unfamiliar with these places. "Well, in Luanda, of course. Miramar was our neighborhood, with a view of the beach, the fort, and the island. And Mussulo is an island south of Luanda. Haven't you been there?"

"No, I've never been to Angola."

"What a shame."

Thomas headed for the door, motioning for her to follow him. Lena came closer. She was about six feet tall. Her soft blue pullover was a perfect complement to her blue eyes and the blond curly hair that tumbled about her shoulders. Thomas struggled not to stare below her neckline.

"So, tell me what brings you to my class," he asked, stepping aside to let her through the doorway first.

"I'm here with the Erasmus Program," she said, moving ahead of him.

"I beg your pardon?" He gulped.

"I'm here with the Erasmus Program," she repeated, turning to look at him.

They walked into the main hall, and she followed him up the stairs. "Erasmus Program?"

"Yes. You're familiar with it, aren't you?"

Thomas shook his head. "Ah, yes. Of course . . . Erasmus." He hesitated, finally grasping what she was saying. "Ah! Then you're here with the Erasmus Program."

She gave a little smile, intrigued by his awkwardness. She had caught on to how nervous she made him. "Yes, that's what I've been telling you."

Erasmus was a European university exchange program, in which students could study at other EU universities for up to one school year. Most of the foreign students who came to the New University of Lisbon's History Department were Spanish, though a few came from northern Europe.

"What university are you from? I wasn't aware you'd be joining us."

"Stockholm."

"Are you studying history?"

"Yes."

They climbed three flights of stairs before they got to his office. Thomas stopped and rummaged in his pocket for the key.

"And why did you choose to come to Portugal?"

"For two reasons," said Lena. "First, because of the language. I speak and read Portuguese fluently, so it isn't difficult for me to follow the lectures. Writing is a little harder."

"If you find it difficult to write in Portuguese, you can always write in English. That's not a problem." He put the key in the lock. "What's the second reason?"

She stopped behind him. "I'm thinking about writing my dissertation on the great discovery voyages. There were the voyages of the Vikings, on the one hand, and I'd like to establish parallels with the Portuguese voyages of discoveries."

The door swung open and Thomas invited her in with a courteous gesture. The office was messy, with piles of exams to grade and papers scattered around the tables and on the floor.

"The Portuguese discoveries are a vast subject," said Thomas, turning his face toward the window to receive the winter sun that spilled in from outside. "Do you know the amount of work you're about to take on?"

"There is no eel so small but it hopes to become a whale."

"What?"

"It's a Swedish proverb. It means that I am more than willing to work hard."

Thomas smiled. "I'm sure you are, but it's important that you define your area of investigation. Exactly what period are you thinking about studying?"

"I want to look at everything that happened up to Vasco da Gama's voyage in 1498. I've been studying and preparing to come here for a year." Her eyes widened. "Do you think I'll be allowed to consult the original journals? Those written by the ship chroniclers who recorded everything?"

"Who? Zurara and company?"

"Yes."

Thomas sighed.

"It'll be difficult. The original texts are precious—fragile relics that the libraries keep zealously protected." He looked pensive. "But you can consult facsimiles and copies. It's almost the same thing."

"Ah, but I want to see the originals!" She gazed at him with pleading blue eyes and almost seemed to pout. "Could you help me? Please . . ."

Thomas fidgeted. "Well, I suppose I could try."

"Great!" she exclaimed, flashing a charming smile.

Thomas was vaguely aware that he had been manipulated, but he was so enchanted by her that he didn't care. "But can you read sixteenth-century Portuguese?"

"A thief will find the grail faster than a sexton."

"What?"

She laughed at Thomas's befuddled expression. "It's another Swedish proverb. It means, where there's a will, there's a way."

"I'm sure there is, but the question remains," he insisted. "Can you read the Portuguese written at that time, with its complicated calligraphy?"

"Not exactly."

"Then what use is it to have access to the texts?"

Lena smiled mischievously, with the confidence of someone who was rarely turned down. "I'm sure you'll give me a helping hand."

Thomas was aware that her drafting him into action would only result in exasperation. If there was one thing he knew about teaching at a university, it was to never get close to his female students. Why, he wondered to himself, was Lena affecting him so? Still, his interest in her was undeniable. There was just something about her that made him exceedingly curious to know more. Much more.

Chapter 3

The afternoon was taken up by a history department meeting, replete with the usual intrigues, political maneuvers, and interminable agenda items. By the time Thomas got home, night had fallen and Constance and Margarida were already halfway through dinner: fried hamburger with spaghetti and ketchup, his daughter's favorite. He hung up his coat, kissed them both, and sat down to eat.

"Hamburger and spaghetti again, I'm shocked," he said dryly.

Constance looked at him and shrugged. "It makes her happy."

"Spaghetti yummy!" burbled Margarida cheerfully, noisily sucking up strands of pasta.

"Well, if she's happy, I'm happy," Thomas said, resigned, as he dished the food onto his plate. He looked at his daughter and stroked her straight, black hair. "Hi, pumpkin. What did you learn today?"

"*A* for apple. *B* for book."

"But remember you learned that last year? Did you learn anything new today?"

"*C* for cat. *D* for dog."

"See that?" he said, turning to his wife. "She's regressing."

"I know," Constance said. "I've requested a meeting with the principal next week."

"*E* for egg."

A year earlier, Margarida had started public school where she had the help of a special-education teacher who worked as a kind of trainer, always pushing her. Unfortunately, budget cuts had made it impossible for him to remain at the school, leaving all of the special needs students without any support—only a regular teacher. Although Margarida was already forgetting much of what she had learned the year before, it was clearly going to be difficult convincing the school that a regular teacher wasn't adequate.

Thomas tried to see his daughter as a stranger would, with her round face, short limbs, almond-shaped eyes, and fine, dark hair. Did the other kids call her names? He was sure they did. A child's mindless cruelty.

He recalled that spring morning nine years ago, in the maternity ward. Overflowing with joy, running to the room holding a bunch of honeysuckles, hugging his wife, and kissing his newborn daughter. He kissed her as if she were a treasure, and was moved to see her bundled up in a blanket, all pink cheeks and sweet soft skin. She looked like a tiny, sleeping Buddha, so wise and peaceful.

That moment of pure, transcendent, celestial happiness didn't last more than half an hour. After twenty minutes, the doctor came into the room and called him into her office with a discreet wave. Her expression was dour as she explained that it looked as though Margarida may have Down syndrome, or trisomy 21.

It was as if he'd been punched in the stomach. The ground seemed to open under his feet, and he was plunged into endless darkness. When he told his wife, she reacted with profound silence and refused to talk about it for a long time; her plans for her daughter had crumbled. There was still a week of tenuous hope, while the karyotype analysis was carried out, the genetic test that would remove all doubt. Besides, Thomas thought she had some of his maternal grandmother's facial expressions, and Constance detected something of her aunt in her nose. The doctors must have made a mistake, they reasoned. But a phone call eight days later confirmed it.

It was a brutal shock. They had spent months projecting their hopes onto their daughter, nursing dreams of the girl who was going to bring new meaning to their lives. Now all that was left was incredulousness, a feeling of injustice, a maelstrom of indignation. It was the fault of the obstetrician who hadn't noticed anything, of the hospitals that weren't prepared for such situations, of the politicians who didn't give a damn about people's real problems; it was, in short, everyone's fault but theirs.

Then came a sense of loss, deep pain, and an insurmountable feeling of guilt. They lay awake at night asking themselves what they had done wrong, questioning their responsibility, searching for errors, faults, reasons, for the meaning of it all.

Eventually, and as was necessary, their concerns stopped revolving around themselves and returned to their daughter. They wondered about her future. How would she mature? Would she be happy? What if something happened to them—who would take care of her? Sometimes they found themselves wishing for an act of God, divine charity, of mercy—so gruesome a secret they could not even share it with each other. Such a thing might spare her so much unnecessary suffering.

But with a simple yawn from the baby, an exchange of looks, a small gesture, everything transformed. As if with the wave of a magic wand, they recognized Margarida as their daughter and loved her fiercely. Before long they concentrated all of their energy on her. When doctors said her heart might have a defect, their lives became a whirlwind of institutes, hospitals, clinics, and an endless stream of exams and tests.

Thomas had managed to finish his Ph.D. in history, though it was extremely challenging to study Renaissance cryptanalysis, with Alberti, Porta, and Vigenère's complex ciphers, amidst so many trips to doctors. There wasn't enough money; Thomas's university salary and what Constance made teaching art at a high school was barely enough to cover their daily expenses. So much stress had inevitable consequences in their marriage. Immersed in their problems, they rarely touched each other anymore. They didn't have time. Money and time. There was never enough of either, and their absence had taken its toll on their relationship. They were cordial and cared for each other, but theirs was a marriage built on habit and duty. Gone were the exciting first years, and gone was the life they had once gleefully imagined living. They both knew it, but no alternative had ever presented itself. Resigned, they continued living as they were supposed to.

Thomas took a bite of hamburger and a sip of Alentejo red. By now Margarida had finished her dessert, slices of peeled apple, and got up to clear the table.

"Hey, Margarida, you can clear it later, okay?" he said.

"No," she said firmly, loading the dirty dishes into the dishwasher. "Have to clean, have to clean!"

"You can clean later."

"No. It's filthy, yucky. Have to clean!"

"This girl's going to end up opening a cleaning service," said Thomas with a chuckle, clutching his plate so she couldn't take it away.

Cleaning and tidying were Margarida's primary fixations. Wherever there was a spot of dirt, there she was, righteous and valiant, to fight it. This had put her parents in some pretty embarrassing situations at friends' houses; at the sight of a simple cobweb or some dust on the furniture, Margarida would screech and point an accusing finger, saying it was filthy. She denounced dirt with such heartfelt repugnance that the startled hosts launched monumental cleaning operations before inviting the Noronha family back to their home.

Margarida went to bed after dinner. Thomas brushed her teeth and Constance helped her put her pajamas on, then Thomas got her things ready for the next day while Constance told her a bedtime story. This time it was "Puss-in-Boots." When she fell asleep, they went to stretch out on the living room sofa to relax a bit from the toils of the day.

"I'm dead on my feet," said Constance, her eyes lost on the ceiling. "Beat."

The living room was small but tastefully decorated. Colorful abstracts painted by Constance when she was a university student hung on the walls. Vases were scattered about the light beech furniture, with bright red flowers poking out from among thick green leaves.

"What flowers are these?" asked Thomas.

"Camellias."

He leaned over a vase on the coffee table and sniffed the luxuriant petals. "They don't smell like anything," he observed, intrigued.

"Of course they don't, silly," said Constance, laughing. "They're camellias. They don't have any fragrance."

"Ah," said Thomas. He leaned back and stroked Constance's palm. "Tell me about camellias."

Constance was crazy about flowers. Oddly, that passion was one of the things that had brought them together as students. Thomas loved riddles and word games, symbols and secret messages, and he was always deciphering codes and ciphers. When they met, Constance opened the door for him into a new world of symbology, that of flowers. She taught him about the women in Turkish harems who had used flowers to contact the outside world, through a brilliant floral code. That practice gave rise to floriography, a system of symbols that became immensely popular in the nineteenth century, aligning the original Turkish meanings with ancient mythology and traditional folklore. To Thomas's delight, flowers, which had once been lovely to look at but nothing more, began to reveal hidden meanings, secretly expressing emotions their bearer or wearer could not. For example, it was imprudent if not unthinkable for a man to tell a woman on their first date that he was in love with her, but it was acceptable for him to give her a bunch of gloxinias, symbols of love at first sight.

Floriography was incorporated in jewelry making, Pre-Raphaelite art, and fashion. The mantle used by Queen Elizabeth II at her coronation was embroidered with olive branches and wheat stalks in the hope that her reign would be one of peace and abundance. Constance, a lover of both the human and natural arts, became a specialist in reading the subliminal meanings in flowers.

"Camellias came from China, where they were greatly appreciated," she explained now, pushing his hair back. "They were introduced to the West by Alexandre Dumas the Younger, who wrote *La Dame aux camélias,* a novel based on the true story of a nineteenth-century Parisian courtesan by the name of Marie du Plessis. Apparently Mademoiselle was allergic to floral perfumes and chose camellias precisely because they had no fragrance." She gave Thomas a mischievous look. "You know what a courtesan is, I assume."

"My *dear,* I am a historian."

"Well, every day Mademoiselle du Plessis wore a bouquet of camellias—white for twenty-five days, to signal her availability, and red on the others, to indicate she was indisposed."

"Oh," exclaimed Thomas, feigning disappointment.

"Verdi was inspired by Dumas's novel and wrote *La Traviata,* slightly adapting the story. In Verdi's opera, the heroine is forced to sell her jewels and wears camellias instead."

"Oh dear," said Thomas with a playful smile. "The poor creature." He glanced at the flowers his wife had placed around the living room. "So judging from the red camellias you bought, there won't be anything for anyone today."

"You're right," said Constance with a sigh. "I'm exhausted."

Thomas looked at his wife. She still carried with her the melancholic air that had seduced him when they met at the School of Fine Arts. He was studying history at the New University of Lisbon at the time, and a friend waxed poetic about the beauty of the girls who studied fine arts. "True masterpieces," joked Augusto in the university courtyard after lunch, early one hot spring afternoon, pleased with his wit. "I'm telling you. One day I'll take you."

Dragged along by his friend, Thomas turned up at the Fine Arts cafeteria one day for lunch and confirmed the rumor; there was no school in Lisbon where beauty was as cultivated. They tried to strike up a conversation with some elegant, well-dressed blondes but were snubbed. After paying, they wandered around with their trays, looking lost, trying to find the best place to sit. They chose a table by the window, partially occupied by three young women, one of whom was a pristine brunette. "Nature is generous," observed Augusto with a wink, leading his friend over.

The brunette had taken an interest in Thomas's green eyes, but he gave his full attention to one of her friends, a girl with milk-white skin, a speckling of freckles on her nose, and brown eyes that held a dreamy, far-off expression. Her soft, languid gestures bespoke a mild, nostalgic nature, although this, as he discovered with time, was sheer illusion. Beneath Constance's sweet demeanor was a volcano; behind the tame cat, an implacable lion. He didn't leave until he'd gotten her phone number. Two weeks later, and after giving her his first honeysuckles, having been informed that they promised undying love, Thomas kissed Constance at Oeiras Station and they walked along the vast sands of Carcavelos Beach holding hands.

This memory of the past became Margarida's face, as if Thomas had traveled forward in time to the present; his daughter's photograph smiled at him from a picture frame next to a vase of camellias.

"We have to take her to Dr. Oliveira next week."

"These visits to the doctor wear me out," said Thomas.

"They wear her out too," said his wife. "Don't forget that she'll have to go in for surgery sometime soon."

"Don't remind me."

"Look, Thomas, like it or not, you're going to have to help me with this."

"Okay, okay."

"It's just that I'm tired of doing it all alone. She needs help and so do I. You are her father." Thomas felt cornered. His wife was overburdened with Margarida's problems, and no matter how hard he tried, he seemed incapable of resolving even half of the things that Constance, with her practicality, resolved all the time.

"I'm sorry. Don't worry. I'll go see Dr. Oliveira with you."

Constance looked calmer. She leaned back on the sofa and yawned. "Time for bed," she said, getting up. "Are you going to stay here?"

"For a bit. I'm going to read awhile."

She leaned over, kissed him lightly on the lips, and left, the warm smell of her Chanel No. 5 lingering. Thomas stood up and walked to the bookcase, where he stood, scratching his head, unsure what to read. As soon as he took down *Selected Tales* by Edgar Allan Poe—he wanted to reread "The Gold Bug"—his cell phone rang.

"Hello?"

"May I speak with Mr. Noronha?"

It was Brazilian Portuguese spoken, Thomas guessed, by a native speaker of English. Judging from his nasal tone, Thomas figured the speaker was American.

"Speaking. Who is it?"

"My name is Nelson Moliarti, and I'm an adviser on the executive board of the Americas History Foundation. I'm calling from New York. How are you?"

"Fine, thanks."

"Sorry for calling so late. Is this a bad time?"

"No, not at all."

"Oh, good," he said. "I don't know if you're familiar with our foundation . . ." He paused, as if waiting for confirmation.

"No, sorry."

"That's okay. We're a nonprofit organization that provides support for research on the history of the Americas. We're based in New York and currently have a massive project under way, but unfortunately we've run into a tricky problem that threatens our work. The executive board has asked me to find a solution, which I've been working on for the last two weeks. Half an hour ago I presented my recommendation. It was accepted, and that's why I'm calling you."

There was a pause.

"Yes?" Thomas said.

"Mr. Noronha?"

"Yes, yes, I'm here."

"You're the solution."

"What?"

"You're the solution to our problem. How quickly do you think you could fly to New York?"

Chapter 4

NEW YORK

A cloud of steam blew up from the ground, as if expelled by a volcano hidden under the street, and quickly dissolved into the cold night air. It brought with it the nauseating smell of fried food, and Thomas recognized the distinct odor of chow mein. Shrinking into his thin overcoat, burying his hands deep in his pockets, he tried to fend off the freezing wind. New York is unpleasant when the wind pummels the streets, even worse when you're not dressed for it. Thomas learned the hard way.

He had arrived at JFK a few hours earlier. An imposing black limousine, placed at his disposal by the Americas History Foundation, had taken him from the airport to the Waldorf-Astoria, the magnificent Art Deco hotel that occupied an entire block between Lexington and Park avenues. Too excited to properly appreciate the superb details of its decor and architecture, he quickly left his luggage in his room, got a map of the city from the concierge, and headed out, forgoing the services of the limousine.

It was a mistake. Night had already fallen on the extraordinary metropolis. At first, when his body was still warm, the cold hadn't bothered him. He'd felt so at ease that he'd turned onto East Fiftieth

Street, awed by the enormous buildings that grazed the sky. But when he crossed the Avenue of the Americas and reached Seventh Avenue, the cold was beginning to seriously affect him. He'd always heard that the only way to get to know New York was on foot, but no one had told him that this was only true when the weather was mild. And a freezing cold, windy night in New York is something you don't forget. The chill was so intense that everything around him seemed to disappear. His vision blurred. His ears were faring the worst. It was as if they were being hacked with a blade.

The sight of Times Square's cauldron of light spurred him south down to Forty-second, beckoning him with successive explosions of color. It seemed day there, not night; multiple suns expelled the darkness and painted the busy square in bright hues. The traffic was chaotic, and pedestrians dodged cars and one another, some walking with purpose, others just wandering, gaping at the spectacle. Neon flashed from buildings, enormous words paraded across long billboards; giant screens showed advertisements or even television broadcasts. It was a tumultuous panoply of images and colors, an inebriating orgy of light.

Thomas felt his cell phone vibrate in his pocket, then heard it ring. Hating to pull his hand from his pocket, he answered it. "Hello?"

"Mr. Noronha?"

"Yes?"

"This is Nelson Moliarti. How are you? Was your trip okay?"

"Oh, hi. Everything's fine, thanks."

"Has the driver been looking after you?"

"Five-star service."

"And do you like the hotel?"

"Wonderful."

"Have you eaten?"

"No, not yet."

"Well, you're welcome to go to one of the hotel restaurants. Just charge it to your room and the foundation will pick up the tab."

"Thanks, but that won't be necessary. I'm going to grab a bite to eat here in Times Square."

"You're in Times Square?"

"Yes."

"Right now?"

"Yes, I am."

"But it's freezing out. Is the driver with you?"

"No, I let him go."

"How did you get there?"

"On foot."

"It's five degrees below zero. And they said on TV a little while ago that the windchill factor is going to make it feel like minus fifteen. I hope you're at least properly dressed."

"Um . . . kind of."

Moliarti made a disapproving sound. "You need to be more careful. If you want, just call me and I'll send the driver to pick you up."

"Oh, that won't be necessary. I'll catch a cab."

"It's up to you. Anyway, I just called to welcome you to New York and to tell you that we're going to meet at our office tomorrow at nine. The driver will be waiting for you at eight thirty in the Park Avenue lobby. The office isn't far from the hotel."

"All right, thanks. I'll see you in the morning."

"Okay. See you tomorrow."

The five-hour time difference between New York and Lisbon had its impact on Thomas that night. It was six o'clock in the morning when Thomas woke up. Outside, darkness still reigned. He tried to get back to sleep, tossing and turning, but after half an hour he realized it was no use and sat up on the edge of the bed. He calculated that it was 11:30 A.M. in Lisbon. Constance had her free period.

He looked around and for the first time was able to appreciate the room. It was decorated in burgundy, with gold trim. The floor was covered with a plush carpet. Plants brightened up the corners of the room, and there was a bottle of Cabernet on a bedside table waiting to be opened. It would be so nice if Constance could see it all.

He called her cell phone.

"Hi, Freckles," he said, using the nickname he'd given her when they were dating. "Everything okay?"

"Hi, Thomas. How's New York?"

"Freezing!"

"But is it amazing?"

"It's a strange city, but yes, it's pretty amazing."

"What are you going to bring me back?"

"Ha!" he chortled. "I am going to bring *me* back, safe and sound. I always had a feeling you were using me."

"You're off waltzing around America while I take care of your home and daughter, and *I'm* using *you*?"

"Okay, okay. I'll bring you the Empire State Building, complete with King Kong."

"You needn't go to so much effort." She laughed. "I'd prefer the MoMA."

"The what?"

"The MoMA. The Museum of Modern Art."

"Of course."

"Bring me Van Gogh's *Starry Night*. But I also want Monet's *Water Lilies*, *Les Demoiselles d'Avignon* by Picasso, and *Divan Japonais*, by Toulouse-Lautrec."

"What about King Kong?"

"What do I need King Kong for if I've got you?"

"You wicked woman." He laughed. "About those paintings—will posters do?"

"Absolutely not. I want you to abscond with the originals."

"Okay then. How's Margarida?"

"Fine. She's fine," she said, then her voice darkened. "But yesterday she told me that her chest felt funny. I'm worried that her heart is acting up again."

Thomas took a deep breath. Grim reality intruded into his city holiday. After a few moments, he said: "We'll just have to take her to her heart specialist again."

"And you should go with me."

"I'm out of the country."

"This time you've got an excuse," she agreed, then quickly changed the subject. "So, have the Americans told you what they want with you?"

"No. I'm going to a meeting with them in a little while. I'll know soon."

"I bet they want your expertise about some manuscript."

"Probably."

Thomas heard a bell ring in the background on the other end of the line.

"There's the bell," she said. "Got to go. I've got a class to teach. Anyway, this call must be costing a fortune. Love you. Be good, okay?"

"Okay. And don't worry. Margarida's going to be fine."

"I know. Or at least I hope. And don't forget to bring me flowers."

He finished breakfast shortly before eight thirty and headed for the hotel lobby at the Park Avenue entrance, per Moliarti's instructions. A beautiful chandelier lit the mosaic set in the marble floor.

"Good morning, sir. How are you today?"

Thomas turned around and recognized the driver from the night before. "Good morning."

"Shall we go?" asked the driver, motioning with his gloved hand for Thomas to follow him.

The morning had dawned cold, but a glorious sun lit the city, especially on wide Park Avenue. Thomas settled into the Cadillac while the chauffeur got into the driver's seat. The security partition rolled down with a soft buzz, and the driver leaned back to point at a tiny TV on the passenger's side, where a bottle of Glenlivet, another of Moët, and a carafe of orange juice sparkled at him from a bucket of ice. "Enjoy the ride," he said with a smile.

The limousine took off and Thomas watched New York slide past him in a busy flurry. They drove up Madison Avenue with its dense traffic until they reached the Sony Building, recognizable by its Chippendale top. The car slowed down and stopped at the corner.

"Here's the office," said the driver, pointing at the entrance to a skyscraper. "Mr. Moliarti is expecting you." Thomas got out and admired the building. It was a striking thirty-seven-story tower of polished green-gray granite, with modern, almost aerodynamic lines. A blast of cold wind whipped down the sidewalk, and a man in a heavy coat hurried out of the building and approached him.

"Mr. Noronha?" Thomas recognized the Brazilian Portuguese with the American accent.

"Bom dia."

"Bom dia. I'm Nelson Moliarti. It's a pleasure to meet you."

"The pleasure's all mine," Thomas said as they shook hands.

Moliarti was a thin, short man with curly gray hair. He reminded Thomas of a bird of prey, with his small eyes and narrow, hooked nose. "Welcome," he said.

"Thank you," said Thomas. "It sure is cold, isn't it?"

"Yes, yes, very cold." Moliarti waved him toward the door. "Let's go inside." Taking refuge in the warmth of the indoors, Thomas admired the sleek lines of the marble lobby, decorated with a surprising sculpture, a block of granite that appeared to be suspended inside a steel tank, with a trickle of water running under it. Moliarti saw him staring at the sculpture and smiled. "It's curious, isn't it?"

"Interesting."

"Come with me. Our office is on the twenty-third floor." There seemed to be no time for further explanation. Moliarti was clearly in a rush.

The elevator was surprisingly fast; the doors opened after a few seconds, and they walked onto the floor occupied by the Americas History Foundation. The main door was made of opaque glass, with the foundation's logo engraved on the front. A golden eagle held an olive branch in one talon, while the other clutched a ribbon bearing an inscription in Latin: *Hos successus alit: possunt, quia posse videntur.* The initials AHF were written in calligraphy beneath it.

Thomas murmured the phrase to himself and tried to remember where it was from. "Virgil," he said finally.

"What?"

"This phrase here," Thomas said, pointing at the ribbon in the eagle's talon. "It's a quote from Virgil's *Aeneid.*" He translated: "Success nourishes them; they can because they think they can."

"Ah, yes. It's our motto," Moliarti said with a smile. "Success breeds success, no obstacle is too great to be overcome." He looked at Thomas with respect. "Are you versed in Latin?"

"Latin, Greek, and Coptic, although I don't get enough practice." Thomas sighed. "I would love to delve into Hebrew and Aramaic. That would open me up new horizons for sure."

The American whistled, impressed, but didn't say anything. Moliarti led Thomas inside and past a reception desk, then down a corridor to a modern office, where they met a stern-looking woman in her sixties.

"This is our guest," he said, motioning to Thomas. The woman stood and greeted him with a nod. "Hi," she said.

"This is Mrs. Theresa Racca, assistant to the chairman."

"Hello," said Thomas, shaking her hand.

"Is John in?" asked Moliarti.

"Yes."

Moliarti knocked on the door and then opened it. The man sitting behind the heavy polished mahogany desk was almost bald. His few gray hairs were combed back, and he had a double chin. He stood and held out his arms. "Nel, come in."

Moliarti walked in and introduced his guest. "This is Thomas Noronha, from Lisbon," he said. "Mr. Noronha, this is John Savigliano, chairman of the executive board."

Savigliano came out from behind his desk holding out both hands, a large, welcoming smile stamped across his face. "Welcome! Welcome to New York."

"Thank you," Thomas said, switching to English, and they shook hands enthusiastically.

"Did you have a good trip?"

"Yes, excellent."

"Splendid! Splendid!" Savigliano waved them over to a pair of comfortable leather sofas in a corner of the office. "Please, have a seat."

Thomas sat and glanced around the office. It was conservatively furnished, with oak-paneled walls and ceiling and eighteenth-century European furniture. An enormous window looked south over Manhattan's forest of buildings. Thomas recognized the radiant steel arches of the spectacular Chrysler Building to his left. On his right was the spire of the Empire State Building. The floor was varnished walnut. Enormous plants graced each corner, and a beautiful abstract painting hung on the wall.

"It's a Franz Marc," explained Savigliano, noting his guest's interest in the painting. "Are you familiar with his work?"

"No," said Thomas, shaking his head.

"He was a friend of Kandinsky's. Together they formed the group Der Blaue Reiter in 1911," he said. "I bought this painting four years ago at an auction in Munich." He whistled. "It cost a fortune, believe me. A fortune."

"John here is a lover of fine paintings," explained Moliarti. "He has a Pollock and a Mondrian at home—just think!"

Savigliano smiled and lowered his eyes. "Oh, it's a little indulgence of mine." He looked at Thomas. "Would you like something to drink?"

"No, thank you."

"How about a coffee? We do a wonderful cappuccino."

"Thanks, a cappuccino then."

Savigliano looked at the door. "Theresa!" he called.

"Yes, sir?"

"Could you bring us three cappuccinos and some biscotti, please?"

"Right away."

Savigliano rubbed his hands together and smiled. "Thomas Noronha," he said. "May I call you Tom?"

"Tom?" Thomas laughed. "As in Tom Hanks? Okay."

"I hope you don't mind. We Americans prefer informality." He pointed at himself. "Please, call me John."

"And I'm Nel," joked Moliarti.

"So that's settled." Savigliano smiled. He glanced out the window. "Is this your first time in New York?"

"Yes. I've never left Europe before," Thomas admitted, slightly embarrassed.

"And are you liking it?"

"Well, I haven't seen much yet, but it looks good so far." Thomas hesitated. "You know, I find myself looking at the streets and thinking that New York looks like something out of a Woody Allen film."

The two Americans cracked up.

"That's a good one!" said Savigliano. "A Woody Allen film!"

"Only a European could come out with something like that." Moliarti said, chuckling and shaking his head.

Thomas sat there smiling, not getting what was so funny. "Don't you think?" he said.

"Well, it's a question of perspective," said Savigliano. "I guess someone who's only seen New York in the movies would think that. But remember, it's not New York that looks like a film set; it's the film sets that look like New York." He winked.

Mrs. Racca came into the office with a tray, served them steaming cappuccinos and chocolate biscotti, and left. The three of them sipped from their cups. Savigliano leaned back on the sofa and cleared his throat.

"So, Tom, let's talk about why you're here." He glanced at Moliarti. "I assume Nel has explained what our foundation is all about."

"Yes, he gave me a rough idea."

"The Americas History Foundation is a privately funded nonprofit organization. It was established here in New York in 1958 to foster study of the history of the Americas. We created a scholarship for American and foreign students, to reward innovative research studies that reveal new facets of our past."

"The Columbus Scholarship," said Moliarti.

"Yes. We've also funded research by archaeologists and professional historians."

"What kind of studies?" asked Thomas.

"Everything to do with the Americas," said the chairman, "from the dinosaurs that lived on this continent to studies of the Native Americans, European colonial occupations, and migratory movements. But let's talk specifically about our problem." He paused, considering where to begin. "As you know, in 1992, the five-hundredth anniversary of the discovery of the Americas was celebrated. The ceremonies were magnificent, and I'm proud to say, the Americas History Foundation played an important role. Soon after, it was time to decide on our next project, we usually focus on one large endeavor at a time. Looking at the calendar, we realized there was one date that failed to catch our attention. It was an incredibly embarrassing failure for the foundation. A date that we should've capitalized on." He gave Thomas an intense stare. "Do you have any idea what it might be?"

"No."

"April 22, 2000."

"The discovery of Brazil," Thomas said matter-of-factly.

"Exactly." replied Savigliano. "The five-hundredth anniversary." He took another sip of cappuccino. "We screwed up in 2000 and didn't commemorate the anniversary at all—no celebration, no proclamation, nothing. For as reputable a foundation as ours is, it was a faux pas I wouldn't want to repeat. So we called a meeting with our consultants. The challenge was working out how to celebrate the date appropriately, after the fact. One of our consultants was Nel, who has taught history at a Brazilian university and who knows the country very well. Nel suggested something that we found interesting." He looked at Moliarti. "It's probably better if you explain your idea."

"Sure, John," said Moliarti. "Basically, it hinges on a long-standing historiographical controversy: Did the Portuguese explorer Pedro Álvares Cabral find Brazil by accident, or did he know precisely what he was doing? As you know, historians suspect that the Portuguese already knew of the existence of Brazil, and Cabral only formalized a discovery that had already taken place. I proposed to the board that we finance a study that could provide a definitive answer to this question. It would add some weight to the scholarship of the epoch and would help bring the foundation some much needed respect in this area."

"The board agreed and the wheels were set in motion," added Savigliano. "We decided to hire the top experts in the area, but we wanted people who were not only thorough in their approach but also daring, who had the courage to challenge fixed ideas, who would not merely consult established sources but be able to piece together underlying truths."

"As I'm sure you know," said Moliarti, "many Portuguese discoveries were originally considered highly classified state secrets, and Portugal's policy to suppress information made a lot of sense. A small country with limited resources wouldn't have been able to compete with the great European powers if everyone had access to the same information. They knew that knowledge was power and guarded it zealously, thereby ensuring their monopoly on this strategic information for the future. This silencing wasn't absolute, it was selective, concealing certain sensitive facts and discoveries. There were, of course, some that were in their interest to publicize, since being the first to explore a territory was the primary criterion in claiming sovereignty over it."

"Precisely," said Savigliano. "Now, since some of the discoveries were kept secret, the official documents were designed to hide the truth, and can't be regarded as reliable. This was why we wanted daring researchers."

Thomas frowned, looking skeptical. "But how can you expect a serious historian to decide to simply ignore the official documents? If everyone gave free rein to his imagination, we'd no longer be talking about history but historical fiction, wouldn't we?"

"Indeed."

"Obviously the documents need to be subject to criticism," insisted Thomas. "We must understand the purpose of the manuscripts, see what their intentions were, and assess their reliability. But surely you believe that historical investigation must be based on documentary evidence."

"Of course," said Moliarti quickly. "Of course. Which is why we wanted reliable researchers. But we also believed that they should be capable of looking beyond the documents, whose purpose—under the Portuguese monarchy's fifteenth-century gag order—*was* to conceal. That meant that our historians had to be able to think outside the box." He bit into a biscotti. "The board put me in charge of finding someone with this profile, and I spent a few months doing my research, going through résumés, asking questions, reading research papers, and consulting friends. Until I found a man who filled the prerequisites."

Moliarti paused for so long that Thomas felt obliged to ask. "Who?"

"Professor Martinho Vasconcelos Toscano, from the School of Letters at the Classical University of Lisbon."

Thomas's eyes bulged. "Professor Toscano? But he—"

"Yes, my friend," said Moliarti, with a grim expression on his face. "He died two weeks ago."

"That's what I heard. It even made the news."

Moliarti sighed heavily. "Professor Toscano caught my attention because of his innovative studies into Duarte Pacheco Pereira, especially his best-known work, the enigmatic *Esmeraldo de Situ Orbis*. I reviewed his studies and was very impressed by his insight, his ability to look beyond appearances, to challenge established truths. Additionally, his work was very well respected at the PUC Department of History."

"PUC?"

"The Pontificial Catholic University in Rio de Janeiro, where I taught," said Moliarti. "So I went to Lisbon to talk to him and convinced him to head up this project." He smiled. "I also think our generous fee helped persuade him."

"The Americas History Foundation prides itself on its ample compensation," bragged Savigliano. "We demand the best, and we pay accordingly."

"Anyway, Professor Toscano appeared to have the right profile," Moliarti went on. "He didn't write so well, it's true. This appears to be a problem among some Portuguese historians, but it was no great obstacle. We have specialists who can deal with questions of style, true Hemingways, who can make Professor Toscano sound like John Grisham."

The two Americans laughed.

"Why not James Joyce?" asked Thomas. "They say he was the greatest writer in the English language."

"Joyce?" barked Savigliano. "Jesus Christ! He was worse than Toscano!"

More laughter. "Well, enough joking," said Moliarti. He took a deep breath. "To be honest, I wouldn't say that Professor Toscano had *exactly* the right profile. But he had the profile I'd been asked to find."

"That wasn't the same thing?"

Moliarti made a face. "Professor Toscano had some issues, as we came to realize." He took a sip of cappuccino. "In the first place, he wasn't one to stay within the limits of his area of investigation. He followed leads that, while interesting, were irrelevant to the study at hand, and he wasted an extraordinary amount of time and money. Second, he didn't care to provide reasonable reports on his work. I wanted to stay abreast of his investigation, but he denied access at every query. Then one day he told me he'd made a very important breakthrough, something that would change everything we know about the Age of Discovery. A true revelation. When I asked what it was, he refused to say. Said we'd have to wait. Whatever he found while doing research on the discovery of Brazil was big. Big enough to turn the man into a paranoid lunatic."

There was silence.

"Did you wait?" Thomas finally asked.

"We didn't have any choice, did we?"

"And then?"

"And then he died," said Savigliano darkly.

"Hmm," murmured Thomas. "Without explaining what the breakthrough was."

"Exactly."

"I get the picture," Thomas said, leaning back on the sofa. "And that's your problem."

Moliarti cleared his throat. "That's our biggest problem." He raised a finger. "We need to find out what Toscano's big discovery was before he died so that our much delayed ballyhoo over the discovery of Brazil keeps respect and donations pouring into the foundation. We're talking a potential windfall of millions. As I explained, Professor Toscano liked his secrets and didn't send us any material, which is why we're empty-handed. We've got nothing. Zilch."

"It'll be the first time in the history of the foundation that we haven't made a contribution on an important day in the history of our continent," added Savigliano.

"An embarrassment," said Moliarti, sighing and shaking his head.

"Also," Savigliano continued, "if what Toscano found was really as big as he made it seem, big enough to transform the old man from a quiet historian to a hoarding paranoid, then the research may in fact help boost our donor contributions to levels we've never seen."

They looked at Thomas expectantly. "That's why we contacted you," explained Savigliano. "We need you to recover Toscano's work."

"Me?"

"Yes, you," he said, pointing at Thomas. "There's a lot to do and you'll have to do it quickly. We need his research first. Our publisher can get the book out quickly, but they can't work miracles. It's crucial that we have things ready by mid-March."

Thomas looked at him, dumbfounded. "I'm sorry, but there must be some mistake." He leaned forward and pressed his palm to his chest. "I'm not an expert in the area of the discoveries. I am a paleographer and cryptanalyst. My work is deciphering hidden messages, interpreting texts, and determining the reliability of documents. If you need a specialist in the discoveries, I can recommend some people in my department who are more than qualified to help in your investigation. Actually, if you're interested, I can already think of one or two people who are right for the job. But I'm not your guy." Thomas looked at the two Americans, smiling helplessly.

The Americans glanced at each other.

"Tom, you've been very clear," said Savigliano. "But it's you we want to hire."

Thomas looked at him for two long seconds. "I don't think I've explained myself very well," he said finally.

"You've explained yourself. I think it is we who haven't explained ourselves very well."

"How so?"

"Look, we don't need an expert in the area of the discoveries," said Savigliano with raised eyebrows. "We need someone who can help us reorganize everything that Professor Toscano investigated about the discovery of Brazil. The New World."

"But that's what I'm trying to tell you," insisted Thomas. "I'm afraid that is just not my area of expertise."

After a terse few seconds, Savigliano looked at Moliarti. "Tell him everything. Otherwise we'll never get out of here."

"So here's the problem," said Moliarti, a sudden change in the tone of his voice. "As I just told you, Professor Toscano really liked to keep things secret. He didn't write progress reports, he didn't tell us anything, and he was always evasive." He took a deep breath. "He took his penchant for concealment to truly ludicrous lengths. He was adamant that no one should know what he had discovered, and since he was always paranoid that everyone wanted to steal his secrets, he hid all the information he had compiled."

"How so?"

"He left all his notes written in code, and we can't make heads or tails of it. Everything he learned, he hid, and we need you to figure out what he was up to." He leaned toward Thomas, narrowing his stare until he looked almost predatory. "Tom, you're Portuguese, you have a basic knowledge of the discoveries, and you're an expert in cryptanalysis. You're the solution."

Thomas leaned back against the sofa, surprised. "Well . . . no . . . that's really . . ."

"And you'll have my help," added Moliarti. "I'll go to Lisbon myself to research images, and I'll always be on call for whatever you need." He hesitated. "I'm also going to want regular updates on your progress."

"Hang on," cut in Thomas. "I'm not sure I've got time for this. I lecture at the university, and besides, I've got some family issues."

Thomas thought of his daughter's health, and his marriage, a union that might not withstand further stresses.

"We're willing to pay whatever is necessary," said Savigliano, playing the ace he had up his sleeve. "Five thousand dollars a week, plus expenses. If you're successful within the period we've established, you'll also get a bonus of half a million dollars." He dragged out the number, pausing between words. "Think about it. Half a million dollars." He held out his hand. "Take it or leave it."

Thomas didn't need to think too hard. Five hundred thousand dollars was a huge amount of money. There was the solution to all his problems. Margarida's endless medical bills, the special-education teacher. They could have a better home, a more secure future, all those little things they missed because money was so tight, like eating at restaurants, spending a weekend in Paris so Constance could go to the Louvre and the little one to Euro Disney.

Thomas leaned forward and looked Savigliano in the eye. "Where do I sign?" He took the contract and signed.

They shook hands enthusiastically. The deal was done.

"Tom, welcome aboard!" bellowed Savigliano with a wide grin. "We're going to do great things together. Great things!"

"I hope so," said Thomas as the euphoric American crushed his hand. "When do I start?"

"Immediately. Professor Toscano died two weeks ago in a hotel in Rio de Janeiro," said Moliarti. "He suffered heart failure while drinking a glass of juice, of all things. We know he'd been looking at documents at the Brazilian National Library. You might find clues there about what he was really on to."

John Savigliano feigned a look of pity. "Tom, I'm sorry to inform you of this, but tomorrow you'll be flying to Rio de Janeiro."

Chapter 5

RIO DE JANEIRO

The bars of the iron gates provided an intermittent view of São Clemente Palace, an elegant, white, three-story edifice whose architecture had clearly been inspired by the mansions of eighteenth-century Europe. The building stood in a well-manicured garden full of tall banana trees and coconut palms, mango trees and flamboyants. The luxuriant vegetation of Botafogo's dense woods closed ranks around the mansion, and behind it, like a silent giant, rose the dark, naked slope of Santa Marta.

It was hot, and Thomas wiped his forehead when he got out of the cab. After clearing security, he followed the mosaic footpath to the consulate building, taking special care not to trample the garden, and climbed a low ramp to the door the guard had pointed at. He made his way up the stairs and through the carved wooden door and found himself in a small foyer. A pair of gilded oak doors stood open, and Thomas walked past them into an enormous hall.

A young man in a dark blue suit, with his black hair combed back, approached Thomas, his footsteps echoing on the marble floor. "Mr. Noronha?"

"Yes?"

"Lourenço de Mello," he said, holding out his hand. "I'm the consulate's cultural attaché."

"How do you do?"

"The consul is on his way." He gestured to a room on his left. "Come, let's wait in the function room."

The room was long and narrow, with high ceilings. They sat in a corner near an enormous painting of John VI, the king who had fled to Rio when Napoleon invaded Portugal, and he noticed a shiny black grand piano at the other end of the room. It looked like an Erard.

"Can I get you something to drink?" asked the attaché.

"No, thank you," said Thomas, settling into his chair.

Lourenço chewed on his bottom lip. "Hmm, I see." He sighed. "Such an unpleasant thing, Professor Toscano's death. You can't imagine the—"

"Good morning." A sprightly, elegant-looking middle-aged man, with gray hair at his temples, burst into the room.

Lourenço de Mello stood and Thomas followed suit. "Mr. Ambassador, this is Thomas Noronha," said the attaché, introducing them. "And this is the ambassador, Álvaro Sampayo."

"How do you do?"

"Please, make yourself at home," said the consul. Everyone sat. "My dear Lourenço, have you offered our guest a cup of coffee?"

"Yes, I have, sir. But he declined."

"You don't want one?" asked the diplomat in surprise, giving Thomas a scolding expression. "It's Brazilian coffee, my friend. The only thing better than this coffee comes from Angola."

"I would very much like to try it, Mr. Ambassador, but not on an empty stomach. It doesn't agree with me."

The consul slapped his knee with the palm of his hand and sprang up.

"You're absolutely right!" He looked at the attaché. "Lourenço, please tell them to serve lunch. It's getting late."

"Yes, Mr. Ambassador," said Lourenço, leaving to relay the orders.

"Come with me," said the consul to Thomas, pulling him along by the elbow. "Let's go to the dining room."

They walked into the enormous dining room, dominated by a long jacaranda table with twenty chairs on either side, all upholstered in burgundy fabric. Three places had been set, with porcelain bowls, silverware, and crystal glasses.

"Please," said the consul, sitting at the head of the table and pointing to a seat on his right. Thomas sat down and Lourenço reappeared and joined them at the table. A man in a white uniform with gold buttons appeared holding a tray and served them vegetable soup.

"Is this your first time in Rio?" asked the consul.

"Yes, it is." They started eating.

"What do you think?"

Thomas swallowed a spoonful of soup. "I only got in late yesterday. But it seems like it would be difficult not to enjoy Brazil. It feels like a kind of tropical Portugal."

"Yes, that's a good definition. A tropical Portugal."

Thomas held his soup spoon in the air. "Mr. Ambassador, forgive me for asking, but if you are an ambassador, why are you also referred to as the consul?"

"Rio de Janeiro is a special place, you know." He lowered his voice, in an aside. "The consulate in Rio is better than the embassy in Brasilia, our capital, you see."

"I see." Thomas was still intrigued. "Why is that?"

"Well, because Rio de Janeiro is much more accessible than Brasilia, which is up on a high plain in the middle of nowhere," replied the consul.

They finished their soup and the server cleared the table. He came back a few minutes later holding a steaming tray of roast leg of pork, accompanied by rice and roasted potatoes. He also filled their glasses with water and red Alentejo wine.

"Mr. Ambassador, it was very kind of you to invite me here."

"Come now, for God's sake, there's no need to thank me. It's a great pleasure for me to be able to help you." They started on the pork. "Actually, after you called from New York, I received instructions from the ministry in Lisbon to give you all the support you need. Research into the discovery of Brazil is considered to be of strategic interest in relations between our two countries. As such, I don't believe I'm doing you any favor; rather, I am merely fulfilling my duty."

"Well, thank you anyway." Thomas hesitated. "Did you manage to get the information I mentioned over the phone?"

"Mm-hmm." The ambassador nodded. "Professor Toscano's death brought everything to a standstill here at the consulate. You can't imagine the headache we had getting his body back to Portugal." He sighed. "It was a pain in the neck, believe me. Good God! There were reams of papers and forms to wade through, plus the police inquiry, problems at the morgue, and endless authorizations, stamps, and bureaucracy. Then there were the hassles with the airline. A horror show, you've never seen anything like it." He looked at the attaché. "Lourenço here went through hell, didn't you, Lourenço?"

"Don't remind me, Mr. Ambassador."

"As for the information you asked me for, we had a look at Professor Toscano's papers and discovered that he did most of his research at the Brazilian National Library."

"Where's that?"

"Downtown." Sampayo took a sip of wine. "Hmm, this red is truly divine!" he exclaimed, holding his glass to the light to examine it. He looked at Thomas. "There shouldn't be too much for you to unearth, right? Professor Toscano was only here for three weeks before he passed away."

Thomas cleared his throat.

"You said you'd been looking through Professor Toscano's papers. . . ."

"Mm-hmm."

"I presume you've already sent them on to Lisbon."

"Of course."

Lourenço coughed, interrupting the conversation. "Not exactly," he said.

"What do you mean, not exactly?" asked the consul.

"There was a problem with the diplomatic pouch, and Professor Toscano's papers are still here. They'll be going off tomorrow."

"Really?" exclaimed the consul. He looked at Thomas. "Well, there you go. The papers are still here after all."

"Can I see them?"

"Of course." He looked at the attaché. "Lourenço, could you fetch them, please?"

Lourenço rose and disappeared through the door.

"How's your roast pork?" asked the consul, pointing at his guest's plate.

"Wonderful," said Thomas.

Lourenço returned holding a briefcase. He sat and opened it on the table, pulling out reams of papers.

"They're mostly photocopies and notes," he said.

Thomas picked up the papers and began to study them. They were photocopies of old books, and from the type of print and text he figured they were from the sixteenth century. There were texts in Italian, others in old Portuguese, and a few in Latin, replete with elaborate miniatures and beautiful illuminations, painted with brushes and quills. His notes, however, consisted of almost unintelligible chicken scratch. Thomas recognized a few names—Cantino, Pinzón, and Cabral, the man officially credited with the discovery of Brazil.

Among the notes, Thomas noticed a loose page with two firm lines of text, three words written with care. The letters seemed to tear the paper, the calligraphy revealing obscure, suggestive contours, as if it contained an ancient magic formula.

Moloc

Ninundia Omastoos

"Strange, isn't it?" said Lourenço, intrigued. "It was found folded up in Professor Toscano's wallet. It doesn't seem to make any sense."

Thomas remained quiet, analyzing the page in his hands.

"Good God!" exclaimed the consul. "It looks like Flemish."

"Or one of those ancient languages," suggested Lourenço.

"Maybe," Thomas said finally, without lifting his eyes from the text. "But something tells me it's some kind of coded message."

The consul leaned forward to study the page.

"In New York they told me that Professor Toscano recorded everything about his breakthroughs in code," explained Thomas. "Apparently, he was paranoid about security and had a penchant for word games." He sighed. "By the looks of things, it's true."

"Does it mean anything to you?"

"Yes, there are a few clues here," murmured Thomas. "This *moloc*, to begin with. It's the first word in the message and the only one whose meaning appears clear, although enigmatic. Moloch was an ancient divinity." He scratched his chin. "The first time I ever came across this word was when I was a child, in a comic book about one of my favorite heroes, Bernard Prince. It was called *Le Souffle de Moloch,* and, if I'm not mistaken, it was set on an island with an erupting volcano called Moloch. I also used to read stories about Alix, whose antiquated adventures involved the god Moloch. I even recall having seen a book by Henry Miller entitled *Moloch*."

"But here it's not Moloch. It's Moloc."

"Moloc, Moloch, or Melech. It's all the same thing. The original word was *melech*. It meant *king* in the Semitic languages. The Jews intentionally distorted it to create the Hebrew Molech, so as to associate *melech*, king, with *bosheth*, or shameful thing. That was how the name Moloch came into being, although the Moloc spelling is more common in Portuguese."

"Which king was that?"

"Molech was a cruel, divine king." Thomas bit his bottom lip. "He was actually a god worshipped by the peoples of Moab, Canaan, Tyre, and Carthage, and they made terrible sacrifices in his name, such as the burning of firstborn children." He glanced around. "Have you got a Bible?"

"I'll go get it," offered Lourenço, getting up from the table again and leaving the room.

"What do you want the Bible for?" asked the consul.

"I think there's a reference to Moloc in the Old Testament," said Thomas.

"Goodness me!" exclaimed the consul. "I see this Moloc fellow was a nasty piece of work." He ran his eyes across the enigmatic message again. "What might Professor Toscano have been suggesting by mentioning such an unpleasant figure?"

Thomas raised his eyebrows, undeniably excited by the prospect of Toscano's great and secret discovery. "That's what I'd like to know."

Lourenço came back holding a Bible, which he placed on the table. Thomas leafed through it, sometimes turning over several pages at a time, other times stopping to study a passage. After a few minutes, he raised his hand. "Here it is." He pointed at a paragraph. "It's the part where God, speaking through Moses, forbids the sacrifice of children to Moloc." He paused and began reading. " 'The people of the community are to stone him . . . cut off from their people both him and all who follow him in prostituting themselves to Molech.' " He looked up. "See?"

"Ah," exclaimed the consul, completely baffled. "And what does that mean?"

"Well, I'm not sure," confessed Thomas. "The Law of Moses forbade the sacrifice of children to Moloc, stipulating the death penalty for any man who ordered or authorized such an offering, although the Old Testament records many violations of this ban."

"But what is the connection between what the Bible says and the strange message Professor Toscano left us?"

"I'll have to look at it carefully. All of the things I'm telling you are elements that may help us decipher the message, that's all. When we're dealing with a ciphered or coded message, we must pay attention to the details we do understand, so that little by little we can break the cipher, or the code."

"Aren't they the same?"

"What?"

"Ciphers and codes."

Thomas shook his head. "Not always. In a code, words are replaced with others, while in a cipher the letters are substituted. We could say, if you like, that a code is the aristocrat of the cipher family, since it's a complex kind of substitution cipher."

"What about this?" asked the consul, pointing at the page written by Professor Toscano. "Is this a code or a cipher?"

"Hmm, I'm not sure," said Thomas. "The word *moloc* clearly suggests a code, but the rest . . ." He trailed off suggestively. After careful consideration, he decided. "No, the rest must also be code." He pointed at the two remaining words. "See how the vowels connect with the consonants to form syllables and make sounds? *Ninundia. Omastoos.* Those, Mr. Ambassador, are words. Ciphers look different. They rarely have syllables, and everything looks more chaotic, in disarray, impenetrable. We see sequences like 'HSDB' and 'JHWG.' But not here. Here, they make words and suggest sounds." Thomas kept his eyes trained on the enigmatic phrase, hoping something he hadn't noticed would leap out at him, something hidden beneath those mysterious words.

"Don't these words mean anything to you?" asked the consul.

"Well, *ninundia* and *omastoos,* to be honest . . . um . . . I don't know what they are," Thomas admitted. He focused on the first word, pronounced it in a low voice, and had an idea. "Hmm," he murmured. "This *ninundia* looks like the name of a land, don't you think?" He smiled, slightly encouraged at having found a potential lead. "The last syllable, *dia,* is reminiscent of place-names in Portuguese."

"A place?"

"Yes. For example, Normandia, Gronelândia, Finlândia . . ."

"And who might the inhabitants be?" joked the consul. "Ninundians?"

"It's just a hunch, that's all. I'm going to have to give it some thought. By using the word *ninundia,* Professor Toscano might be indicating that the key to the cipher involves a geographical place. What we know for sure is that here he mentions a powerful ancient divinity, the terrible Moloc of Canaan. What on earth he intended when he placed this god and this possible terra incognita in the same message is something I have to figure out." He looked at the consul and waved the paper. "Can I keep this page?"

"No," said the consul. "I'm very sorry, but all of this must be delivered to his widow."

Thomas could not conceal his disappointment. "That's too bad."

"But it can be photocopied. That and anything else you want, as long as it's nothing private."

"Great!" exclaimed Thomas, relieved. "And where can I do that?"

"Lourenço will take care of everything for you," said the consul, gesturing to the attaché.

"What would you like me to copy?" Lourenço asked Thomas.

"Everything. I'm going to need everything." He shook the page with the enigmatic message on it again. "But this is the most important."

"Don't worry," the cultural attaché reassured him. "I'll be right back." He took the pile of papers and left the room.

"Thank you," said Thomas to the consul. "This is very helpful."

"Oh, it's nothing. Do you need anything else?"

"Actually, I do."

"What?"

"I need to contact the people in charge of the library that Professor Toscano consulted."

"The Brazilian National Library."

"Yes."

"Not a problem."

It was scorching. The unrelenting sun beat down on the city, and the afternoon stretched out before him, promising and free. Everything was conspiring for Thomas to go to the beach. The foundation had put him up at the same oceanside hotel where Professor Toscano had stayed, and when he got back to his room the ocean looked irresistible. He put on his bathing suit, took the elevator down to housekeeping, got a towel, and headed out. He took Maria Quitéria to the magnificent Vieira Souto, where he crossed the large avenue and promenade and went down to the beach.

The fine, gold sand scalded his feet, and he hopped over to the hotel's beach tent and asked for a deck chair and sun umbrella. Two dark-skinned, well-built employees in blue T-shirts and caps unfolded a white deck chair as close as possible to the water and set up a blue-

and-white umbrella with the hotel logo on it. Thomas tipped them one real. There must have been thousands of people on the beach, shoulder to shoulder, with no more than one square meter of free space anywhere. "Popsicles for sale!" called someone walking by. Thomas sat on the edge of the chair, covered himself in sunscreen, and leaned back to rest.

He looked around. A group of young Italians were lying on the sand to his right. A woman in her sixties was sitting directly in front of him, in a hat and dark sunglasses, and to his left he saw three voluptuous Brazilian women. "Iced tea with lemon! Iced tea!" sang another vendor passing by. The sun's violent rays stung his skin, and he stretched back into the shade of the umbrella.

A pleasant odor wafted up to his nostrils; one of the legion of itinerant vendors—a spectacle in themselves, moving around with heavy loads, sweating, deeply tanned, and wearing colorful caps and T-shirts—made a grilled cheese for a customer on Thomas's left. He pondered a purchase amidst the cries of "Ooorange and carrot juice! Ooorange and carrot juice!" and "Mineral water and Diet Coke! *Maté!*" when his cell phone rang. He reached over to answer it. "Popsicles! Ice cream for sale! Popsicles! Nice and cold!"

"Hello?"

"Mr. Noronha? This is Lourenço de Mello, from the consulate. I've got things arranged for tomorrow. Can you jot this down?"

"Just a minute." Thomas leaned forward to get a pen and notebook from his bag. He pressed his cell phone to his ear. "Yes, go ahead."

"At three o'clock the president of the Brazilian National Library himself will meet with you to help you with whatever you need. He's already been given details about your mission and offered to give you a helping hand. His name is Paulo Ferreira da Lagoa."

"Mm-hmm . . . daaa La-go-a. Got it. At three o'clock. Have you got an address for this library?"

"The National Library is in the square where Rio Branco starts. Any cab can take you there, no problem. If you need anything else, don't hesitate to contact me."

"Great. Thank you very much."

The sounds of the beach filled his ears again. To his right, at the end of the beach, overlooking Leblon, were the twin peaks of Morro dos Dois Irmãos, and spreading up their slopes, above the sea, was the tangled white concrete of the favela of Vidigal.

"Water! *Maté!*"

The tiny Cagarras Islands filled the blue horizon with green.

"Crazy Shorty's sandwiches!"

Thomas wanted to reflect on Toscano's enigmatic message, but the intense heat and hubbub of the beach made it hard for him to concentrate, especially when he became momentarily distracted by blond curls flouncing by in the periphery of his vision. He got up and made his way through the beachgoers to the sea, laughing at himself. Of course it wasn't her. Thomas castigated himself for even thinking that the blond curls he'd glimpsed had belonged to Lena. His hopeful mind was obviously playing tricks on him. He felt embarrassed.

Water kissed his feet. It felt cool, a little too cold for a tropical beach. Thomas made an effort to focus on Toscano and the task that lay ahead as he kicked at the waves.

The first thing to resolve was, naturally, the meaning of the word *moloc,* especially considering that this word appeared on its own. Why would Toscano have used the cruel god of Canaan, the god of sacrifices, to begin the enigma? Was he suggesting that working out the key would involve a sacrifice? On the other hand, he also had to consider the possibility that Toscano had mixed cipher and code systems in the same message; he decided to work from the assumption that he was dealing with a code.

If it was a codified message, what on earth did *ninundia* mean? What was the connection between Ninundia and the god Moloc? If he could get a better handle on the relationship between these two parts, he thought, he would probably be able to decipher the other codified word, *omastoos,* in the same way that Champollion, more than two hundred years earlier, using two simple *s*'s and a *ra,* had managed to unravel the mystery of the hieroglyphics.

Another possibility, one that he must eventually consider should his sleuthing come to naught, was that Toscano may have had a very personal frame of reference—one that Thomas, good as he was, would never be able to conjure. Hoping this was not the case, he stretched out to dry in the sun.

"Agaah!" screamed someone next to him.

Thomas jumped up, his heart beating wildly, and saw a man pointing a knife at the woman in front of him. There was something pink on the tip of the knife. The man looked rather unusual: he was short and dark-haired, with black gloves on his hands and an enormous wicker basket balanced on his head. Kind of bizarre for a mugger.

"Watermelon, ma'am?" the man asked the woman. He was selling it.

"You gave me a fright," complained the woman.

"That's just my manly voice." He gave her a contagious grin. The woman laughed and shook her head no. He thanked her anyway, smiling, and went on his way, the basket of watermelons balanced on his head like a big Mexican sombrero and a piece of fruit on the tip of his knife. He took a few steps toward a young woman, who didn't notice him, and shouted again in her ear.

"*Agaah!* Watermelon, ma'am?"

The girl jumped, glared at him defensively with her hands pressed to her chest, and exclaimed: "You scared the hell out of me!"

Brazil, Thomas thought, was the last place he could have pictured himself. If even the day before yesterday someone had suggested he'd soon be lying on a beach, he'd have thought that person insane. And Moloc. What could Toscano have been thinking? What was the discovery? Too many questions to be answered. For the moment, Thomas sat back and took in the sea air.

Chapter 6

It didn't take Thomas long to discover the delights of Ipanema. He tried the mango and sugarcane in the neighborhood's corner juice bars, along with fluffy, piping-hot cheese rolls, served fresh out of the oven. At nightfall, following the advice of a hotel employee, he went to the Sindicato do Chopp, a busy restaurant that opened onto the street. He ordered a rump steak with white rice, black beans, collard greens, and manioc bread, and washed the meal down with a freshly prepared caipirinha.

As he ate, he went back to the problem of Toscano's enigma. He recalled that one of the oldest works of literature was entitled *The Adventures of Ninurta,* a Sumerian text preserved in Akkad. Could Ninundia be a reference to Ninurta's homeland? But Ninurta was from Nippur, in what is now Iraq, which meant there could be little or no connection to Brazil. No, he decided. Then he worked on unraveling the two words of the second line, but his repeated tries, scribbled on a restaurant napkin, failed.

Frustrated, he began to wonder what the relationship was between Moloc and the discovery of Brazil. Could Brazil be Ninundia? Even more important, he had to work out if the message was in any way related to the great discovery that Toscano claimed to have made, a breakthrough capable of revolutionizing everything that was known about the Portuguese discoveries. Could Toscano have found that the ancients had arrived in Brazil? It would be fascinating, but uncovering that the Canaanites had made it to Brazil, although important, certainly, could not change what was known about the discoveries. Or could it? Thomas tortured himself with the possibilities. He sought solutions, experimented, tried to put himself in Toscano's place and imagine his rationale. His cell phone rang. "Hello?"

"Hej! Kan jag få tala med Thomas?"

"I'm sorry?"

The answer was a woman's laughter. *"Jag heter Lena.* It's me, Lena. I was testing your Swedish." She laughed again. "You need some lessons."

"Ah, Lena," said Thomas, actually blushing at the sound of her voice. "How did you get my number?"

"The department secretary gave it to me." She paused. "Why? Would you rather I didn't call you?"

"No, no," he said quickly, afraid he'd given her the wrong impression. "That's fine. I was just surprised, that's all. I wasn't expecting you to call."

"Are you sure it's not a problem?"

"No, don't worry!"

"Well, first of all, good evening."

"Thanks, Lena. How are you? What's up?"

"I'm fine, thank you." Her tone changed slightly. "I called because I need your help."

"With what?"

"As you know, I only joined the class a few days ago because my Erasmus application was delayed and I enrolled in Lisbon late."

"Yes, the registrar just added you."

"So I need to catch up on the things I missed."

"Well, perhaps the best thing to do would be to get your classmates' notes."

"I'd already thought of that. The problem is that I can't learn everything I need from the notes, can I? Do you think we could meet so you can help me in person? Tomorrow, if you like, or even today if you're available."

"Today? No, I can't—"

"What about tomorrow?"

"Wait. It can't be today or tomorrow. I'm in Brazil. In Rio de Janeiro."

"Wow, lucky you! Have you been to the beach yet?"

"Actually, I have. I went today."

"I'm so jealous! Is it hot out?"

"Eighty-six degrees."

"And your poor Swedish student here is freezing cold," she said. "Don't you feel sorry for me?"

"Actually, I do," Thomas said, laughing.

"So you must help me," she bubbled cheerily.

"Okay. I'm not sure when I'll be back in Lisbon. It depends on how my research goes here in Rio de Janeiro, but I'll definitely be back by Monday, because I have to teach a class. Call me then, okay?"

"Yes, sir. Thanks a lot."

"You're welcome."

"You know," she said in a cheeky voice, "I'm certain it's going to be a pleasure to study with you."

Curious, he thought, as he rode in a cab, momentarily distracted from his concerns about Professor Toscano's research by his student's voice lingering in his mind. Very, very curious.

Returning to the matter at hand, he mulled over the still undeciphered enigma. His mind was bubbling with questions, and he had only grown increasingly perplexed by the relationship established by Toscano between Moloc, *ninundia,* and the discovery of Brazil; no matter how he approached the question, he could not see the solution. Stuck, he decided to go back to the idea he had rejected when he saw the enigma for the first time in São Clemente Palace. What if the message really was a cipher? It seemed unlikely, since nothing in any of those strange verbal structures resembled the chaotic appearance of ciphers. For lack of a better idea, Thomas decided to submit it to a frequency analysis. He first needed to determine in what language the message had been written. Since Toscano was Portuguese, it seemed natural that the hidden message would be written in Portuguese.

He pulled out the photocopy of the enigma that was folded up in his notebook and studied it carefully. He counted the letters of the two words in the second line and discovered that two, *O* and *N*, appeared three times, while *A*, *S*, and *I* appeared twice, and *D*, *T*, *U*, and *M* appeared only once. As a cryptanalyst, Thomas knew that the most common letters in European languages were *E* and *A*, so he decided to place them, respectively, in the place of the *N* and the *O*, the most common letters in the enigma. Other high-frequency letters in the alphabet were *S*, *I*, and *R*, so he tried putting them in the place of *A*, *S*, and *I*. He wrote the phrase in his notebook and began to substitute the letters. When he had finished, he sat there staring at his experiment.

N I N U N D I A O M A S T O O S
E R E ? E ? R S A ? S I ? A A I

What could the first word, *ere?e?rs,* be? He imagined rarer letters in the gaps in his first word and did a series of simulations: first, with *C,* ere*c*e*c*rs; then *M,* ere*m*e*m*rs; and finally, *D,* ere*d*e*d*rs.

He shook his head. Nothing made any sense.

He moved on to the second word, *a?si?aai,* but this one also remained impenetrable. A*c*si*c*aai? A*m*si*m*aai? A*d*si*d*aai? Dissatisfied, he had to admit that the problem lay in the possibility that he had tried the wrong sequence, and to make sure, he swapped the places of the *A*'s and *E*'s and looked at the result.

It was even worse. He shook his head and gave up, convinced it was not a cipher, at least in Portuguese.

All of his hopes now rode on the National Library, where it seemed Toscano had spent most of his time and where he may have made his important discovery.

Thomas got out of the cab and crossed the square and Avenida Rio Branco. He climbed the wide stone stairs of the National Library and was stopped at the entrance by a guard who pointed to a reception desk on his left. Four bored-looking young women were waiting for visitors behind the counter.

"Good afternoon," said Thomas. He consulted his notebook, looking for the name the consul's attaché had given him. "I'd like to speak to Paulo Ferreira da Lagoa."

"Do you have an appointment?" asked a receptionist with dark skin and bright green eyes.

"Yes, he's expecting me."

"Your name is?"

Thomas identified himself, and the receptionist picked up the phone. After a moment, she handed him some credentials and told him to go to the fourth floor, pointing at the elevators. He showed these to a guard, this time a heavyset woman at the elevators, who inspected his pass and frowned when she saw the notebook he was holding.

"You can only use pencils in the reading room. You can borrow one there or, if they don't have one, you can buy one in the gift shop."

He waited a few moments, then the doors opened and he took the already packed elevator up to the top floor. A door on his right said PRESIDENT'S OFFICE; he opened it. His first sensation was a pleasant reminder of air-conditioning. His second was surprise. He expected to see an office but found a vast atrium. The office was, in fact, a wide balcony around a central hall, where there were desks, cupboards, and people working. A large skylight of richly decorated, colorful stained glass covered the entire ceiling, allowing the daylight to spill inside.

"Hello," said a young woman sitting at a desk near the door. "Can I help you?"

"I'm here to see the president."

"Are you Mr. Noronha?"

"Yes, I am."

"I'll go get Mr. Lagoa. He's looking forward to meeting you."

A man of about forty-five with light brown hair that was thinning on top came to greet Thomas. "Mr. Noronha, pleased to meet you," he said, holding out his right hand. "I'm Paulo Ferreira da Lagoa."

"How do you do?" They shook hands.

"The consul called me and explained your mission. I've done a little homework and had someone pull up all of Professor Toscano's requests." He motioned to his assistant. "Célia, have you got the dossier?"

"Yes, sir," said the young woman, handing Thomas a beige file. He examined the documents, copies of the requests made a few weeks before by Toscano. The quality of the list was the first thing that caught his attention. Toscano's first request had been *Cosmographiae introductio cum quibusdam geometriae ac astronomiae principiis ad eam rem necessariis, Insuper quatuor Americi Vespucii navigationes,* by Martin Waldseemüller, dating from 1507, followed by *Narratio regionum indicarum per Hispanos quosdam devastatarum verissima,* a 1598 text by Bartolomé de Las Casas; *"Epistola de Insulis nuper inventis,"* by Christopher Columbus, from 1493; and *De Orbe Novo Decades,* by Peter Martyr of Anghiera, from 1516. There was also *Psalterium,* by Agostino Giustiniani, also from 1516, and *Paesi novamente retrovati et novo mondo,* published by Fracanzano da Montalboddo in 1507.

"Is this what you were looking for?"

"Yes," said Thomas, looking thoughtful.

The president noticed his hesitation. "Is everything okay?"

"Um . . . yes . . . well, there is something strange here."

"What might that be?"

Thomas handed him the copies of the requests.

"Tell me, Mr. Lagoa, which of these works have something to do with Pedro Álvares Cabral's discovery of Brazil?"

The president analyzed the titles. "Well," he began. "Waldseemüller's *Cosmographiae* has one of the first maps with Brazil on it." He consulted another request. "And Montalboddo's *Paesi* was the first book to publish a report of the discovery of Brazil. Until 1507 the details of Cabral's voyage were known only to the Portuguese. They had never been set out in detail in a book. *Paesi* was the first book to do so."

"Hmm," said Thomas. "How about the other books?"

"Not that I know of."

"That's strange."

The men stood silent for a few moments.

"Would you like to see any of these?" asked the president.

"Yes," said Thomas. "*Paesi*."

"I'll have someone show you to the microfilm area."

"Did Professor Toscano read *Paesi* on microfilm?"

Lagoa looked at the request. "No, he saw the original."

"Then, if that's okay, it would be best for me to see the original, too. I want to consult the exact same copies that he used. There may be important notes in the margins of the originals, and the type of paper used is something that may be relevant. I need to see what he saw. It's the only way I can be sure that nothing will escape me."

Lagoa motioned to his assistant. "Célia, could you please send for the original *Paesi*." He looked at the request again. "It's in vault 1.3. Then take Mr. Noronha to the rare-book section and proceed with the consultation according to protocol." He turned back to Thomas and shook his hand. "It's been a pleasure. If you need anything else, Célia will be able to help you."

Lagoa went back to his meeting, and his assistant, after a quick phone call, motioned for Thomas to follow her. They went into the atrium and down the marble staircase to the floor below. Célia took him directly beneath the president's office. They crossed the hall and opened a door with a sign that read RARE BOOKS to a table in front of the librarian's desk covered with a burgundy velvet cloth. On it was a small brown book with gold trim and next to it, a pair of fine, white gloves. Célia introduced him to the librarian, a short, plump woman.

"Is this it?" asked Thomas, pointing at the book on the table.

"Yes," said the librarian. "This is Montalboddo's *Paesi*."

"Hmm." Thomas moved closer, leaning over the book. "Can I see it?"

"Of course," she said. "But I'm sorry, you will have to put on the gloves. It's an old book, and we have to be careful of finger—"

"I know," said Thomas with a smile. "Don't worry, I know how it works."

"And you can only use pencil."

"Now that's something I don't have," he said, patting his pockets.

"You can use this one," said the librarian, placing a sharpened pencil on the table.

Thomas put on the gloves, sat down, and picked up the small brown book, running his hands softly over the leather binding. The first pages contained the title and author, as well as the city, Vicentia, and the publication date, 1507. A note in pencil said, in modern Portuguese, that this was the first report of Pedro Álvares Cabral's voyage to Brazil and that it was the second-oldest collection of voyages. He leafed through the book. Its pages were yellowing and blotchy and exhaled a warm, sweet aroma. He wished he could feel the texture of the pages in his fingertips, but the gloves made them insensitive to touch, as if they had been anesthetized. The text appeared to have been written in Tuscan, and the pages were twenty-nine lines long, with ornate letters at the beginning of each chapter.

It took Thomas two hours to go through the book and take notes. When he finished, he put it down, got up from his chair, stretched, and went to talk to the librarian, who was busy with requests.

"Ah, yes," she said. "Would you like to see another book?"

"I'll come back tomorrow to look at the Waldseemüller." He nodded respectfully. "Thank you very much. See you tomorrow."

Célia returned to the rare-book room and accompanied him to the elevator. They went down to the main entrance and into the atrium, going around the marble staircase. When they reached the reception desk, where Thomas was supposed to leave his credentials, she suddenly stopped, opened her eyes very wide, and put her hands on her head.

"Oh dear, I've just remembered something," she moaned.

Thomas looked at her in surprise."What?"

"Professor Toscano used our safes, and left things in one." She looked at him questioningly. "Would you mind taking them back to the consulate?"

"Of course not."

She hurried toward a security guard on the left-hand side of the hall, directly behind the reception desk, and Thomas followed her. They went through a metal detector and found themselves in front of two heavy black cabinets. Célia located number 67, then took a master key out of its pouch and pushed it into the lock. The door opened, revealing a small safe containing several documents. She took the papers and handed them to Thomas, who watched the operation with mounting curiosity.

"These are the things Professor Toscano left behind." There were photocopies of microfilmed documents and some notes. Thomas tried to read the notes and noticed something strange. There was a page containing two three-word phrases written in capital letters and a crisscrossing alphabet sequence.

ANNA
SEES
MADAM
TOOT
RACECAR
BOB

A D→E H→I M
↓ ↑ ↓ ↑ ↓ ↑
B→C F→G J→L

Thomas closed his eyes and tried to fathom the meaning of these phrases. He considered several possibilities, then broke into a wide grin. He handed Célia the paper, proud and triumphant.

"What do you make of this?" he asked her.

She looked at the words, creased her forehead, and looked up. "Well . . . I'm not sure, but they're weird, aren't they?" She leaned over the page, reading what was written in the first two blocks. "'Anna sees madam' and 'toot racecar Bob.'"

Thomas raised his eyebrow. "Didn't you notice anything strange?"

She examined the page again in vain and pursed her lips. "Well, it doesn't make much sense, does it?"

"Didn't you see anything else?"

"No," she said finally. "Why?"

Thomas pointed at the two phrases.

"They're palindromes. Whether you read them from left to right or right to left, they say the same thing." He stared at the letters. "Look. *Anna, sees, madam.*"

"Oh! And why did he do that?"

"Well, the professor enjoyed word games, and by the looks of things he was busy creating . . ." Thomas suddenly stopped speaking; his eyes went glassy and his jaw dropped. "I bet he was . . . was . . ." he stammered to himself. He plunged his hands into his pockets but didn't find what he wanted, then frantically rifled through the papers folded inside his notebook until he found the one he was looking for. "Here it is."

Célia looked at the page, not understanding.

MOLOC
NINUNDIA OMASTOOS

Thomas ran his eyes across the words, murmuring them under his breath. Then he quickly jotted something down in unintelligible handwriting. Suddenly, his face lit up and he raised his arms effusively in the air. "Got it!" he cried, his voice echoing through the atrium and attracting stares.

"What is it?" Célia looked at him expectantly.

"I've deciphered it!" he exclaimed, his eyes wide open with excitement. "It's ridiculously simple." He slapped his forehead. "Here I was racking my brains like an idiot when all I had to do with the first line was read it from right to left." He picked up the pen and wrote the solution under the cipher. On the line above he wrote:

COLOM

And on the one underneath, comparing it with the alphabetic structure jotted down by Toscano, he wrote a strange equation:

NINUNDIA
OMASTOOS
N I→N U→N D→I A
↓ ↑ ↓ ↑ ↓ ↑ ↓ ↑
O→M A→S T→O O→S
NOMINASUNTODIOSA

He examined the phrase closely, considered the appropriate places for spaces, and rewrote it:

NOMINA SUNT ODIOSA

"What's that?" asked Célia.

"Hmm," murmured Thomas, straining to remember. He frowned, then recalled the citation.

"Cicero. It's the message Professor Toscano left."

"Cicero? But what does it mean?"

"It means, my dear, that I have to go back upstairs and look at everything again," he said, hurrying toward the elevators. He waved the page in the air and excitedly made his way toward a series of events that he would one day marvel over.

Chapter 7

LISBON

The high clouds, emerging slowly like a faraway mantle, threatened to cover the sun. They spread out from the western horizon, grayish clumps of altocumuli, flat and dark at the base, tattered and luminous at the crest. The winter sun spilled clear, cold light over the resplendent surface of the river Tagus and the houses of Lisbon, vividly highlighting the colorful façades and red-tile rooftops that undulated like waves, clung to the curvaceous, almost feminine relief of the Lapa hillside.

Thomas wove his way through the neighborhood's semi-deserted alleys, turning left, then right, unsure which route to take in the narrow urban labyrinth, until, almost by accident, he found himself on the discreet Rua do Pau de Bandeira. Halfway down the steep street stood a beautiful salmon-colored building. He drove his tiny Peugeot through the large gates and pulled up behind two shiny black Mercedes sedans in front of the main entrance to the elegant Lapa Palace Hotel. An impeccably dressed doorman approached the car, and Thomas rolled down his window.

"Hello, sir. Leave your key with me, and I'll take care of the car."

Thomas walked into the cozy hotel lobby, his briefcase at his side. The cream-colored marble floor was like a mirror, its smooth, shiny surface interrupted only by a geometric design in its center, over which stood a gracious, circular table. On top of the table was a beautiful vase of hollyhocks, bright, erect, and full of splendor, fanned out like a peacock's feathers. Thomas recognized these flowers; they were sometimes found in Neanderthal graves and pharaohs' tombs. Constance would know what they meant, he thought.

He noticed a familiar face to his left, with small eyes and a hooked nose. The man put down the newspaper he was reading, stood up, and walked over to Thomas. "Tom, I see you're the punctual sort!" exclaimed Nelson Moliarti with a smile and his characteristic Brazilian accent, complete with American twang.

"Hi, Nelson. How are you?"

"I'm great." He held open his arms and sighed. "Ah, it's so good to be in Lisbon."

"When did you arrive?"

"Three days ago. I've been doing a lot of sightseeing."

"Have you now? Where have you been?"

"Oh, here and there, you know." He motioned for Thomas to follow him to a room on his right, where a sign said RIO TEJO BAR. "Come on, let's get a drink. Are you hungry?"

A shiny, black Kawai grand piano guarded the entrance to the bar like a solitary, silent sentinel, patiently waiting for nimble fingers to bring its ivory keys to life. The gentle melody of a Tchaikovsky ballet wafted softly through the air, lending the bar a calm, gracious elegance. Moliarti chose a table by a window and gestured for Thomas to take a seat.

"What would you like?"

"I think I'll have a cup of tea."

"Waiter," called the American, gesturing to the employee. The young man left the counter and came to their table. "Some tea for my friend here, please."

The waiter took out his notepad. "What kind would you like?"

"Have you got green tea?" asked Thomas.

The waiter nodded and left, and Moliarti gave Thomas a friendly pat on the back. "So, Tom? How was Rio?"

" '*Cidade maravilhosa.*' " Thomas smiled as he sang the famous carnival song. " '*Cheia de encantos mil.*' Enchanting."

"I agree," said Moliarti. "When did you get in?"

"Yesterday morning. I spent the whole night on the plane."

"It's terrible, isn't it?"

"Awful. I didn't sleep a wink."

"So tell me," said Moliarti, his expression growing serious. Placing his elbows on the table, he pressed his fingertips together in front of his nose. "What have you got for me?"

Thomas opened the briefcase at his feet, took out a notebook and some documents, and placed them on the table.

"I've discovered a thing or two," he said, leaning forward to close the briefcase. Straightening up, he looked at Moliarti. "I read all the works Professor Toscano consulted at the Brazilian National Library, and I got access to his photocopies and notes. This morning I went to the Portuguese National Library here in Lisbon to check a few things. I'd say I've made progress." He consulted his notebook.

"Let's start, if you don't mind, with what Professor Toscano was researching about the discovery of Brazil, which was, after all, what the foundation had hired him to do."

"Okay."

"As you told me, his briefing was to conduct a conclusive investigation into what many historians have suspected for a long time—that all Pedro Álvares Cabral did was make official what other explorers had secretly discovered before him."

"That's right."

"Well, one thing at a time. First we must establish whether or not there was a suppression policy, a sort of permanent gag order, in Portugal during the Age of Discovery. This is fundamental. It wouldn't make sense, obviously, for the Portuguese to keep quiet about the discovery of Brazil if there wasn't such a policy."

"Do you believe there was?"

"I think so, it's what Professor Toscano thought, and it's what many other historians think. A number of researchers have abused the notion, using it to justify their filling the gaps in the available documentation, but it is true that many of Portugal's maritime undertakings, even the most important ones, were shrouded in secrecy. For example, official Portuguese records of the time did not mention the fact that Bartolomeu Dias rounded the Cape of Good Hope and discovered the passage from the Atlantic to the Indian Ocean. It was Christopher Columbus, who happened to be in Lisbon when Dias returned, who revealed this extraordinary feat to the world. If it weren't for Columbus's accidental presence in Portugal, Dias might well have remained in obscurity, his remarkable voyage concealed forever. We might now believe that Vasco da Gama was the first to round the cape."

"So it's possible the Portuguese maritime expansion was full of Bartolomeu Diases who have remained anonymous because they weren't lucky enough to have someone like Columbus as their publicist," Moliarti said.

The waiter returned with a tray and placed a steaming teapot, teacup, and sugar bowl on the table. "Japanese gabalong tea," he announced, and left quickly.

"Well, all this shows that the policy was indeed applied in a selective manner, and a lid was kept on many of Portugal's most important expeditions in the name of the higher interests of the state. History consequently forgot these events. They took place, but it's as if they didn't."

"Which brings us to the discovery of Brazil."

"Precisely. The official documents state that Brazil was discovered on April 22, 1500, when Pedro Álvares Cabral's fleet, on its way to India, was blown off course by a storm and came across a large, round mountain, which they christened Monte Pascoal. It was the coast of Brazil. The fleet stayed there for ten days, surveying the new territory, which they named Ilha de Santa Cruz, replenishing stocks, and making contact with the local inhabitants. On May 2, the fleet set sail for India, but one of the ships, a small supply ship, returned to Lisbon under the command of Gaspar de Lemos, carrying some twenty letters about the discovery to King Manuel, including a remarkable report by the ship's clerk, Pêro Vaz de Caminha." Thomas stroked his chin. "The first signs that the discovery wasn't accidental are in the presence of the small supply ship in Cabral's fleet. This vessel was too fragile for the voyage from Lisbon to India. Anyone who knows anything about sailing would know there was no way the ship could have made the entire journey, especially considering the hazardous waters around the Cape of Good Hope, which sailors also dubbed, and rightfully so, the Cape of Storms. The Portuguese were the best sailors in the world, and were more than aware of this fact. Why on earth, then, would they include such a small vessel in that fleet of large ships?"

Thomas let his question hang in the air. "There's only one possible explanation. They knew ahead of time that the ship wouldn't undertake the *entire* voyage. They knew it would only sail a third of the way there before it would return to Lisbon, bringing news of the discovery of a new land. In other words, they already knew there was land in that part of the world, and the smaller ship was included in the fleet on purpose, to return and make the news official."

"It's curious and plausible, but not conclusive."

"I agree. But there's one detail that should be pointed out. When the ship arrived in Lisbon, the sailors kept quiet and the court kept the discovery of Brazil secret until after Cabral's entire fleet returned home. That was highly unusual and would suggest that the entire operation was premeditated."

"Hmm . . . interesting. But it still isn't conclusive."

"I know. This is where another piece of information comes into play. I'm referring to a planisphere by an anonymous Portuguese cartographer, made at the request of Alberto Cantino for Hercules d'Este, duke of Ferrara, in a one-by-two-meter illuminated manuscript on parchment. Since no one knows the name of the anonymous Portuguese cartographer, this enormous map is known as the Cantino planisphere and is now in a library in Modena, Italy. In a letter dated November 19, 1502, Cantino reveals that his mapmaker copied the planisphere from official classified Portuguese prototypes, no doubt in secret. What's important about this map is the fact that it contains a detailed drawing of a large portion of the coast of Brazil. Now, let's do the math."

Thomas picked up his pen and found a clean page in his notebook. "The map was in Cantino's hands by November 1502 at the latest, which means there was little more than two years between Cabral's discovery and the arrival of the planisphere in Italy." He drew a horizontal line across the page and wrote "Cabral, April 1500" on the left, and "Cantino, November 1502" on the right.

"The problem is that Cabral *didn't make* a detailed chart of the Brazilian coast, so the information on the planisphere ostensibly came from subsequent voyages."

He held up two fingers.

"Now, the second official Portuguese voyage to Brazil was apparently made by João da Nova in April 1501, little more than a year before the planisphere reached Cantino. But note, João da Nova didn't make the voyage specifically to explore the Brazilian coast. Like Cabral, he was also on his way to India, and he didn't have enough time to chart the coastline. He also did not return to Lisbon until the middle of 1502."

Thomas held up a third finger. "So it would seem that the information on the Cantino planisphere was the result of a third voyage.

"Now, there was indeed a fleet that set sail from Lisbon with the mission of exploring the Brazilian coast. It was the expedition of Gonçalo Coelho, who left Lisbon in May 1501, and one of the crew members was the Florentine navigator Amerigo Vespucci, the very man who, inadvertently, was to give the continents of the Americas their names. The fleet reached Brazil in mid-August and spent over a year exploring a large portion of the coast. They discovered a large bay, which they named Rio de Janeiro, and continued as far as Cananéia, before returning to Portugal. The fleet's three caravels sailed into the port of Lisbon on July 22, 1502." He scribbled "Gonçalo Coelho, July 1502," three quarters of the way along the horizontal line, near where he had written "Cantino, November 1502."

"Here's the crux of the matter," he said, pointing at the two dates scrawled in the notebook. "Could just four months, from July to November, have been enough time for Lisbon's official cartographers to produce detailed maps from the information supplied by Gonçalo Coelho, as well as for the Portuguese cartographer—the anonymous traitor hired by Cantino—to copy these maps and for the clandestine planisphere to get to Italy?" Thomas underlined the short distance on his horizontal time line between "Gonçalo Coelho" and "Cantino."

He made a face and shook his head.

"Doubtful. Four months isn't enough time. So, how on earth did Alberto Cantino manage to buy a Portuguese planisphere containing information that—if we believe the chronology of the official reports—could not have been placed in detail on maps in that time? Where did this information come from?"

He held up his left palm as if presenting some kind of evidence. "There is only one explanation. The Cantino planisphere was not charted using information collected on the official voyages to Brazil but was based on data obtained *before* Cabral, during clandestine expeditions never known to history, thanks to Portugal's policy of suppressing knowledge on their discovery."

"Hmm," mused Moliarti. "Interesting. But do you think it's conclusive?"

Thomas shook his head. "I find it hard to believe that four months were enough for official detailed maps of the Brazilian coast to be produced, and for a clandestine copy to be made and taken to Italy. He raised his eyebrows. "That is, hard, but not impossible."

The waiter returned with Moliarti's sumptuous snack. Thomas took the opportunity to sip his tea.

"These are interesting discrepancies," said the American, picking up his brioche toast. "But we still don't have . . . a . . . you know . . . a smoking gun as to what Toscano discovered."

"But wait, there's more." Thomas turned back to his notebook. "The Frenchman Jean de Léry was in Brazil from 1556 to 1558, and when he spoke to the settlers who'd been there the longest, they told him that 'the fourth part of the world was already known to the

Portuguese approximately eighty years before its discovery.'" He looked at Moliarti. "Even if we allow that the expression 'approximately eighty years' can mean seventy-five or seventy-six years, we're still talking about a date well before 1500."

"Hmm."

"There's also a letter written by the Portuguese Estêvão Fróis, who was detained by the Spanish, presumably in what is now Venezuela, accused of having installed himself in Castilian territory." Thomas referred back to his notes. "The letter is dated 1514 and addressed to King Manuel. In it Fróis says he merely occupied 'Your Highness's lands, already discovered by João Coelho, the one from Porta da Luz, a neighbor from Lisbon, 21 years ago.'" Thomas computed again. "So, 1514 minus twenty-one is . . . 1493." He smiled at Moliarti. "Once again, that gives us a date well before 1500."

"Do these letters still exist?"

"Of course."

"But don't you think these sources are somewhat dubious? That is, a Frenchman nobody's ever heard of and a Portuguese prisoner, I mean—"

"Ah, my friend, there were four other great navigators who confirmed that Brazil was already known before Cabral."

"Really? Who?"

"Well, I'll start with the Spaniard Alonso de Ojeda, who, along with our friend Amerigo Vespucci, sighted the coast of South America in June 1499, probably around Guyana. Then, in January 1500, another Spaniard, Vicente Pinzón, reached the coast of Brazil three months before Cabral."

"So the Spanish beat the Portuguese to it."

"Not necessarily. The third person was Duarte Pacheco Pereira, one of the greatest navigators of the age, although he is barely known to the general public."

"As well as a navigator, he was an important soldier and scientist and during his time produced the most accurate calculation of the number of leagues per degree and was the best judge of longitude without adequate instruments. Pacheco Pereira also authored one of the most enigmatic texts of his time, a work entitled *Princípio do Esmeraldo de Situ Orbis.*"

Thomas referred to his notes. "At one point, he wrote in *Esmeraldo* that King Manuel had sent him 'to discover the western part,' which he did 'in the year of our Lord one thousand four hundred and ninety-eight, when a large portion of terra firma, with many nearby islands, was found and explored.'"

Thomas stared at Moliarti. "In other words, in 1498 a Portuguese navigator discovered land west of Europe."

"Ah!" exclaimed the American. "Two years before Cabral."

"Yes."

Moliarti ate a piece of toast and washed it down with a mouthful of champagne.

"And what about the fourth great navigator?"

"Columbus."

Moliarti stopped chewing and leveled his eyes at Thomas. "Columbus? Which Columbus?"

"*The* Columbus."

"Christopher Columbus? What do you mean?"

"When Columbus returned from his first discovery voyage to the Americas, he stopped in Lisbon to chat with King John II. In the course of this conversation, the Portuguese king revealed that there were other lands south of the area where Columbus had been. If we look at a map, we can see that South America lies south of the Caribbean. This meeting took place in 1493, which means the Portuguese already knew land existed in that part of the world."

"But where is this conversation recorded?"

"It was Bartolomé de Las Casas, who, on the occasion of Columbus's third voyage to the New World, wrote, 'The Admiral said he wants to go south because he wants to see King John of Portugal's intentions; there he is certain to find valuable things and lands.'"

"So, Tom, what's your opinion on this?" Moliarti asked. "*If* the Portuguese already knew South America existed, why did they wait so long before formalizing their discovery? Why did they only make it official in 1500? Why not before?"

"So as not to raise suspicion," answered Thomas. "The Portuguese believed in the advantages of keeping all strategic information under a lid. The king knew that revealing the existence of these lands would attract undesirable attention, giving rise to inconvenient greed and interests. If the rest of Europe didn't know these lands existed, the king could be sure they weren't going to compete with the Portuguese in exploring them."

"I understand the value of discretion, and that is my conclusion as well," said Moliarti. "But if it was advantageous for the Portuguese to keep a lid on things, what made them change their mind in 1500?"

"I think it was because of the Castilians. When Ojeda, in 1499, and Pinzón, in January 1500, began to snoop around the coast of South America, the king of Portugal realized that it no longer made sense to keep it quiet, that the Castilians might claim for themselves the lands that the Portuguese had already found. It thus became imperative that Brazil's discovery be made official."

"I see."

"Which brings us to the last major piece of information."

"What?"

"The Treaty of Tordesillas. It was an agreement ratified by the Vatican that gave half of the world to the Portuguese and the other half to the Spanish."

"Ah, yes," said Moliarti with a chuckle. "The birth certificate of globalization."

"That's it." Thomas smiled. The Americans had a grandiloquent way of describing things, of making compelling comparisons to modern references.

"Supreme arrogance."

"I know. But in actual fact they were the most powerful nations in the world at the time, and they thought it natural that they should divide the known world's spoils between them." Thomas finished his tea. "When the treaty was negotiated, each country had advantages. The Portuguese were more advanced in terms of navigation technologies, weaponry, and maritime exploration. But the Spanish had a powerful trump up their sleeve—the pope at the time was Spanish. It was kind of like a soccer match—the Portuguese had the best players and the best coach, but the match was presided over by a referee who gleefully awarded the other team unnecessary penalty kicks.

"The Portuguese navigators already sailed up and down the coast of Africa and through the Atlantic as they pleased, while the Spanish only controlled the Canary Islands. The situation was made official in 1479 in the Treaty of Alcaçovas, in which Castile recognized Portugal's authority along the African coast and in the Atlantic islands in exchange for Castile's control of the Canary Islands. The treaty, ratified the following year in Toledo, did not, however, mention the West Atlantic, which became an issue of primary concern following the triumphant return of Christopher Columbus from his first voyage. Since no clause of the document dealt directly with this new parcel of land, it soon became apparent that a new treaty was needed."

"The Treaty of Tordesillas."

"Exactly. Lisbon first proposed that a line be drawn through the world, passing next to the Canary Islands, giving Castile everything north of the line and the rest to the Portuguese. But Pope Alexander VI, who was Spanish, issued two papal bulls in 1493 establishing a dividing line along a meridian 100 leagues west of the Azores and Cape Verde. The Portuguese were not happy about this, and although they agreed to the line, they asked that it be moved 370 leagues west of Cape Verde, which the Castilians and the pope accepted, since they didn't see any reason not to. This negotiation reveals something."

Thomas made a rough sketch of a planisphere in his notebook. The contours of Africa, Europe, and the entire American continents were visible. He drew a vertical line through the Atlantic, halfway between Africa and South America, and wrote "100" underneath it.

"This is what the pope and the Castilians proposed: a line one hundred leagues west of Cape Verde."

Then he drew a vertical line farther left, cutting through parts of South America, and wrote "370" beneath it. "This is the line that the Portuguese requested, three hundred and seventy leagues west of Cape Verde."

He looked at Moliarti. "Tell me, Nel. What's the main difference between these two lines?"

Moliarti leaned over his notebook and examined the lines. "Well, one only cuts through the ocean, while the other one takes in an area of land."

"And what land might that be?"

"Brazil."

Thomas nodded and smiled. "Brazil. Now tell me, why did the Portuguese insist so much on this second line?"

"So they could have Brazil?"

"Which leads me to my third question. How the hell did the Portuguese know that this second line ran through Brazil if Brazil still hadn't been discovered in 1494?" Thomas leaned toward Moliarti.

Moliarti leaned back on the sofa and took a deep breath. "I see your point. There's certainly some food for thought in all this," he said slowly. "But tell me, Tom, is there anything truly new in all you've told me?"

Thomas held Moliarti's gaze. "No," he answered.

"Nothing at all?"

"Nothing at all. I've told you everything that I found in Professor Toscano's research into the discovery of Brazil."

"And there was nothing new? You're absolutely certain?"

"Nothing. Professor Toscano merely revisited what other historians had already discovered or concluded."

Moliarti looked crestfallen. His shoulders and chest slumped; he broke eye contact with Thomas and stared off into space. But soon something began to simmer under the surface; his cheeks went red and his face clouded over with barely contained rage. "That son of a bitch," he growled to himself. He closed his eyes, plunked his elbow on the table, and buried his forehead in his hand. "Damn. I knew it."

Thomas sat in apprehensive silence, waiting to see what would become of Moliarti's controlled anger. Moliarti muttered something else under his breath, spitting the words out in indignation, then took a deep breath, opened his eyes, and looked at Thomas.

"Tom!" he bellowed. "Toscano fooled us. He's been spending our money, patently lying about his new discovery. Now he's dead and all he did in these seven years was revisit the work of other historians, without making any new contributions. As you can imagine, we don't—"

"That's not *exactly* what I said," cut in Thomas.

Moliarti looked at him quizzically. "I'm sorry, but that's what I understood from what you said."

"You understood correctly with regard to what I was able to recover of Professor Toscano's investigations. However, I don't have any concrete answers at present and there are still other important clues that the professor left that I need to follow up on."

"Oh, okay," said Moliarti, suddenly all ears. "There's something else after all."

"Of course," said Thomas cautiously. "I'm just not sure it's directly related to the discovery of Brazil."

"What do you mean?"

"I'm referring to a ciphered clue."

Moliarti smiled strangely, as if he had just received confirmation of something he'd long suspected.

"Tell."

"It has to do with Cicero. He is the person credited with coining the expression *Nomina sunt odiosa*."

"What does it mean?"

"Names are odious."

Moliarti stared at him, perplexed. "Meaning? What does that have to do with what we're talking about?"

" *'Nomina sunt odiosa'* may be a clue Professor Toscano left us, and it may have something to do with his big discovery."

"Was it?" asked Moliarti with mounting anxiety. "A clue? And what does it reveal?"

"I don't know," said Thomas casually. "But I'm going to find out."

Chapter 8

Following class and his usual ten minutes of chatting with students, Thomas went up to his office. He had discreetly watched Lena throughout the ninety-minute lecture. She sat in the same place she had the week before, always alert, her clear blue eyes gazing at him intensely, her mouth slightly open, as if lapping up his words. She was wearing a tight mauve pullover that accentuated the generous curves of her chest and contrasted with her full, cream-colored skirt. When the lesson was over Thomas realized he was disappointed she had not come to him immediately, but he quickly scolded himself. Lena was a student and he was her teacher; she was young and single and he was thirty-five and married. He had to keep his wits about him and not step out of line. He shook his head, as if trying to get her off his mind, and took his lesson plans out of a drawer.

Three raps at the door made him look up. The door opened and a beautiful blond head poked around it. He saw her smile. The curls.

"May I, sir?"

"Come in, come in," he said, perhaps a little too eagerly. "What are you doing here?"

Lena flounced across the office, her body swaying like a cat. She was obviously self-confident, aware of the effect she had on men. She sat in a chair and leaned her torso on Thomas's desk. "I thought today's class was really interesting," she said.

"Did you now? That's good."

"The only thing I didn't understand was how the transition between the idiographic and alphabetic writing systems took place."

"Well, I'd say it was a natural progression, necessary in order to simplify things," explained Thomas, happy for the opportunity to flaunt his knowledge and impress her. "Cuneiform writing, hieroglyphics, and Chinese characters all require that a great number of signs be committed to memory. We're talking about several hundred images to memorize. Obviously, that became an obstacle to learning. The alphabet resolved this problem, because instead of having to memorize a thousand characters, like the Chinese, or six hundred hieroglyphics, like the Egyptians, now all one had to do was memorize a maximum of thirty symbols. Do you see? That's why I say that the alphabet democratized writing."

"And it all began with the Phoenicians. . . ."

"Well, to be really honest, the first alphabet is believed to have appeared in Syria."

"I see," said Lena. "But in class you only mentioned the Phoenicians. Was the Bible written in Phoenician?"

Thomas began to laugh, then quickly stopped, afraid of offending her.

"No, the Bible was written in Hebrew and Aramaic," he explained. "But actually your question isn't completely off track, since there is, in fact, a connection with Phoenician. An Aramaic alphabet similar to the one used by the Phoenicians was found in Syria—known at the time as Aram—which leads us to assume that the two writing systems are related. Many historians believe that the Hebrew, Aramaic, and Arabic writing systems had their origins in Phoenician, although no one knows how they're connected."

"How about our alphabet? Does it also derive from Phoenician?"

"In an indirect way, yes. The Greeks borrowed things from the Phoenicians and invented vowels based on consonants in Aramaic and

Hebrew. The Latin alphabet sprang from the Greek alphabet. Alpha became *a,* beta became *b,* gamma, *c,* and delta, *d.* And here we are speaking Portuguese, which is, as you know, a Latin-based language."

"But Swedish isn't."

"Okay, Swedish is a Scandinavian language, from the Germanic lingual family. But it also uses the Latin alphabet, does it not?"

"What about Russian?"

"Russian uses the Cyrillic alphabet, which also comes from the Greek alphabet."

"But you didn't explain that in today's class."

"Hold your horses," said Thomas, smiling and holding up his left hand. "The semester isn't over yet. Greek is the topic of the next class. We're getting ahead of ourselves here."

Lena sighed. "You know," she said, "I don't really need to get ahead of myself so much as I need to catch up on what I missed in the first few classes."

"Okay, then. What do you need to know?"

Lena leaned over his desk, bringing her head close to Thomas's. He smelled her perfume. "Have you ever had Swedish food?" she asked sweetly.

"Swedish food? Um, yes, had it in Malmö."

"Did you like it?"

"Very much. I remember it was delicious, but very expensive. Why?"

She smiled. "Well, I was thinking, you won't be able to explain everything to me in just half an hour. Why don't you come for lunch at my place and we can talk at leisure, without any rush?"

"Have lunch at your place?" Thomas was taken aback.

"Yes. I'll make you a Swedish dish that'll make your mouth water—you'll see."

He didn't think he could accept. Having lunch at the home of a female student—and this one, of all people—was a dangerous move. He couldn't afford such adventures. On the other hand, he wondered about the real consequences of accepting the invitation. Wasn't he getting ahead of himself? After all, it was just one lunch and one recap session, nothing else. What would be the big deal about spending an hour or two at her house talking about cuneiform writing? Wasn't that a professorial duty? Besides, he thought, it would be an excellent opportunity to try Swedish cuisine again. Why the hell not?

"Okay," he said. "We can have lunch."

Lena gave him an enchanting smile. "It's a date," she said. "How's tomorrow?"

Thomas remembered he had to go with Constance to Margarida's school the next day. They had requested a meeting with the principal to discuss the loss of the special-education teacher. There was no way he couldn't go.

"I can't," he said, shaking his head. "I have to go to . . . um . . . I have a commitment tomorrow. I can't."

"What about the day after tomorrow?"

"The day after tomorrow? Friday? Yes, that sounds fine."

"At one o'clock?"

"One o'clock it is. Where do you live?"

Lena gave him her address and said good-bye, leaving behind the scent of her perfume. He wasn't sure why he'd agreed to the lunch, but he quickly pushed any doubt out of his mind, telling himself he was just being dramatic.

They arrived at São Julião da Barra School in the late morning and went to take a peek at Margarida in her classroom. Peering through a crack in the doorway, they saw her sitting in her place by the window. They knew she was considered a good pupil; she was always standing up for the weak and helping kids who hurt themselves during break. She didn't mind losing games and always volunteered to leave the team if there were too many players. She even pretended not to notice when other kids made fun of her, and she quickly forgot their insults. Thomas and Constance gazed at her admiringly, as if she really were an angel. It was time for their meeting, and they walked quickly to the principal's office, where they did not have to wait long before they were called in.

The head of the school was a tall, bony woman in her early forties, with dyed blond hair and round glasses. She received them politely, but it became evident that she was pressed for time.

"I have a luncheon at twelve thirty," she explained.

Thomas glanced at his watch. It was ten past twelve; they had twenty minutes—not enough time.

"I assume that this is about the problem with the special-education teacher."

"Of course."

"Yes, that's a nuisance."

"I've no doubt it's a nuisance for you," said Constance in a mildly irritated tone. "But believe me, for us, and above all for our daughter, it's a tragedy." She pointed at the principal. "Do you have any idea how bad the loss of that teacher is for Margarida?"

"Please, we're doing everything we can—"

"You're doing very little."

"That's not true."

"Yes, it is," Constance insisted. "And you know it is."

"Why don't you rehire Mr. Correia?" asked Thomas, trying to prevent a verbal showdown between the two women. "He was doing an excellent job."

The sharp tone of their last meeting, when they were informed there would not be Mr. Correia or anyone else to give Margarida special help, had left him feeling that he needed to be on guard. Since then, it had become evident that Margarida was regressing. They were convinced Margarida had the ability to advance just like other children, but because her learning curve was considerably slower, she needed help.

"I would very much like to hire Mr. Correia again," said the principal. "The problem is, as I explained in our last meeting, that the Education Ministry has cut our budget and we don't have the money."

"Nonsense," exclaimed Constance. "You can pay for so many other things, but you can't afford a special-education teacher?"

"No, we can't."

"Did you know that last year Margarida was able to read and this year she can no longer understand a single written word?" asked Thomas.

"I wasn't aware of that."

"The regular teacher, obviously, doesn't understand anything about children with special needs," said Constance.

The principal held up her hands. "You are not listening," she said. "If it were up to me, I would not have fired Mr. Correia. The problem is that I don't have the money. The ministry has cut our budget."

Constance leaned forward. "Excuse me," she said, trying to remain calm. "The law guarantees special-education teachers for children with special needs in public schools. It's not something we've plucked out of thin air, it's not an unreasonable request, and it's not a favor you do us. The only thing my husband and I are asking for is that the school obey the law. No more, no less. So, please do so."

The principal sighed and shook her head. "They voted in a very fair, very beautiful, very human law, but when it's time to cough up, no one's got any money. In other words, the law is there so you can say it exists, so someone can boast that they approved it. That's all."

"So then what are you suggesting?" asked Thomas. "That things stay as they are? That our daughter be left to her own devices in class?"

"Yes," agreed Constance. "What do you intend to do?"

The principal took off her glasses, exhaled on the lenses, and cleaned them with a small orange cloth. "I have a proposal for you."

"What is it?"

"My idea is to have Mrs. Galhardo help Margarida."

"Mrs. Galhardo?" said Constance.

"Yes."

"But does she have any training in special education?"

The principal stood up. "I think it would be better if I called her in," she replied, heading for the door and sidestepping the question, a detail that did not go unnoticed by Constance and Thomas. She opened the door and looked outside. "Marília, could you please send for Mrs. Galhardo?" She returned to her seat, finished cleaning her glasses, then put them back on. Thomas and Constance glanced at each other apprehensively.

"May I come in?"

Mrs. Galhardo was a matronly sort, brimming with good-natured friendliness. She looked like one of those countrywomen with a ruddy complexion and bright eyes who are always surrounded by a horde of children. They greeted one another and she sat down next to Thomas and Constance.

"Mrs. Galhardo," the principal began, "has volunteered to give special-education classes this year."

Mrs. Galhardo nodded. "I'm concerned about Margarida and Hugo's situation." Hugo was another child with Down syndrome at the school.

"Mrs. Galhardo," interrupted Constance. "That is incredibly kind of you, but have you ever worked with children with Down syndrome?"

"No. Look, I'm just offering to help."

"Do you think Margarida will be able to make significant progress with you?"

"I think so. I'll do my best."

Thomas placed his palms together and looked at Mrs. Galhardo. "With all due respect for your kind intentions, Margarida doesn't need classes just for the sake of *saying* she is in classes. The objective is for her to learn. What use would it be to her if, at the end of the day, she still hasn't made any meaningful progression?"

"Well, I hope she does learn something."

"She needs a qualified special-education teacher: I have to be honest. I don't think you're prepared for this task."

"I recognize that perhaps I don't have the qualifications or the knowledge necessary for—"

"Now, let's see," interrupted the principal, who didn't like the direction the conversation was taking. "Things are what they are. Mrs. Galhardo is available. We all agree that she is not a specialist in the area. But like it or not, she's all we've got. So let's take this opportunity and resolve the problem. It's not ideal, but it's a possible solution."

Thomas and Constance looked at each other, irate.

"Look here, ma'am," growled Thomas. "What you're offering us is not a solution for Margarida's problem. It's a solution for *your* problem. What our daughter really needs is a special-education teacher!" He almost spelled it out.

"There is no other choice," said the principal with a peremptory, final gesture. "Mrs. Galhardo will have to be responsible for special education."

"But that's not good enough."

"It'll have to do."

"I'm sorry, but we won't accept it."

The principal narrowed her eyes, staring at the couple in front of her. She sighed heavily, as if she had just made a difficult decision.

"Then you're going to have to put in writing that you won't accept the classes."

"We won't do that."

"Why not?"

"Because it's not true. We want special-education classes. We want them to be taught by a qualified teacher. What we don't want, and we're happy to put this in writing, is a teacher who, in spite of all her good intentions, is not properly trained."

The meeting came to an end without any resolution. The principal said a dry good-bye, frustrated at the impasse, and Thomas and Constance left the school with the impression that they were never going to get anywhere. They would have to hire a private teacher, but they couldn't afford it. With his extra work for the foundation, Thomas hoped to have enough money to help Margarida and lay his wife's mind at ease. If only he knew what Toscano was on to. The half million euros couldn't come fast enough.

Thomas looked at the building with the address Lena had given him. It was old and in desperate need of general repairs. He found the door open and entered a foyer decorated with tiles that were cracked and faded by time. The only light came from the street, spilling through the door's window and invading the tiny foyer with dazzling brightness, casting a geometric shape on the floor. Beyond that was darkness. Thomas began to climb the wooden stairs, which groaned under his weight, as if protesting against the intruder who had interrupted their indolence. He was aware of the stench of mold and moisture that was a trademark of Lisbon's old buildings. When he got to the second floor he checked the numbers on the doors and found the right one on the second door to his right. He pushed the black button on the wall and heard a soft *ding-dong* inside. There were footsteps, the metallic sound of a lock turning.

"Hej!" said Lena, welcoming him in. *"Välkommen."*

Thomas stood at the doorway for a long second, gaping at his hostess. Despite winter temperatures, she was wearing a very tight, light blue silk blouse with an infinitely plunging neckline, and a white miniskirt with a yellow sash that revealed long, shapely legs accentuated by elegant heels.

"Hi," he said finally. "You're looking very . . . pretty today."

"Do you think so?" she said with a smile. "Thank you. That's very nice of you." She motioned for him to come in. "Winter in Portugal reminds me of summer in Sweden. I find it really hot, which is why I'm dressed like this. I hope you don't mind."

Thomas stepped inside. "Not at all," he said, trying to will away his blushing cheeks. "It's a good idea. A very good idea."

The apartment was warm, a sharp contrast to the temperature outside. Its varnished wooden floorboards were old, as were the austere and badly painted pictures on the walls. It didn't smell musty, however. There was a pleasant aroma of food in the air.

"Can I take your coat?" Lena asked, holding out her hand. Thomas took off his coat and handed it to her. She hung it on a hanger by the door and led him down the long corridor, past two closed doors on the left to a kitchen at the end. Next to the kitchen was the living room, where a table was set for two. He peered in at the simple room decorated with old oak and walnut furniture. There were two worn brown sofas, a television on a table, and a wall cabinet displaying several old pieces of porcelain. The cold, diffuse daylight shone through two high windows facing onto an inner patio, where he could see the backs of several other apartments.

"How did you find this place?" he asked.

"I rented it."

"I know, but how did you find out about it?"

"Through the OSO."

"OSO? The university's Overseas Students Office?"

"It's quaint, isn't it?"

"Yes, quaint it is," said Thomas. "Who owns it?"

"An elderly woman who lives on the first floor. This apartment belonged to her brother, who died last year. She decided to rent it to foreigners. She says they're the only tenants she can be sure will leave eventually."

"Smart lady."

Lena checked a pot on the stove, stirred the contents with a wooden spoon, inhaled the steam coming off it, and smiled at Thomas. "It's going to be good." She showed him into the living room. "Make yourself at home," she said, indicating one of the sofas. "Lunch will be ready in a few minutes."

Thomas sat on the sofa and she sat next to him, tucking her legs up underneath her. Eager to avoid an embarrassing silence, Thomas opened his briefcase and pulled out some papers. "I brought some notes about Sumerian and Akkadian cuneiform writing," he said. "You're going to find the use of determiners especially interesting."

"Determiners?"

"Yes," he said. "They're also known as semantic indicators." He pointed at some cuneiform characters in his notes. "See? The function of semantic indicators is to reduce the ambiguity of the symbols. In this example, the determiner *gis,* when placed before—"

"Oh," interrupted Lena imploringly. "Can't we leave this until after lunch?"

"Um . . . yes, of course," said Thomas, surprised. "I thought you wanted to take the opportunity to go over things."

"Never on an empty stomach." She smiled. "Feed your servant well and your cow will produce more milk."

"What?"

"It's a Swedish proverb. It means, in this case, that my head will work better if my stomach is full."

"Oh," he said. "I see you have a penchant for proverbs."

"I love them. They are very wise, don't you think?"

"Yes, I suppose so."

"I think they are," she said peremptorily. "In Sweden we believe very much in proverbs. Do the Portuguese have many?"

"Some."

"Can you teach me?"

Thomas chuckled. "But what do you want me to teach you?" he asked. "Cuneiform writing or Portuguese proverbs?"

"Why not both?"

"That will take a long time."

"That's no problem. We have the whole afternoon, don't we?"

"I see you've got an answer for everything."

"A woman's sword is in her mouth," she retorted. "Another Swedish proverb." She gave him a cheeky look. "And in my case, it has a double meaning."

Thomas found himself at a loss for words, so he raised his hands in surrender. "I give up."

"That's a good idea," she said, leaning back on the sofa. "Tell me, are you from Lisbon originally?"

"No, I was born in Castelo Branco."

"When did you come to Lisbon?"

"When I was young. I came to get a degree in history."

"Which university?"

"Ours."

"Ah," she said, staring at him with her blue eyes, studying him carefully. "Have you ever been married?"

Thomas was caught off guard. He hesitated for a split second, torn between a lie and the truth, which would irremediably place her at arm's length. He lowered his eyes and heard himself say: "Yes, I am married."

He was afraid of her reaction. But much to his surprise, Lena didn't appear at all perturbed. "I'm not surprised," she said. "A handsome guy like you."

Thomas blushed. "Well . . . um . . ."

"Do you love her?"

"Who?"

"Your wife. Do you love her?"

Here was his opportunity to repair things. "When we got married, yes, of course. But we've grown apart over time. Now we're friends, obviously, but it's not the same kind of love."

He studied her, trying to detect her reaction. To his relief, she appeared satisfied with his answer.

"In Sweden we say a life without love is like a year without summer," she said. "Don't you agree?"

"Yes, I do."

Suddenly Lena opened her eyes wide and clapped her hands to her mouth. "Oh! I forgot the food!" she cried, leaping up and hurrying to the kitchen.

Thomas heard the sound of the pot being moved, stirred, and some muffled exclamations. "Is everything okay?"

"I'm fine," she called from the kitchen. "It's ready. You can take a seat at the table."

Thomas went to the kitchen doorway. Lena was holding a hot pot with a dishcloth, pouring soup into an old porcelain terrine that matched the bowls on the table. "Need some help?" he asked.

"No, everything's under control. Go have a seat."

Thomas hesitated, unsure as to whether he should sit or insist on helping. But her resolute expression convinced him to do as he was told. He took his place at the table. A moment later, Lena came in carrying the steaming terrine. She plunked it down on the table and sighed with relief.

"Whew! There it is!" she exclaimed. "Let's eat."

She took the lid off the terrine and ladled soup into Thomas's bowl, then her own. Thomas eyed it curiously; it was white and creamy-looking, with chunks of something floating in it, and it gave off a pleasant, succulent aroma.

"What's this?"

"Fish soup. Try it. It's good."

"So is this a Swedish dish?"

"Actually, it isn't. It's Norwegian."

Thomas tasted it. "Mmm, it's good," he said, nodding. "You're a good cook."

"Thank you."

"What fish did you use?"

"Oh, a few kinds, but I don't know their names in Portuguese."

Thomas ate a piece of fish. It tasted like cod. "This is delicious. Where did you learn the recipe?"

She stopped eating and gazed at him intently. "I don't want to talk about soup anymore. I think you know why I invited you here."

Thomas almost choked. "What?"

"I think you know why I invited you here," she repeated, as if it was a perfectly natural thing to say.

Unable to utter a single word and feeling his throat suddenly dry, he nodded. Lena smiled coyly. She reached over and took his head in her hands and looked adoringly into his eyes.

Thomas gave in.

Any thoughts he may have had of Constance and his daughter were quickly gone as he gave in to lust. Standing up, she reached for his hand, pulled him to his feet, and led him out of the living room.

Chapter 9

The south entrance of Jerónimos Monastery, with its heavy wooden doors, was closed to visitors. Thomas walked around the south side of the building, turned the corner, and slipped through the door on the east side. This was the main entrance, but its location in a tiny galilee under a low arch that obscured its rich Renaissance carvings detracted from its importance. Once he was inside the majestic monastery, his eyes were instantly drawn up to the vaulted ceiling supported on finely carved columns that splayed out at the top like giant palm trees, their leaves interlacing in a network of veins.

Nelson Moliarti, who had been busy admiring the stained-glass windows, saw him come in and went to meet him at the entrance, his steps echoing eerily through the almost deserted church. "Hi, Tom," he said. "How are you?"

Thomas shook his hand. "Hi, Nelson."

"This is incredible, isn't it?" he said, with a sweeping gesture. "Every time I come to Lisbon I drop by. There is no more magnificent monument to the Portuguese discoveries." He pulled Thomas over to one of the columns and pointed at a relief carved in the stone. "Do you see this? It's a sailor's rope. Your ancestors sculpted a sailor's rope in a church!" He pointed at the other side. "And over there are fish, artichokes, tropical plants, even tea leaves."

Thomas smiled at the American's enthusiasm."I know this place well. The maritime motifs sculpted in stone are a part of the Manueline style, which evolved during the reign of King Manuel I, unique in world architecture."

"That it is," agreed Moliarti. "Unique."

"And do you know how the monastery building was financed? With a tax on the spices, precious stones, and gold that the caravels brought from all over the world. It was called the pepper tax."

"How interesting," said Moliarti, looking around.

They wandered about under the high choir gallery near the entrance and strolled over to admire the tomb of Vasco da Gama. A life-size rose-marble statue of the great explorer lay with its hands clasped in prayer on a sarcophagus decorated with motifs of rope, armillary spheres, caravels, and a cross of the Order of Christ. On the other side of the entrance was the tomb of Luíz Vaz de Camões. Portugal's great sixteenth-century epic poet was also represented by a statue on a sarcophagus with its hands clasped in prayer and a crown of bay leaves on its head, which rested on a stone pillow.

"Do you think they're really there?" asked Moliarti.

Thomas chuckled. "It's what they tell the tourists. Let's put it this way. The mortal remains in this sarcophagus are almost certainly Vasco da Gama's." He pointed at the other tomb. "However, the mortal remains in that sarcophagus are almost certainly not Camões's. The travel guides continue saying that he is really there. Tourists seem to like it, and many people buy a copy of *The Lusiads* while they're here."

Moliarti shook his head. "So much for honesty."

"Have you been to Seville to see Columbus's tomb?"

"Yes."

"And are you sure he is really there? What if I told you it's all a big lie, that the mortal remains in Seville are not Columbus's?"

"Aren't they?"

Thomas shook his head. "There are those who say they aren't."

Moliarti shrugged. "What's important is the symbolic value. It may not be Columbus buried there, but that body represents him. It's a little like the Tomb of the Unknown Soldier—although he could be anyone, even a deserter or a traitor—he represents all soldiers."

A Spanish tour bus that had just pulled up outside scattered its passengers through the monastery like hungry ants, with cameras dangling from their necks, disturbing the two historians, who were interested in having a quiet place to talk.

"Come with me," said Moliarti, waving for Thomas to follow him.

Fleeing the tourists, they headed for the cloister. A small French garden brought color to its center; it was simple and flowerless, with a lawn in geometric shapes around a small circular pond. This whole center courtyard was surrounded by the arches and balustrades of the monastery's vaulted galleries. They wandered through until Moliarti lost interest in the symbols sculpted in stone and looked expectantly at Thomas. "So, Tom, have you got any answers for me?"

Thomas shrugged. "I'm not sure if I have answers or more questions."

Moliarti clucked his tongue disapprovingly. "The clock's ticking, Tom. We haven't got time to lose. It's been two weeks since you went to New York and a week since you got back to Lisbon. We really need to have some answers."

Thomas walked over to the fountain, where a stone lion, Saint Jerome's heraldic animal, sat with its front paws raised and a stream of water gushing from its mouth. The continuous gurgling was soothing. He passed his hand through the cold, clear water.

"Look, Nelson, I'm not sure if what I have will please you or not, but it's the result of the cipher that Professor Toscano left us."

"Did you manage to decipher that message?" asked Moliarti.

Thomas sat on a stone bench under the arches with his back to the courtyard and opened his briefcase. "Yes," he said. He pulled out a pile of papers and rummaged through it. He found the document he wanted and showed it to Moliarti, who sat next to him. "See this?" He pointed at some handwritten words in capital letters.

" '*Moloc,*' " read Moliarti. " '*Ninundia omastoos.*' "

"This is a photocopy of the cipher left by Professor Toscano," explained Thomas. "I spent several days trying to work it out, thinking it was a code or even a substitution cipher. Actually, it's a transposition cipher." He looked at Moliarti. "An anagram. Do you know what that is?"

"Of course. Toscano left you an anagram?"

Thomas nodded. "The first line is a very simple one, where everything is reversed, as in a mirror image." He held up the photocopy again. "See? *Moloc* is *colom* back to front. Now, *ninundia omastoos* is more complex, requiring a key to decipher it. Luckily, Toscano left one to remind himself. It conceals the phrase '*nomina sunt odiosa.*' "

"Cicero again. What does it mean?"

"Like I said before, it means 'names are odious.' "

"And what does *colom* mean?"

"It's a name."

"An odious name?"

"Yes."

"So who's this saint of a guy?"

"Christopher Columbus."

Moliarti gave Thomas a long stare. "What did Professor Toscano mean by that?" he asked, scratching his chin.

"That Colom's name was hateful."

"Okay, but in what way?"

"This was the most difficult part to figure out, because the phrase is ambiguous," said Thomas. He pulled another piece of paper out of his briefcase and showed it to Moliarti. "I studied up on it to work out what it was referring to. Apparently, it means that one shouldn't casually mention the names of well-known people without their knowledge when serious matters are at stake."

Moliarti picked up the piece of paper and studied it. "So Columbus's name is connected with something serious? In what respect?"

"Columbus's name wasn't, but Colom's was."

"Didn't you just tell me that he was Columbus?"

"Yes, but for some reason Professor Toscano wanted to draw attention to the name Colom. The only explanation is that it has a meaning."

"What?"

"This is the odious name."

"But in what way? I don't get it."

"That's precisely the question I asked myself. What was so special about the name Colom that Toscano wanted to draw attention to it? And why did he want it to be connected with being hateful?"

They sat there staring at each other, the question hovering like a cloud.

"I certainly hope you've found an answer," said Moliarti finally.

"I've found an answer and several new questions." Thomas flicked through his notes. "For the last few days I've been trying to discover the origin of the name Christopher Columbus. As you know, he spent about ten years in Portugal, studying to navigate the Atlantic. He lived in Madeira and married Felipa Moniz Perestrello, daughter of the navigator Bartolomeu Perestrello, the first governor of the island of Porto Santo. At the time, Portugal was the most advanced nation in the world, with the best ships, the most refined navigational instruments, the most sophisticated weapons, and the most learned individuals. The plan of the Portuguese crown was to find a sea passage to India in order to bypass Venice's monopoly over the spice trade with Asia. The Venetians had an exclusivity agreement with the Ottoman Empire, and at a disadvantage because of this agreement, the other Italian city-states, namely Genoa and Florence, supported this enterprise.

"It was in this context that, in 1483, the Genoese Columbus proposed to King John II that—since the earth was round—he sail west until he got to India, instead of heading south around the tip of Africa. The king of Portugal knew very well that the earth was round, but he was also aware that it was much bigger than Columbus thought and knew the westward route would take too long. We now know that he was right. That was when Columbus, whose Portuguese wife had since died, went to Spain to offer his services to the Catholic Monarchs."

"Why are you telling me all this, Tom?" interrupted Moliarti. "I'm familiar with the story—"

"Hang on," said Thomas. "I'm trying to contextualize what I'm about to tell you. We need to revisit Columbus's story because there was something strange about his name, something pertinent to his life story and the cipher that Professor Toscano left us."

"Okay, go on."

"Very well," said Thomas, trying to remember where he had left off. "As I was saying, Columbus went to Spain. We must remember that Spain was then governed by Queen Isabella, of Castile, and King Ferdinand, of Aragon, thus uniting the two kingdoms. At this time the country was involved in a military campaign to expel the Arabs from the south of the Iberian Peninsula. Columbus presented his project to a committee of Dominican friars. After four years of deliberations, the so-called wise men came to the conclusion that sailing westward in search of a passage to India was pointless, since they believed the earth to be flat. In 1488, Columbus returned to Portugal and was received by the much more enlightened King John II, to whom he renewed his proposal.

"While in Lisbon, Columbus witnessed the arrival of Bartolomeu Dias, who brought news that he had rounded Africa and discovered a passage from the Atlantic to the Indian Ocean, thus forging the long sought after route to India. Naturally, the project went down the drain.

"Discouraged, Columbus returned to Spain, where he married Beatriz de Harana. In 1492 the Arabs surrendered in Granada and the Christians took control of the entire peninsula. In the euphoria of the victory, the queen of Castile gave Columbus the green light, and he set off on the voyage that would lead to his discovery of America."

"Tell me something new, Tom," said Moliarti impatiently.

"I'm telling you this in order to make Columbus's relationship with the Iberian kingdoms clear—not just Castile but Portugal, too. And yet, during the fifteenth century, when he was in Portugal and Castile, Columbus was never referred to as Colombo, the name we call him in Portugal to this day."

"No one ever called him Colombo?"

"There isn't a single document that refers to him as Colombo."

"Then what did they call him?"

"Colom or Colon."

Moliarti was silent for a long moment. "What does that mean?"

"I'm getting there," said Thomas, flicking back through his notes. "I had a look at documents from the era and discovered that Columbus was referred to as Cristovam Colom, or Colon, and his first name was sometimes abbreviated as Xpovam. When he went to Spain, the Spanish started calling him Colomo, but this quickly developed into Cristóbal Colon, with Cristóbal abbreviated as Xpoval."

He rummaged through his papers and held up a photocopy. "Look. This is a letter from the duke of Medinaceli to the cardinal of Mendoza, dated March 19, 1493. Now, look what's written here." He pointed at a line in the letter.

I had in my house for a long time Cristóbal Colomo, who had come from Portugal and wanted to go to the King of France.

He looked up. "See? Here it says Colomo. What's odd is that later on in the same letter, the duke uses another name to refer to him." He pointed at a second passage. "Here it is. Cristóbal Guerra."

"Couldn't this Guerra guy have been someone else whose first name was Cristóbal?"

"No, the duke's letter is very clear. It's the same person. Look. The duke wrote,

In this time, Cristóbal Guerra and Pedro Alonso Niño went exploring, and this witness confirms it, with Hojeda and Juan de la Cosa's fleet."

He looked at Moliarti. "Now, the Cristóbal who went exploring with Niño, Hojeda, and Cosa was—as you are well aware—Columbus."

"Maybe it was just a slip, a mistake."

"It's definitely a slip, but I don't think it's a mistake." He went back to his papers and pulled out two more photocopies. He held the first one up for Moliarti to see. "This is an extract from the first edition of *Legatio Babylonica,* by Peter Martyr of Anghiera, published in 1515. In this book Peter Martyr identified Columbus as Colonus vero Guiarra. In Italian *vero* means 'real,' or 'true,' so Peter Martyr was saying that Columbus was actually Guiarra."

He held up the second photocopy. "This is an extract from the second edition of the *Legatio Babylonica* entitled *Psalterium* and dated 1530. Here, the reference has been changed slightly. It now reads 'Colonus vero Guerra.'" Thomas quickly flicked through his papers looking for another page. "This is document thirty-six from the Simancas Archive, dated June 28, 1500. It's addressed to a certain Afonso Álvares, whom 'their Highnesses order to go with Xproval Guerra to the newly discovered land.'" He looked at Moliarti again. "The surname Guerra again."

"That's three documents that refer to him as Guerra," observed Moliarti. "So you're telling me that in his time Columbus was not known as Colombo but as Guerra."

"Not necessarily. What I'm saying is that for some reason he had many names, but until much later, Colombo wasn't one of them." He made a vague gesture in the air. "You know, there are practically no documents about his time in Portugal, which is *very* curious, but as far as I've been able to determine, he was known in the country as Colom and Colon. In 1484 he went to Spain, where they began calling him Colomo. It was only eight years later that the Spanish began to call him Colon."

"Eight years later?"

"Yes. It was only after his death, in 1506, that the accent was added on the second *o* of Colon, making it Colón."

"Cristóbal Colón."

"Yes. But bear in mind that there's a story behind his first name, too. The Portuguese tended to call him Cristofom or Cristovam, while the Italians preferred Cristoforo. It's curious that Peter Martyr of Anghiera, in the twenty-two letters he wrote about him, always called him Cristophom Colonus, or Christophoro, never Cristoforo. When the Treaty of Tordesillas was being negotiated, Pope Alexander VI himself issued two papal bulls with the same title, *Inter caetera,* which cited the Spanish version of Columbus's name. In the first bull, dated May 4, 1493, he referred to him as Christofom Colon and in the second, dated June 28 of the same year, Christoforu Colon. This evolution is interesting, because Christofom is Portuguese. But the latter usage of Christoforu is the Latin name from which the Portuguese Cristovam and Spanish Cristóbal are derived."

"And what about Guerra?"

"Well, that's another mystery, isn't it? You see, Columbus was known everywhere as Cristofom or Cristovam. His surname was Colom or Colon. From 1492, the Spanish began to call him Cristóbal Colon for the most part, although every now and then he was still referred to as Colom." Thomas pulled out another photocopy. "In this Latin edition of one of the letters about the discovery of the New World, dated 1493, Colom reappears." He straightened up the two copies. "So, we have Guiarra, Guerra, Colonus, Colom, Colomo, Colon, and Colón."

"But why so many names?"

Thomas flicked through his notebook.

"There appears to be some kind of secret," he said. "His Spanish-born son, Ferdinand Columbus, made some very mysterious references to his father's name." He stared at a page of notes. "In a passage in his book, Ferdinand wrote, 'The surname of Colón, which he renewed.' And I'll try to translate what he said in another part of this enigmatic phrase: 'We could cite as examples many names which a hidden cause assigned as symbols of the parts which their bearers were to play.' "

He looked at Moliarti. "Get it? First, this 'renewed' suggests that Columbus changed his surname several times. Second, what should we make of 'We could cite as examples many names which a hidden cause assigned'? Many names? Hidden cause? What on earth is that all about? And what's this story about many names being 'symbols of the parts which their bearers were to play'? What was he insinuating? What, when all is said and done, was his real surname?"

"Hmm," said Moliarti. "So where did the name Colombo come from?"

Thomas turned back to his notes.

"The first time the surname Colombo appeared in a text was in 1494. Everything began with a letter he wrote from Lisbon the year before announcing his discovery of America. This letter was published in several places. On the last page of the Basel edition of 1494, an Italian bishop added an epigram that read '*merito referenda Columbo Gratia,*' thus Latinizing the name Colom. This new version was used by the Venetian Sabellico, in *Sabellici Enneades,* published in 1498. He identified him as '*Christophorus cognomento Columbus.*' Sabellico didn't know him personally, so he must have taken his inspiration from the famous epigram. Later there was a letter written by the Venetian Angelo Trevisan, dated August 1501, in which, citing the first edition of Peter Martyr of Anghiera's *De Orbe Novo Decades,* of 1500, he says the author was a good friend 'of the navigator, whom he called Christophoro Colombo Zenoveze.'

"The problem is that in other letters Peter Martyr gives you the impression that he didn't know Columbus personally, referring to him as 'a certain Cristovam Colon.' It appears that Trevisan altered Peter Martyr's text to make it palatable for Italian readers, Italianizing his name. The oldest surviving chronicle that refers to Columbus as Colombo is Montalboddo's *Paesi novamente retrovati,* published in 1507, which I saw at the Brazilian National Library in Rio de Janeiro.

"The book was very popular during its time—what we would call a bestseller. It even includes the first description of the discovery of Brazil by Pedro Álvares Cabral, and it helped spread a second falsehood, that the man who had discovered the New World was Amerigo Vespucci."

"A second falsehood? What was the first?"

Thomas looked at Moliarti in disbelief. "Isn't it obvious? The first falsehood is that Colom was called Colombo. The name Christopher Columbus is not his real name."

"How can you be so sure?"

"It's common sense. How can we call him Colombo if he referred to himself, in all of the documents he signed, as Colom or Colon?"

"What?"

"Didn't you know that? He never referred to himself in any known document as Colombo, nor did he mention the Latin version of his name. Never. There isn't a single document in Genoa's maritime history that mentions a sailor by this name. Not one. The first known document in which Columbus introduces himself is a letter he sent in 1493, shortly after his discovery voyage to America, to be delivered to the Catholic Monarchs. In this letter he identified himself as 'Christofori Colom.' Colom, with *m* at the end. And later, in his will, he explained that he belonged to the Colom family, which he said was '*mi linage verdadero*,' my true lineage." Thomas smiled. "Isn't it obvious the name Colombo was a misinterpretation?"

"If that's the case, why is he still called by that name?"

"For the same reason we still call the land Amerigo Vespucci didn't discover America. The simple repetition of an original error. Look, he identified himself in all of his documents as Colom or Colon. His contemporaries followed suit or gave him other names. An Italian bishop took it into his head that Colom translated in Latin as Columbo, and then Sabellico came along and, based on this erroneous translation, called him Columbus. A short time later, another Italian, Montalboddo, who didn't know him, took the name Colombo and gave it great visibility in his *Paesi novamente retrovati*.

"*Paesi* was an editorial success; everyone read it, and suddenly he came to be known as Colombo."

"But how do you know the Italian bishop wasn't right?"

"Because on the same page of the Basel edition where he wrote 'Columbo,' his name also appears as Colom. *Colom* means 'dove' in Catalan." He looked at Moliarti. "Now, what's *dove* in Italian?"

"Colomba. Or Colombo, I suppose."

"And in Latin?"

"Columbus."

"Bingo. The bishop, who spoke Catalan, thought *Colom* meant 'dove.' And because he wanted to Latinize the name, he wrote 'Columbo.'"

"Precisely," argued Moliarti. "Colom is a translation of Colombo."

"It would be, if it weren't for the fact that the *name* Colom doesn't mean 'dove.'"

"So what does it mean?"

"Once again it was Colombo's own son, Ferdinand, who enlightened us, when he said that the surname of Colón was a fitting one, because in Greek it means 'member.' Nelson, how do you say *member* in Greek?"

"I don't know."

"*Kolon,* with a *k*." Thomas glanced back at his notes. "In fact, Ferdinand himself, when he reveals that the surname Colón comes from the Greek word *kolon,* says, 'If we give his name its Latin form, which is Christophorus Colonus'"—Thomas grinned at Moliarti—"See? In short, it means that whatever his real name was, it certainly wasn't Colombo, or what we now know as Columbus."

"So it would've been Colonus, would it?"

Thomas cocked his head and made a skeptical face. "Maybe. But it may also be just another pseudonym. Note that Ferdinand wrote: 'We could cite as examples many names which a hidden cause assigned as symbols of the parts which their bearers were to play.' That is, the navigator chose names that predicted something."

"And what prophecy would be connected to the surname Colonus?"

"Ferdinand himself answered that question: 'asking Christ's aid and protection in that perilous pass, crossed over with his company that the Indian nations might become dwellers in the triumphant Church of Heaven.' In other words, the surname Colonus was chosen because it prophesied the colonization of India by the Christian faith."

"Hmm," murmured Moliarti, looking somewhat disappointed. "So in your opinion that was what Professor Toscano discovered?"

"I have no doubt that, when he left the message '*Colom, nomina sunt odiosa,*' Toscano was saying that the name Colom was hateful."

"And that's it?"

"I think there's much more to unravel. As I mentioned earlier, the phrase *'nomina sunt odiosa'* suggests that one should not casually mention the names of well-known people when serious matters are at stake. It seems to me that Professor Toscano was suggesting a connection between Colom and a fact of great importance."

"The discovery of America."

"But we already know about this connection, Nelson. I get the impression that Toscano was referring to something else that no one has ever brought up."

"Such as?"

"If I knew, my friend, I'd have already told you, wouldn't I?"

Moliarti fidgeted on the stone bench. "You know, Tom," he said. "None of this has anything to do with the discovery of Brazil."

"Of course not."

"So why did Professor Toscano spend so much time studying Columbus? Why was he wasting our money on this investigation?"

"I don't know," said Thomas. "But is it worth my continuing this investigation? Regardless of what Toscano discovered, everything suggests that there's no connection with Pedro Álvares Cabral's voyage and his supposed discovery of Brazil." He looked Moliarti in the eye. "Would you like me to continue?"

The American didn't hesitate. "Of course," he said. "The foundation must know what he was spending our money on all this time."

"Which brings us to the second problem. I don't have anything else to investigate."

"What do you mean? What about Professor Toscano's documents and notes?"

"What documents and notes? I've already looked at everything he had in Brazil."

"He did a lot of research in Europe."

"Where did he go? I wasn't told about that."

"To the Portuguese National Library and the Tower of Tombo, here in Lisbon. Then he went to Spain and Italy."

"What was he looking for?"

"He never told us."

Thomas was pensive, his gaze lost in the cloister's ornate arches. "Hmm," he said. "And where are his notes?"

"I assume his widow's got them."

"Have you asked her for them? They're crucial to the investigation."

Moliarti's facial muscles twitched nervously. "Professor Toscano's scholarly digressions created a lot of tension between us. We had several arguments with him, because we wanted progress reports and he refused to write them. Naturally, this tension extended to his wife, with whom our relationship has become just as difficult."

Thomas chuckled. "In other words, she'll have a fit if she sees you."

Moliarti pursed his lips. "Yup. That's why you must go pay the widow Toscano a visit."

"Me?"

"Yes, you. She doesn't know you. She doesn't know you're working for the foundation."

"Sorry, Nelson, but I can't do that. You want me to go to the dead man's house to trick his widow?"

"What other option do we have?"

"I don't know. Talk to her, explain things, try to see eye to eye."

"It's not that easy. Things have already gone past the point of no return. You'll have to go there yourself."

"Nelson, I can't."

Moliarti looked at him with a hard face, his eyes steely, implacable; he was no longer a friendly, laid-back American, warm and good-natured, but a cold businessman. "Tom, we have no intention of wasting our investment with regard to your employment. Do you want the substantial sum we've offered?"

Thomas hesitated. He thought of his daughter, her need for schooling.

"Then go to his house and get everything you can from his fucking wife," snarled Moliarti. "Got it?"

Once his initial surprise at Moliarti's sudden change of humor had subsided, Thomas felt indignation boiling up inside him, galloping through his stomach. He wanted to get up and leave. He didn't let people talk to him like that. He rose from the stone bench, infuriated, not knowing which way to turn. He saw the marble tomb of the Portuguese writer Fernando Pessoa in front of him and, looking for a distraction, an escape, anything, walked over to the monument. A poem leaped out at him from the tombstone:

TO BE GREAT, be whole: exclude
Nothing, exaggerate nothing that is you.
Be whole in everything. Put all you are
Into the smallest thing you do.
The whole moon will then gleam in every pool,
Because it rides so high.

At that moment, Thomas wanted to be great like Fernando Pessoa, to show Moliarti that he was whole, without excluding anything, putting all he was and felt into the words that were choking him. But moments later, when the initial eruption had passed and he was feeling calmer and more rational, he reconsidered. To be great, that great, was a luxury he could not afford; he was a man whose daughter needed a heart operation and a teacher the school could not afford, a man whose marriage was crumbling into an ocean of worries about his daughter's grim future amidst the irresistible advances of a very fresh Scandinavian.

Five thousand dollars a week was a lot of money; and the bonus of half a million dollars, if he managed to recover Toscano's entire study, was a lot more. Thomas knew he *could* recover it.

He restrained himself. He turned around and, resigned, faced the American.

"Okay," he said. "I'll go see the widow."

Chapter 10

The narrow street was quiet, provincial even, in spite of the fact that it was in the center of town, right behind the Marquês de Pombal Square. The old building stood between more modern buildings and had one of those back patios that one sees only in the Portuguese countryside. It had a rustic appearance, with a garden full of lettuces, collard greens, and potatoes; clucking chickens; and a pigsty. An apple tree stood next to it, a silent sentinel.

Thomas checked the number on the door. This was it. He glanced around hesitantly, almost not believing that this was the Toscano residence. But his scribbled annotations left no room for doubt; it really was the address he'd been given at the Classical University. He pushed open the gate and walked onto the grounds. He stood still for a moment and tuned in to the sounds around him, expecting a barking dog to appear. It looked like the kind of place that would be patrolled by hounds with bared teeth. He took another few steps and gained confidence when none appeared.

The door of the building had been left open. He went inside, plunging into the darkness, and felt around for the light switch. No lights came on when he flipped it. He tried again, to no avail. "Shit," he muttered, frustrated.

Once his eyes adjusted to the darkness, he perceived daylight coming through the opening at the door, soft and diffuse; but since the morning had dawned gray, the light was weak and it was still difficult to see. Gradually he made out shapes. On his right was a staircase of rotting wood. Next to it, an outer grating, like a birdcage, contained a rusty elevator that seemed long out of use. The fetid smell of old, abandoned things filled the foyer. The building was a ruin, a pile of debris on the verge of collapse.

He looked for more references in his notebook but couldn't read in the darkness. Stepping back toward the entrance, where the light was stronger, he remembered that he'd been told that Professor Toscano lived on the ground floor. He felt his way down the corridor and found a door. He patted the wall looking for a doorbell but didn't find one. He knocked and heard something scraping against the floor; someone was coming. The door opened a crack, revealing a taut chain attached to a lock. An elderly woman in a blue robe and beige pajamas, with tousled gray hair, peered through the crack.

"Yes?" Her voice sounded frail and apprehensive.

"Good morning. Are you Mrs. Toscano?"

"Yes. What can I do for you?"

"I've come . . . um . . . I've come on behalf of the university, the New University." He paused, hoping these were credentials enough. But the woman's black eyes remained unchanged. "It's about your husband's research."

"My husband is dead."

"I know, ma'am. My sympathies." He hesitated, awkward. "I . . . um . . . I've come precisely to take up where your husband left off."

The woman narrowed her eyes suspiciously. "Who are you?"

"I'm Thomas Noronha, from the History Department of the New University. I've been asked to finish Professor Toscano's research. I went to the Classical University and they gave me this address."

"What do you want with his research?"

"It's very important. It was your husband's last work." Thomas felt he had found a powerful argument and spoke resolutely. "Look, a person's life is his work. Your husband died, but it's up to us to resuscitate his last study. It would be a shame for it never to see the light of day, don't you think?"

She frowned, looking lost in thought. "How do you intend to do this?"

"By publishing it, of course. That would be a just homage. But it would only be possible, obviously, if I manage to reconstruct your husband's research."

She remained pensive. "You're not from the foundation, are you?"

Thomas gulped and felt beads of cold sweat forming on his forehead. "Wh . . . what foundation?" he stuttered.

"The American one."

"I'm from the New University of Lisbon, ma'am," he said, sidestepping her question. "I'm Portuguese, as you can see."

Apparently satisfied with his answer, she unfastened the chain and opened the door, inviting him in. "Would you like a cup of tea?" she asked, leading him into the living room.

"No, thank you, I had breakfast not long ago."

The living room was old-fashioned and had seen better days. Against faded floral wallpaper hung oil portraits of stern men, landscapes, and old ships. Tatty, dirty ottomans were positioned around a small television set, and on the other side of the room, a pine china cabinet with bronze fittings displayed black-and-white photographs of a couple and several smiling children. The house smelled of mold. Shiny dust particles hovered by the windows like ethereal fireflies, tiny points of light slowly dancing in the stagnant air. Thomas sat on the sofa, and his hostess followed suit.

"Please excuse the mess," she said.

"What mess, ma'am?" He looked around.

"Ever since Martinho died I haven't had the energy to keep things tidy. I've been on my own so much."

Thomas remembered the professor's full name. Martinho Vasconcelos Toscano.

"I can't imagine how difficult this must have been for you."

"I know," she agreed, looking resigned. She seemed elegant—or as though she had been—and weary. "Time is ruthless. Look at this. It's all rotting, falling apart. A few more years and they'll tear it down. It won't be long. You know, my husband's grandfather designed this building at the turn of the century."

"Really?"

"It was one of the most beautiful buildings in Lisbon. There weren't as many back then as there are now, all these ghastly high-rises everywhere. No, back then everything was very beautiful, very sophisticated. It was lovely."

"I bet it was."

She sighed, then adjusted her robe and tucked a strand of hair behind her ear. "So tell me. What can I do for you?"

"Well, what I need is to have a look at all of your husband's documents and notes from the last six or seven years."

"The research he was doing for the Americans?"

"Yes . . . um . . . I'm not sure. I'd like to see the material he was compiling."

"It was the research he was doing for the Americans." She coughed. "You know, Martinho was hired by some foundation or other in the United States. They paid him a fortune. He went to a bunch of libraries and the Portuguese National Archives to read manuscripts. He read until he couldn't read anymore. He handled so much old paper that he'd come home with his hands filthy with dust. Then one day he had a breakthrough. He was bursting with excitement when he got home—like a kid. I was over there reading, and all he said was, 'Madalena, I've discovered something extraordinary—extraordinary!'"

"And what was it?" Thomas asked anxiously, perched on the edge of the sofa.

"He never told me. You know, Martinho was special; he loved codes and riddles and spent days doing crossword puzzles in newspapers. He never told me a thing. All he said was, 'Madalena, right now it's a secret, but when you read what I've got here, your jaw is going to drop.' And I let him be, because he was happy when he was absorbed in his things. He traveled, went to Italy and Spain, wandered from place to place, busy with his research." She coughed again. "At one point, the Americans started harassing him. They wanted to know what he was doing, what he'd discovered, that kind of thing. But Martinho wouldn't budge. He told them what he'd told me, to be patient, that he'd show them when everything was ready. They didn't like that and things got messy. Once they came here and got into a shouting match." She pressed both of her hands to her face. "They were so furious that we thought they'd cut the payments. But they didn't."

"Don't you think that's strange?"

"What?"

"If they were so anxious to know everything and your husband wouldn't tell them anything, don't you think it strange that they didn't cut his payments?"

"Yes. But Martinho told me they were scared."

"Really?"

"Yes, they were terrified."

"Of what?"

"He didn't tell me. It was between them. I didn't get involved. I think the Americans were afraid that Martinho would keep his discovery to himself." She smiled. "That really shows how little they knew my husband, doesn't it? When did Martinho ever leave his research in a drawer gathering dust? Unthinkable!"

"Now that he's dead, why didn't you give the material to the Americans? After all, it's a way of getting it published."

"I didn't because Martinho had had a falling-out with them." She chuckled and lowered her voice, as if making an aside. "He was a university professor, but when he got worked up he could have a fiery tongue." She cleared her throat. "He once said, 'Madalena, they aren't going to see a thing before it's all ready. Zip. And if they show up here trying to smooth-talk you, beat them off with a broom!' I knew Martinho very well, and for him to tell me that, it's because someone was up to no good. So I did as he asked. The Americans are actually afraid to come here. One of them did once—he even spoke Portuguese, with a bit of a Brazilian accent—and lurked around the door like a vulture. He said he wouldn't leave until I spoke to him. That was when Martinho went to Brazil. The guy stayed there for hours and hours. Good God! It was as if he'd put down roots. I didn't have any choice but to call the police, did I? They sent him packing."

Thomas laughed, having visions of Moliarti being dragged out of the building by a couple of big-bellied policemen. "And did he come back?"

"When Martinho died, he came snooping around again. I haven't set eyes on him since."

Thomas ran his hand through his hair, trying to find a way to lead the conversation to what had brought him there. "I'm really curious about your husband's research," he began. "Do you know where he kept the material he was compiling?"

"It must be in the study. Would you like to see it?"

"Yes, of course."

She led him down the poorly lit, pungent corridor, her robe dragging along the oak floor. The study was in a state of disarray, with piles of books everywhere. "Please ignore the mess," she said, picking her way through the piles. "I still haven't had the time or the energy to put my husband's study in order."

She opened a drawer and looked through its contents, then opened another. She looked in a cabinet and finally made a sound of satisfaction, having found what she was looking for. "Here it is," she said, dragging out a cardboard box.

The carton was stuffed with papers. On top was a green file with the word *Colom* scribbled across the cover.

Thomas took the box as if it contained a treasure. It was heavy. He carried it to a less cluttered corner of the study, put it on the floor, and sat down with his legs crossed, hunched over the documents. "Would you mind turning the light on?" he asked.

Madalena flipped the switch and a weary yellow light tenuously lit the room, casting ghostly shadows across the ground and cabinets. Thomas dipped into the documents, and almost instantly he lost all notions of time and space, forgetting where he was, becoming deaf to his hostess's comments as he was transported to a faraway world, one that he shared only with Toscano. He organized the photocopies and notes into two piles: relevant and not so relevant. There were reproductions of *History of the Catholic Sovereigns,* by Bernaldez; *Natural and General History of the Indies,* by Oviedo; *Psalterium,* by Giustiniani; *The Life of the Admiral Christopher Columbus,* by Ferdinand Columbus; and documents compiled by Muratori, Columbus's entailed estate, the *Raccolta di documenti e studi, Anotaciones,* and the Assereto Document. There were also photocopies of a letter written by Toscanelli and several letters signed by Colom himself. To complete the list of documents there should have been Montalboddo's *Paesi novamente retrovati,* but Thomas already knew Toscano had found it in Rio de Janeiro. What could it all mean? he pondered.

Night had settled over the city when Thomas stopped working. Looking up from the floor, with documents scattered around him, he realized he'd forgotten to have lunch and that he was alone in the study. He organized the papers and returned them to the box, then he got up. The muscles in his back and legs were stiff and painful, and he practically hobbled down the corridor to the living room. Madalena was lying on the sofa, asleep, a book on Renaissance art open on her lap. Thomas coughed lightly, trying to wake her up. "Ma'am," he murmured. "Ma'am."

She opened her eyes and sat up, shaking her head to wake up. "I'm sorry," she said drowsily. "I dozed off."

"And so you should have."

"Did you find what you were after?"

"Yes," Thomas lied.

"You must be tired, you poor thing. I went in to offer you something to eat, but you didn't even hear me. You looked hypnotized in the middle of all that mess."

"I'm sorry. When I'm concentrating I don't even see what's going on around me. The world could be ending and I wouldn't even notice."

"Don't worry, my husband was the same. When he was off in his own world, it was as if he took a leave of absence from reality." She smiled softly, then waved her hand toward the kitchen. "Look, I cooked you a delicious steak."

"Thank you. You shouldn't have gone to the trouble."

"It's no trouble at all. Won't you sit and eat?"

"I must be off, but thank you so much. I'd just like to ask you a favor."

"What is it?"

"May I take the box so I can photocopy the documents? I'll bring them back."

"You want to take the box?" she asked. "I'm not sure about that."

"Don't worry. I'll bring everything back the day after tomorrow. Everything."

"I don't know. . . ."

Thomas pulled his wallet from his pocket and took out two cards, which he handed to Madalena. "Look, please hold on to my ID and my credit card. I'll leave them as a guarantee that I'll be back in two days with your things."

She took the cards and studied them carefully. Then she looked him in the eye. "Okay," she said, putting them in the pocket of her robe. "Tomorrow. No later."

"Don't worry," said Thomas, heading back to the study.

When he was halfway down the corridor, he heard Madalena's voice coming from the living room, weak but audible. "Would you also like what's in the safe?"

He stopped and looked over his shoulder. "What?"

"Would you like what's in the safe, too? Martinho also kept documents in there. Would you like to see them?"

"Of course I'd like to see them," said Thomas, frustrated. "What are they? Why didn't you tell me about this hours ago?" His tone was almost rude.

The widow looked at him, not a single muscle in her face moving. "I didn't think I could entirely trust you," she said. She bowed her head and patted her robe pocket. Her eyes meeting Thomas's once more, she said, "Now I do." Thomas ran back for his notebook and then followed Madalena.

She led him across the living room and into the bedroom. The bed was unmade. A chamber pot sat on the floor, clothes were draped across a wicker chair, and an unpleasant acidic smell hung in the air. "I'm not sure," she said. "But Martinho told me they were the proof."

"Proof? Proof of what?" Thomas asked.

"That, I don't know. I suppose proof of whatever he was researching, right?"

With mounting excitement, Thomas watched her open the door of a cupboard, revealing a metal safe built into the wall.

The lock had ten digits. "What's the combination?" he asked, barely able to contain his excitement.

Madalena retrieved a folded-up piece of paper from the nightstand and handed it to him. "Here it is."

Thomas unfolded it. It had two columns containing twelve groups of letters and numbers:

W H O   F P E
T A O   F T N
E C H   O F D
U A C   U E I
L T I   S L N
5 4 5   N O G

"Is this the combination?" asked Thomas. "But these are mostly letters and the safe only takes numbers."

"Yes," said Madalena. "Each letter stands for a number. For example, *A* is one, *B* is two, *C* is three, and so on. You see?"

"Of course." He pointed at the digits on the bottom line. "What about these numbers? Do they stand for letters?"

She took a closer look at the paper. "I'm not sure," she admitted. "He didn't tell me."

Thomas copied the combination into his notebook. He tried transforming the letters into numbers, leaving the numbers at the bottom as they were. He finished his calculations and studied the result:

24	8	15	6	16	5
20	1	15	6	20	14
5	3	8	15	6	4
21	1	3	21	5	9
12	20	9	19	12	14
5	4	5	14	15	7

He tried the numbers on the lock, which proved to be time-consuming. When he finished, he waited an instant. The door didn't budge. It was no surprise; the code had to be more complex than a simple translation of letters into numbers. He looked at Madalena and shrugged.

"This is more difficult than it looks," he concluded. "I'm going to take the documents home to get photocopies, and I'll bring everything back tomorrow, okay?" He pointed at the paper with the safe's combination on it. "I'll come back when I've worked out what this means, and, if you don't mind, we can open the safe to see what's inside. Okay?"

Madalena nodded in agreement and both walked silently to the front door.

Chapter 11

Thomas spent the morning at the National Library looking up references he thought might be useful in light of what he had seen the previous day at Professor Toscano's house. Periodically he tried a series of experiments to decipher the safe's combination. At midday he went to pick up his photocopies, took the box of originals back to Madalena Toscano's house, and collected the ID and credit card he'd left. He promised to be back as soon as he'd figured at the combination. By the time he took a break, it was already one o'clock in the afternoon, and Lena called his cell, inviting him for lunch.

They had a light meal dressed in robes in the living room.

"So how's your research going?" asked Lena. "Have you made any progress?"

Thomas had already realized that her interest in his research was genuine. He had been surprised at the start, never imagining that something so dense would arouse her curiosity. Her enthusiasm for his work flattered him, and more important, it was fuel for their conversations, a common interest that strengthened their connection. Constance, it seemed, couldn't care less about his work.

"Would you believe that yesterday I went to Professor Toscano's house and his wife let me photocopy all of his documents and notes from the last few years?"

"Bra!" she exclaimed happily. "Were they any good?"

"Excellent. But apparently the best things are locked in a safe." He found the ciphered message and showed it to her. "The problem is that before I can open it I have to decipher this mumbo jumbo."

Lena leaned forward and studied the cipher. "Are you going to be able to figure it out?"

"I'm going to try using a table of frequencies." He set a book entitled *Cryptanalysis* on the table.

"Is that it?" asked Lena, staring at the cover, which showed what looked like crossword puzzles.

"This book contains several different frequency tables." He flicked through it, and when he found the page he wanted, he held it up. "See? They're in English, German, French, Italian, Spanish, and Portuguese."

"And can you decipher any message using these tables?"

Thomas chuckled. "No. Only substitution ciphers."

"What do you mean?"

"There are three kinds of ciphers. Concealment ciphers, transposition ciphers, and substitution ciphers. A concealment cipher is one in which the secret message is hidden in such a way that nobody even realizes it exists. The oldest known system of concealment was used in ancient times, when the message was written on the shaved head of a messenger, who was generally a slave. The author of the message would let the messenger's hair grow back, and only then would he be sent to the recipient. The messenger made it past the enemy without any problems because it didn't occur to them that there was a message under his hair, you see."

"That wouldn't work for me," said Lena with a smile, running her fingers through her gorgeous curls. "What about the other systems?"

"A transposition cipher is really an anagram, like the one I deciphered in Rio de Janeiro. *Moloc* is *Colom* read from right to left. Obviously, in very short messages, especially those with only one word, these ciphers aren't very safe, since there is a limited number of ways in which you can rearrange the letters. If you increase the number of letters, the number of possible combinations skyrockets. For example, a sentence with only thirty-six letters can be combined in trillions of different ways. It requires a system for ordering them. This was the case with the anagram I deciphered: *Moloc, ninundia omastoos*. It has twenty-one letters, which means there are millions of possible combinations. I realized that the first line, where it said *Moloc*, used an ordering system based on simple symmetry, in which the first letter was the last, the second was the second last, and so on, until you got *Colom*.

"On the second line, however, there was a symmetrical system following a preestablished pattern, luckily one that Toscano had already provided. I had to put one word on top of the other and combine them alphabetically according to the pattern."

"You're a genius," said Lena. She pointed at the cipher Thomas had copied down at Toscano's house. "What about this one? Is it a transposition cipher?"

"I doubt it. My guess is that it's a substitution cipher."

"Why do you say that?"

"Because of the general appearance of the message. Most of the letters look as if they've been thrown together at random."

Lena chewed on her bottom lip. "But what is this substitution, exactly?"

"It's a system in which the real letters are replaced with others. Take the word *dog,* for example. If we establish that *d* is *t, o* is *x*, and *g* is *r, dog* becomes *txr* in the ciphered message. When the cipher alphabet becomes apparent, the rest is easy; anyone can read the message."

"Is this system common?"

"Very. The first known substitution cipher is the one described by Julius Caesar. It was based on an alphabet that involved a forward shift of three places down the normal alphabet. The *a* of the normal alphabet became the letter three places down, which was *d*, while *b* became *e,* and so on. This system came to be known as the Caesar cipher. In the fourth century B.C. the Brahman scholar Vatsyayana recommended in the *Kama Sutra* that women learn the art of secret writing so they could safely communicate with their lovers. These days the practice is highly advanced and the more complex messages can only be deciphered using computers that can test millions of combinations per second."

Lena gazed intently at Toscano's message. "If you think this was written using a substitution cipher, how are you going to read it? You don't know what the cipher alphabet is, right?"

"No."

"So what are you going to do?"

"Try the frequency tables again."

She stared at him, not understanding. "Will they help you find the alphabet?"

"No," he said, shaking his head. "But they contain a shortcut. The idea for frequency tables arose among Arab scholars studying Muhammad's revelations in the Koran. In an attempt to establish the chronology of the prophet's revelations, Muslim theologists decided to count the frequency with which each word and letter appeared. They realized that certain letters were more common than others. For example, *a* and *l*, which make up the definite article *al*, were identified as being the most common letters in the Arabic alphabet."

"I don't follow."

"Imagine the ciphered message was originally written in Arabic. If we know that *a* and *l* are the most common letters in that language, all we have to do is identify the two most common letters in the message. Supposing they are *t* and *d*. Chances are, if we replace *t* and *d* with *a* and *l*, we'll have begun to decipher it."

Lena looked at him, impressed.

"The system isn't infallible. Of course, ciphered texts can contain letters that, for one reason or another, don't appear with the exact frequency recorded in the table. This is especially true of very short texts. Take 'Peter Piper picked a peck of pickled peppers.' Obviously, in a message like this the letter *p* crops up much more often than usual. Longer texts, however, tend to conform to standard frequencies. Unfortunately, that's not the case here. I was too optimistic."

"How many letters does it have?"

"Only thirty-six. That is, thirty-three letters and three numbers. That's not much."

"What now?" she asked. "What are you going to do?"

"I have to find a new approach." He opened his notebook to the page where he'd scribbled down the cipher and put it on his lap. "The first problem is working out which language the message was written in."

"Isn't it in Portuguese?"

"It might be," he said. "But we can't forget that the first cipher was a Latin proverb. There's no guarantee that Professor Toscano didn't choose Latin again, or any other language, for that matter."

"So what happens now?"

"Well, I analyzed it and discovered that the most common letter is *o*, which appears four times, followed by *e*, *f*, *n*, and *t*, which all appear three times. Since *o* is the most common letter, I replaced it with *a*. Then I tried experiments with *e*, *f*, *n*, and *t*, replacing them alternately with *e*, *o*, *r*, and *s*, the most common letters in Portuguese texts after *a*."

"Did you get anywhere?"

"No."

Lena looked at the table. "So if you didn't get anywhere and the most common letter is *o*, don't you think the text might be written in a different language?"

"Well, that would mean it's not a substitution cipher, but—" He stopped midsentence, surprised at what he'd just said.

"But what?" asked Lena.

Thomas was quiet for a moment, as several things dawned on him at once. He ran his hand over his mouth and stared into space as he mulled over the idea.

"What?" begged Lena.

Thomas looked at her, then turned back to the message in his notebook. "Maybe it isn't a substitution cipher," he said finally.

"No? Then what is it?"

Thomas started counting letters. "One, two, three, four, five, six, seven . . ." he murmured, his finger jumping from one letter to the next. "Thirteen," he said, wrote it down in his notebook, and started counting again. He counted up to twenty, then wrote that number under the thirteen. Then he picked up the book and consulted the frequency table. "Hmm," he said with a frown.

"What?" said Lena, not understanding a thing.

Thomas pointed at a figure on a frequency table. "See this?"

"Yes," said Lena. "Forty-eight percent. What does it mean?"

Thomas smiled. "It's the frequency of vowels in Portuguese texts," he explained excitedly. He pointed at other numbers in the book. "See? Only Italian has the same vowel frequency as Portuguese. Spanish has forty-seven percent, French, forty-five, and English and German, forty."

"And?"

"Guess how many vowels there are in Professor Toscano's cipher?"

"How many?"

"Thirteen. And there are twenty consonants. In other words, 39.4 percent of the thirty-three letters here are vowels." He looked her in the eye. "Do you know what that means?"

"That it wasn't written in Portuguese?"

"Probably not," said Thomas. "And I also think we're looking at another anagram. In substitution ciphers, the most common letters in texts are often switched with less common ones. But that's not the case here, is it? There's still a high frequency of letters common in several European languages, such as *e*, *t*, *o*, and *n*, which makes me think they haven't been substituted. They've been transposed, simply changing places."

"Like *Moloc*?"

"Except this time with more letters, more complex, and probably not in Portuguese or Italian—there are too few vowels." He looked at the cipher.

"So now what?"

"I have to test the connections between the vowels and consonants to see if something makes sense. If I manage to pick anything up, I'll be able to figure out the pattern and the language used by Professor

Toscano. For example, for *Moloc* he used a symmetrical mirror-image pattern, where you had to read from right to left." He held up the cipher. "But this isn't symmetrical. Look." He read the first line of the first column from left to right. "'*WHO.*'" He shrugged. "Now, that's a word in English." He read the first line of the second column. "'*FPE.*'" He hesitated. "Doesn't mean anything to me. And if we read from right to left, we get 'EPF,' which doesn't mean a thing."

"How about from bottom to top?"

"It can be any pattern. Left to right, bottom to top, top to bottom, diagonal, skipping letters, zigzagging, whatever—"

"'*WTEUL-5,*'" murmured Lena, reading the left-hand column from top to bottom. Thomas studied the cipher carefully and picked up a pencil.

"Let's try putting the two columns together."

He reproduced it on the next page, no longer in horizontal groups of three, but in a column of six. The result still looked confusing:

W H O F P E
T A O F T N
E C H O F D
U A C U E I
L T I S L N
5 4 5 N O G

"'*WHOFPE,*'" whispered Lena, now reading the first line all the way across. Then she read it from right to left. "'*EPFOHW.*'" She went on, reading the second line and third lines: "'*TAOFTN.*' '*ECHOFD.*' *Tao* and *echo* are both words in English. But the letters on the end don't make any sense."

"'*OLEFTP,*'" continued Lena, now reading each column from the bottom up. "'*LEFT.*' That's a word!"

Thomas was looking for trigraphs, common three-letter clusters such as *the*, *and*, *tha*, *end*, and *ing*. He found *end* and *ing* together in the right-hand column, from top to bottom.

"*Ending*," he said to himself.

Suddenly he smiled. *Pending.* By turning the corner, he connected the *p* to *ending* to make *pending.* He wrote the cipher out again, underlining the letters of the word they'd just found:

W H O F *P* *E*
T A O F T *N*
E C H O F *D*
U A C U E *I*
L T I S L *N*
5 4 5 N O *G*

"That's it!" he exclaimed, almost shouting. "There it is!"

"What? What?"

"A crack in the cipher." He pointed at the underlined letters. "See? It says '*pending.*'"

Lena read it. "Wow, so it does." She frowned, finding the sequence bizarre. "But the *P* isn't in line with the rest of the word."

"That's because of the pattern," said Thomas with growing excitement. "The words must turn corners according to a specific pattern." He picked up his pencil and studied it. "Let me see. If we turn the corner again after '*pending,*' it says '*on545.*' That must be meant to read '*pending on 545.*" He went back to the other lines. "And here's your *left*, reading from the bottom up." He scratched his nose. "Hmm. *Left pending on 545.*"

Working his way backward, he followed the entire sequence of letters to the beginning according to the pattern he'd just identified. The sentence looped around like a game of snakes and ladders. He wrote out the deciphered text.

WHATECHOOFFOUCAULTISLEFTPENDINGON545

He analyzed the line and rewrote it, now inserting logical spaces between the words. When he was done, he looked from his work to Lena, a triumphant grin on his lips.

"Voilà!" he said.

Lena stared at the scribbled sentence and was amazed at how that impenetrable jumble of letters had magically become an intelligible sentence.

WHAT ECHO OF FOUCAULT IS LEFT PENDING ON 545?

"What does that mean?" Lena asked.

Thomas shook his head. "I'm not sure. But I know someone who may."

Chapter 12

The gulls swooped low, and their forlorn cries could be heard over the waves that rhythmically washed up and down the vast Carcavelos Beach, leaving fingers of foam on the sea-beaten sand. Cold and windy under a gray winter sky, the beach was populated by only a handful of surfers, two or three couples, and an old man walking his dog by the water's edge. Its gloomy, monochromatic appearance was a far cry from its colorful exuberance in summer, when it brimmed with life and energy.

In the beach restaurant Thomas had entered ten minutes earlier, the waiter brought him a steaming cup of coffee. Thomas took a sip and glanced at his watch. It was three forty in the afternoon; his colleague was ten minutes late. He sighed. The night before he had called Alberto Saraiva, from the Department of Philosophy, to request an urgent meeting. Saraiva lived in Carcavelos, a stone's throw from Oeiras. Apart from being an obvious meeting place, the beach, even in winter, was much more pleasant than the university's small offices.

"Mon cher, sorry I'm late," he heard from behind him.

Thomas stood and shook Saraiva's hand. Saraiva was about fifty, with sparse gray hair, thin lips, and a squint—à la Jean-Paul Sartre. There was something extravagant about him, slightly harebrained; he had the aura of the mad genius, with a cultivated *negligé charmant*. His wild appearance had stood him in good stead in his area of philosophy, the French deconstructionists he had studied so intensively while doing his Ph.D. at the Sorbonne.

"Hello, Alberto," said Thomas. "Please, have a seat." He gestured at the chair next to him. "Would you like something to drink?"

Saraiva sat down and looked at Thomas's coffee. "I think I'll have coffee, too."

Thomas waved at the waiter, who was walking toward them. "Another coffee, please."

Saraiva took a deep breath, filling his lungs with the salt air, and looked around, taking in the ocean from one end of the horizon to the other.

"I love to come here in the winter," he said. He spoke pompously, enunciating his syllables carefully, as if he were reciting a poem and the right cadence was essential in order to express the indolence of the place. "This ineffable peace and quiet inspires me. It gives me energy, stretches my horizons, fills my soul."

"Do you come here often?"

"Only in autumn and winter. When there are no summer tourists around." He made a face of disgust, as if one such lamentable specimen had just walked by. The waiter set a second cup of coffee on the table, and the clink of the china jolted Saraiva out of his reverie. He opened his eyes and saw the cup in front of him. "This is where I'm best able to delve into the thinking of Jacques Lacan, Jacques Derrida, Jean Baudrillard, Gilles Deleuze, Jean-François Lyotard, Maurice Merleau-Ponty, Michel Foucault, Paul—"

Seeing his opportunity, Thomas faked a cough. "In fact, Alberto," he interrupted, "it's precisely about Foucault that I need to speak to you."

Saraiva stared at him with raised eyebrows, as if he had just committed blasphemy, taking both God's and Christ's names in vain.

"*Michel* Foucault?"

"Yes, Michel Foucault," said Thomas diplomatically, accepting his unspoken rule. "You know, I am currently doing some historical research and have come across, don't ask me how, Michel Foucault's name. I'm not exactly sure what I'm looking for, but something about him is relevant to my research. What can you tell me about him?"

The professor waved his hand vaguely, implying that there was so much to say that he didn't know where to begin. "Oh, Michel Foucault! He was the greatest philosopher after Immanuel Kant. Have you read the *Critique of Pure Reason*?"

"Um . . . no."

Saraiva sighed. "It's the most important philosophical text ever written, *mon cher*," he proclaimed, gazing steadily at Thomas. "Kant observed that we do not know the world as it is 'in itself,' the ontological truth of things, but only representations of it. We do not know the nature of objects themselves, but only our perception of them, which is unique to humankind. For example, human beings experience the world differently than bats do. Humans see images, while bats detect sonar echoes. Humans see colors, while dogs see in black and white. No experience is truer than another. They are just different. No one has access to truth itself, and everyone has a different idea of it. If we revisit Plato's famous 'Allegory of the Cave,' what Immanuel Kant is saying is that we're all in a cave chained to the limits of our own perception. We only see the shadows of things, never the things themselves." He turned to Thomas. "Do you understand?"

Pensively, Thomas watched a wave deposit white spume on the sand. He nodded without taking his eyes off it. "Yes. Is that what Foucault says as well?"

"*Michel* Foucault was strongly influenced by this, yes. He realized that there was no such thing as one truth, only several truths."

Thomas frowned. "How can you say that there is no truth? If I say that this chair is made of wood, am I not telling the truth?" He pointed at the ocean. "If I say the ocean is blue, am I not telling the truth?"

Saraiva smiled. This was his territory. "This is a problem that the phenomenologists had to resolve in the aftermath of the *Critique of Pure Reason*. It had become necessary to redefine the word *truth*. Edmund Husserl, one of the fathers of phenomenology, found that judgments are not objective and only express a subjective representation of the thing-in-itself."

"Hmm, I'm not sure," said Thomas hesitantly. "It sounds like wordplay to me."

"It isn't," insisted Saraiva. "Take your field, history, for example. The history books speak of the Lusitanian leader Viriathus's resistance to the Roman invasions. But how can I be sure that Viriathus really existed? Only through texts that mention him. But what if these texts are fictional? As I'm sure you know better than I do, a historical text does not deal with what is real but with accounts of what is real, and these accounts may be incorrect, if not invented. As such, truth in historical discourse is not objective but subjective. Karl Popper observed, nothing is definitely true; there are just things that are definitely false and others that are provisionally true."

"That's valid for everything," said Thomas. "It doesn't really answer my question." He pointed at the horizon again. "I can see the ocean there, and I can see that it is blue. How can you say that that is a subjective reality?" He pursed his lips. "As far as I know, the blue of the ocean is an objective truth."

"The ocean isn't blue—it is our eyes that see it as such, as a result of the fact that the wavelength of blue light scatters better than the other colors in the spectrum and makes the ocean *appear* blue. This is the real problem with truth—because I know my senses can betray me, my rationale can lead me to incorrect conclusions, my memory can play tricks on me, and I don't have access to the thing-in-itself. You look at the ocean and see it as blue, but when a dog looks at the ocean, he sees it as black, because he is color-blind. Neither of you has access to the thing-in-itself, only to a vision of it. Neither of you has access to the objective truth, only to something less categorical. The subjective truth."

Thomas rubbed his eyes. "Is this where Foucault comes in?"

"*Michel* Foucault built on these realizations. What he showed was that claims of truth depend on the dominant discourse of the era in which they are stated. Working almost like a historian, he came to the conclusion that knowledge and power are so intrinsically connected that they become power/knowledge, almost as if they were two faces of the same coin. Essentially, it was around this fundamental axis that he developed all of his work." He gestured at Thomas. "Have you ever *read* any Michel Foucault?"

"Actually," Thomas said hesitantly, afraid of offending his colleague, "I haven't."

Saraiva shook his head in paternal disapproval.

"Tell me about him."

"What would you like me to tell you, *mon cher*? He was born in 1926 and was gay. After discovering Martin Heidegger, he stumbled across Friederich Nietzsche and his theory about the central role of power in all human activity. This revelation marked him deeply. He came to the conclusion that power underpinned everything and set out on a mission to analyze the way in which power manifests itself through knowledge, using knowledge to establish social control. The power/knowledge nexus."

"But where is this written?"

"In several books. In *Order of Things,* for example, he analyzes the dominant discourse and prejudices that organize thought in any given era. It was perhaps Michel Foucault's most Kantian work, in which words are a manifestation of what is real, while things themselves are actually real. In a way, this book helped destroy the absolute notion of truth. Because if our way of thinking is always determined by the dominant discourse and prejudices of the era, then it isn't possible to arrive at an objective truth."

"That's what Kant said."

"Of course. That's why many people consider Michel Foucault to be a new Immanuel Kant, though Michel Foucault put these ideas in a new context," said Saraiva, intent on making sure his favorite philosopher wasn't seen as a kind of plagiarist. "I'll tell you a story. When he was invited to lecture at Collège de France, they asked him what his title was. Do you know what he said?"

Thomas shrugged.

"Professor of the history of systems of thought." Saraiva cracked up. "They must have looked at him as if he had two heads." His laughter faded into a contented sigh. "Michel Foucault defined truth as a construct, a product of the knowledge of each era, and extended this understanding to other concepts. He believed an author was not just one who wrote books but a construct built on a series of factors, including language, the literary schools of the time, and several other social and historical elements. In other words, an author is nothing more than the product of his circumstances."

"Ah," said Thomas, as if he finally understood. Truth be told, he didn't see anything extraordinary or innovative about it, but he didn't want to argue with Saraiva or diminish his enthusiasm. "What else?"

Gazing out at the horizon, the philosopher launched into a long summary of Foucault's work.

"That's all," said Saraiva when he'd finished. "Two weeks after delivering the manuscript of the third volume of *The History of Sexuality*, Michel Foucault collapsed and was taken to hospital. He had AIDS. He died in the summer of 1984. Now, why so interested?"

"I'm investigating a riddle."

"A riddle involving Michel Foucault?"

Thomas ran his hand across his face, rubbing it distractedly. "Yes. Kind of."

He looked at the vast ocean before him, the water glittering as if a bright carpet of diamonds had been scattered across the restless surface, heaving with the waves. The sun was sinking to his right, behind a mantle of clouds.

"What's the riddle?"

Thomas looked at Saraiva hesitantly. Was it worth showing him? To be honest, what did he have to lose? In his notebook he found the page on which he'd written the phrase and showed it to Saraiva. "See?"

Saraiva leaned forward and stared at the strange question:

WHAT ECHO OF FOUCAULT IS LEFT PENDING ON 545?

"What on earth?" said Saraiva. "Echo of Foucault?" He looked at Thomas. "What echo?"

"I don't know. You tell me."

Saraiva studied the phrase again.

"Mon cher, I haven't the foggiest. Perhaps someone who echoes Michel Foucault?"

"Now, that's an interesting idea," said Thomas thoughtfully. He looked at Saraiva with a slightly anxious expression. "Do you know if there is anyone who echoes Foucault?"

"Only if it was Immanuel Kant. However, it was Michel Foucault who echoed Immanuel Kant, not the other way around."

"But hasn't anyone followed Foucault?"

"Michel Foucault had many followers."

"And are any of these followers 'left pending on 545'?"

"I don't know how to answer that because I don't know what it means. What's this '545'?"

Thomas didn't take his eyes off Saraiva. "Doesn't any of it sound even remotely familiar?"

Saraiva bit his bottom lip. "Nothing," he said, shaking his head. "Nothing at all. What is this all about anyway?"

Thomas snapped closed his notebook with a great to-do and sighed. "Can I promise to tell you when it's all over?"

Saraiva jotted down the mysterious phrase and put it in his jacket pocket. "I'll have a careful look through my books," he promised. "Maybe I'll find something."

"Thanks."

"What are you going to do now?" asked Saraiva.

"I'm going to stop off at a bookshop and buy Foucault's books, to see if I can find a clue. The key to the riddle is probably there, in some small detail."

They left the restaurant together and said good-bye in the parking lot. "Michel Foucault was a curious character," said Saraiva before he left.

"In what way?"

"Do you know what he once said about all his work in search of truth?"

"What?"

"That all his life he did nothing but write fiction."

Chapter 13

Lisbon's old hillside neighborhood of Alfama was quaint and colorful, the run-down façades of its old houses almost hidden behind potted flowers and clothes hanging out to dry in front of their large windows and stretched across iron balconies. Oblivious to the busy neighborhood, Thomas kept his head down, and it was with relief that he reached the top and entered the wide perimeter of the castle.

Thomas arranged to meet Moliarti at São Jorge Castle to update him on the progress he'd made. His meeting with Saraiva had only intensified Thomas's curiosity about what Toscano's investigation had to do with Michel Foucault. Thomas knew he had to decipher the connection with Foucault in order to really make headway into Toscano's work. And, more important, to get into Toscano's safe.

Moliarti waved at him from a table at the castle's café between an old olive tree and a huge sixteenth-century cannon. Thomas sat with him, even though the cold air and gray clouds didn't make sitting outdoors very appealing.

After ordering lunch, Moliarti was the first to break the silence.

"I trust your research is progressing."

"Absolutely," Thomas replied. "But my problem at the moment is getting into Professor Toscano's safe. The combination is a puzzle he left. That safe may hold all the information I need."

"Can't you just break in to it?"

"What?" Thomas laughed, amused at the brashness of Americans. "I can't. His widow won't let me."

"Why don't you just stage a burglary?" Moliarti seemed annoyed by Thomas's honesty.

"Good God, Nelson. I'm a university lecturer, not a thief. If you want to break in to the safe without the widow's consent, go hire a thug to do the job. I'm not your guy."

Moliarti sighed. "Okay, okay. Forget I said that."

"Fine," Thomas began. "Based on the photocopies I found at Toscano's house and library records in Lisbon, Rio, Genoa, and Seville, I've been able to establish beyond a doubt that Professor Toscano spent most of his investigation verifying Christopher Columbus's origins. It seems he was especially interested in analyzing the documents that connect him to Genoa and determining their reliability. I'm about to show you the information he collected and the conclusions I believe he came to."

"Allow me to clarify that," said Moliarti. "Are you actually in a position to assure me that Toscano hardly spent any time studying the discovery of Brazil?"

"I'm pretty sure he dedicated himself to that topic in the early days of the project. But in the middle of his investigation he must have come across some document that sidetracked him."

"What?"

"That, I don't know."

Moliarti shook his head. "The son of a bitch!" he muttered under his breath.

"Shall I go on?" asked Thomas cautiously.

"Yes, do."

"Well, let's have a look at which documents connect Columbus to Genoa." Thomas leaned over his briefcase and pulled out a small bundle of photocopies. "Actually, a recurrent problem with the documents about Columbus's origins is their lack of reliability. The originals were lost and we don't know how careful the scribes were and to what extent attempts were made to appropriate his nationality. In some cases documents may have been forged, while in others, probably the majority, certain key points may have been changed. As you know, sometimes merely moving a comma can completely alter the meaning of a text."

"So, what have you got?"

"As I mentioned the last time we met, in 1501, Angelo Trevisan, from Venice, sent a fellow countryman an Italian translation of an early version of Peter Martyr's *De Orbe Novo Decades,* where he mentions his friendship with 'Christophoro Colombo Zenoveze,' thus clearly establishing for the first time the explorer's connection to Genoa."

"Mm-hmm."

"The problem is that Toscano doubted the veracity of parts of this edition and quoted the scholar Enrique Bayerri y Bertomeu's suspicions in his notes. I read Bayerri y Bertomeu and saw that he questioned the authenticity of Peter Martyr's text because it all seemed to have been written for an educated Italian public. It's almost as if *De Orbe Novo* was a sensationalist text, like the ones Amerigo Vespucci published on the New World. It didn't necessarily tell the truth; rather it told what the public wanted to hear. And the Italians wanted to hear that it was an Italian who had made the great discovery of America."

"I see," murmured Moliarti, scratching his chin. "What else is there?"

Thomas took some photocopies out of the bundle. "In 1516, ten years after Columbus's death, a Genoese friar who became bishop of Nebbio, Agostino Giustiniani, published a text in several languages entitled *Psalterium Hebraeum, Graecum, Arabicum, et Chaldaeum,* which proved to contain a wealth of hitherto unknown information. Giustiniani revealed to the world that the man who discovered America, a Christophorus Columbus, of '*patria Genuensis,*' 'born in Genoa,' was of '*Vilibus ortus parentibus,*' meaning 'of humble birth,' and his father was a '*carminatore,*' or wool carder, whom he did not name. According to Giustiniani, Columbus was also a wool carder, having received only a rudimentary education. Before he died it is said that he left a tenth of his income to the the Bank of Saint George in Genoa. Giustiniani reiterated this information in a second work, *Castigatissimi Annali di Genova,* published posthumously in 1537, in which he only corrected the profession of this Christophorus. He was no longer a wool carder but a silk weaver."

"That coincides with what we know today about Columbus."

"True," said Thomas. "But in his notes, Toscano listed some of the problems he identified in the information presented by Giustiniani in *Psalterium* and *Castigatissimi Annali.* First, Columbus couldn't have left the Bank of Saint George one-tenth of his income because he died penniless. One-tenth of nothing is zilch." He smiled. "But this is just a humorous detail. Much more serious is the allegation that Columbus was an uneducated silk weaver, because it raises some big questions. If he was a silk weaver and an uneducated man, where the hell did he acquire the advanced knowledge of cosmography and sailing that would allow him to navigate unknown seas? How is it possible that he was entrusted with not just one ship but entire fleets? How could he have earned the title of admiral? Is it likely that a commoner like him would have married Dona Felipa Moniz Perestrello, a Portuguese noblewoman, descended from Egas Moniz and a relative of the general Nuno Álvares Pereira, in an era of great class prejudice when marriages between commoners and nobility didn't take place? How could such an uneducated individual have gained access to the court of the great King John II, at that time the most powerful and knowledgeable monarch in the world?" He waved the copies of Toscano's notes in the air. "It's clear to me that Toscano didn't find any of this very plausible. Additionally, Giustiniani didn't know Columbus personally. All he did was cite secondhand information. Columbus's own Spanish son, Ferdinand, accused Giustiniani of being a false historian and pointed out several easily verifiable factual errors to suggest that the Genoese author had also given false information about 'a matter of which little is known'—an enigmatic expression in Ferdinand's book presumed to be about his father's origins."

"I see," murmured Moliarti. "Is there anything else?"

Thomas tucked his pen back into his jacket pocket and pulled a book out of his briefcase.

"Let's see the most important witness of all, after Columbus himself," he said. "Ferdinand, the admiral's second son, born of his relationship with the Spanish Beatriz de Harana, and author of *The Life of the Admiral Christopher Columbus.*" He held up the book. "This is what should be, beyond a doubt, a true gold mine of information. No one dares challenge whether Ferdinand knew his father. He had access to privileged information. Ferdinand makes it immediately clear that he wrote this biography because others had tried to do so without getting their facts right."

"But does Ferdinand confirm that his father was from Genoa?"

"Well, that's the problem. He doesn't state unequivocally that he was. On the contrary. He says he traveled to Italy three times, in 1516, 1529, and 1530, to try and see if there was any truth to the information being bandied about at the time. He went looking for relatives, interviewed people with the surname Colombo, and searched the public records. Nothing. He didn't find a trace of a relative on any of his three visits to Genoa. He did, however, locate his father's origins in Italy, more specifically in Piacenza, in whose cemetery he claimed to have seen tombs with arms and epitaphs bearing the name Colombo. Ferdinand revealed that his ancestors were of illustrious stock, although his grandparents had been reduced to great poverty, and refuted the argument that his father was uneducated, pointing out that only someone with a high level of instruction could have drawn maps or done such great deeds. *The Life of the Admiral Christopher Columbus* also provided details of his father's arrival in Portugal. He claims it was because of 'a renowned man of his name and family, called Colombo,' whom Ferdinand goes on to identify as Colombo the Younger. During a battle at sea, somewhere between Lisbon and Cape Saint Vincent, in the Algarve, the admiral is said to have leapt into the water two leagues offshore and swum to land, clutching an oar. He then went to Lisbon, where, according to Ferdinand, 'many of his Genoese nation' lived."

"There you go!" exclaimed Moliarti with a triumphant smile. "Proof, from Columbus's own son."

"I'd agree with you," said Thomas, "if we could be sure it really was Ferdinand who wrote that."

Moliarti pulled his head back in surprise. "Huh! Wasn't it?"

Thomas glanced at his copies of Toscano's notes.

"From the look of things, Toscano had his doubts."

"What doubts?"

"About the reliability of the text and some strange contradictions and inconsistencies in it," said Thomas. "Let's start with the manuscript. Ferdinand finished his book, but he didn't publish it. He died without leaving any descendants, so the manuscript was passed down to his nephew, Luís de Colón, the oldest son of his Portuguese half brother, Diego. Luís was approached in 1569 by a Genoese gentleman by the name of Baliano de Fornari, who offered to publish *The Life of the Admiral* in three languages: Latin, Spanish, and Italian. Ferdinand's nephew agreed and gave the man the manuscript. In 1576 Fornari published the Italian version, saying he was doing it so 'this story whose first glory should go to the state of Genoa, the great explorer's homeland, can be universally known.' He forgot the other two versions and spirited away the manuscript." Thomas held up the Spanish copy of Ferdinand's book again. "In other words, what we have here is a translation from the Italian, which is, in turn, a translation from the Spanish commissioned by a Genoan who professed to want to attribute glory to Genoa." He placed the book on the table. "So in a way, this is yet another second-hand source."

Moliarti rubbed his eyes, exasperated. "What are the inconsistencies?" The waiter set down their plates.

"First of all, the reference to the tombs with the family coat of arms and epitaphs in Piacenza. When you visit the city cemetery, you can see that these tombs actually exist, but the surname is Colonna." He smiled. "Professor Toscano seems to have thought the Genoese translator changed the Latinization of Colón to Colonus, not Columbus, thus contradicting the story that the tombs belonged to the Colombo family."

"But didn't Ferdinand say his father jumped into the sea because of a certain Young Columbus, who was a relative?"

Thomas chuckled. "It's Colombo the Younger, Nelson." He leafed through *The Life of the Admiral.* "The book does say that. But it's yet another contradiction. Colombo the Younger was a corsair whose name wasn't even Colombo. He was Jorge Bissipat, whom the Italians nicknamed Colombo the Younger to distinguish him from Colombo the Elder, as the Frenchman Guillaume de Casenove Coullon was known."

"What a mess."

"I know. But that's the thing. How could Colombo the Younger have been of the same name and family as Ferdinand's father if Colombo was not his actual name but a nickname? The only possibility is that the translator also had a hand here, establishing of his own accord a family connection between Christopher Columbus and Colombo the Younger that obviously wasn't possible."

Moliarti leaned back in his chair, fidgeting. He had finished his fish and pushed his plate away.

"Well, regardless of whether it was Colonna or Colombo, in Piacenza or in Genoa, the fact is that Ferdinand places his father's origins in Italy."

"It seems Professor Toscano wasn't so sure about that," said Thomas, leafing through his notebook. "In his notes, and beside the references to Piacenza as Columbus's true hometown in *The Life of the Admiral,* he made an observation in pencil that the person who came from Piacenza wasn't the explorer himself but the ancestors of Felipa Moniz Perestrello, Columbus's Portuguese wife and the mother of his son Diego. Toscano appeared to believe that Ferdinand, in the original text, had mentioned Piacenza as one of Felipa's distant origins and that the Italian translator fiddled with this passage, changing Felipa to Christopher. In fact, Toscano jotted down the Italian saying '*traduttori, tradittori,*' which literally means 'translator, traitor.'"

"That's speculative."

"True. But almost everything about Columbus is speculative, so great are the mysteries and contradictions surrounding his life." Thomas looked back at *The Life of the Admiral.* "Let me show you some other inconsistencies that Toscano found. For example, this story that after swimming to shore his father went to Lisbon, 'knowing that many of his Genoese nation lived in that city.'"

"Well, you can't argue with that."

"But think about it, Nelson. Didn't Ferdinand state only a few pages earlier that he had visited Genoa and never located a single relative there? Wasn't it Ferdinand who supposedly said that his father's origins were in Piacenza? After writing that, why would he then lead us to believe that his father was from Genoa?" Thomas went back to Toscano's notes. "Again, Professor Toscano seems to have suspected tampering by the Genoese translator, writing '*traduttori, tradittori.*'" He picked up some other photocopies. "In fact, there are so many contradictions in *The Life of the Admiral* that Father Alejandro de la Torre y Velez, canon of the Salamanca Cathedral and a scholar of Ferdinand's work, also came to the conclusion that 'someone had tampered with and adulterated it.'"

"So you're saying it's all false?"

"No. *The Life of the Admiral* was definitely written by Ferdinand. That is something no one disputes. But in the published text there are certain contradictions and inconsistencies for which there are only two possible explanations. Either Ferdinand didn't have his head screwed on properly, which doesn't seem probable, or someone fiddled with key details of his manuscript, adapting them to the taste of readers in Italy, where it was first published."

"Who?"

"Well, the answer seems obvious to me. It could only have been Baliano de Fornari, the Genoese who got the manuscript from Luís de Colón and only published the Italian translation, openly confessing to wanting the 'first glory' of the discovery of America to go 'to the state of Genoa, the great explorer's homeland.'"

Moliarti made an impatient gesture. "Go on."

"Well," said Thomas, "let's move on to the most important witness of them all."

"Who?"

"Columbus himself."

"What did he say?" asked Moliarti.

Thomas took a deep breath as he put the photocopies in his briefcase back in order. "We now know that Columbus spent his entire life hiding his past. We call him Columbus, but there isn't a single document in which he refers to himself by this name. Not one. Columbus always referred to himself, in the surviving manuscripts, as Colom or Colón. Not only did the man we now call Christopher Columbus never, as far as we know, use this name to introduce himself, he also deliberately kept his origins shrouded in mystery."

"Do you mean he never said where he was born?"

"Put it this way. Columbus was always very careful to hide his origins, except on one occasion." He held up some photocopies he had set to one side. "His *mayorazgo*."

"His *mayor*-what?"

"*Mayorazgo,* or entailed estate. It was a will, dated February 22, 1498, establishing the rights of his Portuguese son, Diego, shortly before Columbus took off on his third voyage to the New World." Thomas scanned the text. "In this document, Columbus reminded the crown of his contribution to the nation and appealed to the Catholic Monarchs and their eldest son, Prince Juan, to protect his rights and 'my offices of admiral of the ocean, which is to the west of an imaginary line, which His Highness ordered to be drawn, running from pole to pole a hundred leagues beyond the Azores, and as many more beyond the Cape de Verd islands.' Columbus indicated that such rights should pass to his firstborn son, Diego, 'being a man of legitimate birth, and bearing the name of Colón derived from his father and ancestors.' If Diego were to die without leaving any male heirs, the rights were to pass to his half brother, Ferdinand, then to Columbus's brother Bartolomeu, then his other brother, and so on successively as long as there were male heirs." Thomas looked up at Moliarti. "This detail is important. Note that Columbus didn't say 'bearing the name of Columbus' when he referred to himself and his ancestors. He said, 'bearing the name of Colón.'"

"I get it," complained Moliarti, a dark look on his face. "But what about where he was from?"

"I'm getting there," said Thomas, gesturing for Moliarti to be patient. "His will also established that a part of the revenue to which the admiral was entitled should be deposited with the Bank of Saint George and provided strict instructions about how his heirs should sign all documents. Columbus didn't want them to use their surname, but just the title *el Almirant,* beneath a strange pyramid of initials and dots." Thomas held up another page. "Here's the part you're interested in, Nelson. You and Toscano, so it seems. At a certain point in his will, Columbus did something unprecedented. He reminded the Catholic Monarchs that he had served them in Castile, although he had been born in Genoa."

"Aha!" exclaimed Moliarti, almost leaping out of his chair. "Proof!"

"Whoa! Hold your horses!" said Thomas, laughing at Moliarti's eagerness. "In another part of his will, he urged his heirs to always maintain one person of their lineage in Genoa, 'inasmuch as I was born there, and came from thence.'"

"See? What's not to believe?"

"It's all very clear," agreed Thomas with a smug smile. "If it's true."

A dark cloud obscured Moliarti's enthusiasm. His smile faded, but his mouth remained open and his eyes bulged in disbelief. "What the fuck?" he said, flying off the handle. "No way! You're not going to tell me it's all false, are you? Come off it, man. Don't bullshit me!"

"Whoa!" said Thomas again, unnerved by the explosion and holding up his hands in surrender. "Wait a minute. I'm not saying things are true or false. All I'm doing is studying the documents and witnesses, consulting Toscano's notes, and reconstructing his thought processes. After all, that's what you hired me to do, isn't it? Now, what I've seen is that Toscano was highly suspicious of certain aspects of the traditional biography of Christopher Columbus. What I'm doing is showing you their problems as far as reliability goes. If we accept all of the documents and witnesses as good, the admiral's life story doesn't make sense. He would have been born in several places and had several different ages and names. That's not possible. At the end of the day, you're going to have to decide what's true and what's false. If you want Columbus to be Genoese, all you have to do is ignore the contradictions and inconsistencies in the documents and witnesses that uphold this theory, resorting to pure speculation to solve them. The opposite is also true. But I'm not here to destroy the Genoese hypothesis. To be honest, Christopher Columbus's origins are irrelevant to me. Why should I care?" He paused for emphasis. "All I'm trying to do is reconstruct Toscano's research, which is what I was hired to do."

"You're right," said Moliarti, calmer now. "Sorry, I flipped my lid for nothing. Go on, please."

"Well," said Thomas. "As I already mentioned, in his will Columbus made two explicit references to Genoa as his city of birth."

"So Columbus made two references to Genoa, openly claiming to have been born there."

"That's right," said Thomas. "Which means that now everything depends on an assessment of the reliability of this document. There is a royal ratification of his *mayorazgo,* dated 1501, which was only discovered in 1925, and is held at the General Archive of Simancas. I brought photocopies of the notarized copy of the draft of his will, which is in the General Archive of the Indies, in Seville." He waved some photocopies. "I imagine it's the copy that was at the center of the *Pleyto Sucessorio,* very important judicial proceedings that opened in 1578 to determine the admiral's legitimate heir after the death of Don Diego, his great-grandson. We mustn't forget that the *mayorazgo* stipulated that all heirs were to be males bearing the name Colón. Now, directly disobeying the provision supposedly established by the admiral, the court decided the name Colombo was also valid, notice of which soon spread throughout Italy. Since Christopher Columbus was entitled to a part of all the income from the Indies, the news that anyone by the name of Colombo could be a candidate for succession aroused enormous interest among Italians. The name Cristoforo Colombo proved to be quite common in Italy, so the court stipulated that candidates must have in their ancestry a brother Bartolomeo, another brother Jacobo, and a father called Domenico. One candidate by the name of Baldassare Colombo, from Cuccaro Monferrato, had to face other Spanish descendants of Columbus, and it was during these hearings that a Spanish lawyer named Verástegui produced a copy of the draft, showing that it had been ratified by Prince Juan on February 22, 1498, the date on which the will was executed."

"Who is this Prince Juan?"

"The firstborn son of the Catholic Monarchs."

"So you have a copy of the draft ratified by the crown prince, and you're still unsure as to its reliability?"

"Nelson," said Thomas in a low voice. "Prince Juan died on October 4, 1497."

"So?"

"How could he have ratified the copy of a draft in 1498?" He winked. "Huh?"

Moliarti remained still for a long moment, his eyes frozen on Thomas as he mulled over the problem.

"Well . . . um . . . ," he finally mumbled.

"This, my dear Nelson, is a very serious technical problem. It totally undermines the credibility of the copy of the *mayorazgo*. And the worst thing is that it isn't the only inconsistency in the document."

"There are more?"

"Of course there are. Check this out." He picked up a photocopy of the text. " 'And I also pray the king and queen, our sovereigns, and their eldest-born, Prince Don Juan, our lord' "—Thomas looked up at Moliarti. "It's the same problem. Columbus addresses Prince Juan as if he were alive, when he had died the year before, at the age of nineteen. It was such a big thing at the time that the court dressed in mourning, public and private institutions closed down for forty days, and symbols of mourning were placed on the walls and gates of Spanish cities. Under these circumstances, how could the admiral, being a person close to the court, especially the queen, not have known of the prince's death?" He smiled and shook his head.

"Now look here," Thomas went on, looking at his photocopies. " 'The said Don Diego or any other inheritor of this estate, shall possess my offices of admiral of the ocean, which is to the west of an imaginary line, which His Highness ordered to be drawn, running from pole to pole a hundred leagues beyond the Azores, and as many more beyond the Cape Verde islands.'" He looked at Moliarti. "This short passage contains as many inconsistencies. In the first place, how on earth could the great Christopher Columbus have said that Cape Verde sat on the same meridian as the Azores? Is it possible that the man who discovered America, who had actually visited these two Portuguese archipelagos, could have made such a great blunder?

"Second, we mustn't forget that this business of the hundred leagues had cropped up in the papal bull *Inter caetera,* dated 1493, which culminated in the Treaty of Alcaçovas. The problem is that in 1498, when the *mayorazgo* was signed, the Treaty of Tordesillas was already in effect. So how is it possible that the admiral used papal expressions from a treaty no longer in force? Had he lost his mind?

"Third, he said 'to the west of an imaginary line, which His Highness ordered to be drawn,' at a time when Queen Isabella was still alive. She only died six years later, in 1504. How on earth could Columbus have referred to the Catholic Monarchs in the singular? It was custom, as one can see in any document from that era, to refer to them as Their Highnesses, in the plural. Might Columbus have decided to insult the queen, insinuating that she did not exist? Or might this document have been written after 1504, when there was in fact only one monarch, by a forger who overlooked this detail and put the date as 1498?"

"I see," said Moliarti, looking downcast. "Is that all?"

"No, there's more. The fact that Columbus makes two references to Genoa in his will deserves special analysis." He held up two fingers. "Two. These references are explicitly saying that this was his city of birth." He leaned back in his chair and tidied his photocopies. "I mean, Columbus spent his entire life hiding his origins. He was so obsessive about it that the criminologist Cesare Lombroso, one of the greatest detectives of the nineteenth century, classified him as paranoid." He stared at Moliarti. "The more famous Columbus became, the less he wanted people to know about his birthplace and family. So for years this guy goes to great lengths to keep the location of his birth secret, then suddenly, out of the blue, he changes his mind and makes an orgy of references to Genoa in his will, dashing all of his hard work in one stroke? Does that make any sense?"

Moliarti sighed. "So this means the will is a fake, does it?"

"That's the conclusion the Spanish court arrived at, Nelson. And the estate ended up being given to Dom Nuno, from Portugal, another of Columbus's great-grandsons."

"Now, Nelson, pay attention to what I'm about to tell you. There was a real will, but it disappeared. Some historians, like the Spaniard Salvador de Madariaga, believe his will was forged, although they think many aspects of the forged will are based on the lost original document." He consulted his notes. "This opinion is shared by the historian Luís Ulloa, who discovered that the forged copy of the *mayorazgo* presented by the lawyer Verástegui had at one stage been in the possession of Luísa de Carvajal, who was married to a certain Luís Buzon, a man known for altering documents."

"What about Professor Toscano? What did he think?"

"Toscano clearly believed the will had been forged from a real original, the one that was lost. Like I said, everyone wanted to be Columbus's heir, and it was natural that under such circumstances, with so much money at stake, impostors were going to come out of the woodwork. Now, it is possible that this Luís Buzon guy forged the will—very well, from a technical point of view—and accurately copied the more innocuous sections, including the essential parts of the executive clauses." Thomas waved his hand as if wanting to add something else. "In fact, you have to agree that it's strange that this will didn't show up when Columbus died in 1506. It only materialized in 1578, more than seventy years later, in a period in which it appeared to favor one of the parties that came forward. Under these conditions, how can we trust anything written in it?" Thomas looked a little weary. "We can't."

Moliarti gave a resigned shrug. "So let's forget the *mayorazgo*. Is there anything else as far as documents go?"

"There are others that are allegedly from the same era but they only came to light much later, especially in the nineteenth century. Their details and inconsistencies will be in the written report I'll submit to you. Let us focus on the most important one, shall we?"

"All right."

"In 1799, Filippo Casoni, from Genoa, published *Annali della repubblica di Genova*, which included the silk weaver Cristoforo Colombo's family tree. Since it had yet to be established whether the explorer's name was Colom or Colón, he sidestepped the issue and decided that Colombo was a variation on Colom, meaning 'of the Colom family.' This was a bold move and opened the floodgates for an endless stream of official texts. Now, the most important discovery was announced in 1904 by the academic journal *Giornale storico e letterario della Liguria,* which said that the Genoese colonel Ugo Assereto claimed to have found a notarial record, dated August 25, 1479, that recorded Christophorus Columbus's departure for Lisbon the following day. The Assereto Document, as it is now known, also reveals that Columbus's age was *'annorum viginti septem vel circa,'* approximately twenty-seven years old, which would mean he had been born in 1451."

"You're not going to tell me it's all false, are you?" asked Moliarti.

"Nelson," said Thomas, smiling, "do you really think I could be so cruel?"

"Yes."

"You're wrong, Nelson. I could never do such a thing."

Moliarti's face took on an expression of cautious relief. "Good."

"However—"

"Please—"

"We must always assess the reliability of any document, look at it with a critical eye, try to see intentions and make sure there are no discrepancies."

"You're not going to tell me there are anomalies in these documents, too."

"Unfortunately, I am."

Moliarti let his head roll back in discouragement. "Fuck!"

"The first thing to consider is that they didn't appear when they should have, but much later. In his notes, Toscano even used the French expression *'le temps qui passe c'est l'évidence qui s'efface.'* The more time passes, the more evidence is erased. In this case, by the look of things, the opposite is true. The more time passes, the more evidence appears."

"You're saying the notarial records are all fake?"

"No, I'm not saying that. What they prove is that there was a Cristoforo Colombo in Genoa who was a silk weaver and had a brother called Bartolomeu, another called Jacobo, and a father who was a wool carder by the name of Domenico Colombo. This is probably true. No one disputes it. What the records don't prove, however, is that this silk weaver who lived in Genoa was the person who discovered America. There is only one record that explicitly makes this connection." He held up some photocopies. "It's the Assereto Document. This clearly established a connection between the Genoese Colombo and the Iberian Colom, by recording the day the silk weaver left for Portugal."

"Let me guess," said Moliarti somewhat sarcastically. "The document isn't entirely reliable."

"No," said Thomas, ignoring his tone. "Let's try to reconstruct the whole picture, always bearing in mind that documents regarding Columbus in Genoa only began to pop up like mushrooms during the nineteenth century. When the explorer returned from his first voyage to the New World, the Genoese ambassadors in Barcelona in 1493, Francesco Marchesi and Giovanni Grimaldi, sent news of the feat to Genoa but forgot to mention one tiny detail, something obviously of little importance: that the admiral was a fellow countryman. Nor did anyone in Genoa remind them of such a fact. Does that make any sense? And there's more. In 1492, when America was discovered, the father of the weaver Cristoforo Colombo was still alive. But there isn't a single record saying that he or any family member, neighbor, friend, or acquaintance celebrated or was even aware of Cristoforo's great feat. Additionally, official documents from Genoa show that Domenico died in poverty in 1499, with all of his assets mortgaged. The explorer ignored his impoverished father until his death. And in turn, none of Domenico's many creditors asked his famous son to settle his late father's debts.

"Even more remarkable, during the famous *Pleyto Sucessorio,* the legal proceedings begun in 1578 to determine the admiral's legitimate heir after the death of his great-grandson, countless candidates from all over Liguria showed up in Spain, all claiming to be Columbus's relatives." Thomas stared at Moliarti. "Guess how many of these candidates were from Genoa."

Moliarti shook his head. "No idea."

Thomas made a circle with his thumb and forefinger. "Zero, Nelson." He let his answer hang in the air like the echo of a gong. "Not one of these candidates was from Genoa." He paused again to emphasize the significance of this revelation. "Until documents began springing up everywhere in the nineteenth century. We must bear in mind, however, that historical research in this period mixed dangerously with political interests. The Italians were in the midst of a process of national unification and affirmation, led by the Ligurian Giuseppe Garibaldi. This was when the first theories that Columbus might not have been Italian appeared. This proved unacceptable to the new state. The Genoese Columbus was a symbol of unity and pride for the millions of Italians in the recently created country, as well as those who had begun to emigrate to the United States, Brazil, and Argentina. The debate became chauvinistic. It was in this political and social context that the Genoese theory suddenly ran into a crisis. On the one hand, many documents were found that proved that a Cristoforo, a Domenico, a Bartolomeo, and a Jacobo had indeed lived in the city, but there was no way of establishing beyond a doubt that there was any relationship between these people and the explorer. Besides which, such a connection seemed absurd, seeing as the Genoese Colombo was an uneducated weaver and the Iberian Colom was an admiral versed in cosmography, sailing, language, and letters. Considering what was at stake, especially in the political scenario and against this backdrop of

Italian nationalism, this was unacceptable. Then, providentially, the Assereto Document appeared, providing the necessary proof. The fact that this document was discovered precisely when it was most needed is clearly suspicious. Even more suspicious in the light of the fact that Colonel Assereto, after providing such sought-after proof, was honored by the Italian state for his services to the nation and promoted to general."

"That might all be true, but I'm sorry, once again, it's speculative. Is there some element of the notarial record discovered by Assereto that can be questioned?"

"Yes, there is."

The two men stared at each other for a long moment.

"What?" asked Moliarti finally, almost gulping.

"Columbus's date of birth."

"What's abnormal about it?"

"The Assereto Document's insistence that 1451 was the year in which Columbus was born is contradicted by an important witness." He gave Moliarti a challenging stare. "Guess who challenged the date given in the Assereto Document?"

"I haven't the slightest idea."

"Christopher Columbus himself. We now know that, among so many other things, he went to great lengths to conceal his date of birth. His son Ferdinand merely revealed that his father began his life as a sailor at the age of fourteen. Columbus himself, however, kept quiet about his age, but he let it slip on two occasions." Thomas referred to his notes. "In his diary of his first voyage, on December 21, 1492, he wrote, 'I have sailed the seas for twenty-three years, without leaving it for any length of time worth counting.' Based on this statement, we just have to do the math." Thomas started scribbling on a fresh page of his notebook. "If we add twenty-three years at sea and eight in Castile, which *is* time 'worth counting,' while he waited for authorization to sail, and the fourteen years of his childhood before he became a sailor, we get forty-five. In other words, Columbus was forty-five when he discovered America in 1492. Now, if we subtract forty-five from 1492, we get 1447. The year he was born."

Thomas looked back at his notes. "Later, in a letter dated 1501 and transcribed by Ferdinand, Columbus told the Catholic Monarchs: 'I have been engaged in this endeavor for more than forty years,' referring to his time as a navigator." He went back to the page where he'd done his previous figuring. "If we add forty to the fourteen years of his childhood, we get fifty-four. So he wrote this letter in 1501 at the age of fifty-four. If we subtract fifty-four from the year 1501, we get 1447 again. In both references Columbus leads us to believe he was born in 1447, four years before 1451, which is when the Assereto Document says he was born. This completely undermines its credibility. Additionally, the Assereto Document is, strictly speaking, no more than a draft, which was not signed by the declarant or the notary and does not mention Columbus's paternity, which was standard practice in similar documents at the time."

Moliarti sighed heavily. He leaned back in his chair and stared at the rampart in front of the restaurant and the city behind it. "Tell me something, Tom," he said, breaking the silence that had momentarily fallen over them. "Do you believe Columbus wasn't Genoese?"

Thomas picked up a toothpick and started fiddling with it, twirling and turning it between his fingers as if it were a miniature acrobat. "It's pretty clear to me that, in Professor Toscano's opinion, he wasn't Genoese."

"I understand that," said Moliarti. "But I'd like to know your opinion," he said, pointing at Thomas.

Thomas smiled. "Would you?" He chuckled to himself. "Here we are faced with two paths. We either consider the Genoese documents and accounts to be true, in spite of their discrepancies, in which case Columbus was Genoese. Or we take on board the innumerable objections to this theory, in which case he wasn't Genoese." He raised another finger. "There's still a third hypothesis, perhaps the most plausible of all. This falls somewhere between the two first versions, but it requires a leap in our reasoning. This third possibility is that the evidence and signs on both sides are, overall, correct, although both contain certain falsehoods and inaccuracies."

"I like this one."

"You like it, my friend, because you still haven't worked out the implications of such a hypothesis." Thomas laughed.

"Implications?"

"Yes, Nelson." He held up two fingers. "It implies that we're dealing with two Columbuses." He paused to allow the idea to sink in. "Two. One, Cristoforo Colombo, Genoese, an uneducated silk weaver, perhaps born in 1451. And the other, Cristóvão Colom or Cristóbal Colón, of uncertain nationality, an expert in cosmography and the nautical sciences, versed in Latin, an admiral, and the man who discovered America, born in 1447."

Moliarti looked at Thomas in shock. "That can't be."

"Yet, my dear Nelson, that's where it all leads." He smiled. "Two Columbuses. The Genoese silk weaver and the discoverer of the New World." Thomas's two fingers became one. "Two different men out of whom history made one."

Moliarti sighed, his shoulders dropping as if in surrender. "I see."

"This, of course, raises a big, big question, doesn't it?"

"What?"

"You see, if the discoverer of the New World was not the ignorant Genoese silk weaver Cristoforo Colombo, then who the hell was he?"

After Moliarti had left, Thomas, lost in thought, wandered the grounds of the castle and into the surrounding neighborhood.

He thought about Lena, and how much of a help she'd been to him over the past weeks. She asked questions, got involved in his work, helped him with his research, questioned colleagues who studied philosophy, tried to find clues that might help him solve the riddle, and had even brought him essays on Michel Foucault in the hope that they might provide some overlooked detail. In fact, Lena was so dedicated to his cause that she had taken it upon herself to read *História da Loucura,* the Portuguese translation of *Madness and Civilization,* always looking for the numbers 545 or words reminiscent of the riddle that tormented him. In spite of her help and his great effort to concentrate on the details, he hadn't found a single clue.

There were other books to be read and a lot of work ahead of him.

He stopped in a bookshop and located a copy of *Order of Things,* hoping it would help him in his quest. Being around books had a way of relaxing his body and mind, enabling him to think clearly, make connections, and he spent a while browsing. He found two books by Amin Maalouf that he examined carefully—*The Rock of Tanios* and *Samarkand*. He was tempted to buy both but reined in the impulse; it was unlikely he'd get to read them any time soon.

Even so, he hung around the section absentmindedly looking through the titles. His gaze was caught by an enigmatic title on a beautiful cover, *The God of Small Things*, by Arundhati Roy, but he only smiled again when he saw *The Name of the Rose,* by Umberto Eco. A great book, he thought; difficult but interesting.

Next to Eco's classic was his *Foucault's Pendulum*. Thomas pursed his lips; Eco had the good sense to wrestle with the physicist Léon Foucault, and stay away from the philosopher Michel. Léon had, in the nineteenth century, demonstrated the earth's rotation using a pendulum, which was now exhibited in the Paris Observatory. As Thomas gazed at the cover of the book, three words leapt out at him: *Eco, pendulum, Foucault*. He froze, staring.

Eco, pendulum, Foucault.

In fumbling, febrile excitement, he whipped his wallet from his jacket pocket and pulled out the tiny piece of paper on which he had jotted down Toscano's riddle. There was the historian's question, interrogating him with all the splendor of an enigma he had begun to fear was unsolvable:

WHAT ECHO OF FOUCAULT IS LEFT PENDING ON 545?

His eyes danced from the book's cover to the question on the piece of paper. Echo, Foucault, pending. Eco, pendulum, Foucault. The book was titled *Foucault's Pendulum* and had been written by Umberto Eco. Professor Toscano had asked, "What echo of Foucault is left pending on 545?" Thomas felt as if he'd been struck by lightning.

Dear God.

The key to the riddle lay not in Michel Foucault's books but in Umberto Eco's novel about the pendulum invented by the other Foucault—Léon. Echo, Eco. How could he have been so stupid? He cursed himself. The answer to the riddle had always been right under his nose, so simple and obvious, and it had merely been his ridiculous insistence on Michel Foucault that had kept him from seeing it. Anyone would have quickly realized that it was an explicit reference to Foucault's pendulum, not to the the man of letters, Ph.D., lover of history.

Idiot.

He studied the book and the piece of paper again, his eyes jumping from one to the other, until his attention stuck on the last element of the question, the three numbers before the question mark.

545.

With the clumsy movements of a starving man before a banquet fit for kings, he quickly flicked through the book, in a shaky rush to finally discover the solution, and only stopped when he got to page 545.

Chapter 14

Thomas pulled **Foucault's Pendulum** from his briefcase and held it out. Lena cocked her head to the side. "What's that?" she asked as she stretched her long legs out and placed her pedicured feet on Thomas's lap.

"Apparently, Professor Toscano was referring to *this* book by *Umberto* Eco."

Lena took the book and scrutinized it. "What's on page 545?"

Thomas took it back, turned to page 545, and showed Lena. "It's a scene in a cemetery. He describes a partisans' funeral during the German occupation at the end of World War II. I've read it and reread it dozens of times, but I didn't find a thing."

"Can I have a look?" she asked, holding out her hand. She read page 545 with great attention.

"This really . . . looks pretty useless," Lena said finally, laughing. She turned the first few pages and looked at the diagram with the Tree of Life, showing the ten Hebrew *sefirot,* before the text began. She read the first epigraph and hesitated. She placed her hand on Thomas's arm and sat up. "Have you seen this quote before?"

"What?"

She read it aloud, her voice rising dramatically. "'Only for you, children of doctrine and learning, have we written this work. Examine this book, ponder the meaning we have dispersed in various places and gathered again; what we have concealed in one place we have disclosed in another, that it may be understood by your wisdom.' It's a quote from Heinrich Cornelius Agrippa's *De occulta philosophia.*" She looked at Thomas, slightly giddy. "Do you think it's related?"

"It sure sounds like it." He took the book and studied the epigraph. "'What we have concealed in one place we have disclosed in another'?" He carefully leafed through the novel. After the epigraph was a blank page, followed by a page with the number 1 and a strange word, "*Keter.*"

"What's that?"

"The first *sefirah.*"

"What's a *sefirah?*"

"*Sefirah* is the singular and *sefirot* is the plural. They're the structural elements of the Jewish Kabbalah—the emanations through which God reveals himself." He turned to the first page of text. It contained a second epigraph, this one in Hebrew, with the number 1 again, smaller now, to the left. He read the first sentence of the novel to himself. "'That was when I saw the Pendulum.'"

He flipped through the book and, six pages along, found another subchapter with a new epigraph, a quote from Francis Bacon, and a small number 2 on the left. He turned another eight pages and found a new blank page, with only the number 2 and the word *Hokhmah,* which he recognized as the second *sefirah*. He flipped to the back of the book and looked for the index.

There were the ten *sefirot,* each with subchapters, in some cases few, in others, many. The *sefirot* with the most subchapters were 5, *Gevurah,* and 6, *Tipheret*. He ran his eyes across the subchapters of 5. They went from 34 to 63. His attention was drawn from the book for a few moments to the crumpled bit of paper with the disquieting question:

WHAT ECHO OF FOUCAULT IS LEFT PENDING ON 545?

He returned to the subchapters of *Gevurah,* the fifth *sefirah,* his eyes roving between the list of numbers and the riddle. Suddenly, what had previously been no more than a mere point of light surrounded by the darkness of ignorance became a blinding radiance, like an all-illuminating sun.

"Oh my God!" he exclaimed, almost leaping up off the sofa.

"What? What?"

"Oh my God, oh my God!"

"What is it?"

Thomas showed Lena the index. "See this?"

"What?"

He pointed at the number 5, with *Gevurah* beside it. "This."

"Yes, it's a five. So?"

"What's the number in Toscano's question?"

"545?"

"Yes. What's the first number?"

"Five."

"And what are the other two numbers?"

"Four and five."

"Four and five, right? Is there a subtitle forty-five in chapter five?"

Lena looked at the index. "Yes, there is."

"Then what Toscano was saying wasn't 545, but 5:45. Chapter five, subchapter forty-five. See?"

Lena's jaw dropped. "I *see.*"

"Now look," said Thomas, showing her the index. "What's the title of subchapter forty-five?"

Lena found the line and read aloud. "'And from this springs the extraordinary question.'"

"Get it?" Thomas laughed. "'And from this springs the extraordinary question.' What could it be?" He held up the crumpled paper again. " 'What echo of Foucault is left pending on 545?' " He raised an eyebrow. "Now, there's an extraordinary question."

"Wow!" exclaimed Lena. "We found it!" She leaned over the index again. "What page is this chapter on?"

They located the page number. "Page 236."

Lena laughed in excitement. "It's what the epigraph of the book says, remember?" she said. " 'What we have concealed in one place we have disclosed in another.' " She beamed.

Thomas paged frantically through the book to 236. He found it and held the book still, carefully analyzing the text. In the top left corner was the number 45 in a small font, and on the right an epigraph by Peter Kolosimo, taken from *Terra senza tempo*.

" 'And from this springs the extraordinary question,' " read Thomas. " 'Did the Egyptians know about electricity?' "

"What's that about?"

"I don't know."

Thomas scanned the page hungrily. It looked like a mystic text, with references to the mythical lost continents of Mu, the legendary islands of Atlantis and Avalon, and the Mayan complex of Chichén Itzá, variously populated by the Celts, the Nibelungs, and the vanished civilizations of the Caucasus and the Indies. But it was when he read the last paragraph that Thomas's heart started beating wildly. "Oh my God," he murmured.

"What?"

He handed Lena the book and pointed at the paragraph. She read it breathlessly:

> *A text on Christopher Columbus: it analyzes his signature and finds in it a reference to the pyramids. Columbus's real aim was to reconstruct the Temple of Jerusalem, since he was grand master of the Templars-in-exile. Being a Portuguese Jew and therefore an expert cabalist, he used talismanic spells to calm storms and overcome scurvy.*

Lena finished the passage with a combination of satisfaction and confusion on her face. She turned to Thomas.

"Columbus was *Jewish*?"

• • •

The knock at the door was unfamiliar. Madalena Toscano had learned to recognize the usual knocks. This one was different, fast and strong, betraying a sense of urgency.

"Who is it?" called Madalena in her shaky voice.

"It's me," a man answered from the other side. "Thomas Noronha."

"Who?" she asked warily. "Noronha who?"

"The professor from the university who's recovering your husband's research. I was here the other day, remember?"

Madalena opened the door slightly, keeping the security chain on, and peered through the crack, as was her habit. Lisbon wasn't the village it used to be, she told people. It was full of robbers, thugs, and the worst kind of no-goods; you just had to watch the news. One couldn't be careful enough. On the other side of the door, however, she didn't see any kind of threat. Looking at her from the corridor was a man with dark hair and bright green eyes, a smiling face that she quickly recognized.

"Oh, it's you," she exclaimed good-naturedly. She carefully removed the security chain and opened the door. "Come in."

The old apartment enveloped Thomas with the same stale, musty air, and the same dim light, with slivers of sun squeezing through gaps in the heavy curtains, incapable of illuminating the room's dark corners. Thomas handed a white package tied with string to his hostess, who was wearing a dressing gown. "This is for you," he said.

Madalena Toscano looked at the small package.

"What is it?"

"Some sweets I brought from the patisserie. They're for you."

"Oh, good God. You needn't have gone to any trouble—"

"It's my pleasure."

She led him into the living room and opened the package. "How lovely!" she said. She fetched a plate from the buffet and arranged the sweets on it. "Which one would you like?"

"They're for you."

"Oh, it's too much. I wouldn't be able to eat it all. Besides, my doctor would kill me." She held out the plate. "Take one, go on."

Thomas took a *duchaise;* he hadn't sunk his teeth into one of those sweet, fluffy cakes for a long time. Madalena took a crunchy *palmier.*

"I told my son, the oldest one, 'You know, Manuel, I'd still like to see your father's work published one day.' I told him a young man from the university had come looking for his documents, but I hadn't heard from him since."

"And here I am."

"Yes. Have you found what you wanted?"

"Almost everything. All I need now is to see what's in your safe."

"Ah, yes, the safe. But I told you I don't know the code."

"It's a code of numbers, isn't it?"

"Yes."

"The last time I was here you told me that, once I'd worked out the key words, all one had to do was convert the letters into digits."

"Yes, that's what my husband always did."

Thomas smiled. "Then I know what the key words are."

"You do?" said Madalena. "How do you know?"

"Remember that cipher you gave me?"

"That jumble of letters?"

"Yes."

"I remember. I've got it here."

"I've deciphered it and I think I have the answer. Can we try it?"

Madalena led him to the bedroom. They crouched in front of the safe and Thomas took his notebook out of his briefcase and flicked through it until he found the page he was looking for. He had written down the key words with the corresponding numbers underneath each letter:

P	O	R	T	U	G	U	E	S	E	J	E	W
16	15	18	20	21	7	21	5	19	5	10	5	23

Thomas plugged in the numbers. Nothing happened. They exchanged a look of disappointment, but Thomas didn't give up. He tried the first sequence of numbers by itself, but the safe door refused to budge.

"Are you sure that's the key to the code?" asked Madalena.

"We can never be sure, can we? But I did think it was right, from the way the letters match up with numbers."

"Couldn't it be a synonym? Sometimes Martinho liked to play with synonyms."

"Did he now?" said Thomas, surprised. He rubbed his chin thoughtfully. "Well, in the sixteenth century they started calling converted Jews New Christians."

He took his pen out of his jacket, and wrote the words in his notebook. Then he wrote the corresponding numbers underneath:

N	E	W	C	H	R	I	S	T	I	A	N
14	5	23	3	8	18	9	19	20	9	1	14

He entered the two sequences into the lock and waited a moment. Nothing happened again; the tiny door remained closed. He sighed and ran his hand through his hair, disappointed and out of ideas. "No," he said, shaking his head. "That's not it." He and Madalena stared at each other, not knowing what to make of the locked safe in front of them.

There were bunches of large flowers in the clay vases, the blossoms peering up over the leaves as if on tiptoes, trying to get a breath of fresh air. The petals, various shades of pink, were fine, as light as feathers, and leaned toward the center of the flower like tattered shells. They were beautiful, voluptuous, sensual flowers.

"Are these roses?" asked Thomas, holding a glass of whiskey.

"They look like roses," said Constance. "But they're peonies."

They had just finished dinner and were relaxing in the living room, while Margarida changed into her pajamas.

"What do they mean?" he asked. "Tell me about them." Thomas needed to get his mind off his research. Since he'd started seeing

Lena, he hadn't felt much like talking with Constance and now was relieved to simply listen.

"Paiōn was the physician of the Greek gods. According to legend, he cured Pluto with the seeds of a special flower. They were named peonies, in homage to Paiōn. Pliny the Elder claimed that peonies were able to cure twenty diseases, but it has never been proven. Peony roots, however, were used in the eighteenth century to protect children from epilepsy and nightmares, and as a result, the flowers came to be associated with childhood."

Thomas stared at the flowers."I could have sworn they were roses."

"They're like roses, but without the thorns. This led the Christians to compare them to the Virgin Mary. A rose without thorns."

"And what do they represent?"

"Shyness. The Chinese poets always used peonies to describe the shy flush of young girls, associating the flower with a certain virginal innocence."

Thomas got up and went into his daughter's bedroom. He tucked her into bed, then kissed her rosy cheeks and stroked her fine hair as he told her a bedtime story. Lulled by the cadence of her father's whispered words, she surrendered to the sweet drowsiness invading her body. Her eyes closed and her breathing became deep and regular. Thomas kissed her again and turned off the lamp. He left the room on tiptoes, almost without breathing, softly closed the door, and went back to the living room.

Constance was asleep on the sofa, her head nodding toward her shoulder. He picked her up and carried her in his arms to the bedroom, removed her jacket and shoes with one hand, and laid her on the bed, pulling a blanket up to her chin. She murmured something inaudible and rolled onto her side, hugging the pillow, the heat of the blanket making her freckled cheeks flush. She looked like a baby. Thomas turned off the light and was about to head back to the living room, but he hesitated. He stopped in the doorway and turned to look at his wife, who was now fast asleep. He approached her slowly, taking care not to make any noise, gazed at her for a moment, then sat on the edge of the bed. He stared at her in silence, watching the blanket rise and fall softly, in time with her breathing.

What future did he want for himself, for his wife and daughter, for his mistress? Didn't he want to live in truth? Saraiva had told him we don't have access to an objective truth. But as a human being, a man, he always had access to another truth, a subjective truth. A moral truth.

Honesty.

Hugging her pillow as she slept, Constance looked innocent and fragile, her ringlets spilling across the pillow and sheets. He sighed and ran his fingers through her curls, playing with them absentmindedly. He felt her soft breathing and admired the spirit with which she faced the difficulties that made him stumble. He stroked her face; her skin was warm and soft. He imagined he was holding two tickets, one that allowed him to stay, the other allowing him to leave. He'd have to make a decision. He thought about how he had projected all of his own unrealized dreams and aspirations onto his daughter, and how the news of her limitations had been too hard a blow, a setback that he had never properly digested, in spite of appearances. Constance had faced her disappointment with courage, looking it in the eye. But he had reacted differently. After nine years of resistance, he had fled. Perhaps it was time to come back.

He looked around as if trying to memorize the shadows of the bedroom, his wife's soft, steady breathing, the trace of Chanel No. 5 hovering in the air. He took a deep breath, and right there and then, as he tenderly stroked Constance's placid face, he came to a conclusion. He knew what he had to do.

Chapter 15

The palace rose up out of the fog as if it were suspended in the clouds, hovering melancholically over the shadowy slope of the Sintra hills. The light stone façade, replete with sphinxes, winged creatures, and bizarre, frightening animals, all tied in knots or wrapped in acanthus leaves, was reminiscent of a fifteenth-century construction in all its Manueline Gothic magnificence, but with the gloomy, almost sinister touch of an evil fortress. Floating above the thick tufts of vapor that clung to the green of the hill, the palace stood proud in the gray refracted light of the misty afternoon. With its stone lacework of spires, pinnacles, battlements, towers, and turrets, it looked like a fantasy castle, a mysterious, haunted mansion, lost forever in time.

Sitting on a bench facing the garden, Thomas still didn't know what to think of the enigmatic palace. There were moments when Quinta da Regaleira looked so beautiful and otherworldly, but under the mantle of mist its beauty was somewhat frightening and dismal, a labyrinth of darkness and shadows. He felt shivers run through his body and glanced at his watch. It was five past three. Moliarti was late. The palace was deserted. It was a weekday in mid-March, a time when one wouldn't expect to see visitors wandering through the grounds. He really hoped Moliarti would hurry up, as the thought of spending any more time alone here was not at all appealing.

He tore his eyes from the palace and gazed at the statue in front of him. It was Hermes, messenger of Mount Olympus, and the god of eloquence and self-expression—but also the deceitful, unscrupulous divinity who conducted the souls of the dead to hell, the name that gave rise to Hermeticism, symbol of all that was inaccessible. Thomas looked around and thought that he was definitely an appropriate god to watch over Quinta da Regaleira, a place where the rocks themselves guarded secrets, where even the air was thick with enigmas.

"Hi, Tom!" called Moliarti, his head gradually coming into view as he climbed the garden stairs. "Sorry I'm late. I had a hard time finding this place."

Thomas stood to greet him, relieved to finally have company. "No problem. I was just enjoying the landscape and this pure mountain air."

Moliarti looked around. "This place gives me the creeps."

"Quinta da Regaleira is perhaps the most esoteric place in Portugal."

"Why do you say that?" asked Moliarti, gazing at the deserted palace.

"In the late nineteenth century, when Portugal was still a monarchy, this estate was bought by a man named Carvalho Monteiro. He decided to make Quinta an esoteric, alchemical place, where he could found his mission of resuscitating Portugal's grandeur based on its mythical tradition and feats in the Age of Discovery. Look at this. What does it remind you of?"

Moliarti studied the palace's intricate, silvery structure. "Hmm," he murmured. "Perhaps the Belém Tower . . ."

"Exactly. Neo-Manueline style. Quinta was built during an era of revivalism, when old values were revisited. That's why there are innumerous references to the Order of Christ, which succeeded the Templars in Portugal and was fundamental in the country's maritime expansion. The magical symbols scattered around the place are in accordance with an alchemical formula from Templar Christianity and the classical Renaissance tradition, with deep roots in Rome, Greece, and Egypt." He made a sweeping gesture to his left. "See those statues?"

Moliarti contemplated the row of silent figures standing around a geometric French garden, full of straight lines and angles."Yeah."

"Meet the guardians of the secrets of this place, vigilant sentinels protecting Quinta da Regaleira's mysteries. Want to go for a walk?"

They strolled along the path in front of the statues toward the loggia at the back of the garden."So, tell me," said Moliarti. "Did you figure out how to get into the old girl's safe?"

Thomas shook his head. "I didn't manage to get it open. But I'm sure I'm close. Professor Toscano's riddle is undoubtedly connected with a passage in *Foucault's Pendulum*."

"Are you sure?"

"Absolutely. Toscano was researching Christopher Columbus's origins, he had serious doubts that he was from Genoa, and the passage in question mentions Columbus." He ran his hand through his hair. "But I think I slipped up somewhere in my formulation of the key."

They passed Orpheus and Fortuna, and when they reached the loggia, with its intricately carved canopy, they turned right to climb the slope. The geometric garden gave way to a romantic garden that harmoniously integrated lawn, rocks, bushes, and trees. There were magnolias, camellias, tree ferns, palm trees, redwoods, and exotic plants from all over the world. Amidst the lush foliage a strange lake became visible, its surface covered with a dense emerald-green mantle, making it look like a moss soup. Two quacking ducks slid across the water, opening dark furrows that closed behind them, sealed once more by the thick blanket of green.

"The Lake of Nostalgia," said Thomas. He pointed at some enormous dark arches around the rim of the lake and extending back under the earth. They looked like the gloomy cavities of a skull, dripping with strands of ivy and ferns. "That's the Grotto of the Cathars. The lake extends into it."

"Wow," said Moliarti. They took the path around the lake, crossed the small bridge, overhung by a giant magnolia tree, and came upon a tiny building covered in quartz and a mosaic of other tiny stones. An enormous shell in the center of the wall caught a clear stream of water.

"This is the Egyptian Fountain," said Thomas, pointing at the upside-down shell that served as a basin. "See these pictures?" He pointed at two birds in mosaic on the wall. "They're ibises. In Egyptian mythology, the ibis represented Thoth, the creator of language and god of esoteric knowledge, who gave origin to the hieroglyphs. Do you know who the Greeks identified him with?"

Moliarti shook his head. "No idea."

"Hermes. The mysterious alchemical treatises of Hermes Trismegistus were born of this syncretism of Thoth and Hermes." He pointed at the beak of the ibis on the left, which appeared to be holding an enormous worm. "This ibis is holding a serpent, the symbol of *gnosis,* or knowledge, in its beak." He made a sweeping gesture with his arm. "Nothing was put here by chance. Everything contains a meaning, an intention, a hidden message, an enigma that harks back to the early days of civilization."

"But the ibis doesn't have anything to do with the Age of Discovery."

"Everything here has to do with the Age of Discovery. In the Book of Job, where this bird represents the power of foresight, God asks: 'Who gives the ibis wisdom?' Now, what was the world of the fifteenth and sixteenth centuries if not a profound place, an oracle to be read, a mystery to be solved?"

He gazed at the walls of the palace in the background. "The Portuguese discoveries were related to the Templars who found refuge in Portugal from the persecution initiated in France and approved by the pope. In fact, the Templars brought to Portugal the knowledge necessary for the great maritime adventures of the fifteenth and sixteenth centuries. That's why there's a mystic culture surrounding the discoveries, a mysticism with roots in the classical age and the idea of the rebirth of mankind.

"There are four texts that are fundamental in order to understand the architecture of this place. Virgil's *Aeneid;* its Portuguese equivalent, *The Lusiads,* by Luíz de Camões; Dante Alighieri's *Divine Comedy*; and an esoteric Renaissance text, equally packed with enigmas and allegories, called *Hypnerotomachia poliphili,* by Francesco Colonna. All of them have been, in one way or another, immortalized in the stones of Quinta da Regaleira." Thomas indicated a carved stone bench in front of the lake, next to the Egyptian Fountain. "Shall we take a seat?"

They walked over to the bench, which had greyhounds standing guard at both ends, and a statue of a woman holding a torch in the middle.

"This is the 515 bench," said Thomas. "Do you know what 515 stands for?"

"No."

"It's a code in *The Divine Comedy.* It is the number that corresponds to God's messenger, who will avenge the end of the Templars and announce the third age of Christianity, the Age of the Holy Ghost, which will bring eternal peace to earth. As you can see, like everything else here, this bench is also an allegory."

They sat down and Thomas opened his briefcase, pulling out his notebook. "I've got a story to tell you."

"Have you, now?"

Thomas flicked through his notebook and leaned back on the hard bench.

"Remember Toscano's cipher? I finally realized it was a reference by Umberto Eco to the effect that Columbus was, in fact, a Portuguese Jew."

"You're kidding."

"Check *Foucault's Pendulum,* it's all there." He ignored Moliarti's stunned facial expression. "Eco made me redirect my search, and I discovered a few things I'm sure you'll find interesting." He glanced at his notes. "The first is that we really can't debate Columbus's nationality in terms of today's sovereign states. In his day, countries didn't exist in the modern sense. Spain was the entire Iberian Peninsula. The Portuguese considered themselves Spanish and protested when the Castilians insisted on using this name to refer to them. Nor were there Portuguese explorers in today's sense of the term, but explorers in the service of the king of Portugal or the queen of Castile. Ferdinand Magellan, for example, was an experienced Portuguese navigator who sailed around the world with a Castilian fleet. While he did so, he was Castilian."

Thomas continued, "The second important thing to consider is that the big debate about Columbus's true nationality began somewhere around 1892, which was an era of rampant nationalism throughout the world. Spanish historians began finding inconsistencies in the Genoese arguments and put forward two hypotheses, that Columbus was either Galician or Catalan. The Italians, in the grip of the fervor of the time and determined to assert their recently established country both politically and culturally, fiercely denied such a possibility. Forged documents began to emerge from both countries.

Thomas took a small book from his briefcase. "This is a study of Columbus's true identity by Simon Wiesenthal, a Jew who hunted fugitive Nazis after living through the Holocaust. Wiesenthal says he spoke to an Italian historian about his study and got the following reply." He translated the Italian historian's words straight from the book: " 'What you find is of little importance. What matters is that Christopher Columbus doesn't become a Spaniard.' " He fixed his eyes on Moliarti. "In other words, he was interested not in the truth but in the need to preserve Columbus's Italian identity at any cost."

"Let's not make a big thing of it." He ran his hand through his hair, as if trying to reorganize his thoughts. "Tell me, Tom. Do you really think it plausible that Columbus was Spanish?"

"No, I don't. There are strong indications that Columbus wasn't born in Castile or Aragon. The first document to certify his presence in Spain is dated May 5, 1487, and refers to a payment made to 'Cristóbal Colomo, foreigner.' Additionally, Columbus's foreign origin was even proven by a Spanish tribunal when his Portuguese son,

Diego, sued the crown for failing to observe clauses of a contract between the Catholic Monarchs and Columbus, signed in 1492. During the hearing, several witnesses swore under oath that Columbus spoke Castilian with a foreign accent. The tribunal ended up dismissing the accusation, arguing that the monarchs, who were allowed to grant such favors to Spanish citizens, couldn't grant them to a foreigner who hadn't lived in the country for at least eighteen years." He glanced at his notes. "The tribunal's findings can be seen in *Codex V.II.17,* at El Escorial library in Madrid, and read: 'The said Don Cristóbal was a foreigner, neither a native or neighbor of the Kingdom, nor a resident of it.' Columbus was a foreigner."

"Genoese," said Moliarti.

"You are persistent," said Thomas, laughing. "Maybe he really was. Who knows? But we still must consider the hypothesis that he was Portuguese, which, by the look of things, was what Professor Toscano believed. And so did Umberto Eco." He paused, looking through his notes. "The first big clue was provided by one of the most famous cosmographers and geologists of the fifteenth century, Paolo Toscanelli, of Florence. This great scientist exchanged correspondence with the canon of Lisbon, Fernam Martins, and Columbus himself. Of particular interest is a letter he sent to Lisbon in 1474, addressed to the explorer and written in Latin." He cleared his throat. "Toscanelli began by saying, 'I have received your letters. I do not wonder that you, who are of great courage, and the whole Portuguese nation, which has always distinguished itself in all great enterprises, are now inflamed with desire to undertake this voyage.'"

"So?" said Moliarti haughtily.

"So?" Thomas laughed. "This letter's very revealing! It contains at least four curious facts. The first is that it shows that Columbus corresponded with one of the greatest scientists of his time."

"I don't see what's so curious about that."

"Nelson, don't those who believe he was Genoese argue that Columbus was just an uneducated silk weaver? How could such a person correspond with Toscanelli?" Thomas paused, as if to emphasize his question. He looked back at his notebook. "The second thing is that 'you, who are of great courage, and the whole Portuguese nation' implicitly shows that Toscanelli believed Columbus to be Portuguese. He smiled. "The third is that the letter, sent to Lisbon, was dated 1474." Thomas shook the paper he was holding.

"Remember the notarial document saying that the silk weaver Cristoforo Colombo only arrived in Portugal in 1476? How could Toscanelli have corresponded with Columbus in Lisbon if Columbus only set foot in the city two years later?"

"Couldn't someone have been mistaken?"

"No one was mistaken. The historian Bartolomé de Las Casas, describing a meeting between Columbus and King Ferdinand in Segovia in May 1501, cited the admiral as having said he spent fourteen years trying to convince the Portuguese crown to support his endeavor. Now, if Columbus left Portugal in 1484, and if we subtract fourteen from that, we get 1470." Thomas looked at Moliarti. "Columbus would have had to have been in Lisbon in 1470. Four years later, in 1474, he received Toscanelli's letter in Lisbon. How is that possible if he hadn't even arrived in Portugal until 1476 according to the Genoese notarial documents?

"Nelson, contrary to what it may seem, this is not a minor detail but a very, very big problem. So big that historians spent the entire nineteenth century debating these bizarre discrepancies. This was because for a few years there had been two Columbuses at the same time. A Colombo in Genoa weaving silk, and a Colom in Lisbon trying to convince the Portuguese king to send him sailing west to the Indies."

Moliarti was fidgeting. "What's the fourth problem?"

"Toscanelli's letter is written in Latin. Toscanelli was Italian. If they were both Italian, wouldn't it have been natural for them to correspond in Tuscan, rather than a dead language?"

"True. But it wasn't impossible for two Italians to correspond in Latin at that time. They came from different cities and were learned men, and Latin was a way of demonstrating this learning."

"So Columbus was a learned man?" Thomas laughed. "I thought he was just an uneducated silk weaver."

"Clearly he studied."

"It's possible, Nelson. But remember that at that time the lower classes didn't have easy access to education."

"Perhaps he had a tutor, or maybe he was an autodidact."

Thomas laughed. "Maybe. Who knows? Allow me, however, to point out that it was not just with Toscanelli that Colombo did not write in a living Italian language. His correspondence was all in Castilian or Latin."

Moliarti gave him an inquisitive look. "I don't believe you."

"Its true." Thomas pulled out photocopies of handwritten letters. "See?" He held up a page. "This is a letter from Columbus to Nicolo Oderigo, the Genoese ambassador to Spain, dated March 21, 1502. It is held in the Palazzo Municipale di Genova archives. What do you know, it's written in Castilian. In this letter, to the same Oderigo, also in Castilian, Columbus even asks him to *translate* the letter for another Genoese gentleman." He stared at Moliarti. "You have to agree it's odd, right?"

He pulled out one last photocopy. "This is a letter to another Italian, Friar Gaspar Gorricio. Yet again, surprise, surprise, in Castilian. Curious, isn't it?"

"I don't get it, Tom. You told me yourself you didn't think Colombo was Spanish."

"I don't."

"But here you are, telling me that he only wrote in Castilian or Latin."

"I am, and it's true."

"Where are you going with this? As far as I know, Castilian wasn't spoken in Portugal—"

"It wasn't."

"So where does that leave us?"

"Well, I still haven't told you everything. Columbus's personal documents have been lost over time." Thomas held up his hand. "Take note of what I'm going to say now, Nelson, because it's important. Columbus's own diary wasn't conserved, and all we have left is a handwritten copy, discovered in the nineteenth century, *believed* to have been written by Bartolomé de Las Casas. Of course, amidst all this confusion, many forgeries have appeared. In some cases, the forgers merely altered small details of the text to support their theories. In other cases the documents were completely forged. In some situations this was either to claim Columbus's nationality, or it was simply to get money.

"I spoke to experts in original manuscripts, accustomed to acquiring rare letters at auctions, who told me that if a manuscript written in Columbus's own hand were to turn up, and proven to be authentic, it would be priceless. The only thing worth more, they told me, would be a letter signed by Jesus Christ himself. As you can see, these astronomical values are a great encouragement for falsifications."

"So you're telling me everything's forged."

"I'm telling you that many of the letters attributed to Columbus are probably partial or total falsifications."

"Including these letters to his Genoese acquaintances?"

"Yes."

Moliarti smiled. "Then that solves the problem you presented a little while ago, doesn't it? If these letters are forged, the fact that they were written in Castilian doesn't prove anything."

"They prove a lot of things, Nelson. They prove that not even forgers dared to write Columbus's letters to Genoese citizens in Tuscan, since that would discredit them. They prove that the originals they were based on were also written in Castilian. Finally, they prove that there really was a conspiracy to make Columbus Italian."

"That's ridiculous."

"It's not ridiculous, Nelson. There were many falsified documents in which the word *Genoa* was deliberately planted."

"So the notarial documents found in the archives of Savona and Genoa were forged?"

"No, those are probably genuine. There really was a silk weaver by the name of Cristoforo Colombo. There's no doubt about it. The falsifications affect some of the navigator Cristóbal Colón's documents and everything that tries to connect Colombo and Colón, such as the Assereto Document and these letters sent by the admiral to people in Genoa. All we know about Columbus was written by Italians and Spaniards, in some cases innocently, in others not so much."

"Right. So go on," said Moliarti impatiently, gesticulating at Thomas's notebook. "Isn't there anything we are sure was written by Columbus himself?"

"There are only two things that are above all suspicion. The first thing is his letters to his son Diego, since they've been conserved and handed down by properly identified people and institutions in a sequence that can be retraced with precision.

"The second is the marginal notes in the books that belonged to Columbus, which were donated by his Spanish son, Ferdinand, to the Columbine Library in Seville. Although in this case it's possible that some of the notes were made by Columbus's brother Bartolomeu. At any rate, there are some we know were written by the admiral himself."

"And what language are these letters and notes in?"

"Mostly Castilian. There are a few in Latin and two in Tuscan; only one of these two in Tuscan is Columbus's beyond all doubt. But that's not the best part."

Moliarti rolled his eyes.

"All of the texts written in Columbus's own hand, whether in Castilian, Latin, or Tuscan, are full of Portuguese quirks."

"What?"

"Columbus's texts are *riddled* with Portuguese quirks. In fact, he didn't write in Spanish, he wrote in *portuñol,* a blend of Portuguese and Spanish. If I go to Madrid and say, '*Necesito un carro para ir al palacio,*' that is, 'I need a car to go to the palace,' they'll know I'm Portuguese, because in Spanish they don't say '*carro.*' *Car* in Spanish is *coche.*"

Moliarti leaned back on the bench, his eyes lost in the carpet of green covering the lake. "Ah!" he said. "And what were Columbus's quirks?"

Thomas laughed heartily. "I think that's the wrong question, Nelson. The question should be what weren't his Portuguese quirks?" He winked playfully.

Moliarti didn't laugh.

"The only attempt to write in Tuscan that we are sure was really his is in the margin of his *Book of Prophecies* at the beginning of Psalm 2.2. In his copy of Pliny's *Natural History* there are twenty-three notes in the margins. Twenty are in Spanish, two in Latin, and the last in Tuscan. Experts are not sure if this was written by Columbus or, perhaps, his brother Bartolomeu. Both sentences in Tuscan are hilarious attempts, as they are packed with fifteenth-century Portuguese and Spanish words."

"What about the other notes?"

"For the most part they're in *portuñol*." Thomas looked at his notes. "So much so that the Spanish academic Altolaguirre y Duval said that the traces of Columbus's dialect are undoubtedly Portuguese. Columbus spent twenty-four years of his life in Italy, then, in the blink of an eye, he forgot Tuscan and his native Genoese. The same Columbus spent only ten years in Portugal and, voilà, never again forgot Portuguese, using it to the end of his life. Amazing, isn't it?"

"Give me some examples."

"Well, to start with, take the *ie* diphthong in Spanish words. Many words in Portuguese and Spanish are almost the same, the only difference being that in Spanish they're written with *ie* and in Portuguese with just *e*. For example, Columbus wrote *'se intende'* instead of *'se entiende'* and *'quero'* instead of *'quiero.'* He also used the *ie* in Spanish words when it shouldn't be there, such as *depende*, which Columbus spelled *depiende*. Spaniards know that only the Portuguese, in a bumbling effort to speak Spanish, stick in an *ie* where there shouldn't be one."

"What about his general vocabulary?"

"Same thing. For example, Columbus wrote *algun,* while the Spanish word for 'some' is *alguno* and the Italian is *alcuno*. He used *ameaçaban*, when the Spanish for 'they threatened' would be *amenazaban* and the Italian, *minacciàvano*. Another word was *arriscada*, meaning 'risky' or 'hazardous' in Portuguese, which is *arriesgado* in Spanish and *rischiosa* in Italian. He also—"

"Okay, okay, enough. I get it." Moliarti took a deep breath and cleared his throat. "There has to be a logical explanation for these anomalies, for why he wrote in this mixture of Castilian and Portuguese—"

"A logical explanation? Such as?" Thomas leaned forward. "At the Genoa State Archives they told me that at that time, Italians who lived abroad mostly used Tuscan to communicate among themselves."

"That's true," said Moliarti.

"Then why didn't he?"

"Maybe Columbus only spoke the Genoese dialect. Since it wasn't written, he couldn't have used it in his correspondence with other people from Genoa, could he?"

"I think that's a very imaginative explanation. Starting with the fact that it's not true that the Genoese dialect wasn't written. A Genoese professor of languages assured me that the dialect was written in the Middle Ages. Which poses two questions. Columbus didn't speak Tuscan because he was uneducated—but he knew Latin, which only the educated knew? And he didn't write in Genoese dialect, spoken by all Genoese and written by the educated, but he produced oodles of texts in Castilian with Portuguese quirks? Which brings us to the crux of the matter. Why not simply allow that, if Columbus didn't write in any Italian dialects, the logical explanation is that he didn't actually speak any? And, if he didn't speak any Italian dialects, one has to conclude that he probably wasn't Italian." He paused. "And that's not all, Nelson. There's more."

"What?"

"I haven't had a chance to read everything that the witnesses who knew Columbus said about him, especially in the legal battles of the *Pleyto con la Corona* and the *Pleyto de la Prioridad,* where it was established that he was a foreigner. But two researchers whose work I consulted, Simon Wiesenthal and Salvador de Madariaga, found some incredible testimonies." He checked his notes again. "According to Wiesenthal, witnesses claimed that Columbus 'spoke Castilian very well but with a Portuguese accent.' And Madariaga, in turn, also observed that Columbus 'always spoke in Castilian with a Portuguese accent.'" Thomas smiled triumphantly at Moliarti, his green eyes sparkling, like a chess player who had just checkmated his opponent. "Do you see?"

Moliarti remained silent for a long moment, gazing into space with an absent look.

"Shit!" he finally muttered to himself. "Are you sure?"

"That's what they said." Thomas stood up and stretched to get his circulation going. "There are a lot of things about Columbus that don't add up, Nelson. When he arrived in Spain, presumably in 1484, do you know who the first person he contacted was?"

Moliarti also stood and stretched, stiff from having sat still for so long. The 515 bench was beautiful but uncomfortable.

"I have no idea, Tom."

"A friar by the name of Marchena. Guess what his nationality was."

"Portuguese?"

"Of course." He smiled.

"That doesn't prove a thing."

"Of course not, but it's still curious." Thomas started down a dirt path, wandering between the trees with Moliarti beside him. "There are many questions in need of answers. For example, if Columbus was Genoese, why was he so guarded about his origins? After all, Castilian-Genoese relations were good at the time. In fact, having Genoese contacts was even a thing of prestige. The English sailed the Mediterranean under the protection of the Genoese flag of Saint George, which was white with a red cross, and which was later adopted on the English flag. Now, if we consider the rivalry between the Portuguese and the Castilians, a Portuguese national commanding a Castilian crew could be a problem, just as the opposite was also true. Look at what the Portuguese explorer Ferdinand Magellan went through at the helm of the Castilian fleet that sailed around the world for the first time. If he was Genoese, Columbus wouldn't have had any reason to hide his origins. But if he was Portuguese . . ."

Moliarti didn't respond; he walked along with his eyes glued to the ground, his shoulders slumped, a brooding expression on his face.

They climbed the sloping dirt path in meditation, immersed in the mysteries that Toscano had spirited out of old manuscripts, secrets kept by time behind a thick curtain of dust and strange silences, contradictions and omissions. Red and yellow magnolias colored the green path, weaving between the beeches, palms, pines, and oaks. The air was fresh, light, perfumed by the romantic beds of roses and tulips, whose feminine grace contrasted with the carnal beauty of the orchids. The afternoon stretched out, drowsy, to the slow rhythm of nature's great waltz; the woods sprang to life, the treetops rustling lightly in the breeze wafting softly down from the mountains, as if blown by the low, gray-brown mantle of clouds. From the luxuriant branches came the high, cheerier notes of siskins chirping, battling to be heard over the low cooing of the hummingbirds and the melodious warbling of the nightingales.

The narrow path suddenly opened out onto what looked like a patio. There was a wall on one side, with a fountain gushing water, and a stone semicircle opposite it. "The Fountain of Abundance," announced Thomas. "In spite of the name, it's actually something much more dramatic. See if you can guess."

Moliarti studied the open structure in the wood. At either end of the semicircle stood a vase. Carved on each was the head of a satyr and a ram. "The satyr represents chaos. The ram is a symbol of the spring equinox; it represents order. With a satyr and a ram side by side, each of these vases means *ordo ab chao*—order out of chaos."

In the middle of the semicircle was an enormous chair carved out of the stone, and in front of it was a large table. Set in the wall of the fountain was a shell, and above it a mosaic of a set of scales.

"I've got no idea what that is," said Moliarti.

"That, Nelson, is a court. It's the judge's throne." Thomas pointed at the large stone chair. "Those are the scales of justice." Pointing at the mosaic, he continued, "In Templar and Masonic symbolism, light and darkness, representing justice and equity, strike a balance on the spring equinox, and for this reason, this is the day the new grand master takes office, assuming command when he sits on the throne." He waved at the fountain wall, where there were other pictures in mosaic. "This wall imitates decorations from Solomon's Temple in Jerusalem. Have you ever heard of Solomon's justice?" He looked up at the two pyramid-shaped obelisks at the top. "The obelisks connect the earth to the heavens, as if they were the two columns at the entrance to Solomon's Temple, true pillars of justice."

They headed down a new trail between the trees and came upon another patio, this one bigger. It was the Guardians' Portal, protected by two tritons. Thomas led the way down a path that went around this new structure and they zigzagged through the woods, climbing the hillside until they came upon what looked like a dolmen, a megalithic mound, covered in moss. Thomas led Moliarti to the mound, through an archway formed by stones sitting on top of one another, like Stonehenge, and pushed on a large one. To Moliarti's surprise, the stone turned on its axis to reveal an internal structure. They went through the secret passage, and a well appeared before them. Leaning over the balustrade, they gazed into the well and saw a spiral staircase and handrail carved into the stone walls, under a series of arches supported by columns, areas of shadow dug into the walls, the daylight shining in from above.

"What's this?" asked Moliarti.

"An initiation well," explained Thomas, his voice reverberating between the cylindrical walls. "We're inside a dolmen, a reproduction of a funeral monument. This place represents the death of man's primary condition. We have to go down the well in search of spirituality, the rebirth of man, enlightened man. We go into the well as if we were going into our soul, in search of our deepest selves." He gestured with his head for Moliarti to follow him. "Let's go, come on."

They started down the narrow stone steps, following the walls of the well in a clockwise spiral. The ground was wet and their footsteps rang out in raspy, metallic echoes, mixing with the twittering of the birds that flew into the abyss through the opening at the top, and resounded through the dark, coiled hole. The walls and balustrades were moist and covered in moss. They leaned over the handrail and peered into the depths. The well now looked like an upside-down tower, dug into the earth.

"How many levels are there?"

"Nine," said Thomas. "They didn't arrive at this number by chance. Nine is a symbolic number, and in many European languages the word for it is similar to the word for 'new.' In Portuguese, *nove* is nine and *novo* is new. In Spanish, *nueve* and *nuevo*. In French, *neuf* and *neuve*. In English, *nine* and *new*. In Italian, *nove* and *nuovo*. In German, *neun* and *neu*. Nine thus means the transition from old to new. There were nine original Templars, the knights who founded the Order of the Temple, which was later succeeded by the Portuguese Order of Christ. Solomon sent nine masters in search of Hiram Abiff, the architect of the temple. Demeter traveled the world in nine days looking for her daughter Persephone. Zeus's nine muses were born as a result of his nine nights of love. Nine months are needed before a human being to be born. As the last of the single numbers, nine heralds in both—and in this order—end and beginning, old and new, death and rebirth, the end of a cycle and the beginning of another; it is the number that closes the circle."

"Interesting."

They finally reached the bottom and stared at the center of the initiation well, which was a circle in white, yellow, and red marble covered in mud and tiny puddles. Inside the circle was an eight-pointed star with the suggestion of an orbicular cross inside it; it was the cross of the Templars, the religious order that brought the octagonal shape to the Christian temples of the West. One of the yellow points of the star pointed toward a dark hole in the wall.

"This star is also a wind rose," explained Thomas. "The extremity of the rose points east. The sun rises in the east, and churches are built facing east. The prophet Ezekiel said: 'The glory of the Lord came into the temple through the gate facing east.' Let's go through the cave."

He plunged into the darkness of the opening in the stone wall, and after holding back a moment, Moliarti followed him. They walked cautiously, almost groping their way along the walls like blind men.

After they had rounded the corner, a row of tiny yellow lights became visible on the ground to their left, and they were able to walk with more confidence, weaving through the long irregular tunnel carved out of the granite. Another dark shadow appeared on their right. It was a new path through the cave, an indication that the place they were in was more of a labyrinth than an underground connection. Familiar with the route, however, Thomas ignored this alternative passage and continued on, sticking to the main path until a sliver of light announced the outside world. They headed toward the light and saw a stone arch over a clear lake, with a thin stream of water cascading into it. They stopped beneath the arch. The path forked in front of the lake and they had to choose which way to go.

"Left or right?" asked Thomas.

"Left?" asked Moliarti, unsure of himself.

"Right," said Thomas, pointing at the correct path. "The end of the tunnel is a reenactment of an episode from Virgil's *Aeneid*. This represents the scene in which Aeneas goes into the underworld looking for his father and has to choose which way to go at a fork in the road. Those who turn left are condemned, fated to burn in hell. Only the path to the right leads to salvation. Aeneas chooses the right and crosses the Lethe River to get to the Elysian Fields, where his father is. So we should follow his footsteps."

They went right and the tunnel grew darker, narrower, and lower. At one point they were immersed in utter darkness and had to go slowly, feeling their way along the moist walls. The outside world finally became visible and the tunnel was flooded with light, terminating in a path of stepping-stones across the lake. They jumped from rock to rock until they reached the other side, then found themselves back in the woods, surrounded by color, breathing in the perfumed afternoon air and listening to the soft trilling of the linnets flitting from branch to branch.

"What a weird place," said Moliarti.

"You know, Nelson, this estate is a text."

"A text? Do you mean the four texts you mentioned earlier?"

Now they walked trails through the trees until they reached the

Guardians' Portal again, where Thomas led his guest into a narrow, medieval-style tower built into the hillside, with battlements at the top. They entered at the top of the tower and headed down the spiral staircase.

"In the past, during the Inquisition, when society was ruled by an intolerant church, certain works were prohibited. Artists were persecuted, new thoughts were silenced, books burned, paintings torn. That's where the idea came from to sculpt a book in stone. That, after all, is what Quinta da Regaleira is. A book sculpted in stone. It's easy to burn a book made of paper or tear a painting on canvas, but it's much more difficult to demolish an entire property. Remember this estate contains conceptual constructions that reflect esoteric thinking, inspired by Colonna's *Hypnerotomachia poliphili* and upheld by the philosophy behind Portugal's maritime expansion. In a way it is through the myths in the *Aeneid, The Divine Comedy*, and *The Lusiads*—that this place becomes a great monument to the Portuguese discoveries and the role the Templars played in them."

They reached the base of the tower and emerged, then headed down a wider path, passing through Leda's Cave on their way to the chapel. They marched along in silence now, listening to the sound of their footsteps and the delicate rustling of the woods.

"What now?" asked Moliarti.

"We're going to the chapel."

"No, that's not what I meant. What's left to be done in order to wrap up the investigation?"

"Ah," said Thomas. "I'm going to carefully study that passage by Umberto Eco to see if I can find the key that will open Professor Toscano's safe. I also need to clarify a few things about Columbus's origins. So I'm going to need to make one last trip."

"Okay. You know it's in the budget."

Thomas stopped next to a large tree a few steps from the chapel. He opened his briefcase, pulled out a piece of paper, and held it up. "This is another mystery about Columbus," he said.

"What is it?"

"It's a copy of a letter found in the Veragua archives."

Moliarti took the photocopy. "What letter?" He studied the text and shook his head, returning the page to Thomas. "That's fifteenth-century Portuguese."

"I'll read it to you," said Thomas. "This letter was found among Columbus's papers after his death. It's signed by none other than the great John II, nicknamed the Perfect Prince, the king of Portugal who signed the Treaty of Tordesillas, the man who told Columbus, and rightfully so, that it was quicker to sail around Africa to get to the Indies than to sail west, the monarch who—"

"I know who John II was," said Moliarti impatiently. "So he wrote to Columbus, did he?"

"Yes." Thomas studied the back of the page and pointed at some horizontal and vertical lines. "See these lines? This is where the letter was folded." He started folding it. "If we fold it along these lines, the words on the back join up and we can see the addressee." He held up the folded letter. "It's addressed 'to Xpovam Collon, our special friend in Seville.'" He unfolded the letter to read the text on the other side. "It says:

Xpoval Colon. We Dom John by the grace of God King of Portugal and the Algarves, of either side of the sea in Africa, Lord of Guinea send you our highest regards. We saw the letter you wrote us and through it the good will and affection you demonstrate being in our service. We thank you greatly. As regards your visit, certainly, for the reasons you cite as well as other matters for which we require your skill and ingenuity, we wish and shall be greatly pleased that you come since that which pertains to you shall transpire in a manner that will surely please you. And seeing as you may be wary of our judiciary because of certain obligations, we hereby guarantee that during your journey here, stay, and return journey, you will not be arrested, held, accused, summonsed, or indicted for anything civil or criminal, of any nature. And we herein order all of our judiciaries to so comply. And we thus implore and urge you to come quickly and with no hesitation and we will show you our gratitude and be much indebted. Written in Avis, on the twentieth of March of 1488. The King."

"Strange letter, isn't it?" said Moliarti, intrigued.

"I'm glad you agree. It looks like Columbus sent a letter to King John II offering him his services again. He apparently voiced his concerns about the possibility of having to face the king of Portugal's legal system."

"But why?"

"Because of something he supposedly did here in Portugal. Don't forget that Columbus left Portugal in a hurry sometime in 1484, four years before this exchange of letters. Something happened to make Columbus and his son Diego flee to Spain, but we don't know what. One of the mysteries surrounding the admiral is precisely the lack of documents regarding his life in Portugal. It's as if this period has disappeared into a black hole."

"What about the letter from Columbus to King John? Where is it?"

"It's never been found in the Portuguese archives."

"That's a shame."

"And there's another curious detail."

"What?"

"The almost intimate way in which King John refers to Columbus before he became famous, calling him 'our special friend in Seville.' It isn't a formal letter between a powerful sovereign and an uneducated foreign silk weaver. It's a letter between people who know each other well."

Moliarti raised an eyebrow. "It doesn't appear to be relevant to the problem of Columbus's origins."

Thomas smiled. "Maybe not," he admitted. "But at least it shows that they knew each other much better than we thought and that Columbus had frequented the Portuguese royal court, which raises the question of his belonging to the nobility, a possibility in keeping with two other points. The first is, as we've already seen, his marriage to the noblewoman Felipa Moniz Perestrello, which in that era would have been unthinkable for a commoner. If he was a nobleman, the marriage makes sense."

"Hmm," grumbled Moliarti. "And what's the other thing that supports the hypothesis that Columbus belonged to the nobility?"

Thomas pulled another piece of paper out of his briefcase. "The second is this document. These are the letters of patent issued by Isabella the Catholic, dated May 20, 1493, granting him the coat of arms." He pointed at the passage on the page he was holding. "She says here, '*armas vuestras que soliades tener*,' that is, 'the arms you already have.'" Thomas gave Moliarti a quizzical look. "'The arms you already have'? So Columbus already had a coat of arms? How could a silk weaver from Genoa have had a coat of arms?" He pulled out a piece of paper and held it up, pointing at the image on the left. "Now look, this is Columbus's coat of arms. As you can see, it is made up of four images. At the top are a castle and a lion, representing the kingdoms of Castile and León. In the bottom left-hand corner are some islands in the sea, representing his discoveries." He pointed at the last quarter of the coat of arms. "This is the image that Isabella the Catholic referred to as 'the arms you already have.' What does it show?"

He paused, then answered his own question. "Five golden anchors in the form of a cross on a blue field. Now look at this."

He pointed at the Portuguese coat of arms on the right.

"As you can see, the five golden anchors in the last quarter of Columbus's coat of arms is extraordinarily similar to the royal Portuguese coat of arms, where the five escutcheons are composed of five bezants also arranged in the form of a cross, a design that can still be seen on the Portuguese flag. Columbus's coat of arms is directly linked to the symbols of León, Castile, and Portugal."

"Incredible. But did anyone at that time confirm in writing that Columbus was Portuguese?"

Thomas smiled. "As it happens, someone did. In *Pleyto de la Prioridad,* two witnesses, Hernán Camacho and Alonso Belas, referred to Columbus as a 'son of Portugal.'"

"Doesn't seem like that big a deal. Apparently people lie and forge *all* the time."

"There's something else I want to tell you," said Thomas, checking his notes again. "At the peak of the dispute between Spanish and Italian historians over Columbus's true origins, one of the Spaniards, the president of the Spanish Royal Geographical Society, Ricardo Beltrán y Rózpide, wrote a text that ended with a cryptic phrase. He said: 'The man who discovered America was not born in Genoa and was originally from somewhere in Iberian territory on the western part of the peninsula between capes Ortegal and Saint Vincent.'" He looked Moliarti in the eyes. "This is an extraordinary observation."

"I'm sorry," said Moliarti, "but I don't see what's so extraordinary about that—"

"Nelson, Cape Ortegal is in Galicia—"

"Precisely. At that time it would be natural for a Spaniard to claim he was from somewhere in Spain."

"And Cape Saint Vincent is at the southern tip of Portugal."

"Oh."

"Like you said, it would have been perfectly natural, in an atmosphere of great nationalist debate, for a Spanish historian to claim that Columbus came from Galicia. But for him to explicitly mention the entire Portuguese coast as the admiral's place of origin, in that context, was not at all normal." He held up a finger. "Unless he knew something he wasn't revealing."

"Well, did he?"

Thomas nodded. "It appears he did. Beltrán y Rózpide had a Portuguese friend by the name of Afonso de Dornelas, who was also a friend of the famous historian Armando Cortesão. On his deathbed, Beltrán y Rózpide told his friend that among João da Nova's papers, which were held in a private archive in Portugal, there were one or more documents that completely explained Christopher Columbus's origins. Dornelas asked him several times which private archive he was referring to. Beltrán y Rózpide told him that, with Columbus's origins the topic of such heated debate in Spain, he'd risk causing a riot if he revealed where such a document might be found. He died a short time later, taking his secret to the grave."

Thomas turned and started walking again, toward the miniature cathedral that was the chapel, yet another mysterious place within the walls of Quinta da Regaleira.

But not so mysterious as his next destination, a new port in this strange journey.

Chapter 16

The hustle and bustle of the crowd was what most disturbed Thomas when he had to go to Chiado. After driving around the neighborhood looking for a place to park, he left his car in an underground parking garage and walked through a busy cobbled square to Rua Garrett, dodging the other pedestrians, some heading up the slope to the upper part of town, others on their way down to the lower districts, all staring into space, thinking about money or their girlfriends, hating their bosses, preoccupied with life.

He finally reached Rua Garrett's sidewalk, which, though wide, was crowded with tables and chairs occupied by idle customers—including the statue of the famous poet Fernando Pessoa, in a hat and round glasses, sitting with his legs crossed. Thomas looked around for Lena's golden hair, but she wasn't there. He turned the corner and headed for the large arched entrance to the Café A Brasileira, where Lisbon's bohemians and literary crowd once gathered.

His first step through the door was like a leap back in time to the 1920s. The room was long and narrow, richly decorated in an Art Nouveau style. The floor was black and white, and period paintings decorated the walls. Old chandeliers hung from carved designs on the wood-paneled ceiling. They looked like spiders with legs arching upward and downward, holding small candles. A beautiful gold-framed mirror ran the entire length of the wall, making the place look twice its size. The tiny tables were pushed up against the mirror, while a long counter festooned with lots of twisted, spaghetti-like ironwork ran down the right side. Bottles of wine and spirits lined the wall behind the counter.

Thomas found a place at a partially occupied table and sat down, leaning his right shoulder against the mirror, his eyes on the ceiling. He realized Lena had entered the café when he noticed customers' heads turning to look at the door, like troops obeying a silent order. She was wearing a tight, black, knee-length dress and a bright yellow sash around her waist. Her long legs were set off by a pair of dark gray stockings and shiny black heels. She carried several large shopping bags, which she deposited next to her chair when she leaned over to kiss Thomas.

"*Hej,*" she said. "Sorry I'm late. I was doing some shopping."

"No problem." Chiado, with its fancy stores and fashion boutiques, attracted lots of customers and brightened the steep, cobbled streets of the city's oldest quarter.

"Whew!" she exclaimed, tossing back her long blond hair. "I'm exhausted and the day has barely begun."

"Did you buy a lot?"

She leaned over to get one of the bags by her chair. "A few things," she said. She opened the bag and showed him some red lace. "Do you like it?"

"What is it?"

"It's a bra, silly," she explained, arching her eyebrows in a naughty expression. "To drive you crazy. I also went to that old elevator on Rua do Ouro."

"The Santa Justa Elevator?"

"That's the one. Have you ever been there?"

"No, I haven't."

"Of course." She smiled. "A foreigner's eye sees farther than a local's. Yes, another Swedish proverb. It means that foreigners visit more places in a country than the people who live there do."

"Very true," agreed Thomas. "Would you like something?"

"No thanks, I've already eaten."

Thomas shook his head at the waiter, who disappeared down the noisy corridor, which was now packed with people; he had no time to waste.

Lena leaned across the table and sought his eyes. "What's up?" she asked, looking intrigued. "I haven't seen you in two days, and you're acting mysterious. You look far away. What's going on?"

He finally allowed his eyes to rest on her. "I don't think I've been fair to you, you know."

Lena raised an eyebrow in surprise. "Oh. Haven't you?"

"I still love my wife."

She narrowed her eyes and stared at him, her expression suddenly comprehending. "Ah." Lena laughed and playfully shoved his shoulder. "It's adorable that you're concerned—but you are married, and I would be shocked if you didn't love your wife."

"You don't mind?"

"Of course I don't mind. You can have us both. It's not a problem for me."

"But . . ." He hesitated, confused. "You don't mind if I sleep with my wife and you at the same time?"

"Not in the *least*," she replied, still giggling at his earnestness.

Thomas leaned back in his chair, dazed. He really didn't know what to say. He hadn't expected this reaction. "Well, I'm not sure my wife would be too happy about it."

Lena shrugged. "So you shouldn't mention it to her, should you?"

He ran his hand through his hair nervously. "That's also a problem. I can't live like this. . . ."

"What do you mean you can't live like this? You've been with two women for the last two months and you haven't seemed even remotely worried about it. What's got into you now?"

"Well, that's just it. I'm having doubts about what we're doing."

Now it was Lena's turn to be taken aback. "Doubts? What doubts? Are you crazy? You've got a wife at home who doesn't suspect a thing.

You've got a girlfriend who, all modesty aside, any man would like to have and who doesn't give you any trouble. What's more, a girlfriend who doesn't mind if you *keep* this cushy little lifestyle of yours. So what's your problem? What exactly is there to doubt?"

"The problem, Lena, is that I don't know if I want this cushy little lifestyle."

Lena was incredulous. "You don't know if . . ." She frowned, trying to understand him. "Thomas, what's really going on?"

"I just don't want to go on like this."

"Then what do you want?"

"I want to break up."

Lena's shoulders slumped and she fell back in her chair, bewildered. She stared at Thomas as if he were a madman.

"You want to break up?" she finally said, making sure she'd heard correctly.

He nodded. "Yes. I'm sorry."

"Are you nuts? Why?"

"Because I feel guilty all the time. Because I love my wife. Because I have a little girl. Because I'm living a lie and I want the truth."

"Oh, give me a break!" she exclaimed. "The coat of truth is often lined with lies."

"No more proverbs."

Lena leaned across the table and grasped his hands. "Tell me what I can do to make you feel better. Do you want more space? More sex? What do you want?"

Thomas was more than a little surprised that Lena was clinging to their relationship. He had thought she would leave the café in a huff and it would be over.

"Look, Lena, I'm really fond of you. You're an amazing woman, and you've been a great help in my research. But I love my family. My wife and daughter are why I wake up in the morning. One moment I was dazzled by you, and the next, I began to see how maniacally selfish I've been."

"So you're dumping me. Is that it?"

"You're young, single, and very beautiful. Like you said yourself, all you have to do is snap your fingers and you can have any man you want. What do you need me for? We'll each go our own way and be friends."

She shook her head, disheartened. "I can't believe my ears."

Thomas looked at her and thought that if he said anything else, he'd only be repeating himself. After a moment, he stood up and held out his hand to Lena. She stared at it and did not return the gesture. He pulled his hand back awkwardly and turned to face the door. "See you in class," he said, leaving some money on the table.

Lena followed him with her eyes.

"The rooster that crows in the morning," she whispered, "will be in the falcon's beak by nightfall."

Chapter 17

JERUSALEM

Like a ballerina's feet gliding gracefully across a stage, the yellow and brown leaves lightly lifted from the ground, fluttering intermittently until they began to whirl, turning and turning around an invisible axis, blown by a warm zephyr that gradually, almost imperceptibly, whipped itself into a fury, a whirlwind of dust, dragging the leaves along the sidewalk and on to the busy street next to Jerusalem's Old City wall.

Thomas avoided the narrow corridor of twisting winds and quickened his step, crossing Sultan Suleiman Street at the plaza in front of the Damascus Gate and losing himself in the crowd. Ancient stones, strong as metal and soft as ivory, peered from every corner, holding memories made of blood, pain, hope, faith, and suffering.

The day had dawned bright and dry, although the sun proved harsh and intolerable for those who ventured out into it with no protection on their heads. Hordes of people came from all directions and flocked down the vast stairs, converging on the large gate in an ever-tightening squeeze, like greedy ants flowing toward a drop of honey, looking serious as they passed the vigilant gaze of the men in olive-green uniforms and helmets. The Israeli Defense Force soldiers, M16's swinging from their shoulders, stopped a few passersby here and there, asking for ID and rummaging through bags; their weapons looked neglected, but everyone knew that was just an impression. Around the monumental Damascus Gate the movement intensified as people streamed toward it, dodging the itinerant vendors selling fruit and vegetables and sweet rolls, people muttering under their breath, cursing, and elbowing one another. Many had come from afar to do their shopping at the souk or pray to Allah in the huge al-Aqsa Mosque.

Nearly squashed by the mass of humanity, Thomas felt himself carried by the human current through the gate. The route passed between the low buildings of the Muslim Quarter. Unable to resist the tremendous pull of the crowd, Thomas allowed himself to be led to a narrow street seething with activity.

Here there was a fork in the road and the crowd drained away in three directions. Thomas looked around for street names and consulted his map. He decided it was the street in the middle that interested him, so he took it, heading south. He passed under a building that arched over the street and found himself at a new fork in the road. On the corner was the Austrian Hospice complex, and the street running off on his left boasted a wall with a sign on it, saying, in Hebrew, Arabic, and Latin, a name that made him stop short. VIA DOLOROSA.

Thomas wasn't religious, but at that moment he couldn't help but imagine the bent figure of Jesus staggering through the narrow street with a cross on his back, escorted by Roman legionaries, blood trickling from his head and dripping onto the stones. The image was a product of his upbringing, almost a cliché. He had seen reproductions of that fateful route so many times that, once there, confronted with the name on a wall, he was flooded with imagined sequences of events that had taken place there two thousand years before, and involuntarily seized up with emotion.

The map told him he'd have to take the long street in front of him across the entire Old City. He headed down al-Wad Street and passed the Yeshivat Torat Chaim, leaving behind the street Christ had traveled in his last hours of life. At the next intersection on his left, Israeli soldiers had set up a post and were controlling access to the street leading to the sacred Haram al-Sharif complex and the al-Aqsa Mosque, stopping all non-Muslims from entering. It appeared there was an Islamic religious ceremony under way that no one wanted to disturb. Hemmed in by buildings and passing through a series of tunnels and arches, al-Wad was protected from the sun and cooled by a breeze that ran end to end, giving Thomas goose bumps. After passing al-Ain Bathhouse, he headed west along the Street of the Chain. At the Tashtamuriyya Building he turned left, entering the Jewish Quarter.

Here the commotion of the Arab alleys gave way to something very different; the spaces were quieter and more open, almost bucolic, and not a soul was to be seen. All that could be heard was the happy cooing of birds and the placid murmur of the treetops rustling in the wind. Thomas located Shonei Halakhot and looked for the street number he wanted. Next to a doorbell was a shiny golden sign in Hebrew, with English in smaller letters: THE JEWISH QUARTER KABBALAH CENTER. He pressed the black button and heard an electric buzzer sound inside, followed by footsteps approaching. The door opened and a young man with round glasses and a very fine, sparse beard stared at him questioningly.

"Boker tov," he said, greeting Thomas in Hebrew and asking how he could be of assistance. *"Ma uchal laasot lemaancha?"*

"Shalom," replied Thomas. He consulted his notebook, looking for a phrase he had jotted down at the hotel to say he didn't speak Hebrew. "Um . . . *eineni yode'a ivrit*. Do you speak English?"

"Ani lo mevin anglit," said the young man, shaking his head.

Thomas stared at him. " Um . . . Solomon . . . um . . ." he stuttered, trying to ask for the rabbi with whom he had an appointment. "Rabbi Solomon Ben-Porat?"

"Ah, *ken,*" said the young man, opening the door to invite him in. *"Bevakasha!"*

His host led him to a small, sparsely decorated room, let out a short *"Slach li,"* gestured for Thomas to wait, bowed quickly, and disappeared down the corridor. Thomas sat on a sofa and looked around the room. The furniture was made of dark wood, and the walls were covered with paintings of Hebrew characters. There was a trace of camphor and old paper in the air, mixed with the acidic smell of wax and varnish. A tiny window looked onto the street, but only a small amount of diffuse light made it through the curtains, enough to illuminate the flecks of dust floating in the air.

Minutes later he heard voices drawing near and a corpulent man appeared in the doorway; although he looked to be about seventy, he seemed robust. He was wearing a white cotton tallith with purple stripes and a blue-and-white fringe. He had a thick, gray beard, like Santa Claus or an Assyrian king, and a black velvet skullcap atop his bald head.

"Shalom aleichem," he said, holding out his hand cordially. "I'm Rabbi Solomon Ben-Porat," he said in English with a thick Hebrew accent. "With whom do I have the pleasure of speaking?"

"I'm Thomas Noronha, from Lisbon."

"Ah, Mr. Noronha!" the rabbi exclaimed effusively. They shook hands vigorously. Thomas noticed that the rabbi's hand was chubby but strong, almost squishing his. *"Na'im le'hakir otcha!"*

"I beg your pardon?"

"Nice to meet you," he said in English. "Did you have a good trip?"

"Yes, thank you."

The rabbi gestured for Thomas to follow and led him down the corridor, chattering about the wonders of airplanes nowadays, fantastic inventions that allowed one to travel faster than Noah's dove. He walked with some difficulty, his enormous body swaying from side to side. At the end of the corridor he entered what looked like a library with a large oak table in the middle, invited Thomas to take a seat, then sat opposite him.

"This is our meeting rrroom," he explained in a gravelly voice. "Would you care for something to drink?"

"No, thank you."

"Not even a glass of water?"

"Okay. Some water would be nice."

The rabbi looked at the doorway.

"Chaim!" he bellowed. "*Mayim*."

A few moments later a man appeared in the doorway with a jug of water and two glasses on a small tray. He looked to be in his thirties. He was thin, with a long dark beard, curly brown hair, and a knitted yarmulke on his head. He came into the room and left the tray on the table.

"This is Chaim Nasi," said the rabbi, and chuckled. "The Prince of the Jews."

Thomas and Chaim exchanged *shaloms* and shook hands.

"So, are you the professor from Lisbon?" asked Chaim in English.

"Yes."

"Ah," he said. He seemed to want to say something else, but he held back. "I see."

"Chaim here has a Portuguese background," explained the rabbi. "Don't you, Chaim?"

"Yes," said Chaim. "My family is Sephardic. The Sephardim were expelled from the Iberian Peninsula sometime around 5250. By the Jewish calendar, that is. The end of the fifteenth century according to the Christian calendar."

The rabbi added, "The expelled Sephardim totaled somewhere in the vicinity of a quarter of a million people. They settled in North Africa, the Ottoman Empire, South America, Italy, and Holland."

"Interesting," said Thomas. "Didn't Spinoza's family flee to Holland?"

"Yes," said the rabbi. "The Sephardim were very cultured, perhaps among the most highly educated Jews of that time. They were the first to go live in the United States and to this day consider themselves to be of the most prestigious Jewish lineage."

Thomas leaned an elbow on the table to rest his chin in his hand.

"I've always thought that the expulsion of the Jews was tragic," he said sadly, "possibly one of the most senseless acts ever committed in Portugal. And not just in terms of human rights. Their leaving was directly related to the country's decline. What makes a country wealthy isn't money. It's knowledge. Now, what happened in Portugal during the Age of Discovery? The country opened itself to knowledge. Prince Henry the Navigator brought together some of the greatest minds of his time, from Portugal and abroad, people who invented navigation instruments, designed ships, developed more sophisticated weapons, made advances in cartography. It was a period of great intellectual wealth. Many of these Portuguese and foreigners were Christian, but not all of them."

"Some were Jews. . . ."

"Precisely. There were Jews in his think tank that conceived the Portuguese discoveries, and some were very important. They were leaders in their fields and brought new expertise to the country, opened doors, made contacts, found financing. While the Spanish were persecuting the Jews, the Portuguese were taking them in and they were protected by King John II. The problem arose when his successor, Manuel I, began to dream of becoming king of the entire Iberian Peninsula, making Lisbon the capital, and hatched a plan to seduce the Catholic Monarchs. A fundamental step in this plan was his marriage to one of the Catholic Monarchs' daughters, in order to unite the two dynasties, but the bride imposed her own condition for the marriage to take place."

"She wanted the Jews expelled." The rabbi shook his head.

"Exactly. She didn't want Jews in Portugal. Under normal circumstances, King Manuel would have told his bride and the Catholic Monarchs to get lost. But those weren't normal circumstances. The king of Portugal wanted to rule all of Iberia. Faced with his bride's condition, and also under pressure from the Portuguese Church, that idiot King Manuel gave in. He attempted a kind of subterfuge, however. Instead of expelling the Jews, he tried to convert them by force. In a massive operation in 1497, he baptized them against their will, thereby converting to Christianity seventy thousand Portuguese Jews, who were dubbed New Christians. But of course, most continued practicing Judaism in secret. As a consequence, the first massacre of Jews took place in Lisbon in 1506, a pogrom carried out by the populace that left two thousand dead. This was common in

Spain, where there had been widespread intolerance for some time, but not in Portugal."

"The result was catastrophic," said Chaim. "Jews began to flee the country, taking with them a priceless treasure: their learning, their curiosity, and their inventive spirit. This was followed in the 1540s by the installation of the Inquisition in Portugal, and the disaster was completed forty years later, when King Manuel's dream of uniting Portugal and Spain finally became a reality, but with the Spanish at the helm. Spain introduced an even more radical form of obscurantism. Portugal was closed to outside influences and knowledge. Scientific texts were prohibited, education became the exclusive domain of the church, and the country floundered in fanatical ignorance. With the prohibition of Judaism, Portugal entered a period of decline that has only occasionally been reversed."

"Now, that's an interesting way to get to know a country's history," said the rabbi with a smile. "Through its bad decisions."

"Small mistakes, big problems," said Thomas.

The rabbi placed his hand on Chaim's shoulder in an affectionate gesture but kept his eyes on Thomas. "Well, our Prince of the Jews here is from one of the most important Sephardic families in Portugal." He turned to his protégé. "Aren't you, Chaim?"

Chaim nodded humbly. "Yes, sir."

"What was your family's surname?" asked Thomas.

"The Portuguese or Hebrew name?"

"Both, I guess."

"My family adopted the name Mendes, but it was really Nasi. Years after the persecution had begun in Lisbon, my ancestors fled to Holland and then Turkey. The matriarch of the family was Gracia Nasi, who used her influence with the Turkish sultan and her many commercial contacts to help the New Christians get out of Portugal. She even tried to organize a trade embargo on the countries that persecuted the Jews."

"Gracia Nasi became famous," added the rabbi. "The poet Samuel Usque dedicated a book to her in Portuguese, *Consolaçãm às tribulaçõens de Israel,* and dubbed her 'the heart of her people.'"

"Gracia's nephew Joseph also fled Lisbon for Istanbul," said Chaim, taking up the story. "He became a famous banker and statesman, and was friend to European monarchs and adviser to Sultan Suleiman, who made him a duke. Joseph and Gracia were the Jews who assumed control of Tiberias, here in Israel, encouraging other Jews to come resettle here."

Thomas smiled. "Are you suggesting that it was the Portuguese Jews, your ancestors, who initiated resettlement in the Middle East?"

The two Israelis gave him half-smiles.

"That's one way of looking at things," said Chaim, stroking his curly beard. "I prefer to think that they were God's instruments in returning the Promised Land to us."

"But the best bit," said the rabbi, "is that Joseph Nasi became incredibly rich and even today is known as the Prince of the Jews, not least because the word *nasi* means 'prince' in Hebrew." He patted Chaim's head. "That's why, as a descendant of Joseph's family and because his name is Nasi, I call Chaim here the Prince of the Jews."

"Now, that's my country's loss," said Thomas. "Imagine what we might have done if Chaim's family had remained in Portugal."

Solomon glanced at the large clock on the wall. "That and many other families," he said sadly. He took a deep breath. "But here we are, talking and talking, and we haven't even gotten to the subject of our meeting, have we?"

That was Thomas's cue to reach for his old briefcase and pull out a bundle of photocopies. "Very well!" he exclaimed. "As I said on the phone, I would very much appreciate your help in analyzing these documents." He set the bundle on the table and pushed it toward the rabbi; he pulled out one page and pointed to it. "This is the most intriguing."

Solomon put on a small pair of glasses and leaned over the photocopy, examining the letters and symbols. "What's this?" he asked without taking his eyes off the page.

"Christopher Columbus's signature."

The old Jew stroked his thick white beard thoughtfully, then took off his glasses and looked at Thomas. "This signature says a lot of things," he said.

Thomas nodded. "That's what I thought," he said. "Do you think it's Kabbalistic?"

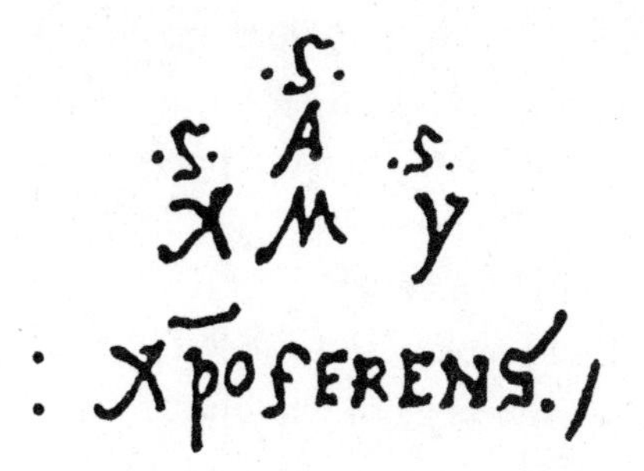

Solomon put his glasses back on and studied the page again. "It's possible, it's possible," he said after a few seconds. He laid the photocopy on the table, stroked his thin lips with his fingers, and sighed. "I need you to give me a few hours to consult some books, talk to some friends, and study this signature." He looked at the clock. "It's eleven o'clock, so let me see . . . Why don't you go do some sightseeing and come back at around five this afternoon?"

"Great." Thomas got up, and the rabbi pointed at Chaim.

"Chaim will go with you. He's a good guide and can show you around the Old City." He made a vague wave of good-bye with his hand. *"Lehitra'ot."*

The old Kabbalist turned back to the page and delved into the mysteries it contained.

Outside, the air was still cool and dry, in spite of the strong sun bathing the buildings and squares of the Jewish Quarter. As they left the building, Thomas zipped up his jacket and followed Chaim.

"What would you like to see?" asked his guide.

"The usual things, I think. The Holy Sepulcher and the Western Wall."

"The Western Wall," said Chaim, pointing to his right. "It's about five minutes from here."

They set out toward the sacred wall of Judaism. Turning south, they headed for Hurva Square. This was the first large space Thomas had seen in the Old City. There were cafés, restaurants, souvenir shops, and a few trees in a square dominated by four Sephardic synagogues built by the Spanish and Portuguese Jews in the sixteenth century, the ruins of the Hurva Synagogue, and the slender minaret of the now closed-up Sidna Omar Mosque. They turned east, heading through the arched passages of the busy Tipheret Yisrael, and wove their way through a maze of alleys.

"Do you think the rabbi will be able to decipher the signature?" asked Thomas, walking next to Chaim, his eyes roaming the sidewalk.

"Solomon Ben-Porat is one of the world's finest Kabbalists, and the greatest in Jerusalem. People come from all over to consult him about the secrets of the Torah."

They passed the Yeshivat HaKotel, and a vast plaza opened out before them. Behind it was an enormous old wall of large, rough limestone blocks, and at the base were rows of Jews in yarmulkes, rocking back and forth. The prayer area was cordoned off from the rest of the plaza.

"The Kotel HaMa'aravi," announced Chaim. "The Western Wall. Everything started here, under that golden dome. There is the rock on which the patriarch Abraham, obeying an order from God, prepared to sacrifice his son Isaac. This rock is called Even ha-Shetiyah in Hebrew and is the foundation stone of the world, the primordial rock. It was here that the Ark of the Covenant later rested. This whole elevation, where the Rock of Abraham is situated, is called Mount Moriah, or Temple Mount, as it was here that King Solomon had the First Temple of Jerusalem built. When Solomon died, a series of conflicts led to the division of the Jews, who, after being defeated by the Assyrians, were enslaved by the Babylonians, who destroyed the temple. The Babylonians were later defeated by the Persians, and the Jews were allowed to return to their lands. That was when the Second Temple was built. Alexander the Great's presence here sowed the seed for a period of Greek domination of the Middle East, then Roman. Although they controlled things, the Romans allowed the Jews to be governed by Jewish kings. That was how, shortly before the birth of

Jesus the Nazarene, Herod the Great widened the temple and built a large wall around it. The Western Wall was a part of it and is the only section that has survived.

"In the year 66 of the Christian era, the Jews rebelled against the Romans, beginning what we know as the Wars of the Jews. In response, the Romans conquered Jerusalem and razed the temple in 68, an event that proved profoundly traumatic for our nation." He gestured toward the wall. "That's why the Western Wall is also known as the Wailing Wall. The Jews come here to mourn the destruction of the temple."

They entered the large plaza and strolled toward the wall. Thomas noted its rough surface, with green tufts of henbane poking out here and there and vestiges of snapdragon growing out of the cracks at the top. The lower stone blocks were enormous, clearly from the original wall, while the higher ones were much smaller and revealed later additions. In the gaps between the rocks he spotted two nests, possibly belonging to the swallows and sparrows flying over the plaza, filling it with a delightful duel of celestial warbling and twittering.

"The temple was the center of the spiritual universe," Chaim continued, "through which goodness entered the world. In this place there was respect for God and his Torah. It was here that Abraham almost sacrificed Isaac and where Jacob had a vision of a ladder to heaven. When the Romans destroyed the temple, the angels came down to earth and covered this part of the wall with their wings to protect it, saying that it would never be destroyed. That's why the prophets say the Divine Presence will never abandon the last remnants of the temple, the Western Wall. Never. They say it is eternally sacred." He pointed at the enormous stone blocks at the wall's base. "See those rocks? The biggest one weighs four hundred tons. Four hundred. It's the largest rock ever carried by man. There are no rocks this size in the monuments of ancient Greece or the Egyptian pyramids, or even the modern buildings of New York and Chicago. Believe it or not, there's no crane strong enough to lift this rock."

He took a deep breath. "The Talmud teaches that when the temple was destroyed, all the gates of heaven were closed, except for one, the Gate of Tears. The Western Wall is the place where Jews come to weep; it is a place for mourning. Jews all over the world pray facing the Western Wall, and it is here, through the Gate of Tears, that their prayers ascend to heaven. The Midrash says that God never leaves this wall. The Song of Songs refers to his presence, saying, 'Behold, He standeth behind our Wall.' "

"If the Temple is so important, why don't you rebuild it?"

"Reconstruction will begin when the Messiah comes. The Third Temple will be built in the exact place where the First and Second Temples stood. The Midrash says that this Third Temple has already been built in heaven and is just waiting for preparations to be made for it on earth. Everything indicates that this time is nigh. A very strong sign is the return of the Jewish people to the Promised Land. The Messiah will build the temple on Mount Moriah, Temple Mount."

"How will you recognize the Messiah?"

"Precisely through his taking responsibility for rebuilding the temple. That will be the sign that he is the true Messiah."

"But the al-Aqsa Mosque and the Dome of the Rock are there," said Thomas, pointing at the Islamic domes behind the wall. "To build the Third Temple you'll have to destroy the mosques, which belong to the third holiest site in Islam, as well as everything else there. Haram al-Sharif is sacred to the Muslims. How do you think they're going to react to that?"

"That will be resolved by God and his envoy, the Messiah."

Thomas looked at Mount Moriah and started toward it. "Chaim, tell me how, with so many hills around, the Jews and the Muslims chose exactly the same mount as their holy place?"

"The answer to that is in history. The Romans expelled the Jews from Jerusalem and also persecuted the Christians on a large scale until, in the fourth century of the Christian era, the Roman emperor Constantine converted to Christianity. Constantine's mother, Helena, came to Jerusalem and ordered the first Christian churches to be built in the areas related to the life of Jesus. Jerusalem was once again important. In 614, the Persian army invaded the region and, with the support of the Jews, massacred the Christians. The Romans, who were Byzantine by this time, reconquered Palestine in 628, the same year that an army led by the prophet Muhammad took Mecca and brought a new religious force into the world: Islam. Ten years later, Muhammad was dead and his successor, the caliph Umar, defeated the Byzantines and conquered Palestine. Since Islam recognizes Abraham and the Old Testament, its followers also considered Jerusalem to be a holy place. Additionally, the Muslims believed that Muhammad, years before, had ascended to heaven from the Even ha-Shetiyah, the stone where Abraham almost sacrificed his son and over which the Jews had built their two temples. The rubble the Romans had left behind on Mount Moriah was removed, and the Muslims built their two shrines there, the Dome of the Rock, in 691, and al-Aqsa Mosque, in 705, both within the holy site Haram al-Sharif." He made a sweeping gesture, taking in the entire hill behind the Western Wall, including the golden dome shining in the sun to his left, as if it were the crown of the Old City.

He continued. "Christians and Jews were not allowed to enter this place built here on Mount Moriah but continued living in Jerusalem. A period of relative tolerance ensued until the eleventh century, when the Muslims changed their policy and denied Christians and Jews access to Jerusalem. That was the beginning of our problems. Christian Europe reacted badly and launched the Crusades. The Christians recovered Jerusalem and even constituted a religious order with the name of the temple."

"The Poor Fellow-Soldiers of Christ and of the Temple of Solomon."

"Exactly. The Knights of the Order of the Temple, also known as the Knights Templar. They established their headquarters here on Haram al-Sharif, or Temple Mount, and set about excavating. They found important relics, but which ones we don't know. Some say they found the Ark of the Covenant and the chalice Jesus drank from at the Last Supper and where drops of his blood were collected at the Crucifixion."

"The Holy Grail."

"Yes. There are even those who say that the Shroud of Turin, the cloth supposedly used to cover Jesus' body after the Crucifixion, was also found here by the Templars. They remain unsolved mysteries and help make Mount Moriah a mythical place for Christians, too."

They approached the prayer area and stood watching the faithful wash their hands in a basin to remove any impurities before going to pray. In front of the wall, men and women, separated by the *mechitza,* rocked their heads and torsos in a rhythmic prayer. Some held small books.

They left through the north corner of the plaza, turning onto the Street of the Chain outside the Khalidi Library, where the brutal Tartar prince Barka Khan was buried, then continued on until they got to David Street. It was already after two in the afternoon, and they were hungry. Chaim took his guest to a restaurant in the peaceful Jewish Quarter. They had hummus, tabbouleh, and two kebabs in pita bread with spicy *harif* sauce. They finished off with *katzar,* strong coffee served in copper bowls.

As their food digested, they strolled down David Street, which separated the Armenian Quarter from the Christian Quarter, admiring its cheery bazaar atmosphere, chockablock with stores selling clothes, rugs, trinkets, and religious statues carved in olive wood—everything imaginable to catch the eye of tourists and the devotion of pilgrims. Eventually they found themselves before the dark, sinister structure of the Church of the Holy Sepulcher.

Walking through the arched doorways with marble pillars they went up to the rock of Calvary, where the Romans crucified Christ, hidden by the structure of the two chapels. The Latin chapel on the right occupied the tenth and eleventh stations of the cross, the place where Jesus' executioners had nailed him to the crucifix. An arch next to it marked the Altar of Stabat Mater, where Mary wept beneath the cross. The Orthodox chapel on the other side marked the place where the cross was erected. Two glass cases next to the Orthodox altar allowed one to see the uneven surface of Calvary emerging from the ground.

"Amazing!" said Thomas in a low voice, leaning forward to get a better look at the stone where the Crucifixion had taken place. "So, this is the exact spot where Jesus died."

"It isn't necessarily the exact spot. In 325 Constantine called an ecumenical council to discuss the nature of the Holy Trinity. Sitting on the council was Bishop Macarius of Jerusalem, who convinced Constantine's mother, Helena, to come to the Holy Land to locate the neglected places where Jesus had been. Helena came here and found the cave he was born in, in Bethlehem, and the cave on the Mount of Olives, where he predicted the destruction of Jerusalem. She came to the conclusion that Golgotha, the large rock where he was crucified, was underneath the pagan temples built by the Roman emperor Hadrian two hundred years earlier in the northwestern part of the Old City."

"Golgotha?"

"That's the Hebrew word for the rock, meaning 'the place of the skull.' The Latin derivation is Calvary." He paused. "She arbitrarily determined the places where Jesus had prepared for his execution, where he was nailed to the cross, and where the cross was erected, that is, the tenth, eleventh, and twelfth stations of the Way of the Cross. But it was based on guesswork, and the truth is that no one is absolutely certain that the rock beneath the basilica is really Golgotha, although everything seems to indicate that it is. It says in the gospel that Jesus was crucified on a rock located outside of what were then the Old City walls, at the foot of a hillock with caves used as catacombs, and archaeological studies have revealed that this place fits the description precisely."

They got on the queue to enter the Holy Sepulcher, the part of the catacomb where the body of Christ was believed to have been laid after his death, now concealed within a shrine built right in the middle of the Romanesque Rotunda, the majestic circular room directly beneath the basilica's large white and gold dome, with arched passages on the ground and first floors, circling the small tomb. Chaim preferred to go admire the Catholicon, the neighboring dome that covered the central nave of the Crusader church and was considered the center of the world by the Orthodox Church. So Thomas went alone through the small passage and looked around the hot, humid chamber of the Holy Sepulcher. With unexpected reverence, he observed the marble slab over the place where Jesus' body was said to have been laid, and gazed at the bas-reliefs in the claustrophobic crypt, showing a scene from the Resurrection. He only stayed for a few seconds, so great was the pressure to leave and allow those behind him to enter. At the exit, Chaim was waiting for him with his arm out, pointing at his watch.

"It's four thirty," he said. "We should be getting back."

Solomon Ben-Porat's hefty body was facing away from the door as he talked with a bony man with tiny eyes and a long, pointy black beard, who was wearing a *bekishe,* a somber Hassidic coat. The rabbi sensed their arrival and twisted around in his chair, a smile of satisfaction visible through his thick beard.

"Ah!" he exclaimed. *"Ma shlomkha?"*

"Tov," answered Chaim.

"Come in, come in," said Solomon in English, wiggling his fingers at them. "Misterrr Norrronha!" he boomed. He turned back to the man sitting on his right. "Allow me to introduce a friend of mine, Rabbi Abraham Hurewitz."

The thin man stood to greet Thomas and Chaim. *"Na'im me'od,"* he said.

"Rabbi Hurewitz has come to help me," explained Solomon, distractedly stroking his white beard. "I looked over the documents you gave me and called a few friends. I discovered that Rabbi Hurewitz had studied Christopher Columbus's texts some time ago, especially his *Book of Prophecies* and diary, and when I called him he said he was available to come clarify things for you."

"Excellent," said Thomas appreciatively, without taking his eyes off Hurewitz.

"First I think it's important to give you something by way of an introduction." Solomon looked at Thomas curiously. "Mr. Noronha, forgive me for asking, but what do you know about the Kabbalah?"

"Very little, I think," Thomas said, getting his old notebook ready. "This is the first time I've come across it in my research."

"Well, Mr. Noronha, the Kabbalah contains the symbolic code of the mysteries of the universe with God at the center. The word *Kabbalah* comes from the verb *lekabel,* meaning 'to receive.' We are thus dealing with a system of transmission and reception, a system of interpretation, an instrument for deciphering the world, the key that allows us to know the designs of the Ineffable One." Solomon spoke with great eloquence, his voice slow and deep. "Some say that the Kabbalah dates from Adam, while others believe it goes back to the patriarch Abraham, and many point to Rabbi Moshe Alshich, believed to be the author of *Torat Moshe,* a commentary on the Pentateuch, as the first Kabbalist. As far as we know, the original systematized traces of the Kabbalah appeared in the first century B.C.E. and passed through a total of seven phases. The first was the longest and lasted until the tenth century. This initial stage predominantly used meditation as a means of reaching the spiritual ecstasy that allows one access to God's mysteries, and the Kabbalistic writings from this period describe the higher planes of existence. The second phase took place from 1150 to 1250 in Germany, with the practice of absolute ascetism and an extreme form of altruism. The next phase lasted until the beginning of the fourteenth century and marked the birth of the prophetic Kabbalah, mostly thanks to the work of Abraham Abulafia. This was when methods were developed for reading and interpreting the mystic nature of the sacred texts, and combining Hebrew letters with the names of God. The fourth phase occupied the entire fourteenth century and gave rise to the most important work of Kabbalistic mysticism, the *Sefer Ha-Zohar,* or *Book of Splendor.* This rich text appeared in the Iberian Peninsula at the end of the thirteenth century, and its authorship is attributed to Moses de León."

"What's it about?"

"It's an enormous work on the Creation and understanding the hidden meanings of the mysteries of God and the universe." He cleared his throat. "The fifth phase also began in the Iberian Peninsula, when

Judaism was banned in Spain in 1492, and Portugal in 1496. Its greatest proponent was Isaac Luria, who, in an effort to find a mystical explanation for the persecution, developed a theory of exile, combining the Kabbalah with messianism in the hope of attaining collective redemption. That's why the sixth phase, in the seventeenth and eighteenth centuries, was marked by pseudo-messianism, which caused many misunderstandings and paved the way to the seventh and last phase, known as Hassidism, which arose in eastern Europe as a reaction to messianism. The Hassidic movement, founded by Ba'al Shem Tov, popularized the Kabbalah, making it less obscure and elitist and more accessible to everyone."

"And what about the counting of letters and the Tree of Life?" asked Thomas, scribbling furiously in his notebook. "Where does that come in?"

"You're talking about two different things, Mr. Noronha," said Solomon. "What you call the counting of letters is, I imagine, gematria. This technique involves obtaining the numerical value of words by assigning numbers to the letters of the Hebrew alphabet. In gematria, the nine first letters are associated with the nine single numbers, the next nine letters are associated with the nine decades, or multiples of ten, and the remaining four represent the first four hundreds." He opened his hands and waved them around, as if embracing all of the world.

"God created the universe with numbers, and each number contains a mystery and a revelation. Everything in the universe is part of a chain of cause and effect and forms a unit that can be multiplied endlessly. Nowadays mathematicians use chaos theory to understand the complex workings of things, while physicists prefer the uncertainty principle to justify the odd behavior of subatomic particles in a quantum state. We Kabbalists choose gematria.

"Almost two thousand years ago, sometime between the second and sixth centuries of the common era, a small, enigmatic, metaphysical work entitled *Sefer Yetzirah,* or *Book of Creation,* appeared, describing how God had made the world using numbers and words. Like today's mathematicians and physicists, the *Sefer Yetzirah* argued that it was possible to tap into divine power through numbers. That is basically what gematria is all about. This system attributes creative power to words and numbers and is based on the assumption that Hebrew was the language used by God in the Creation. Numbers and Hebrew are divine in nature. Using gematria, one can transform letters into numbers and make very interesting discoveries." These last words he pronounced "verrry interrresting discoverrries," giving the statement an air of mystery. "For example, the Hebrew word for 'year,' *shanah,* is equivalent to 355, which is precisely the number of days in the lunar year. And the word *herayon,* or 'pregnancy,' is equivalent to 271, the number of days in nine months, the duration of a pregnancy."

"Like an anagram."

"Exactly, a divine anagram of numbers and letters. See what happens when we apply gematria to the Holy Writ. Another of God's names, *YHVH Elohei Israel,* equals 613. And *Moshe Rabeinu*—Moses, our teacher—also adds up to 613. Now, 613 is the number of commandments in the Torah. That means that God gave Moses the 613 laws of the Torah." He made a circular gesture with his hands. "The Holy Writ contains a holographic complexity; many different meanings are multiplied within the text. Another example is in Genesis, where it says that Abraham led 318 servants into battle. But when Kabbalists analyzed the numerical value of the name of his servant Eliezer, they discovered that it was 318. It is thus presumed that Abraham actually only took Eliezer with him."

"Are you saying the Bible contains subliminal messages?"

"If that's what you want to call them," said Solomon, smiling. "Do you know what the first word of the Pentateuch is?"

"No."

"*Bereshith*. That means 'in the beginning.' If we divide *bereshith* into two words, we get *bere*, or 'he created,' and *shith*, which means 'six.' God created the world in six days and rested on the seventh. The entire message of the Creation is contained in a single word, the first word of the Holy Writ. *Bereshith. In the beginning. Bere* and *shith. He created* and *six*. The six corresponds to the hexagram, the double triangle of the Seal of Solomon, which we now call the Star of David and which is on the flag." He pointed at the white-and-blue Israeli flag in a corner of the room. "There are also anagrams in the Pentateuch. For example, God says in Exodus: 'I send an angel before thee.' In Hebrew, 'my angel' is *melakhi,* an anagram of Mikhael—the Hebrew spelling of *Michael*—the guardian archangel of the Jews. In other words, God sent the angel Mikhael."

"Does this system of interpretation also apply to the Tree of Life?"

"The Tree of Life is something else," said the rabbi. "For a long time, two questions dominated man's relationship with God. If God made the world, what is the world if not God? The second question, stemming from the first, is why is the world so imperfect if the world is God? The *Sefer Yetzirah,* the mystical text I just mentioned that describes how God created the universe using numbers and words, appeared, in part, to answer to these two questions. This work was originally attributed to Abraham, although it was probably written by Rabbi Akiva. The *Sefer Yetzirah* reveals the divine nature of numbers and equates them with the thirty-two paths of wisdom traveled by God when he was creating the universe. The thirty-two paths are composed of the ten primordial numbers, the *sefirot,* and the twenty-two letters of the Hebrew alphabet. Each letter and each *sefirah* symbolizes something. For example, the first *sefirah* represents the spirit of the living God expressed in voice, breath, and speech. The second *sefirah* represents air emanated from the spirit, the third *sefirah* is water emanated from the air, and so on.

"The ten *sefirot* are emanations of God, manifested in the act of the Creation, and are structured in the Tree of Life, which is the elementary unit of Creation, the smallest indivisible particle containing elements of the whole. Naturally, this concept evolved and the *Sefer Ha-Zohar,* the classical text of Kabbalism that appeared in the Iberian Peninsula in the late thirteenth century, defined the *sefirot* as the ten divine attributes. The first *sefirah* is *keter,* crown. The second is *chokhmah,* wisdom. The third is *binah,* understanding. The fourth is *chesed,* mercy. The fifth is *gevurah,* might. The sixth is *tipheret,* beauty. The seventh is *netzach,* eternity. The eighth is *hod,* glory. The ninth is *yesod,* foundation. And the tenth is *malkhut,* kingdom."

"Hold on," begged Thomas, frantically scribbling all the information in his notebook. "Could you go slower, please?"

By this time, Thomas had already lost track of things, tangled in that mesh of Hebrew words, but Solomon calmly continued. He paused briefly to allow Thomas to get the Tree of Life down on paper, then resumed.

"The *Sefer Ha-Zohar* established multiple ways of interpreting the Tree of Life, with horizontal and vertical, descending, and ascending readings of the *sefirot*. For example, the path from top to bottom represents the act of Creation, in which the light filled the first *sefirah*, *keter*, and spilled downward to the last, *malkhut*. The path from bottom to top represents the developmental act that leads the creature to the Creator, moving from matter to spirituality. Each *sefirah* is associated with one of the names of God. *Keter*, for example, is *Ehieh*, and *malkhut* is *Adonai*. And each *sefirah* is governed by an archangel. *Keter*'s is the archangel Metatron. The Tree of Life applies to everything. To the stars, to vibrations, to the human body."

Thomas felt as if he was finally beginning to grasp it all. "The human body?" he asked.

"Yes, the Kabbalah suggests that the human being is a microcosm, a simulation of the universe in miniature, and integrates it with the Tree of Life. *Keter* is the head; *hokhmah*, *chesed*, and *netzach* are the right side of the body; *binah*, *gevurah*, and *hod* are the left side; *tipheret* is the heart; *yesod*, the genitals; and *malkhut*, the feet." He took a deep breath and made a sweeping gesture with his hands. "Much, much more can be said about the Kabbalah. Believe me, one can study it for an entire lifetime, there's no way I can explain all of its mysteries, all of the enigmas it contains, in this brief summary. For now, I think I've given you enough for you to follow our interpretation of the documents and the signature you gave me this morning."

Thomas stopped taking notes for a minute and leaned on the table. The conversation seemed to have arrived at the crucial point. "Yes, let's take a look at Christopher Columbus's signature. In your opinion, is it Kabbalistic?"

Solomon smiled. "Patience is a virtue of the wise, Mr. Noronha.

Before we get into the signature, I think there are a few things you should know about Columbus."

"I already know a thing or two," said Thomas with a chuckle.

"Perhaps," said Solomon. "But I'm sure you'll also be interested in what Rabbi Abraham has to tell you."

Solomon turned to his right, motioning for Hurewitz to speak. The rabbi hesitated a moment, his eyes dancing among the three men looking back at him, and took a deep breath before he began.

"Mr. Noronha," he said in a whispery, submissive voice that contrasted with Solomon's guttural rumble. "I heard you say you already know a thing or two about Mr. Christopher Columbus. Could you be so kind as to enlighten me about the date on which Mr. Columbus set sail on his first voyage to America?"

"Well, I believe he left the port of Palos, in Cádiz, on August 3, 1492." Thomas smiled, recognizing the rhetorical technique he used with Nelson, which wasn't nearly as fun to be on the receiving end of.

"And now, Mr. Noronha, could you tell me the deadline decreed by the Catholic Monarchs for the Jews to leave Spain?"

"Hmm," pondered Thomas. "That . . . that I don't know. It was sometime in 1492."

"Yes, Mr. Noronha, but what was the exact date?"

"I don't know."

The rabbi paused theatrically. He kept his eyes trained on Thomas, gauging his reactions. "What if I told you that the royal edict ordered the Sephardic Jews to leave Spain by August 3, 1492?"

Thomas felt his eyes open wide. "What? August 3? You mean . . . you mean, the day Columbus left on his first voyage?"

"The same day."

Thomas shook his head in surprise. "I had no idea!" he exclaimed. "That's a curious coincidence."

Rabbi Hurewitz's thin lips twisted into a humorless smile. "Do you think so?" he asked, almost mocking Thomas's choice of words. "Shimon bar Yochai wrote that all of the Supreme King's treasures are guarded by a single key. That means, Mr. Noronha, that there are no coincidences. Coincidences are subtle ways the Creator chooses to transmit His messages. Is it a coincidence that God and Moses' names correspond to the same number as the laws of the Torah? Is it a coincidence that Christopher Columbus left Spain on exactly the same day that the Jews were expelled from the country?" He consulted a small book resting on the table with Columbus's face on the cover and a title in Hebrew. "These are Mr. Columbus's own diaries of his discovery of America. Listen to what he says in his very first entry." Hurewitz read in a low voice, translating the Hebrew text into English as he went. "'So after having expelled the Jews from your dominions, Your Highnesses, in the same month of January, ordered me to proceed with sufficient armament to the said regions of India.'" He looked up and stared at Thomas again. "What do you think of this passage?"

Thomas, who had started taking notes again, bit his bottom lip. "I've read the diary, but I have to admit I didn't pay much attention to that sentence."

"It's near the beginning," said the rabbi. "Actually, Mr. Noronha, this sentence tells us several things. First, that the decision to send Mr. Columbus to the Indies was made in January 1492. Second, that the decision to expel the Jews, set forth in the royal edict dated March 30, which gave the Sephardim until August 3 to get out of Spain, was made in the same month." He cocked his head. "Do you think that's a coincidence, Mr. Noronha?"

"I don't know," said Thomas, shaking his head without taking his eyes off his notes. "I really don't know. I'd never realized these events took place simultaneously."

"None of this is coincidental," said the rabbi with conviction. "Because the sentence I read you reveals something else. Mr. Columbus's intention. As Rabbi Shimon bar Yochai wrote, it is not the act itself that rewards men, but the intention behind it. What did Mr. Columbus intend when he mentioned the expulsion of the Jews at the beginning of his diary? Did he just feel like it? Was it just a detail? A throwaway reference to something going on at the time?" He raised an eyebrow to show he disapproved of such an interpretation. "Or was it on purpose?" He held up both index fingers and brought them together. "Isn't it obvious he tried to relate the two events?"

"Do you think they're connected?"

"Beyond a doubt. Did you know that on the eve of his departure on his first voyage, Mr. Columbus demanded that all crew members be on board by eleven o'clock at night?"

"Meaning?"

"It was highly uncommon, quite the opposite of sailors' habits at the time. But he insisted on it. And guess what happened an hour later."

"What?"

"The edict expelling the Jews came into force." He smiled. "There were Jews in the fleet."

"Rabbi, you mean Columbus himself—"

"Exactly." The rabbi flicked through the diary again. "Look what he wrote in his entry on September 23, when the sea rose with no winds, bringing an end to a dangerous calm." He started translating. "'I was greatly favored by the high seas, which hadn't risen like that since the time of the Jews, when Moses led them out of captivity in Egypt.'" He looked at Thomas. "Isn't it odd for a Catholic to cite the Pentateuch like this, especially a description from Exodus, an event of supreme importance to Jews?" He consulted a large notebook full of Hebrew writing. "In some research I did on Mr. Columbus a few years ago I made some other curious discoveries. The first was that, a few days before setting off on his first voyage, he received astronomical tables from Lisbon, which had been prepared by Mr. Abraham Zacuto for the king of Portugal."

"King John II."

"Yes. A copy of these tables is now on display in Seville. At the time I popped over to see them. Do you know what I discovered?"

"I have no idea."

"That the tables were written *in Hebrew.*" He allowed this revelation to sink in. "Now, where did Mr. Columbus learn to read Hebrew?"

"Good question," said Thomas. He couldn't help himself and lowered his voice in an aside: "Especially if one believes he was a humble silk weaver."

"I beg your pardon?"

"Don't mind me. I was just talking to myself," said Thomas, scribbling in his notebook. "This story obliges us to ask another question. How is it possible that an instrument was sent from King John II to Columbus two days before he set off on a voyage that supposedly was not in Portugal's interests?"

"I don't have the answer to that, Mr. Noronha," said the rabbi.

"You don't need to, sir. You don't need to. It's just an additional mystery, indicating close relations between the admiral and the king of Portugal."

Rabbi Hurewitz delved back into his notes. "There are still other things that caught my attention," he said. "There was a very curious letter sent to Queen Isabella the Catholic by her confessor, Hernando de Talavera. The letter is dated 1492, and in it Talavera questions the Catholic Monarchs' authorization of Mr. Columbus's expedition. In one passage of this document, Talavera asks: 'How will Colón's criminal voyage give the Holy Land to the Jews?' " He looked up, an intrigued expression on his face. " 'Give the Holy Land to the Jews'? Why did the queen's confessor explicitly link Mr. Columbus to the Jews?" He let the question hang in the air for a few moments. "And there's more. In his *Book of Prophecies,* Mr. Columbus based his writings almost exclusively on prophets from the Pentateuch, with countless references to Isaiah, Ezekiel, Jeremiah, and many others. His son Ferdinand, in his book about his father, actually referred to him as being descended 'from the royal blood of Jerusalem.' " He looked at Thomas again. " 'Royal blood of Jerusalem'?" He laughed discreetly, almost hiding his mouth. "It's hard to be more direct than that."

Rabbi Hurewitz closed his notebook, indicating that he had finished. Solomon Ben-Porat took the bundle of pages Thomas had given him that morning, cleared his throat, and resumed the conversation.

"Mr. Noronha," he boomed, in sharp contrast to Hurewitz's soft speech. "I read the pages you gave me with great interest and detected a few things that are very revealing." He pulled out a piece of paper and showed it to Thomas. "What is this?"

Thomas stopped writing and leaned forward to study the photocopy.

"That's a page from *Historia rerum ubique gestarum,* by Pope Pius II, one of the books that belonged to Christopher Columbus and which is now at the Columbine Library in Seville."

Solomon pointed at a marginal note. "And who wrote this?"

"Columbus himself."

"Very well," said the rabbi. "Had you noticed that he converted the Christian date here into the Jewish year 5241?" He cocked his head. "Tell me, Mr. Noronha. Are Christians in the habit of converting Christian dates into Jewish dates?"

"Certainly not."

"Which begs a second question. How many Catholics would know how to make this conversion?"

Thomas chuckled.

"None, as far as I know," he said, scribbling furiously in his notebook. Solomon pointed at another note in the margin of *Historia rerum.*

"Look at this detail. Referring to the razing of the Second Temple, Columbus calls it 'the destruction of the Second House' and, in an implicit allusion, established that this took place in A.D. 68." The rabbi stared at Thomas, who shrugged.

"Meaning?"

"In the first place, there is only one people who refer to Solomon's Temple as a house. Do you know who?"

"The Jews?"

"Naturally. In those days the Christians always referred to the destruction of Jerusalem, never the temple and much less the house. There is also a historical discrepancy regarding the year of the destruction of the temple. Jews tend to say it happened in the year 68, while Christians claim it took place in 70. Now tell me, what identity does Columbus reveal when he refers to the temple as house, talks about the destruction of the house instead of the destruction of Jerusalem, and states that it took place in the year 68?"

Thomas smiled. "I see."

The old Kabbalist pulled a second page from the bundle. "This photocopy has yet another strange marginal note."

Thomas looked at the page. "This note is also in Columbus's handwriting. What does it mean?"

"Gog and Magog."

"What?"

"Gog and Magog. Or, more correctly, Gog uMagog."

"I don't understand."

Solomon glanced at the others. Chaim and Hurewitz were gazing at the page in awe, as if it were a relic or something shocking.

"Prince of the Jews," said the rabbi, addressing Chaim. "You're a Sephardi of Portuguese origin; tell our friend from Lisbon here what this means."

"Gog uMagog is a reference to a prophecy by Ezekiel about Gog, from the land of Magog," said Chaim, speaking for the first time since the meeting began. "According to this prophecy, in the period immediately preceding the coming of the Messiah, Gog and Magog will wage a large-scale war against Israel, bringing great destruction." He looked at Thomas. "When the Jews were expelled from the Iberian Peninsula, the Sephardim saw this act as a sign that the prophecy was fulfilling itself in their time, with the Catholic Monarchs in the roles of Gog and Magog and the Jews as Israel."

While Thomas busily scratched away in his notebook, Solomon located another photocopy. Thomas finally finished and looked up. "What else?"

"I was having a look here at the letters Columbus sent his son Diego and came across something very interesting." He held up the page, pointing at what was written at the top.

"'*Muy caro fijo*'—dearest *fijo*?" Thomas laughed. "He slipped into Portuguese here. The Spanish word for 'son' is *hijo,* and the Portuguese word is *filho.*" He shrugged. "We refer to this jumble of Portuguese and Spanish as *portuñol.*"

"Mr. Noronha," rumbled Solomon, "the expression *muy caro fijo* means nothing to me. What's surprising is the symbol above it."

"The symbol?" asked Thomas. "What symbol?"

"This here," he said, pointing at the squiggle above the words.

"What's that?"

"It's a Jewish acronym."

"A Jewish acronym?"

"Yes. Although it's written in a strange way, this squiggle combines two Hebrew letters, *he* and *bet*. Since we read from right to left in Hebrew, that reads *bet he. Bet he* is a traditional Jewish reference, corresponding to the greeting *Baruch HaShem*, meaning "Blessed be the Name," which is how the Orthodox refer to God, and it is placed over the first word of the text, as was their habit. In the case of the Sephardim forcefully converted to Christianity, this was a secret sign, meaning 'Don't forget your origins.' It's interesting that I've only found these initials on the photocopies of Columbus's letters to his son Diego. He didn't use *bet he* in any other letters. In other words, by using a Hebrew acronym, Columbus was asking Diego not to forget his origins." He tilted his head. "It's not hard to imagine what origins these might be, is it?"

Thomas was busy taking everything down. "What else?" he asked, when he had finished writing.

"Let's take a look at what you're most curious about," he announced. "Columbus's signature."

"Ah, yes!" exclaimed Thomas. "What can you tell me about it?"

"The first thing is, yes, it is Kabbalistic."

Thomas's face broke into a triumphant grin. "I knew it."

"But it is important, Mr. Noronha, that you understand that the Kabbalah is an open system of interpretation. Traditional ciphers and codes, when cracked, reveal an exact text. The Kabbalah doesn't work like that. It points at double meanings, subliminal meanings, subtly concealed messages."

He took the photocopy with Columbus's signature on it and placed it on the table, where everyone could see it.

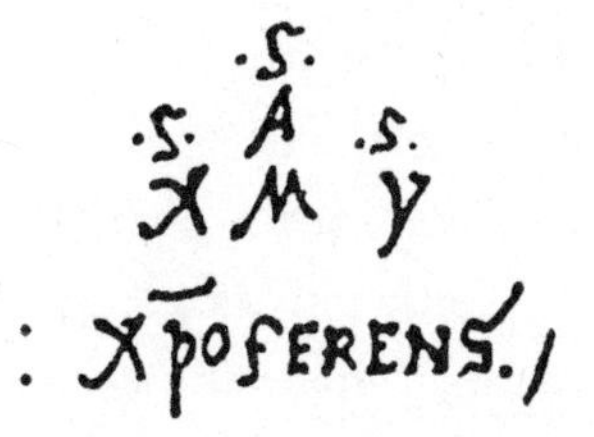

Thomas pointed at the letters. "What are these initials?"

"This signature has many possible interpretations," said Solomon. "In this case, several texts appear to be occupying the same space, mixing the Hebrew tradition with innovations introduced by the Christian Templars."

Thomas looked at him in surprise. "The Templars?"

"Yes. Not many people know this, but a number of Christian mystics, magicians, and philosophers have dedicated themselves to studying the Kabbalah. Among them were the Knights Templar, who, here in Jerusalem, developed Kabbalistic analyses that were later incorporated into the traditional schools of Judaism. It seems Columbus was familiar with these innovations." He pointed to the *s* at the top. "The Christian, or Templar, reading should be in Latin. These *s*'s, arranged in a triangle, represent the Sanctus. *Sanctus, Sanctus, Sanctus.* The *A* means *Altissimus* and allows us to read upward from the third line, which starts from matter and ascends to the spirit. The *X*, *M*, and *Y* should thus be read from the bottom up. The *X* connecting to the *S*, the *M* to the *A* and *S* at the top, and the *Y* to the *S* on the right. In other words, *XS* is *Xristus, MAS* is *Messias*, and *YS* is *Yesus*. Therefore, the Templar interpretation, in Latin, is *Sanctus. Sanctus Altissimus Sanctus. Xristus Messias Yesus*. There's no doubt about it. It's definitely a Christian signature."

"Christian?" said Thomas in surprise. "So he wasn't a Jew after all?"

"We're getting there," said Solomon, gesturing for Thomas to be patient. "Remember I told you a little while ago that the Kabbalah sees the Holy Writ as containing a holographic complexity, combining many meanings? Well, this is precisely what happens in Columbus's signature. Underlying the Christian Templar signature in Latin, there is actually a subliminal Jewish Kabbalistic message in Hebrew. One of the greatest Kabbalists ever, Rabbi Eleazar ben Judah, once observed that there are two worlds, one hidden and the other disclosed, but they are really only part of a single world." He tapped the photocopy with his finger. "That's the case with this signature. A Kabbalistic interpretation starts by observing that the initials in his signature correspond to Hebrew words. If we consider that the letter *A* corresponds to the Hebrew *alef* for *Adonai,* one of the names of God, and the *S* is the Hebrew *sheen* for *Shaddai,* another name for God, or the Lord, we get *Shaddai. Shaddai Adonai Shaddai.* That translates as 'Lord. Lord God Lord.' And what happens when you take the last line, *XMY,* and read it from right to left, as Hebrew is read? You get *YMX. Y* for *Yehovah, M* for *maleh* and *X* for *xessed. Yehovah maleh xessed*. God full of compassion. In other words, beneath the Christian prayer in Latin, we have a Jewish prayer in Hebrew. The two worlds, hidden and disclosed, are part of a single world."

"Brilliant."

"You haven't seen anything yet, Mr. Noronha," said Solomon. "Just you wait. Things get even more complicated if I read *XMY* from left to right, considering that *y* corresponds to the Hebrew letter *ayin*. We get *shema,* or *hear,* the first word of Deuteronomy 6:4: 'Hear, O Israel, the Lord our God, the Lord is One.' Among Jews, this prayer is known as the Shema and is recited twice daily, in the morning and evening, as well as at bedtime and on one's deathbed. The Shema is a monotheistic prayer, asserting the oneness of God, and this verse is believed to have been written on the battle flag of the Ten Lost Tribes. When they recite it, Jews are accepting the Kingdom of Heaven and the Commandments. This is the Hebrew word Columbus chose to put in his signature." He held up a finger. "But look at this double meaning. If *Y* corresponds to the Hebrew *yod* here, *XMY* can be read *XMI*, or *shmi*, which means: 'my name.' Presumably, the name of the author of this signature, Christopher Columbus."

The old Kabbalist leaned over the page, as if it was about to reveal something astonishing. "Pay attention, Mr. Noronha, because this is very important. Let's read *XMY* from right to left, in the Hebrew manner. We get *YMX*. If *y* represents *yod* in this case, a new word appears here. *YMX*. *Yemax*. Together with the reading from left to right, we get *yemax shmi*. Do you know what that means?"

"I have no idea."

"It means 'may my name be erased.'"

"Oh my God!" exclaimed Thomas, glassy-eyed, the puzzle falling into place in his mind. "*Colom, nomina sunt odiosa*."

"I beg your pardon?"

"*Nomina sunt odiosa*. Names are odious. It's a Latin proverb. Adapting it to this situation, it means that Columbus's name is inconvenient. Based on what you're telling me about the Kabbalistic interpretation of his signature, it's clear that the admiral's contemporaries weren't the only ones who wanted to create confusion around his identity. For some reason Columbus himself wanted to erase his original name." He scratched his chin thoughtfully. "Now I get it. Colom wasn't his real name. It was just a surname he adopted, a kind of . . . disguise. He erased his original name himself."

"Why?"

"I don't know."

"*Yemax shmi*. May my name be erased. It ties in."

"His name was hateful and thus had to be erased," said Thomas, connecting the Latin and Hebrew expressions. "What was his real name?"

"That I don't know," said the rabbi. "But I can give you another clue. He also renounced his first name."

"Which one? Cristóvão, Cristóbal, or Cristoforo?"

"All of them."

"What do you mean?"

Solomon Ben-Porat picked up the piece of paper with Columbus's signature on it and pointed at the triangle of *s*'s.

"See these dots between the *s*'s?"

"Yes."

"They weren't put here by accident," said the rabbi. "In Hebrew, dots next to letters can mean many things. It can be a sign that the letter is an initial or that it requires a vowel. We have already seen that the dots indicated letters that were initials. The *sheen* for *Shaddai* and the *alef* for *Adonai*. In ancient languages the little dots could be a sign that something should be read from top to bottom. Now, the Kabbalah says that everything in the universe is connected by a magic thread and that inferior things bear the secrets of superior things. Rabbi Shimon bar Yochai, an important Kabbalist, observed that the lower world is made in the image of the higher world; the lower is but a reflection of the higher. The *Book of Kabbalistic Mysteries* says that the world we inhabit is an inversion of the world of the soul. The axiom inscribed on the emerald tablet of Hermes revealed: As above, so below. The words *reflection* and *inversion*, *above* and *below,* all point to the notion of mirroring, which is very dear to the Kabbalah. Since the dots indicate that something must be read from top to bottom, I decided to do an experiment and invert the letters of his signature." He picked up the page he had written on and showed it to Thomas. "The result was surprising."

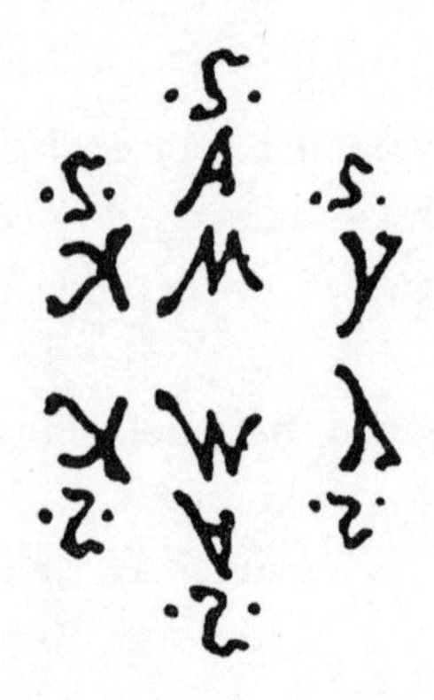

Thomas looked at the symbols in the lower part of the mirror image.

"What is it?" he asked.

"A headless Tree of Life."

"That's the Tree of Life?"

"Yes. Look." The rabbi opened a book and showed Thomas a structure of circles. "This is the Tree of Life."

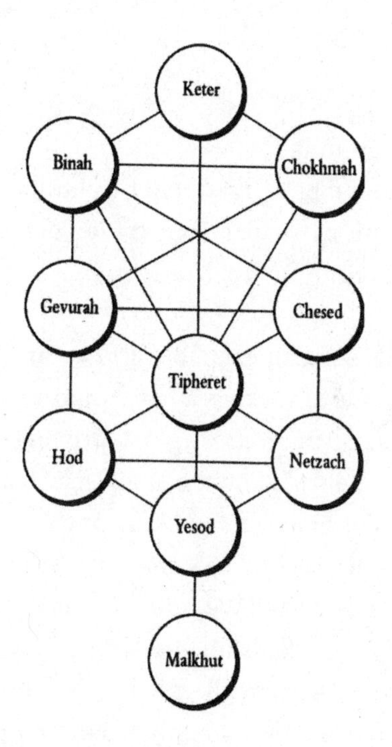

"There are ten circles," said Thomas.

"Yes, they are the ten *sefirot*. The traditional representation of the Tree of Life has ten. But the second most important has seven *sefirot*. In this case, eliminating the upper part of the signature, we get a headless Tree of Life."

He cut off the three higher *sefirot*—*keter*, *chokhmah*, and *binah*—and held it up, placing it next to the mirror image of Columbus's signature.

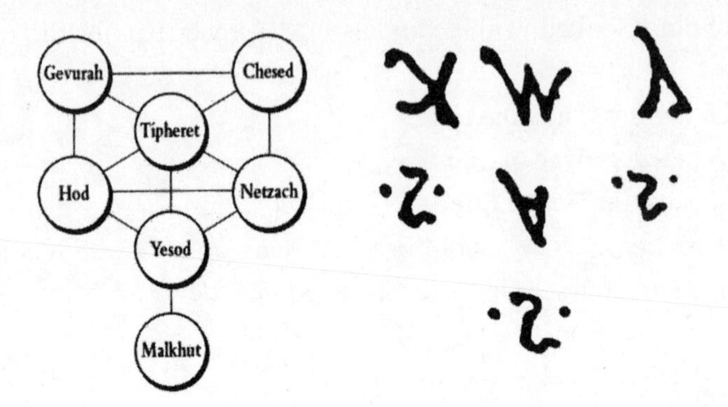

"Oh!" exclaimed Thomas, comparing the two structures. "They're . . . quite similar."

"Yes," said the rabbi. "Christopher Columbus's Kabbalistic signature reproduces this particular Tree of Life. Each letter is a *sefirah*."

"Doesn't reducing the Tree of Life to seven *sefirot* mean it's incomplete?"

"No. Some have five or even four *sefirot*. But the one with seven is particularly significant. Seven is a very important number in Kabbalism. It represents nature in its original, pristine state. God made the world in six days and rested on the seventh." He pointed at the reflection of Columbus's signature. "Looking at the mirror image, you see clearly that this was Columbus's way of revealing his true identity. Because the top line reads XWλ. The *X* is associated with the *chet* in *chesed,* the *sefirah* that stands for the right arm and symbolizes kindness. The λ is associated with *gimal,* the first letter of the *sefirah gevurah,* or the left arm, which symbolizes strength. Between them is *W,* which the Hebrew alphabet associates with *tet,* the first letter in the *sefirah tipheret,* beauty, represents a synthesis of kindness and strength. Columbus removed the top of the Tree of Life and structured it using the middle and lower members. His Kabbalistic intention was unmistakable." Solomon pointed again at the first line of the signature, XWλ. "Take a look at this, Mr. Noronha. Reading this line from right to left, you get λWX. That reads *Yeshu*." He looked at Thomas and frowned. "This is a terrible thing."

"Terrible?" said Thomas. "In what way? What does it mean?"

"The deification of Jesus by Christians is considered idolatry by some Jews. Which brings us back to the line that reads λWX in the reflection of Columbus's signature. In Hebrew, the name Jesus is pronounced 'Yeshua.' Since the Jews didn't like this name, they removed the last letter, leaving us with Yeshu. This is precisely how the line λWX should be read. Yeshu. This is not an innocent name. *Yeshu* means *'yemax shmo vezichro.'* That is, 'May his name and memory be obliterated.' "

"Wow!" said Thomas. "That's strong stuff."

"Mr. Noronha," said Solomon, "what I'm trying to tell you is that Christopher Columbus, a Catholic, put the Hebrew name Yeshu in his Kabbalistic signature, stating his wish that the name and memory of Jesus be erased."

Thomas fell silent for a moment, stunned. "But . . . why?" he finally managed to say. "How could Columbus have done that?"

"Don't forget he lived in late-fifteenth-century Iberia. If he was Jewish, as everything seems to indicate, life at that time and in that part of Europe for the Sephardim mustn't have been easy. Which brings us to his first name." He picked up the page. "Underlying the Kabbalistic signature is his name, Xpoferens. Can you tell me what it means?"

"Xpoferens? *Xpo,* in Greek, means Christ, while *ferens* is a form of the Latin verb *fero,* meaning "to carry" or "to bear." Xpoferens is Cristoferens. He who bears Christ. Christ is at the root of the names Cristóvão, Cristóbal, and Cristoforo."

"And that's a name no Jew would ever use," added the rabbi. "Christ. No one in Israel would ever name his child Christ. How could Columbus, a Jew, have gone by the first name of Cristóvão or Cristóbal and signed Cristoferens?" He raised his finger. "There's only one kind of Jew capable of doing that."

"What kind?"

"A Jew desperate to pass himself off as Christian, but who still professed his Jewish faith in secret. Such a man could take on the name Christ, but to make peace with God, he would include in his Kabbalistic signature an unequivocal rejection of the name Jesus, erasing the name and its memory. Yeshu. What I mean, Mr. Noronha, is that the expression *'yemax shmi,'* 'may my name be erased,' is a simultaneous rejection of his first and last names. He clapped his hand down on the photocopy with the signature on it. "Judging from everything I've seen here, I can tell you that the man we know today as Christopher Columbus was, in all probability, a Sephardi and originally had another name that remains unknown. He hid his true religion under a Christian mantle but did not become a New Christian. He was what they referred to as a Marrano."

Solomon Ben-Porat rested his elbows on the oak table and was quiet. He had finished. A heavy silence fell over the office, only broken by the sound of Thomas's pen scribbling frantically in his notebook, recording the old rabbi's extraordinary thought process. He wrote quickly in almost indecipherable scrawl, until he finished his notes with the last word Solomon had uttered.

Marrano.

He was about to close his notebook, but something made him hesitate. The word drew his eye like a magnet, a snag, a disturbing inkblot in his fluid handwriting. He stared at it for a moment, then looked at the rabbi.

"What do you mean by 'Marrano'?"

"Marrano?" said Solomon in surprise. "Surely you know. What does it mean in Portuguese?"

"It's an archaic word for 'pig.'"

"There you go. In Portugal and Spain, Marrano was a derogatory name given to the New Christians who remained Jews in secret. They were called Marranos because, like all good Jews, they refused to eat pork, as pigs were considered impure, nonkosher, and their consumption was forbidden by the dietary laws."

"Hmm," murmured Thomas, lost in thought. "A Marrano was a Jew who pretended to be Christian?"

"Yes."

"And Columbus was a Marrano?"

"Definitely."

"Could he have been a Genoese Marrano?"

The rabbi laughed. "'Marrano' refers to an Iberian Jew," he explained. "At any rate, being a Jew, Columbus could never have been Genoese."

"Couldn't he? Why not?"

"Because since the twelfth century, the Jews had been banned from staying in Genoa for more than three days at a time. In the fifteenth century, when Columbus was alive, this ban was still in force."

"I see."

"In fact, there's something very interesting you should know. According to a curious Jewish tradition, the word *Genoese* was a euphemism for 'Jew' in the fifteenth and sixteenth centuries."

"You're kidding."

"I'm not. When someone wanted to say that such and such a person was Jewish, it was common to say that they were 'of the nation.' The Jewish nation, it was understood. Apparently, during that era of anti-Semitic persecution, many Jews, when interrogated by Christians, said they were Genoese. It was an ironic or discreet way of saying someone was a Jew. Understand?"

"Is there proof of this?"

"It's something that has been passed down through the oral tradition, but there is nothing to document it. However, there is an implicit confirmation in a letter sent in 1512 by Friar António de Aspa, of the Order of Saint Jerome, to the great inquisitor of Castile. In this letter, Aspa wrote that Columbus had taken 'forty Genoese' with him on his first expedition to the New World. We now know that almost all of these crew members were Castilians, although among them a few dozen were supposedly of the Jewish nation, probably Marranos. In other words, António de Aspa was actually informing the Inquisition that forty Jews were on board."

"Hmm," said Thomas, mulling over a question he'd already asked himself a thousand times. "What echo of Foucault is left pending on 545?"

"What?"

Thomas suddenly came alive. "It's a question someone asked me. 'What echo of Foucault is left pending on 545?'" He stood up, excitement galloping through him. He couldn't keep quiet. "Based on a revelation by Umberto Eco, I imagined the answer to this question was 'Portuguese Jew' or 'New Christian.' But it isn't after all. The right answer is something else."

The rabbi shrugged.

Thomas grinned. "Marrano."

Chapter 18

LISBON

Thomas's fingers slowly turned the dial of the lock, and the metal box answered with a soft *click-click* as the numbers went around clockwise with mechanical precision. Madalena peered over Thomas's shoulder, her eyes wide open and expectant. "Are you sure it's right?" she whispered.

Thomas glanced at the paper on which he'd jotted down the combination.

M	A	R	R	A	N	O
13	1	18	18	1	14	15

"We're about to find out," he murmured.

Thomas had made arrangements to head toward Toscano's the second he landed in Portugal. Bypassing home, he simply had to find out if he had deciphered the combination of the safe, and if that would be his entrée into whatever Toscano believed was the proof of his great discovery.

He dialed the numbers one by one. Thirteen, one, eighteen, eighteen again. *Click-click-click-click*. Their deep, heavy breathing was the only sound besides the cold, metallic clicking, so precise and serene, so small and so incredibly nerve-racking. It was the sound of a covetous safe, guarding its secret with jealous zeal. It was the contemplative noise of a suspicious, possessive device, forced to face the possibility of what it most feared: its own unveiling. It was as if the safe preferred to hold its treasure in obscurity, and it was this mute duel between man and safe, combination and secret, that fueled the tension in the half-light of the stuffy bedroom. When Thomas was nearing the end of the sequence, he paused, took a deep breath, and dialed the last few numbers. One, fourteen. *Click-click-click.*

Fifteen. *click.* The door swung open.

"Yes!" exclaimed Thomas, raising his fist victoriously. "We did it!"

"Thank God!"

He plunged his hand into the safe's gaping mouth and timidly, almost fearfully, like an explorer about to brave an unknown jungle, touched the smooth, cold surface of paper. He gingerly took hold of the pages he believed to hold an ancient mystery and pulled them out slowly, as if they were a forgotten relic, into the light of day.

There were three pages.

The first two were photocopies, which he studied carefully. At first sight they appeared to be a sixteenth-century document. He scanned them quickly to get the gist of them, then resorted to his experience as a paleographer and read from the miniature at the bottom of the first photocopy, carefully deciphering the apparently impenetrable contents.

"'In the following year . . .'" He hesitated, couldn't make out the date, and went on: "'The King was in Paraíso Valley, which is above Santa Maria das Virtudes Monastery, because of the great plague, which was in most parts of that district, on the sixth day of March, Xpova Colonbo, Italian, sailed into Restelo, in Lisbon, coming from his discovery of the islands of Cipango, and Antilia, which he had done at the bidding of the King and Queen of Castile . . .'"

"What is it?" asked Madalena.

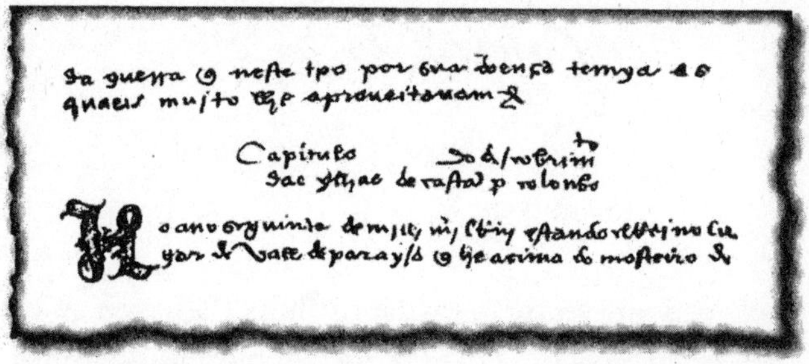

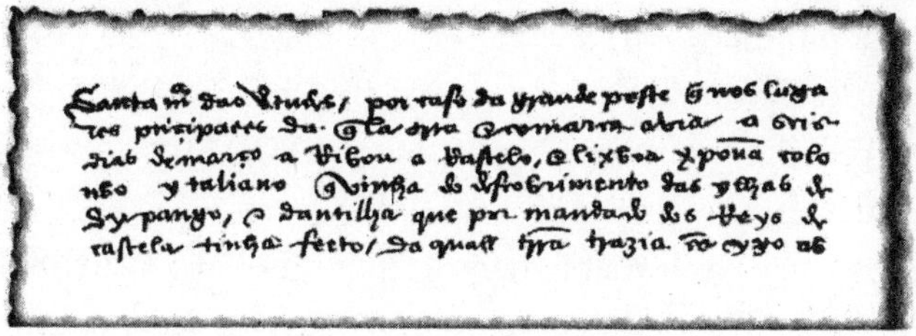

Thomas stared at the pages, intrigued. "This," he said hesitantly, "looks like *Chronicle of King D. John II*, by Rui de Pina. I think this is the passage that describes the meeting between King John II of Portugal and Christopher Columbus, after Columbus's return from his first voyage—the one on which he discovered America."

"Is it important?"

"Well, yes, it is. But unexpected." Somewhat disconcerted, he looked at Madalena. "First, because this text has been well known for a long time. It's no secret. And second, because this chronicle contradicts your husband's theory." He pointed at the third and fourth lines of the second page. "See here? It says *'Xpova colo nbo y taliano,'* that is, 'Christopher Columbus, Italian.' Your husband believed exactly the opposite, that Columbus wasn't Italian."

"But Martinho told me he'd put the proof in the safe—"

"Proof? Proof of what? That Columbus was Italian?" He shook his head, perplexed. "I don't get it. It doesn't make any sense."

Madalena took the two photocopies and examined them carefully.

"What about this? What is it?" she asked, pointing at something written in pencil on the back of the first page.

Thomas read the note.

Codex 632

"Strange," he murmured.

"What is it?"

He shrugged, not knowing what to think. "I haven't a clue." He pursed his lips. "'*Codex 632*'?" He scratched his chin. "It must be the manuscript number."

"Manuscript number?"

"It's a reference number librarians use to locate things in archives. It makes life easier—"

"I know very well what a manuscript number is," said Madalena.

Thomas gave her a sheepish look. Madalena's tired, neglected appearance made her look like a woman of humble origins, but her aged face and withered body belied a highly educated woman, who had frequented academic circles and was used to being surrounded by books. The dirty jumble of her house, realized Thomas, was not just a case of sloppy housekeeping after her husband's death but was also due to the fact that she was unaccustomed to domestic chores.

"I'm sorry," he said sincerely. "I think your husband must have jotted down this manuscript number so he could look it up in a library."

Madalena studied it again. "But it says 'codex.'"

"Yes." Thomas smiled. "A codex is actually an ancient manuscript on papyrus, parchment, or paper, bound like a book. Because this is a sixteenth-century manuscript, I'd say it's probably on parchment."

Madalena took the third page from him. "Have you seen this?" she asked.

It was a sheet of white paper, with a name and a number beneath it. Thomas's eyebrows shot up when he saw the name.

"Count João Nuno Vilarigues," he read.

"Do you know him?"

"Never heard of him." He looked at the numbers under the name. "This looks like a phone number."

Madalena took a closer look. "Let me see." She thought for a moment. "That's funny. I recognize the area code. Martinho used to call there a lot."

"This number?"

"I'm not sure. But the area code's the same."

"And what area is it?"

Madalena got up and left the room without a word. She came back moments later with a phone book under her arm, opened it to the list of Portuguese area codes, and ran her finger down the columns.

"Here it is!" she exclaimed. "Tomar."

On his way home from Toscano's, Thomas determined what he had to do next. Contacting this Count Vilarigues was now his priority. Thomas had never heard of him, and he had to wonder what this count had to do with Toscano's discovery. Having gone this far, though, he couldn't have been more relieved to know that his next trip was to Tomar, so close to home.

It was ten o'clock at night when he unlocked the door to his apartment. He was exhausted and wanted to shower, eat, and go to bed.

"Girls, I'm home!" he announced, dropping his travel-worn bags in the foyer, the dust of Jerusalem still settled on the leather.

The apartment remained dark.

That's odd, he thought. He switched on the light and noticed that everything was clean and tidy but no one seemed to be home.

"Girls!" he called again. "Where are you?"

He looked at his watch and figured they'd probably turned in for the night. He crossed the tiny apartment in six steps, trying not to make any noise, and peeked into the two bedrooms, but they were both deserted. He carried his suitcase to the bed, put it down, and looked around, disoriented. Where on earth were they? He scratched his head. Could something have gone wrong? He stood there a moment wondering what to do. He could call Constance's cell phone again, but he had called her only two hours earlier when he landed and got her voice mail. What should he do now?

He was starving—he couldn't stand the food they served on planes—so he headed for the kitchen. If he raised his blood sugar, he reasoned, he'd be better able to decide what to do next. He feared the worst—that Margarida had had to go into the hospital—but surely Constance would have left a note, were that the case. As he walked down the hall again on his way to the kitchen, he noticed that the vase on the hall stand was full of orange bell-shaped flowers with long curved stalks, mixed with other yellow flowers that resembled roses. He gazed thoughtfully at the flowers, then bent over to smell them. They seemed fresh. He hesitated, stroking his chin, then touched the petals lightly. He did an about-face and headed for the living room.

The vases there had the same flowers in them. He picked up a piece of paper lying on the table, and saw it was a florist's receipt for roses and foxgloves. He stood there thinking for a moment, then, holding the receipt, turned to the bookshelves and looked for a book he finally found on the top shelf: *The Language of Flowers,* Constance's favorite book. He flipped to the glossary at the back, looking for foxgloves. The entry said that foxgloves represented insincerity and selfishness. He looked up at the flowers with a start.

Frantically, with panic setting in, he clumsily flipped through the pages until he reached *r,* then scanned for a reference to yellow roses. His finger froze on their meaning.

Infidelity.

Chapter 19

TOMAR

The pigeons in Praça da República filled the square with their gurgling music. They were fat and well fed, pecking at the pavement and fluttering short distances, flapping here and there, covering the rooftops, lining anything that jutted out from the façades of buildings, draping themselves over the enormous bronze statue of Gualdim Pais in the center of the square.

Some were strutting about at Thomas's feet, cooing, indifferent to the man sitting on the wooden bench. They looked like little gray pawns wandering across a giant chessboard. Thomas looked around, admiring the elegant Tomar Town Hall and square, until the Gothic architecture of the church on his right caught his attention. São João Baptista Church had a faded whitewashed façade with an intricate Manueline door, the imposing octagonal steeple of the neighboring bell tower hovered over it, proudly boasting a symbolic trio beneath the bells: the royal coat of arms, the armillary sphere, and the cross of the Order of Christ.

Thomas's mind momentarily slipped away from the riddles of Toscano, Columbus, and the foundation, as well as the count Thomas had, with incredible difficulty, tracked down and was now waiting to meet. Since Constance had moved out, Thomas withdrew; he felt as though he was wandering through the confusion his life had become. All the hours he spent at home alone, like a hermit, led him to an analysis of his relationship with his wife and the reason behind his affair. He now realized his liaison with Lena had been more than a sexual adventure. His infidelity was a symptom of the way in which he'd isolated himself from Constance, an isolation that was possibly the result of the disappointment and silent resentment he felt when his high expectations for their future together had crumbled.

He spent hours lying in bed or on the sofa, always waiting for a phone call that Constance did not make, getting up countless times to wander around his tiny apartment, unshaven and in his pajamas, talking to himself. It was only Toscano's discovery that motivated him. It was his reason to rise in the morning. Aside from the money he knew would help make his daughter's life easier, his search for some apparent truth had led him to the bench he now sat on. And to a meeting with a count he hadn't been able to learn a thing about. Only his phone number, which he'd gotten from Madalena's old phone bills. Nothing more.

A man in a dark gray suit, silver vest, and bow tie approached him with an inquisitive look on his face. "Mr. Noronha?" he asked hesitantly.

Thomas smiled. "Yes. You must be Count Vilarigues?"

"João Nuno Vilarigues," said the man, straightening his vest and bowing his head ceremoniously.

The count was thin and enigmatic-looking. His black hair, graying at the temples, was combed back, showing a receding hairline atop a high forehead. He had a thin mustache and a pointy goatee. But the most striking thing about him were his penetrating eyes. He looked like a time traveler from Renaissance Italy.

"Thank you for coming," said Thomas. "Although, to be honest, I don't even know what we're here to talk about."

"You told me over the phone that you got my number from some notes left by the late Professor Toscano concerning Christopher Columbus."

"Yes."

The count sighed and gazed at Thomas for a moment as if caught up in debate with himself. After several very long seconds, he broke the silence. "Are you acquainted with the study Professor Toscano was conducting?" he asked, clearly feeling out the terrain and testing Thomas.

"I am," Thomas said. The count remained silent, as if waiting for more, and Thomas realized he was going to have to demonstrate his familiarity with the research. "Professor Toscano believed Columbus wasn't Genoese but a Marrano, a Portuguese Jew."

"Why do you want to revisit his research?"

This wasn't an innocent question, thought Thomas; it was a test. He would have to proceed with caution if he wanted to get anything out of this mysterious character. "I teach history at the New University of Lisbon, and I paid Professor Toscano's widow a visit to see the documents he'd left. I think it will make an exceptional article, capable of changing everything we know about the Age of Discovery."

The count allowed a long pause, keeping his eyes trained on Thomas, as if trying to scrutinize his very soul. "Have you heard about the American foundation?" he asked finally.

The way he worded the query put Thomas on alert. This was, for some reason he couldn't fathom, the most important question of all, the one that would determine whether the count cooperated or clammed up. Since Toscano's allies seemed to have a negative reaction to the name of the foundation that had financed the study, Thomas decided it would be best to keep his connection to Moliarti under a lid. At least for now.

"What foundation?" he heard himself asking.

The count did not take his eyes off Thomas. Thomas stared back, trying to look sincere.

"It doesn't matter," said the count, apparently satisfied. He glanced around the square, then gazed up at the hill and smiled, relaxing. "Have you ever been to Tomar Castle and the Convent of Christ?"

Thomas followed his gaze and saw the walls poking up over the greenery at the top of the hill behind the town.

"Yes, I have. But it was a long time ago."

"Then come with me," said the count, signaling for Thomas to follow him.

They crossed the square and headed through the quaint, cobbled side streets, with colorful pots hanging from balconies. They came to an enormous black Mercedes, parked next to a white wall that stretched as far as the old synagogue. Count Vilarigues got into the driver's seat and, once Thomas had seated himself next to him, took off, sliding through the quiet alleys of Tomar.

After several seconds of driving in silence, the count spoke. "Have you ever heard of the Christi Militia?"

"The Knights Templar?"

"No, the Christi Militia."

"Never heard of it."

"I'm a representative of the Christi Militia, the successor organization to the Order of the Temple, or Knights Templar."

Thomas wrinkled his forehead, astounded. "But the Order of the Temple hasn't existed for a very long time."

"That's precisely why the Christi Militia is its successor. When the Order of the Temple was suppressed, some knights decided to keep it going in secret and formed the Christi Militia, or Military Order of Christ, a clandestine organization with its own statutes, whose existence is known by only a few. A handful of Portuguese noblemen, descendants of the old Knights of the Order of the Temple, come together in Tomar every spring to renew the old customs and register the oral tradition of the never-revealed secrets. They are the guardians of the last mysteries of the Order of the Temple."

"Wow, I had no idea."

"What do you know about the Order of the Temple?"

"A thing or two, not much. I'm a historian, but my area of expertise is cryptanalysis and ancient languages, not the Middle Ages or the Age of Discovery. Let's just say I kind of fell into this investigation by chance . . . because I knew Professor Toscano, not because it's my main area of interest."

The car arrived at a fork in the road, with a statue of Henry the

Navigator at its center. The count turned right and left the town's arterial roads, weaving his way up the green mountainside through the shade of the lush Mata dos Sete Montes, heading for the old castle walls.

"Then let me tell you the story from the beginning," said Count Vilarigues. "When the Muslims barred Christians access to the Holy City of Jerusalem, a cry of revolt resounded throughout Europe and the Crusades began. Jerusalem was taken in 1099, and Christianity was installed in the Holy Land. The problem was that, as the crusaders started returning to Europe, Christian pilgrimages to Jerusalem became very dangerous. This was when two new military orders appeared. The Hospitalers, who cared for the sick and wounded, and a militia of nine knights who set out to ensure the pilgrims safe passage to Jerusalem. Although there were only nine of them, these men managed to make the routes they traveled much safer. In return, they were given headquarters at al-Aqsa Mosque, at the top of Mount Moriah, in Jerusalem, the exact place where the legendary Temple of Solomon had stood. That is how the Knights of the Order of the Temple came into being." He paused. "The Knights Templar."

"A story told a thousand times over."

"True. And a story so extraordinary that it captured the imagination of all of Europe. Some say that the Templars, when picking through the abandoned ruins of the Temple of Solomon, came across precious relics, eternal secrets, divine objects. The Holy Grail. Whether due to these mysteries or simply as a result of their ingenuity and persistence, the Templars grew and spread throughout Europe."

"And they reached Portugal."

"Yes. The order was formally established in 1119, and a few years later they were already here. This town of Tomar, taken when the Moors were conquered in 1147, was granted in 1159, by the first king of Portugal, Afonso Henriques, to the Knights Templar. Led by Gualdim Pais, they built the castle the following year."

The Mercedes took the last curve and entered a small parking area among the trees. The castle's massive keep could be seen behind the great stone walls, whose battlements looked as if they had been cut out of the blue sky. They left the car in the shade of some tall pines and walked along the path that circled the walls of the citadel and keep, heading for the imposing Porta do Sol entrance. For a few moments it was as if they had returned to the Middle Ages, to a rustic, simple time, lost in the memory of the centuries, of which only those proud ruins were left. A crude wall topped by battlements ran off to their left, flanking the path and the dense forest. A breeze made its way up the hillside, rustling the trees, whose branches seemed to dance to the rhythm of a soft, natural melody. Swallows twittered, nightingales warbled, and the cicadas answered with a high-pitched chirring, the bees with a laborious drone. On the right side of the path there was only the arid, stony slope, rising up in dry, empty silence toward the castle, which reigned at the top like a feudal lord, imposing and arrogant.

"So this is the Templars' castle," said Thomas, gazing at the old walls.

"It is. The Templars were offered large tracts of land in Portugal for their services in combat, including the conquests of Santarém and Lisbon, but nowhere was their presence more evident than here, at Tomar Castle, their headquarters. The order came to an abrupt end, however, as a result of the persecution that began in France in 1307, culminating in the papal bull *Vox in excelso,* which extinguished it in 1312. The pope called upon European monarchs to arrest the Templars, but King Dinis of Portugal refused to obey. The pope determined that the Templars' assets should go to the Hospitalers, but once again King Dinis did not obey. He came up with an ingenious legal interpretation of the matter, alleging that the Templars were merely occupying properties that belonged to the crown. Should the Templars cease to exist, the crown would then reclaim its land. The king's attitude attracted the attention of the French Templars, who were being mercilessly persecuted in their own country. Many came to Portugal seeking refuge. King Dinis let things simmer for a while, until he proposed the creation of a new military order, with its headquarters in the Algarve, to defend Portugal from the Muslims. The Vatican agreed, and in 1319 the Military Order of Christ was officially created. Dinis gave this new organization all of the assets of the former Order of the Temple, including ten cities. Even more important, its members were Templars. In other words, the Order of the Temple became the Order of Christ. The resuscitation of the Templars in Portugal was completed in 1357, when the Order of Christ transferred its seat to Tomar Castle."

They walked through the magnificent Porta do Sol entrance and found themselves in a large square with a beautiful geometrical garden overlooking the valley on their left. There were hedges shaped in half-spheres, untrimmed bushes, tall, slender cypresses, sycamores, and flower beds.

"So why are you telling me all this?" asked Thomas.

Count Vilarigues laughed and pointed at the walls on their right and the medieval buildings in front of them, dominated by the stairs leading up to the cylindrical structure of the magnificent rotunda, which looked like a fortress, its walls marked by thick buttresses running up to the roof, with sixteenth-century battlements at the top and a bell tower crowning the entire building. On the other side of the complex were the compact outer walls of the main cloister and the ruins of the Chapter House, which stood behind a giant sycamore casting its protective shade over the monastery.

"My good man, I'm telling you this to help you understand this wonderful place better. After all, it is in Tomar, behind these mysterious medieval walls, that the pure spirit of the Holy Grail resides, the enigmatic, esoteric soul behind Portugal's development and maritime discoveries." He winked. "I'm also telling you this because these details are pertinent to the extraordinary story I'm about to tell you. And of course because you're connected with Toscano."

"What story might that be?"

"My good man, surely you know. What I'm about to tell you is the true story of Christopher Columbus, the explorer who gave America to the Castilians."

"The . . . the true story of Columbus? Do you know it?"

They strolled through the garden, passing under a bush in the shape of an arch, and went to sit on a blue-and-orange-tiled bench set in the wall.

"This is a story whose prologue goes back to the Templars." The count observed the walls below them. "Tell me, have you ever noticed the crosses on the sails of the Portuguese caravels used in the discovery voyages?"

"They were red, if memory serves me correctly."

"Red crosses on a white background. Doesn't that mean anything to you?"

"Um . . . no."

"The crosses worn by Crusaders were red on a white background. The crosses of the Portuguese Templars were red with curved arms on a white background. The crosses of the Order of Christ were red on a white background. And the Portuguese caravels also bore red crosses on white sails. These were the crosses of the Order of Christ, the crosses of the Templars, hoisted through the seas in search of the Holy Grail." He leaned forward, staring intensely at Thomas. "Do you happen to know what the Holy Grail was?"

"It was the chalice Christ drank from at the Last Supper. It's said that Joseph of Arimathea collected drops of Christ's blood in it as he was dying on the cross."

"Superstitions, my good man! The Holy Grail is only a chalice in a figurative sense, metaphoric if you will." He pointed toward the town of Tomar, whose buildings could be seen behind the trees and walls, at the foot of the hill. "If you go to the baptismal chapel of São João Baptista Church, down there in Tomar, you'll see a triptych showing a picture of John the Baptist holding the Holy Grail. Inside the Grail is a winged dragon, a mythical animal mentioned in the legend of the Knights of the Round Table. In this legend, Merlin the Magician told the tale of a fight in an underground lake between two dragons, one winged and the other not, one representing the forces of good, and the other, the forces of evil, one symbolizing light, and the other, darkness. This fight between dragons can also be seen at the top of a column in the same church, giving it an undeniable initiatory value."

"Are you talking about the church in the square where we met a little while ago?"

"Yes."

"Hmm," murmured Thomas, recalling the white façade and the imposing bell tower.

"The dragon is the Templar symbol of wisdom, associated with the Egyptian Thoth and the Greek Hermes. The dragon in the Holy Grail represents Hermetic wisdom." He paused. "So what is the Holy Grail? It's knowledge. And what is knowledge, if not power? This was something the Templars quickly realized. When they came to Portugal to escape persecution elsewhere in Europe, they brought the chalice and the dragon, the Holy Grail, or the wisdom—scientific and occult—gained over two centuries of exploration in the Holy Land. They were navigators, inventors, and had the spirit of discovery, Hermetic learning. Portugal was their destination, but it was also their point of departure for their discovery of the world, their new quest for knowledge. This country is called Portugal, after all. The name comes from *Portucalem,* but it can also be connected to the Holy Grail. Portugal. Porto Graal. The port of the Grail. It was from this great port that they set off in search of the new Grail. The Holy Grail of wisdom. The Grail of knowledge. The discovery of a new world."

"Are you saying the maritime explorations came about as a result of the Templars' quest for the Holy Grail?"

"In part, yes. The Templars and the Jews, with their secrets and mysterious Kabbalistic practices, some openly seeking the Holy Grail and others discreetly searching for the Promised Land. United by their nostalgia for Jerusalem and the holy Temple of Solomon, the Sephardim and the Portuguese made for an explosive mix, brought together at the beginning of the fifteenth century by one of the greatest statesmen in the history of Portugal and one of humanity's greatest visionaries, Prince Henry of Portugal, the mind behind the movement we now call globalization. The third son of King John I, Henry became governor of the Order of Christ in 1420 and later came to be known as Henry the Navigator. He brought together men of science—Portuguese, Templars, Jews, and others—and came up with an ambitious plan to launch the quest for the Holy Grail." The count held up a hand and began to recite: " 'May Portugal wake up to itself,' wrote the poet Fernando Pessoa. 'Surrender to its own soul. In it, it will find the tradition of chivalry, where, near or afar, the Secret Tradition of Christianity, Super-Apostolic Succession, and the Quest for the Holy Grail live on.' "

He altered his declamatory tone of voice. "Henry the Navigator's grandiose plan to brave the unknown seas and discover the world was carried out by the Portuguese over several decades. The knights became navigators, and Portugal's discovery voyages, the new Crusades. The country was full of new crusaders. We know many of them. But others were involved in secret voyages, making discoveries that have never been revealed, and their names have remained hidden in the shadows of history."

"Are you saying Columbus was one of them?"

"I'm getting there. Let's set aside the great mystical designs of the Age of Discovery and concentrate on the trivial events of everyday life in late-fifteenth-century Portugal. When Henry the Navigator, and later King Afonso V, died, another man took control of maritime expansion. King Afonso's son, the new King John II, referred to as the Perfect Prince. Shortly after he'd acceded to the throne, an event took place that was to shape Christopher Columbus's destiny."

"The discovery of the Cape of Good Hope by Bartolomeu Dias."

The count laughed. "No, my good man, that came later." They got up from the tiled bench and crossed the square, strolling among the orange trees. Vilarigues went over to the ruins of the castle's royal chambers, now missing their roof, and rested his hand on the rough, bare wall, as if stroking it. "Prince Henry, the man who planned everything before King John II, lived between these walls. As did another statesman, someone whose life was to be changed by the same event that marked Columbus's life. It was Manuel the Fortunate, King John II's successor."

"What event was this?"

The count cocked his head and gave Thomas an odd look. "The conspiracy to assassinate King John."

Thomas frowned. "I beg your pardon?"

"The plot against John II. Haven't you ever heard of it?"

"I vaguely remember something to that effect."

"Listen carefully," said the count, motioning for him to be patient. "In 1482, the royal council, led by the recently crowned King John II, determined that royal magistrates could enter the properties of the feudal lords to ensure that the law was being applied correctly and confirm their privileges and properties. This decision constituted a direct attack on the power of the nobility, until then absolute masters of their dominions. The most powerful of these noblemen was Ferdinand II, duke of Braganza and a distant cousin of the king. The duke decided to produce the legal documents proving the property and privileges he and his ancestors had been granted. He asked his finance manager, João Afonso, to go get them from the safe. But instead of going himself, João Afonso sent his son, who was young and inexperienced.

"When his son was going through the safe looking for the documents, a clerk by the name of Lopo de Figueiredo appeared and tried to help him. During their search, however, Lopo de Figueiredo discovered some strange letters between the duke of Braganza and the Catholic Monarchs of Castile and Aragon. Intrigued, he spirited them away and, once outside, got a secret audience with the king and showed him the letters, some of which included observations made in the duke's own handwriting. John II examined them and quickly realized that they revealed a conspiracy against the crown. Portugal's duke of Braganza was a secret agent for the Catholic Monarchs in Castile and had promised to help them invade the country." Vilarigues lowered his voice, as if uttering an evil word. "A traitor. The letters showed that the duke of Viseu, the queen's brother, was also involved, as was her mother. John II had the documents copied and told Lopo de Figueiredo to put them back in the safe he'd gotten them from. The king spent more than a year secretly assessing the extent of the conspiracy and preparing to dismantle it. He even discovered details of how the conspirators were planning to execute him.

"Then, one day in May 1483, he had the duke of Braganza arrested and tried. Found guilty of treason, Ferdinand II was beheaded a few days later in Évora. The conspiracy continued, however, now led by the duke of Viseu, until 1484, when King John decided to put an end to it for good. He called a meeting with the duke and, after a short conversation, stabbed him to death. Other noblemen involved in the plot were beheaded or poisoned, or fled to Castile. While all this was going on, however, a strange event took place. King John summoned the duke of Viseu's brother. Manuel came, fearing for his life—after all, his brother had been executed by the king in that same place. But the outcome was very different. King John granted Manuel all of his brother's assets and, interestingly, informed him that, if his own son Afonso were to die without leaving an heir, Manuel would be heir to the throne. This actually ended up being the case."

"What a strange story," said Thomas, impressed by the details of the palace intrigue smack in the middle of the Age of Discovery. "But I still don't understand why you're telling me all this."

Count Vilarigues folded his arms across his chest and raised an eyebrow. "Do you mean to tell me you're conducting an investigation into Christopher Columbus and the year this large-scale royal cleansing took place doesn't mean anything to you?"

"When did you say it happened?"

"In 1484."

Thomas scratched his chin thoughtfully. "That was the year Columbus left Portugal and went to Castile."

"Exactly." The count smiled, a spark dancing in his eyes.

Thomas was still for a moment, mulling it over in his mind, considering the implications, adjusting the pieces of the puzzle. "Are you insinuating that Columbus was a part of the conspiracy against King John?"

"Exactly."

"Ah . . ." Thomas struggled, unable to organize the whirlwind of thoughts racing through his mind. "Ah . . ."

Seeing him speechless, the count helped him. "Tell me something. Have you ever noticed that there are scads of documents about

Columbus's time in Spain, but regarding his presence in Portugal, you'll find only an enormous void? Nothing. Not a single document. The little that is known comes from brief references left by Las Casas, Ferdinand Columbus, and the admiral himself. Nothing else." He shrugged. "Now, why would that be? It is because Columbus had another name. We've been searching high and low for documents with the name Colom, when we should actually be looking for a different name."

"Wha—what name?"

"Nomina sunt odiosa."

"Names are odious," said Thomas, translating almost mechanically. "Cicero."

The count looked at him in surprise. "That was quick."

"Professor Toscano left this quote as a clue to unraveling the mystery of Columbus."

"Ah," said the count. "Did you know I was the one who told him that? I hoped he'd taken note." He shrugged. "Anyway, for all intents and purposes, Columbus's true name remains unknown. *Nomina sunt odiosa*. What matters is that he had another name. A nobleman's name."

"How do you know that?"

"Columbus was a nobleman who was also a member of the Order of Christ. His true story is a part of the Templars' oral tradition. And there are many facts to back it up. Did you read the letter King John sent Columbus in 1488?"

"What didn't I read?"

"What do you think of that passage in which the king mentions Columbus's problems with his legal authorities?"

Thomas opened his notebook, looking for his notes on that letter. "Wait, here it is," he said. "The king wrote: 'And seeing as you may be wary of our judiciary because of certain obligations, we hereby guarantee that during your journey here, stay, and return journey, you will not be arrested, held, accused, summonsed, or indicted for anything civil or criminal, of any nature.'" He looked at the count. "That's it."

"So? What crimes are these that made Columbus flee to Spain with his son in 1484?"

"The conspiracy."

"Exactly. The conspiracy dismantled in 1484. Many noblemen fled to Spain with their families that year. There was a general exodus of everyone involved in the plot engineered by the dukes of Braganza and Viseu."

Thomas grabbed his briefcase, fumbled around in it, pulled out a copy of *The Life of the Admiral Christopher Columbus* written in Spanish, and flipped through it quickly. "Hang on, hang on," he said, as if afraid the idea might escape him. "If memory serves me correctly, Columbus's Spanish son, Ferdinand, wrote the same thing in a brief reference to his father's arrival in Castile. Let me see . . . here it is. It says, 'who toward the end of the year 1484 secretly departed from Portugal with his little son Diego, fearing that the king might seek to detain him.' "

"Columbus secretly departed from Portugal?" asked the count ironically. "Afraid the king might detain him?" He smiled. "It would be hard to be any clearer than that, wouldn't it?"

"Do you think it's natural for the king to forgive Columbus if he really was involved in the conspiracy?"

"It depends on the circumstances, but considering what we know, it's perfectly plausible. Columbus wasn't one of the masterminds behind it; he was no more than a pawn in the plot, a secondary figure. Additionally, he was pardoned four years after these events, at a time when no one posed a threat to the king anymore. King John himself named the brother of one of the conspirators heir to the throne. It would have been even easier for him to forgive a smaller player like Columbus if he thought he might be useful." He pointed at the notebook and book Thomas had pulled from his briefcase. "And did you notice the way the king addressed Columbus in his letter of 1488?"

Thomas read from his notes.

" 'To Xpovam Collon, our special friend in Seville.' "

"Special friend? What kind of intimacy is this, for God's sake, between the great king of Portugal and an unimportant foreign silk weaver, a nobody?" The count shook his head. "No, this is a letter from a monarch to someone he knows well, a nobleman who has frequented his court. More important, it's a letter of reconciliation."

"So who was Columbus really?"

The count started walking again, heading for the stairs at the end of the square.

"Christopher Columbus was a Portuguese nobleman, of Jewish extraction, connected to the duke of Viseu's family, who played a minor role in the plot against King John II. When the plot was overturned, the conspirators fled to Spain. The more important players went first, and their accomplices followed them later. Columbus was one of them. He left behind his former name and rebuilt his life in Seville, where he made good use of the navigational skills he'd acquired in Portugal. He went by the name Cristóbal Colon and decided to hide his past, not least because of the strong anti-Semitism in Spain. After the discovery of America, Italian authors insinuated that he was Genoese. It was a convenient insinuation for Columbus, who encouraged it without confirming or denying it. It helped allay suspicions about his true origins, distracting people with something much less offensive." He cocked his head. "Did you notice that not even his Spanish son knew the truth of his origins?

"Ferdinand even went to Italy to verify what people said, that his father had come from Genoa." He looked at Thomas. "Can you believe it? Columbus didn't even reveal his origins to his own son! Imagine what lengths the admiral went to in order to keep his secret. It's evident that Ferdinand didn't find anything in Genoa, as he revealed in his book, which led him to actually pose the theory that his father had been born in Piacenza, thus confusing his origins with those of some paternal ancestors of the admiral's Portuguese wife, Felipa Moniz Perestrello, who actually were from Italy."

"So not even the Catholic Monarchs knew who he was?"

"No, they knew, all right." The count nodded. "Columbus had played a part in the conspiracy against the Portuguese crown. Among the documents found in the duke of Braganza's safe were letters from the Catholic Monarchs. Since Columbus was involved in the plot, the monarchs had to have known him, if remotely. In fact, it's the only explanation for why they gave him credit." He held out his hand for the book by Ferdinand Columbus. "Let me see that." The count flicked through it. "Somewhere here . . . there's a revealing reference. It's a passage in a letter from Columbus to Prince Juan. Here it is. He says, 'I am not the first Admiral of my family.' " He stared at Thomas, his head hanging to one side in an expression of mockery. "Columbus said he wasn't the first admiral of his family? Wasn't he supposed to have been an uneducated Genoese weaver?" He laughed. "In other words, the admiral himself made an indirect reference to his noble origins, of which the Spanish monarchs already knew. If Columbus really had been a humble Genoese weaver, as the ridiculous official version would have it, the Catholic Monarchs would have laughed at his request for an audience.

"Given the rivalry between Portugal and Spain, it wouldn't have been convenient to publicize the fact that the admiral of the Spanish fleet was Portuguese, especially of Jewish origins. That would have been unacceptable, so his true identity remained a secret. So great were the efforts to keep his origins quiet that the Spanish naturalization certificate of his younger brother, Diego, didn't mention his original nationality. Now, according to Spanish law, such certificates always had to show the original nationality of the citizen being naturalized. Diego's was the only exception. That shows how far the crown was prepared to go to conceal the admiral's origins. If he had really been Genoese, there wouldn't have been any reason to hide his nationality. It was convenient for the Catholic Monarchs to allow the Italian rumor to spread freely; through this conspiracy of silences and implicit understandings, fed by the explorer and his protectors, Columbus's origins remained obscure."

They passed between a giant sycamore and a doleful walnut tree, unmoving sentinels and silent witnesses to centuries of life in that strange monastery, and started up the wide stone staircase of the Templar complex.

"If Columbus was involved in the conspiracy, why did King John call him to Lisbon in 1488?" Thomas asked.

Count Vilarigues stroked his pointy beard. "Matters of state, sir. Matters of state. Christopher Columbus believed it was possible to get to India by sailing west, but the Catholic Monarchs weren't convinced. King John knew the voyage probably wasn't possible, for two reasons. The first was that the world was considerably bigger than Columbus imagined. The second was that the king of Portugal already knew there was a landmass in the middle of the route."

They were crossing the church courtyard near the entrance, heading for the south portal of the monastery, when Thomas stopped and looked at the count.

"So King John knew all along that America was there."

The count laughed. "Of course he knew. In fact, that was no big deal. As far as I know, America was discovered thousands of years ago by the Asians, who colonized the two Americas from tip to tip. The Vikings, in particular Erik the Red, were the first Europeans to arrive there. This knowledge was preserved by the Nordic Templars, some of whom came to Portugal. And the Portuguese had definitely explored those parts during the fifteenth century, always in secret. Admiral Gago Coutinho, the first man to cross the South Atlantic in an airplane, concluded that fifteenth-century sailors had sailed to the American coast before 1472. He also suspected that explorers in the service of the Portuguese crown had been the first post-Viking Europeans to get there. In fact, during the *Pleyto de la Prioridad* hearings, set in motion in 1532 by the sons of Captain Pinzón—who had served under Columbus—with the curious theory that the admiral had discovered a land whose existence was already known, several witnesses who had come into contact with the great explorer were heard. One of them, a certain Alonso Gallego, referred to Columbus as a 'person who had served the King of Portugal and heard of the said lands of the said Indies.' Which is confirmed by the biographer Bartolomé de Las Casas, Columbus's contemporary, who said a Portuguese sailor had told the admiral there was land west of the Azores. The same Las Casas traveled through the Antilles and said that the indigenous people of Cuba had told him that other sailors, white and bearded, had already visited those parts before the Spanish. Have you ever seen the Cantino planisphere?"

"Of course."

"And have you ever noticed that it shows the coast of Florida?"

"Yes."

"The planisphere was drawn by a Portuguese cartographer in 1502 at the latest, but Florida was only discovered in 1513. Curious, isn't it?"

"It's obvious they knew more than they let on."

"Of course they did. What do you make of the fact that Columbus took Portuguese coins to the New World on his first voyage? Why not Spanish coins? It only makes sense if the admiral was convinced that the local populations were already familiar with Portuguese currency, doesn't it?"

The ornate, Manueline-style south portal was closed. They went around the right side of the rotunda, still in the main courtyard, and, just after the bell tower, passed through the small sacristy door to the penumbra of the sanctuary. They bought tickets, crossed the cemetery cloister, with its small orange trees decorating a flamboyant Gothic courtyard, and headed down the dark corridors until they finally reached the heart of the Templar monastery. The rotunda.

The building exhaled the mildewy aroma of old things, a smell Thomas associated with museums. Its sixteen-sided outer structure housed an internal octagon, where the high altar was located. There were frescoes covering the walls and gilded statues in the pillars; the round nave was topped with a Byzantine dome. Here was the place of worship of the Tomar Templars, modeled on the rotunda of the Holy Sepulcher in Jerusalem. It was the jewel of the monastery, with its sober, imposing architecture. The south portal, seen from the inside, was flanked by two twisted pillars, like those that, according to the Scriptures, protected the Temple of Solomon. Thomas and the count were so engrossed in their conversation that, after a quick look around the inside, they soon forgot their surroundings.

"I'm sorry, but there are things I don't understand," said Thomas, glancing around the central octagon. "If the Portuguese already knew America existed, why didn't they go explore it?"

"They didn't think there was anything there," answered the

count, with the air of one presenting evidence. "My friend, the Portuguese wanted to get to the Orient. On an esoteric level, they believed the knowledge they sought was somewhere in the mythical Christian kingdom of Prester John, as suggested in the German epic poem *Parzival,* by Wolfram von Eschenbach, knowledge of which must have been brought here by the German Templars. On an economic level, their ambition was to find a route to India in order to bypass Venice and the Ottoman Empire's trade monopoly and buy spices at their source at a much more affordable price. The quest for the Holy Grail—or the knowledge it represents—was Henry the Navigator's motivation, as it was the priority for his team of Templars. But commercial interests gradually eclipsed mystic ones. They believed that America was home to only indigenous peoples and trees, as they quickly realized when they disembarked there. Which is why King John began to take an interest in Columbus's plans.

"Christopher Columbus knew there was land to the west of the Azores. I think he thought this land was Asia, of which Marco Polo had spoken. He tried to convince the king of Portugal to explore to the west, but King John already knew that the real Asia was much farther away, which was why he kept rejecting the young nobleman's suggestions. In 1484, after the conspiracy against the king fell through, Columbus fled to Castile, where he tried to sell his theory to the Catholic Monarchs. It's important to note that this development was convenient for King John. He was an astute strategist and quickly realized that as soon as Spain saw the Portuguese making millions in trade with the Indies, they'd want in. War would break out. King John considered the Spaniards a potential threat to his plans. He needed to distract them with something apparently very valuable but that was not the ultimate prize."

"America," said Thomas.

"The one and only." The count winked. "America met these requirements; it was the perfect decoy. The problem was, due to their extreme lack of information and the fact that they were still busy trying to expel the Moors from the south of the Iberian Peninsula, the Spanish rejected his proposals. Disheartened and feeling homesick,

Columbus wanted to return to Portugal, but there was still the old problem of his involvement in the assassination conspiracy. So he wrote to King John in 1488, claiming his innocence and begging pardon for any offense taken. The monarch seized the opportunity and sent him the letter of reconciliation that you've already seen, guaranteeing that he would not be arrested for any crime committed. With this letter of safe conduct, Columbus went to Portugal to insist on his plan. To his surprise, however, he saw that King John had no intention of setting up an expedition to the west but wanted him to convince the Catholic Monarchs to undertake such a voyage. He promised to secretly help Columbus with whatever he needed and to do everything in his power to ensure his voyage was a success. While in Lisbon, Columbus witnessed Bartolomeu Dias return with the news that he had discovered a passage to the Indian Ocean and realized King John really did have good reason not to follow his suggestion. Resigned, he accepted the offer of secret help and returned to Spain."

"The return of Bartolomeu Dias is a key point," said Thomas. "It has always been assumed that King John discarded the idea of trying to reach India by sailing west because Dias's arrival with the news that he had discovered the Cape of Good Hope showed him that this was a better route."

"Nonsense," exclaimed the count with a weary gesture. "King John had known that for a long time!" The count patted Thomas on the shoulder. "My dear man, think about it. If King John were really entertaining the idea of sailing west, do you think he would have hired a Genoese navigator from Seville, as the official theory goes? Did he not have far more experienced men among his subjects, top-notch navigators such as Vasco da Gama, Bartolomeu Dias, Pacheco Pereira, Diogo Cão, and many others, all better equipped to successfully carry out such a mission? Anyone who thinks King John let Columbus go to Lisbon to discuss the possibility of an expedition to the west can only be joking!" The count shook his head. "Do you not think it odd that Bartolomeu Dias discovered the passage to the Indian Ocean in 1488, but Portugal only sent Vasco da Gama to explore the passage ten years later?" He looked perplexed. "Why wait ten years?"

"Well, I imagine it was to prepare the voyage—"

"Ten years to prepare a voyage? Come now. If the Portuguese had been green at this business of navigation, okay, I'd understand, I'd be able to believe it. But they conducted regular maritime expeditions. It was a part of everyday life for them, which rules out that theory." He leaned forward. "Ten inexplicable years separate the voyages of Dias and Da Gama." He shrugged. "Why? What made them put off their anxiously awaited voyage to India? This, my friend, is one of the greatest mysteries of the Age of Discovery, the subject of much speculation among historians." He pointed at Thomas. "In a way, you were correct in your explanation. The Portuguese were indeed preparing the Spanish."

"Preparing the Spanish for what?"

"The king of Portugal knew they could only embark on their adventure to India when they'd resolved the problem of the Spaniards. The 1480 Treaty of Toledo, following the Treaty of Alcaçovas, gave Portugal the right to explore the coast of Africa, as well as 'to and including the Indies,' but King John II feared that when push came to shove, the Spanish would go back on their word. After all, hadn't the Catholic Monarchs, while signing the treaties of Alcaçovas and Toledo, been simultaneously conspiring with Portuguese noblemen to assassinate the king? How could King John trust them? He needed Columbus to convince the Spanish to send an expedition west, and it was important that they believed that America was actually Asia. The Portuguese were waiting for Columbus's voyage and the subsequent geopolitical renegotiations."

"That voyage took place in 1492."

"Yes. And with the secret support of King John II."

"How so?"

"In the first place, with financing," he said, counting on his thumb. "Isabella the Catholic promised a million *maravedis* to pay for the expedition. But that wasn't enough, and Columbus himself put in a quarter of a million. Tell me, where on earth did an impoverished nobleman get that kind of money? Those who believe the Genoese theory say the money was advanced to him by Italian bankers, but if that were true, they would have come knocking on his door later. Anyway, whoever lent him the money didn't turn up to claim a slice of the profits from trade with the West Indies. Why not? Because the real dividends from this investment were not in money but in geostrategic gains. In short, because the secret financier was the king of Portugal.

"Second, King John supplied Columbus with navigational instruments. Just days before he set sail, Columbus received from Lisbon a set of astronomical tables called the *tábuas de declinação do sol,* written in Hebrew, an essential tool for correcting imprecision in the use of the astrolabe. Who sent them?" He smiled. "The Portuguese king, obviously. He bent over backward to ensure the voyage was a success." The count pretended to rock a baby in his arms. "King John played the Spanish all the way to America."

"That's all true, but Columbus's voyage took place in 1492 and Vasco da Gama only reached India in 1498. Why wait another six years?"

"Because they needed to clarify the geopolitical developments that had taken place in the meantime, tying the Spanish in to a new treaty, signed with the Vatican's approval, that ensured the most favorable situation for Lisbon. This came to pass in 1494, when Portugal and Spain signed the Treaty of Tordesillas, dividing the world into halves, one for each Iberian kingdom. The Spanish believed their part was the best, since it included what they thought was India—that is, the land recently discovered by Columbus." The count held up his hand. "Now, my good man, do you really think King John would have signed this treaty if he thought India was in the Spanish half? The only plausible answer is that King John accepted this division of the world because he already knew that the Spanish half didn't include the real India. The Portuguese handed the 'American India' to their rivals and kept the real India for themselves. The risk of a future war was eliminated, and the Portuguese finally began planning Vasco da Gama's great voyage."

"Even so, Vasco da Gama only set sail three years after the signing of the treaty."

"Yes," said the count. "The Perfect Prince died in 1495, delaying the process, and the fleet didn't set sail until 1497, in the reign of King Manuel."

"How can you state with such certainty that Columbus was the pawn intentionally used by King John to throw the Spanish off the scent of the real India?"

"There's nothing speculative about it," said Count Vilarigues. "This information about the agreement between Columbus and King John is part of the secret inheritance of the Order of Christ and is backed up by a mixture of circumstantial and hard evidence."

"What evidence?"

The count smiled. "We're getting there," he said. "Let's start with the circumstantial evidence. Are you familiar with the documents on which the theory that Columbus was Genoese is based?"

"Yes, of course."

"Do you happen to think they are reliable?"

"No, they're weak, full of contradictions and discrepancies."

"So you believe he was Portuguese?"

"Yes. But I must say, there's no hard evidence."

"Would you like a home movie of Columbus looking at the camera and singing the Portuguese national anthem?"

"No. But, even with all its inconsistencies and absurdities, the Genoese theory is the only one that gives Columbus an identity, a family, home, and documents. Everything else is shaky, it's true. The Portuguese theory is the opposite. Regardless of the fact that it makes sense and explains the mysteries surrounding the admiral, there is no document to clearly identify him."

"Very well, we're getting to the proof," said the count, signaling for Thomas to be patient. "Let's focus on the circumstantial evidence for now. Based on what you've seen, does the story I've told you make sense?"

"Yes, I'd say so. Things seem to fit together."

"Now let's examine the strange events that took place on the first and crucial voyage of 1492. Columbus arrived in the Antilles and made contact with the native people, whom he called Indians, thinking he was in India. But it was the return journey that the strangest decisions of the voyage began. Instead of returning by the same route they had come, sailing east toward the Canary Islands, as the captain of the *Pinta* did, the admiral headed north, toward the Arctic, on the caravel *Niña*. In fact, we know that this was the easiest route, since the more favorable trade winds blew there at that time of year. But if no one had ever sailed those waters before, how on earth did Columbus know to take this route? He had obviously been informed. He sailed north-northeast for two weeks, until he turned east, in the zone of prevailing westerlies, heading for the Azores. Las Casas claims that the admiral did not correct his course because he still hadn't arrived at the Portuguese archipelago, which shows his intention to go there. He ran into a storm and sailed to the island of Santa Maria, where he anchored.

"A curious episode followed. The Spanish caravel was well received by the Portuguese, who even went as far as to send a boat with supplies. The interim governor of the island, a certain João Castanheira, said he knew Columbus well. The admiral sent part of his crew ashore to pray in a chapel, but the men were late returning, and Columbus realized they had been detained by the Portuguese. The men of Santa Maria then sent a boat for Columbus, demanding that he turn himself in, as they had orders from the king to arrest him. The admiral did not obey and tried to sail to the island of São Miguel, but with so few crew members and a new storm brewing on the horizon, this proved impossible and Columbus returned to Santa Maria. The next day the Portuguese let the crew go. When they got back to the *Niña,* they said they'd heard Castanheira say he only wanted to arrest Columbus, on the king's orders, and that the Spanish were of no interest to them."

The count looked skeptical. "Now, all this, obviously, is very odd. Columbus took a spin through the Azores instead of going straight to Castile? What about the admiral's reaction when he learned that the king had ordered his men to detain him? Instead of sailing away to escape the enemy, as anyone with a smidgen of common sense would have done, he decided, amazingly, to head for the island of São Miguel, where the king's order would presumably be carried out equally as efficiently. Isn't that a weird way to behave?"

"True," said Thomas. "What's the explanation?"

"He assumed that the king's previous order for the traitor's arrest was still in force. We mustn't forget that Columbus had been involved in the assassination plot. Castanheira knew of this old warrant for his arrest but, being isolated on a remote island, was not aware that it had been revoked. The Admiral, instead of fleeing to Castile, as would have been expected of one being accosted by the king of Portugal, decided to head for São Miguel. Why would he have done that if his neck was on the line? The answer is simple. Columbus knew that there were authorities in São Miguel who were aware of the truth." He waved his hand brusquely, as if wishing to sweep the matter aside. "Well, let's go on. After this bizarre visit to the Azores, what do you think would be the normal thing for Columbus to do next?"

"Return to Castile?"

"Exactly." He covered his eyes with the back of his hand, in feigned suffering. "However, destiny's cruel. Another storm forced him to stop in Lisbon, would you believe it? Of all places! The winds conspired to throw him into the lion's den, the enemy's lair!" He winked and laughed, enjoying himself. "Our friend anchored in Restelo on March 4, 1493, alongside the king's own ship. The captain visited the *Niña* to ask Columbus what he was doing in Lisbon. The admiral answered that he'd only speak with his 'special friend,' the king of Portugal. On the ninth, Columbus was taken to a villa in Azambuja, where he met with King John. He kissed his hand in one room, and they exchanged a few words in private. Then, the king took the admiral into another room where there were several illustrious members of his court. The chroniclers' accounts of what took place here differ from one another.

"Ferdinand Columbus, citing his father, said that the king listened to his story of the voyage with a happy expression on his face, only making the observation that, according to the Treaties of Alcaçovas and Toledo, the lands he had discovered were his. Rui de Pina, however, says the king looked displeased as he listened to the tale of his former subject's feats and that Columbus addressed him in an exalted manner, accusing him of negligence for not having believed in his project earlier. According to Pina, the terms he used were so offensive that the noblemen present decided to execute Columbus. However, not only did King John forbid them to kill him, but—surprise, surprise—he treated his aggressive, rash visitor most graciously. The next day, Columbus and King John resumed their conversation, and the king promised him help with whatever he needed, telling him to take a seat in his presence, always very ceremonious showering him with honors. They said good-bye on the eleventh, and the Portuguese noblemen saw him off, going to great lengths to show him respect." The count looked at Thomas. "What do you make of all this?"

"Well, in light of what you've told me, it's a surprising story."

"Very, isn't it? Starting with the storms." The count tilted his head mockingly. "Convenient, don't you think?"

"What are you implying?"

"That the third storm was no more than a heavy rainfall, enough to give Columbus a pretext to stop in Lisbon. In the famous lawsuit *Pleyto con la Corona,* in which all of the participants on this voyage served as witnesses, the Spanish sailors vividly remembered the storm in the Azores, but there is no mention of one near Lisbon. In other words, Columbus went to Lisbon because he wanted to. As he told the captain of the royal vessel anchored in the Tagus, he wished to speak with the king."

The count arched his eyebrows. "Do you see? Columbus was informed in Santa Maria that the king wanted him to be detained, and the first thing he did when he left the Azores was head precisely for Lisbon to request an audience with the king! Is that normal? Why did he go so calmly to the lion's den?"

"You've got a point," said Thomas. "What was discussed?"

"No one knows, but it seems logical that they agreed to put on a show."

"A show?"

"Las Casas describes Columbus as polite and sober, incapable of using rude words. It appears his most violent outbursts were 'God take you!' How did he speak to the king in such a brutal way that the noblemen wanted to kill him? And what about the reaction of the great, implacable King John II? This was the king who had some of the most powerful noblemen in Portugal beheaded and poisoned. This was the king who had stabbed his own brother-in-law. Standing before this king was a foreign silk weaver, offending him in his own house in front of his subjects. Such offenses were enough of a reason for King John to kill Columbus. And what did this merciless and calculating king—the first absolutist ruler of Portugal—do?" The count let his question hang in the air for a moment. "He stopped the noblemen from killing Columbus and showered the admiral with honors. Additionally, he helped him stock the *Niña* with supplies for the voyage back to Castile, asking Columbus to send his regards to the Catholic Monarchs, and even made his nobles see him off with great pomp!" He held up a finger as if giving a public speech. "This, my good man, is not the behavior of a foreigner forced to visit his archenemy. Nor is it the behavior of a king offended by the man who, to top it all off, has just thwarted his greatest ambition. These are two men in cahoots putting on a show. With the Spanish now occupied with the wrong India, King John was finally free to prepare Vasco da Gama's voyage to the true India, which was indeed the greatest feat of the Age of Discovery. Do you know what Columbus did after saying good-bye to King John?"

"Um, he went to Castile."

"No. He went for another waltz around Portugal, to Vila Franca de Xira."

"What on earth did he go there for?"

"To talk to the queen, who was at a monastery. Las Casas says that Columbus went to pay his respects, and that the queen was accompanied by the duke and marquis. Don't you think that's odd?"

"Of course I do! What did they talk about?"

"Family matters, I assume."

"What family matters?"

"My good man, consider Columbus's trajectory. Here is a Portuguese nobleman forced to flee to Castile with his son because of his role in the conspiracy against the king. Who were the masterminds in this conspiracy? The queen's mother and brother, the duke of Viseu. Columbus had connections with the queen herself. I can't tell you exactly who he was, but I can assure you he was someone on intimate terms with the queen, possibly even a blood relation." The count held up his finger to stress the importance of his point. "How else can we understand such a meeting? And how do we understand that they talked until nightfall? Why was the new duke of Viseu, none other than the future King Manuel, the queen's brother, present at this meeting?" He made a resigned gesture. "The only explanation is that it was a reunion of family members who hadn't seen one another in a long time." He leveled his gaze at Thomas. "Do you have any other explanation?"

"No," Thomas admitted. "But that doesn't necessarily mean all this is true."

"Columbus slept in Alhandra on the night of the eleventh," said the count. "The next morning the king sent an escort offering to take him overland to Castile, arranging accommodation and animals for the journey." He winked. "Nice of the king, wasn't it? Helping Columbus deliver the secret route to India to Castile. Going out of his way to help in his own defeat." He shook his head skeptically. "At any rate, Columbus returned to the *Niña,* and weighed anchor in Lisbon on the thirteenth."

The count looked at Thomas again. "Do you know what Columbus's next destination was?"

"You don't mean to tell me he went somewhere else in Portugal."

"Oh, yes I do. The man went to Faro!" They both laughed. The story of Columbus's return voyage was becoming a farce.

"Faro?" said Thomas. "What did he go to Faro for?"

"God knows," said the count with a shrug. "Columbus arrived in Faro on the fourteenth and spent almost an entire day there, only leaving in the evening. Being a Portuguese nobleman, he no doubt went to visit someone he knew. Finally, on the fifteenth, he reached Castile." Vilarigues stroked his beard. "Now look. Columbus's Spanish crewmen were itching to get home. Columbus must have been eager to present himself to the Catholic Monarchs with the story of his great discovery of India. Nevertheless, he went traipsing around the whole of Portugal, as cool as a cucumber, chatting with the king and queen, dropping in on people, zipping here and there—it's almost as if the fellow was on holiday. Christopher Columbus, my good man, was a Portuguese nobleman who had been of great service to his country in luring Castile away from the true route to India."

Thomas ran his hand over his face, massaging it. "Okay," he agreed. "But tell me something. Didn't the Spanish crew find this all rather odd?"

"Of course they did." He pointed at Thomas's briefcase. "Have you got copies of Columbus's letters with you? Have you got the one he wrote in 1500, when he was in captivity, to Dona Juana de la Torre?"

Thomas pulled a wad of photocopies out of his briefcase, found the letter, and handed it to Vilarigues.

The count scanned it. "Now, look at this sentence," he said. " 'I think Your Grace will remember, when the tempest tossed me into Lisbon with no sails, that I was falsely accused of having gone there to give India to the King.' "

He gazed at Thomas. "In other words, the crew also thought his behavior very strange, and had regarded his talks with King John with particular suspicion. Columbus did not meet with King John in Lisbon in 1493 to offer him America. He went there so they could take stock of the situation and plan their next move, which would lead to the Treaty of Tordesillas."

"Okay," said Thomas. "Regardless of whether all the details are correct, this story does tie in exceptionally well with what we know. But where is the hard evidence? Where is the document that confirms everything?"

"You're not hoping to find a document stating that Columbus was a secret agent for Portugal, are you?"

"It's to be expected that that was kept under wraps. What I want is proof that Columbus was Portuguese."

Vilarigues stroked his pointy beard. "Well," he said, "you know, the former president of the Spanish Royal Geographical Society, Beltrán y Rózpide, claimed that there was proof in a private Portuguese archive—"

"Yes," said Thomas. "I already knew that. Armando Cortesão

mentions it. The document has never been found, because Beltrán y Rózpide died without revealing the location."

Count Vilarigues took a deep breath, looked up, and observed the large gilded Gothic baldachins pointing toward the top of the dome, decorated with the heraldic symbols of King Manuel and the Order of Christ. Here the Templar church was at its most splendid. Finally, he looked back at Thomas.

"Have you ever heard of *Codex 632*?" Thomas ran his hand over his face.

"It's curious you should mention it," he said. "I found a reference to this codex on the back of some photocopies in Professor Toscano's safe, together with the piece of paper that had your phone number on it. Here," he said, taking them out and showing them to the count.

Vilarigues took the papers, glanced over them, and looked back at Thomas. "Do you know what this is?"

"It's the *Chronicle of King D. John II* by Rui de Pina. The passage that tells of Columbus's famous meeting with the king."

The count sighed again. "This, my friend, is an extract from *Codex 632*."

Thomas stared at the pages in the count's hands. "*Chronicle of King D. John II* is *Codex 632*?"

"No, my friend. *Codex 632* is a version of the *Chronicle of King D. John II*. Sometime at the beginning of the sixteenth century, King Manuel had Rui de Pina write the chronicle. Pina had been a personal friend of the late king and knew his life in great detail. This manuscript went to the copyists, who made copies on parchment and paper. The original was lost, but there are three main duplicates, all from the sixteenth century. The most beautiful is locked in a vault at the Tower of Tombo archive, where almost all of Portugal's most valuable books are kept. It is *Parchment 9*, an illuminated manuscript written in Gothic letters and replete with colorful miniatures. The other two copies are at the Portuguese National Library. One is known as the *Códice Alcobacense*, because it was found at the Monastery of Alcobaça, and the other as *Codex 632*. All three tell the same story, in different calligraphy. But there is one detail, one tiny detail, that betrays the uniform version."

He picked up the photocopies. "This detail is in *Codex 632*, where Pina describes the meeting between Columbus and King John." He held the photocopies up for Thomas to see. "Do you notice anything abnormal about this text?"

Thomas took the papers and studied the bottom of the first page and the top of the second.

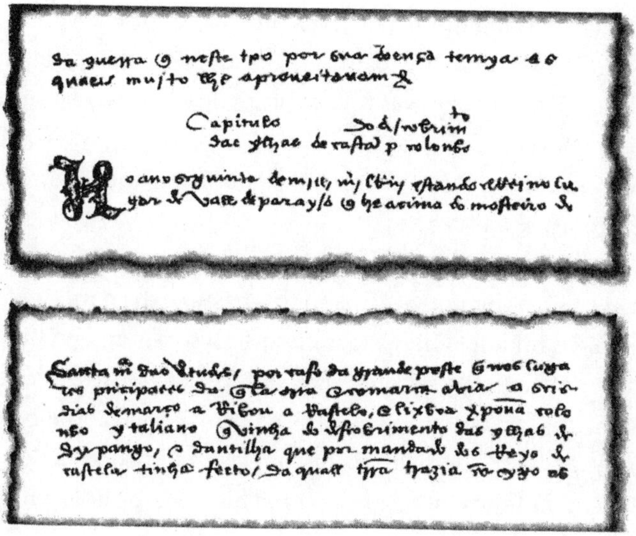

"No, I don't," he finally confessed. "It's the description of Columbus's arrival in Lisbon, on his way back from America. It looks okay to me."

The count raised his left eyebrow slightly, as if he were a teacher and Thomas a student who had given him the wrong answer. "Does it really? Look carefully at the spaces between the words. They are all uniform. But there's one place where the copyist strayed from his pattern. Can you see it?"

Thomas leaned over the two pages again, staring at the text. First he looked at the whole, then the details. "There's a blank space after the word *Capítulo,* at the bottom of the first page—"

"Which means that the copyist didn't fill in the number of the chapter, waiting for instructions from a superior. What else?" the Count asked patiently.

"And there's an abnormally large space before and after *'y taliano.'* It's a small detail, but it stands out compared with the spaces between the other words."

"Yes, my friend. What does that mean? Go on. Don't be afraid. Give it a try."

"Well, off the cuff . . . it looks like . . . it looks like the copyist left a blank space in the part that refers to Columbus's origins. It's almost as if he were waiting for instructions on what to put there."

"Bingo!" exclaimed the count. "Like all court chroniclers, Rui de Pina only wrote what he was told to write or what they let him write. Many things were suppressed."

"Yes," said Thomas. "There's no doubt they only recorded what was of interest to the crown."

Count Vilarigues pointed at the third and fourth lines of the second page. "Have you noticed that in this passage the name *'Colo nbo'* is divided in the middle? On the third line it says *'colo'* and on the fourth, *'nbo.'* It's as if the copyist later received instructions to write *'nbo y taliano'* instead of something else in the blank space at the beginning of the fourth line." He held up his finger and opened his eyes very wide. "Instead of the truth." He lowered his voice, almost whispering. "Instead of the secret."

"Incredible!" Thomas said, his eyes glued to the fateful spot.

The count fidgeted on the hard pew, uncomfortable from having sat so long in the same position. "When I talked with Professor Toscano shortly before he died, he posited another hypothesis. It had always seemed to me that these abnormal spaces around the *'y taliano'* showed that, when it was first being written, a blank space had deliberately been left so whatever was most convenient could be added later. Professor Toscano thought that the spaces were signs of tampering. In other words, he thought the copyist had included the information about Columbus's true identity from Pina's original manuscript, which has since been lost. It was erased and *'nbo y taliano'* was written over the top. He was going to look into it but never got back to me about it." He shrugged. "I suppose his suspicion proved to be unfounded."

"Perhaps," said Thomas. He waved the two pages at the count. "Do you know if these photocopies were taken from the original document or a facsimile?"

"Ah, no. This photocopy was taken from the microfilm at the National Library. As you know, no one has access to the originals. *Codex 632* is a rare manuscript and is kept in a vault. You can't consult it at the drop of a hat."

Thomas got up from the pew and stretched. "That's what I wanted to know," he said.

The count got up, too. "What are you going to do now?"

"Something very simple, sir," Thomas said, straightening his clothes. "I'm going to do what I should have done already."

"What?"

Thomas headed for a small door near the pew they'd been sitting on. He was about to leave the Charola and head down to the Main Cloister when he stopped, turned around, and stared at the count, his face partially visible in the half-light.

"I'm going to the National Library to see the original *Codex 632*."

The count smiled.

"One question," ventured Thomas, almost as an afterthought. "Why haven't you told other scholars all this? Why Toscano? Why me? Why now?"

The count nodded, looked up at the sky, and said, "I was instructed to let this secret go. That's all I can tell you. It's time the world knew. Those I represent have reasons for everything they do."

Chapter 20

The elevator door opened with a hum, and Thomas walked onto the third floor of Lisbon's National Library, a sullen, empty place. A soft light insinuated itself through nooks and crannies, emerging from deserted corridors, draping itself over the naked walls, only overcome by the bright light gushing through the wide windows overlooking the terrace and treetops in the distance. With his footsteps echoing across the polished marble floors, Thomas crossed the bare space and pushed open the glass doors of the reading room.

Windows filled the entire outer wall, flooding the room with light and offering a view of the greenery outside. The inner walls were covered in shelves, replete with catalogues and all manner of old books, priceless volumes sitting side by side with their clothbound spines on display. Hunched over the tables, arranged in rows, several people were perusing ancient manuscripts, here a worn parchment, there an elegant illuminated book, everywhere weary treasures to which only academics had easy access. Thomas recognized a few faces; at the back a professor from the Classical University of Lisbon, a thin, cranky old man with a prickly white beard, was examining a medieval codex; in a corner, an ambitious young lecturer from University of Coimbra, with a thick mustache and round face, was poring over a worn book of hours; in the first row, a thin, nervous young woman with unkempt hair and rumpled clothes was leafing through a tattered old catalogue.

"Good day, sir," said the librarian, a middle-aged woman with tortoiseshell glasses, well known to habitual visitors to the archives.

"Hi, Alexandra," said Thomas. "How are you?"

"Fine, thanks." She got up. "I'll go get your request."

Thomas had put in a request the day before. He waited at a seat by the window, opened his notebook, and scanned the information he had collected on the author of the document. Rui de Pina, he had read, was a high-ranking palace employee who had enjoyed King John II's unwavering trust. He had followed Portugal's great disputes with Castile as a diplomat and had been the Portuguese crown's envoy to Barcelona in 1493, where he met with the Catholic Monarchs about the situation created by Columbus's voyage to "Asia." He had helped prepare for the negotiations that led to the Treaty of Tordesillas, the famous document that divided up the world between Portugal and Spain. After the death of the Perfect Prince, whose will he executed, he had become the court chronicler, writing the *Chronicle of King D. John II* no later than the early sixteenth century, during the reign of King Manuel.

The sound of approaching footsteps interrupted Thomas's train of thought, wrenching him from his notes. It was Alexandra holding a heavy-looking manuscript in her arms. She plunked it down on the table, looking relieved. "Here it is!" she exclaimed, almost out of breath. "Treat it well."

"Don't worry," said Thomas, smiling, his eyes glued to the manuscript.

The heavy volume had a brown leather cover with the manuscript number on the spine. *Codex 632.* He leafed through it carefully, deferentially even, using his fingertips to turn the pages affectionately, as if caressing a relic. The pages were yellow and stained with time, with illuminated first letters. On the first page was the title: *Chronicle of King D. John II.* The pages weren't numbered, and Thomas went through it slowly, scanning each page, sometimes reading every word, sometimes skipping paragraphs or entire pages, always looking through the difficult sixteenth-century Portuguese calligraphy for the enigmatic extract from his photocopies.

He stopped on the seventy-sixth page. There was the illuminated initial beginning the sentence "In the following year . . . the King was in Paraíso Valley. . . ." He turned the page and studied the top of the next, looking for the blank spaces around the reference to Christopher Columbus. He found them and his heart leapt. His eyes glued to the page, he was seeing but refusing to believe. At the beginning of the fourth line, on the left, a white mark over the words *nbo y taliano* showed evidence of tampering. It was an erasure.

The erasure.

Thomas tugged at his collar, feeling hot. Short of breath, he looked around, as if he was drowning and looking for someone to save him. He wanted to shout out his discovery, the fraud he had finally unmasked, but everyone in the room seemed oblivious to his moment of revelation, immersed in the drowsiness of monotonous study.

He focused on the manuscript again, afraid that what he saw might have disappeared. But no, the alteration was still there, subtle but unmistakable. It seemed to be laughing in his face. Thomas shook his head, mentally repeating an inescapable conclusion. Someone had fiddled with *Chronicle of King D. John II.* The passage that identified Columbus's nationality had been tampered with; an unknown hand had erased the original words and replaced them with '*nbo y taliano,*' so it would read: '*Xpova Colonbo, Italian.*' Who had done it? And more important, what did the original text say? This last question began to rattle through his mind, insistent, stubborn, and insidious. What secret had been erased? Who was Columbus? He held the codex up to the window to see if the light against the page could show him what was underneath the alteration. But the page remained opaque and dense.

Impenetrable.

After spending more than ten minutes trying to see the invisible, Thomas decided to change tactics. He'd have to talk to an expert in electronic imaging about the possibility of recovering any vestiges of the original text. He took the manuscript back to the reception counter and set it down.

"Are you done already?" asked Alexandra, looking up from her novel.

"Yes. I'm off."

She picked up the codex to take it back to the archive. "This manuscript has been in demand lately," she said, positioning it under her arm.

Thomas was already at the door when he heard her comment. "What?"

"*Codex 632* has been in demand lately," she repeated.

"In demand? By whom?"

"Well, a professor looked at it about three months ago."

"Aah," said Thomas. "Yes, Professor Toscano must have been studying the codex, that's for sure."

"You knew him? The poor man. Dying like that in Brazil, so far from his family."

Thomas clucked his tongue and sighed, an appropriately resigned expression on his face. "Yes, a bit. It's a shame."

"I know," said Alexandra. "And here I was with an answer to his request. Now I don't know what to do with it."

"What request?"

She held up the manuscript. "This codex," she said. "He asked our labs for an X-ray. It came back about two weeks ago, and I don't know what to do with it."

"What?" Thomas said, his heart skipping a beat. "Professor Toscano asked for an X-ray of the manuscript?"

Alexandra laughed. "No, just of one page."

It could only have been of the page that had been meddled with. "Where is it?" asked Thomas.

"There," she said, pointing under the counter. "In my drawer."

Thomas leaned over the counter to see the drawer, his heart pounding. "May I see it?"

Alexandra put the manuscript back on the counter, opened the drawer, and pulled out an enormous white envelope with the Lisbon National Library logo on it. "Here," she said, handing it to him.

Thomas tore open the envelope and pulled out the X-ray. A glance was enough to tell Thomas that it was indeed the page of *Codex 632* that had been tampered with. His eyes were drawn to the left side of the fourth line. The words *'nbo y taliano'* could still be seen, but mixed in with their letters were other markings, confused, half erased, the lines twisting around one another. Thomas stared more closely at the text and concentrated on the shape of the letters and the way they connected to make words. He tried to distinguish what the original writing said.

Suddenly, it became clear. Thomas was finally able to see what Rui de Pina had actually written in his first version. The truth sprang from the text.

He knew what Toscano had discovered.

The white stone structure rose up out of the resplendent green surface of the water with cool vigor under the hot midday sun. Like a medieval castle in the middle of the river, it stood aloof and proud, as if it were a stone ship, unmoving in the liquid roll of the waves, a Gothic monument to times of greatness. It was a sentinel watching the entrance of the Tagus and guarding Lisbon from the unknown, from the giant beyond the horizon, a phantom submerged in the infinity of the ocean.

Thomas walked along the jetty over the calm waters at the river's edge, his eyes fixed on Belém Tower, which stood before him with imposing refinement. The lookouts were crowned with ribbed domes, like Almohade mosques, and pairs of arched windows faced onto narrow balconies enclosed by ornate balustrades. The Order of Christ cross, the symbol of the Portuguese Templars, was everywhere, especially on the battlements, in addition to proud armillary spheres sculpted in the stone walls.

Thomas went inside and headed for the meeting place, secretly amused by Moliarti's obsession with the most emblematic monuments of the Age of Discovery. Nelson Moliarti was leaning against the lower battlements near one of the front lookouts, chewing gum.

"I have good news," said Thomas with barely contained euphoria as he shook the American's hand. He held up his brown briefcase. "I've finished the investigation."

Moliarti smiled. "That's great, excellent. Tell me about it."

Leaning against the battlements, Thomas revealed what he had discovered on his trips to Jerusalem and Tomar. He spoke with such intensity that he became oblivious to the opera of color, sound, and fragrance around him. The seagulls flapped about noisily, cawing melancholically. A salty sea breeze perfumed the air and the deep sigh of the ocean filled the wind with its cool, reinvigorating breath, as the waves lapped softly at the base of the tower, kissing its feet. Moliarti listened to Thomas's report with an impassive expression, almost bored. His face only changed at the end, when Thomas extracted the X-ray from his briefcase.

Moliarti stared at the X-ray, barely able to hide his anxiety, then quickly looked back at Thomas.

"The texts are superimposed," Thomas explained. "You'll see that the new version is darker. It says '*nbo y taliano*.' But these lighter gray lines are what you need to focus on. See?"

Moliarti brought the X-ray closer to his eyes, as if he was near-sighted. "Yeah," he said. "There's something there all right."

"Can you make it out?"

"Yeah. There's an *n* and . . . an *a* . . ."

"Good. And what comes next?"

"It looks like . . . an *l*?"

"It's a *d*. What else?"

"And an *o*."

"Exactly. So what does it say?"

"*Nado*."

"Excellent. What about the next words?"

"Well, it looks like there's an *e*, followed by an *n*, right?"

"Yes."

"Which gives us *en*."

"And what's beneath the end of *y taliano*? Look closely, because it's hard."

"Well," said Moliarti, "it starts with a *c*, and then . . . then there's an *n*?"

"A *u*."

"Ah, yes. A *c* and a *u*. Then there's a *b*. That's a *b*, isn't it?"

"Yes, it is."

"And an *a*."

"Excellent. So, go ahead and read the whole phrase now."

"Nado en cuba."

Thomas beamed a knowing smile at Moliarti. "Get it?"

Moliarti read it again, unsure of himself. "No."

"Then let's go to the last word of the third line," said Thomas, pointing at the spot. "Here it says *'colo,'* which, in the corrected text, gives us *'colo nbo y taliano,'* that is, 'Colonbo, Italian.' The word *colo* wasn't tampered with, as you can see from the X-ray. But it reveals two letters that were originally a part of this word. What are they?"

Moliarti stared hard at the spot. "An *n* and an *a*."

"So what does that give us?"

"Na?"

"Yes. What do we get when we add this to *colo?"*

"Colo*na*?"

Thomas waited, hoping a light would come on in Moliarti's mind. "Go ahead. What's the original phrase as Rui de Pina originally wrote it?"

"Okay. It says *'colona nado en cuba.'* "

"Get it?"

"Not really."

Thomas ran his hand through his hair, impatient. "Okay, look. At the beginning of the sixteenth century, Rui de Pina wrote *Chronicle of King D. John II*. When he mentioned the famous meeting between Columbus and King John II on Columbus's return from the New World, Pina thought that this confidential detail was now obsolete. This original text was given to a copyist, who started working on the manuscript we now know as *Codex 632*. When he finished, someone who read it, presumably King Manuel himself, was horrified that Columbus's identity was revealed and had the information changed. At the end of the third line, where it said *'colona,'* the *na* was erased, leaving just *colo*. On the fourth line, where it says *'nado en cuba,'* the text was erased and *'nbo ytaliano'* was written over it. Since this last phrase is slightly shorter than the original, the copyist had to stretch out the word *ytaliano*, leaving *'y taliano.'* Even so, the spacing remained off. Pina's original manuscript was destroyed, and the other copies, known as *Pergaminho 9* and *Códice Alcobacense,* were copied from *Codex 632*. That's how *'Xpova colona nado en cuba,'* became *'Xpova colo nbo y taliano.'* " He paused. "Do you follow?"

"Yes," said Moliarti, still hesitant. "But what does *'colona nado en cuba'* actually mean?"

"Let's start with *'nado en cuba.' Nado en* is archaic Portuguese for *nascido em*, or 'born in.' 'Cuba' is his place of birth. *'Nado en cuba.' Nascido em Cuba*. Born in Cuba."

"Born in Cuba? But how is that possible? When he was born, as far as I know, Cuba hadn't been discovered."

Thomas laughed. "Come on, Nelson. He wasn't born on the island of Cuba."

"Oh. Well, where was he born then?"

"There's a village in the south of Portugal called Cuba. Now do you see?"

Moliarti finally understood.

"This information, incidentally, ties in perfectly with Columbus's family connections. Remember I told you that he fled to Castile in 1484 after the conspiracy to assassinate King John II, led by the duke of Viseu, who was also the duke of Beja? Beja is an important city in the south of Portugal. It's near the village of Cuba. The duke of Viseu and Beja had, as one would expect, family and friends in those regions. Columbus, born in Cuba, near Beja, was one of them.

"When the admiral arrived on the island we now call Cuba, he named it Juana. A short time later, however, he decided to change its name to Cuba." He gave Moliarti a questioning look. "Why? Why did he only change the name of one island? What was special about it?

Why didn't he do the same thing with the other islands? There's only one explanation. When he heard the natives calling it Colba, Columbus noted a certain similarity between this name and the name of his native village in Portugal and decided to rename the island. Instead of calling it Colba, as the locals did, he called it Cuba. Cuba, his true birthplace." Thomas winked. "A kind of private homage to his roots."

"I see," murmured Moliarti. "And what does *colona* mean?"

"It seems that this was Columbus's real surname. Colona. There really was a Portuguese family called Colona at the time. Their name was written both with one *n* and two. They were the Sciarra Colona, or Colonna family. Sciarra is a version of Guiarra. Or Guerra. Which ties up the loose ends of the mystery. Remember all that confusion about the admiral's names, which cropped up all over the place as Colon, Colom, Colomo, Colonus, Guiarra, and Guerra? His original name was not Columbus, a name he himself never used, but Sciarra Colonna. Do you remember that Ferdinand said he'd gone to Piacenza and found his ancestors' tombs? Well, the Colonna family was originally from Piacenza, like Columbus's first wife's paternal ancestors, the Palestrello family, whose name became Perestrello."

"So you're telling me Columbus was Portuguese of Italian extraction?"

"Cristóvam Colonna was a Portuguese nobleman of Italian and Portuguese origin, with Jewish ancestry. When the Sciarra Colonna family came here from Piacenza, they married into Portuguese nobility. It's no accident that Ferdinand said his father's true name would have been Christophorus Colonus in Latin. And since he was also called Sciarra, that explains how many different people, including Peter Martyr and witnesses who testified in the *Pleyto de la Prioridad* hearings, claimed that his true name was Guiarra or Guerra. Cristóvam Sciarra Colonna. Cristóvam Guiarra Colon. Cristóvam Guerra Colom."

"Where did his Jewish blood come from?"

"There were many Jews in Portugal at that time. They were protected by the nobility, who were their friends. It was natural that they should intermarry, or even have children out of wedlock. In fact, most Portuguese have Jewish blood in their veins, they just don't know it."

Moliarti gazed across the smooth surface of the water. The breeze began to pick up, and he took a deep breath, filling his lungs with the invigorating air of the vast estuary, savoring the aroma given off by the meeting of the river with the sea.

"Congratulations, Tom," he said finally in a monotone, without taking his eyes off the Tagus. "You've solved the mystery."

"I think so."

"You deserve the bonus." He fixed his gaze on Thomas. "Half a million dollars." He winked and gave him a strange, humorless half smile. "That's a lot of money, isn't it?"

"Um . . . yes," admitted Thomas. He felt embarrassed talking about the bonus, but at the same time, it had now become his main concern. Half a million dollars really was a lot of money. Lots and lots of money. It would, without a doubt, be a big help for Margarida.

"Okay, Tom," said Moliarti, resting his hand on Thomas's shoulder in an almost paternal gesture. "I'm going to tell New York and present my report. I'll call you to make arrangements to deliver the check. Okay?"

"Fine, of course."

Moliarti slipped the X-ray back into the giant envelope and waved it at Thomas. "This is the only copy, right?"

"Yes," said Thomas warily.

"So there aren't any others?"

"No."

"I'll keep this," he said.

He turned and crossed the fortress courtyard somewhat hurriedly, disappearing into the dark mouth of the small tower door under the elegant balcony that graced the south façade.

Thomas didn't hear from Moliarti for four days. Then, on the fifth evening, he called to arrange a meeting. The following morning Thomas drove along the seaside avenue with the car windows down, craving the cool ocean breeze on his face. He felt terribly alone. His nights were spent in agonizing solitude that he fought with pathetic attempts to drown himself in his work, preparing lessons, marking tests, reading any new paleographic studies he could get his hands on. Constance had cut all ties, reducing her contact to delivering Margarida for her every-other-weekend outings, but even this had been interrupted lately by spells of fever, which had forced his daughter to spend much of her time in bed. In a moment of desperation Thomas had even tried to contact Lena, but she had stopped coming to class and her cell phone no longer worked. He concluded that she'd probably given up her course study and left the country.

Rossio Square teemed with people, some in a hurry, their eyes glued to the sidewalk, others taking their time, staring into infinity, and still others sitting watching the mass of humanity scurrying about. Thomas sat outside at the Café Nicola, his legs crossed, gazing into his coffee with a vacant expression on his face.

Nelson Moliarti emerged from the crowd, wearing a suit and tie. He was forty minutes late.

"Sorry I'm late," he said. He pulled up a chair and sat down. "I was talking to John Savigliano in New York and time got away from me."

"No problem," said Thomas, forcing a smile. "It was my turn to wait. That's fair."

"Yes, but I don't like to be late."

Thomas called the waiter over and ordered. "How's Savigliano?"

"Oh, fine," said Moliarti, his gaze flitting about behind Thomas, as if he didn't want to look him in the eye. "John's fine. Now then, Tom, my instructions are to pay you the salary of five thousand dollars a week and the bonus of half a million, as agreed in New York." He cleared his throat. "When would you like it?"

"Well . . . now would be good."

Moliarti opened his briefcase and took out a check.

"I'll give you the check now then, Tom, but there's one matter to clear up."

"What?"

"It has to do with confidentiality."

"Confidentiality?" said Thomas in surprise. "I don't understand."

"All the work you did for us is confidential."

"Confidential?"

"Yes. Not a word about these discoveries."

Thomas scratched his chin, intrigued. "Is this some kind of commercial strategy?"

"It's our strategy."

"Yes, but what's the idea? To keep quiet for the time being and then make a big bang with the publication?"

Moliarti stared at Thomas. "Tom," he said, matter-of-factly. "There isn't going to be a publication. Not now, not ever."

Thomas sat for a long moment, unable to articulate his shock. "But . . . but . . . ," he stuttered. "It doesn't make sense. Aren't they convinced by the material? The proof is quite solid, Nelson. The subject is controversial, it's true. There'll be a negative reaction on the part of the establishment. Some historians will be furious if the official version is contested, and they'll say it's all a bunch of nonsense—"

"Tom."

"I can already see them, hysterical, beside themselves, cursing and shaking their fists at the sky. But when all said and done, the evidence we have is solid."

"Tom, we're not going to publish the investigation. Period."

Thomas leaned forward, getting as close as he could to Moliarti. "Nelson, we've made an extraordinary discovery. We've dug up a five-hundred-year-old secret. We've solved an enigma that has intrigued historians for centuries. We've shone a light on a dark area of scholarship. Why keep people ignorant?"

"It's for the best."

"I'm sorry, Nelson, but that's not an answer. Why don't they think these discoveries should be revealed?"

Moliarti ignored the question. "Tom, you already signed a confidentiality agreement."

"What?"

Moliarti placed a legal document on the table, the contract he'd signed in New York. "You will get nothing if you go public. In addition, the foundation can sue you for breach of contract." Moliarti read it aloud from start to finish. It stated that the Americas History Foundation agreed to pay Thomas Noronha five hundred thousand dollars in exchange for his work and the promise not to reveal anything about the investigations he had conducted on behalf of the institution. He was forbidden to discuss the discoveries in articles, essays, interviews, and press conferences, and was not allowed to reveal the names of anyone involved in the process under any circumstances. There was also a penalty clause stating that in the event of breach of contract, Thomas would have to pay the foundation double what he had been paid. All told, that came to a million dollars. The document seemed ironclad.

"You can't do this."

"Yes, I can."

"Do you think I'm for sale? Do you really think it's possible to shut me up with money, however much it is?"

"Tom, the discoveries you made in the course of the investigation *belong* to the foundation, and the foundation will decide what to do with them."

"This investigation, Nelson, belongs to Professor Toscano. I merely followed the clues he left."

"Toscano was working for the foundation."

"He was studying Brazil for the foundation, not Columbus."

"He used the foundation's funds to study Columbus's origins; therefore, his work belongs to us. He signed the same contract you did."

"Now I see why Toscano's widow loathes you."

"That's neither here nor there. What matters is that your investigation and Toscano's work belong to the foundation."

"They belong to humanity."

"Humanity didn't pay the bills, Tom. We also explained all this to Professor Toscano."

"And what did he think?"

Moliarti was momentarily at a loss for words. He cocked his head and smiled. "He had a different point of view."

"I'm sorry, Nelson, but none of this makes sense."

Moliarti was quiet for a moment, deciding what to reveal. Almost instinctively, he glanced around at the people near their table, took a deep breath, and leaned toward Thomas again. "Tom," he said, almost whispering. "What do you know about the Americas History Foundation?"

"Well, um . . . it fosters . . . American studies," he said impatiently. "You're a part of the foundation. You should know."

"I'm just an employee," said Moliarti, pressing his hand to his chest. "I'm not the owner. The boss is John Savigliano. He's the president and chairman of the executive board. Do you know the other people on the board?"

"No."

"Jack Mordenti is the vice president. And there's Paul Morelli and Mario Ghirotto. Don't these names mean anything to you?"

"No."

"Look, Tom." He held up a finger for each name. "Savigliano, Mordenti, Morelli, Ghirotto. Even John's secretary, Mrs. Racca, that sour-looking woman you met in New York. What names are these?"

"What names are these? I'm sorry, but I don't understand the question—"

"What's their ethnic origin?"

"Italian?"

"Yes, but where from?"

Thomas looked sideways at Moliarti.

"From Genoa, Tom. Italians from Genoa. The Americas History Foundation is an institution financed by the Genoese." He clenched his teeth. "These people are very proud to share a hometown with the man who discovered America, the most famous man in history after Jesus Christ. Do you really think they would publish a study that proves that Columbus wasn't Genoese after all, but Portuguese?" He tapped his forehead. "Never."

Thomas sat paralyzed, understanding everything but unable to believe it.

"You . . . you're Genoese?"

"*They* are Genoese," he said, offering a strained smile. "I'm not. I was born in Boston and my family's from Brindisi, in the south of Italy."

"Whatever, Nelson, what difference does nationality make? Didn't Umberto Eco among others recognize that Columbus wasn't Italian?"

"Umberto Eco isn't Genoese," said Moliarti.

"But he's Italian."

Moliarti sighed. "Let's not be naïve, Tom," he said patiently. "If the foundation were run by Americans originally from Piacenza, you can be sure these discoveries would be published immediately. Other Italians or Italian Americans, even if they weren't happy about it, would be willing to divulge these revelations. But you have to understand that it's too much to ask of the Genoese."

"The truth is the truth. I'm sorry, Nelson, but I don't understand. Even if I promise to keep my mouth shut and receive your bribe, what's to say I won't have a word on the side with a colleague and tell him to go see *Codex 632* for himself?"

Moliarti smiled and leaned back in his chair, strangely confident. "Do you know why I was late to our meeting?"

"You already told me you were talking to Savigliano."

"That's what I told you. The truth is that I was glued to the radio and the television." He winked. "Have you seen the news today, Tom?"

"What news?"

"The news about the break-in. At the National Library last night."

A repairman was standing on a table working on replacing the glass in the window, when Thomas burst into the archives reading room. A cleaning lady was sweeping up shards of glass scattered across the floor, and there was a hammering back in the archives, no doubt the sound of a carpenter at work.

"That door should be locked; we're closed, Mr. Noronha," said a voice. It was Alexandra behind the counter, flushed and nervously wringing her hands.

"What happened?" asked Thomas.

"When I got to work this morning I found that window over there smashed in, and the door to the manuscript archive open." Alexandra waved her hand in front of her face like a fan. "Good God, my cheeks are still burning." She sighed. "I'm sorry, Mr. Noronha. I'm really shaken up."

"What did they take?"

"They took my peace of mind, Mr. Noronha. They took my peace of mind." She pressed her hand to her chest.

"But what did they take?"

"We still don't know. We're taking an inventory of the manuscripts to see if there's anything missing." She sighed heavily, as if there was still steam bottled up inside her. "If you ask me, it was the work of drug addicts. There are these kids that hang around the place—pretty rough around the edges, all unshaven and dirty. They're not students, no siree. I know what they're like. These ones are real hoodlums, you know?" She held her fingers to her mouth, pretending to hold a cigarette. "They're on dope, hashish, and God knows what else. They go around stealing computers to sell for peanuts. So—"

"Let me see *Codex 632*," cut in Thomas, impatient.

"What?"

"Go get *Codex 632*, please. I need to see it."

"But, Mr. Noronha, we're closed. You'll have to—"

"Bring me *Codex 632*." He opened his eyes very wide to show he was unwilling to discuss the matter. "Now."

Alexandra hesitated, surprised at his vehemence, but decided not to argue and disappeared into the room where the ancient manuscripts were kept. Thomas sat down and drummed nervously on a table with his fingers, preparing for the worst. Instants later, Alexandra came back into the reading room.

"And?"

"Here it is." She was holding a brown leather-bound book. Seeing it safe and sound, Thomas sighed with relief. "Moliarti, you bastard. You scared the shit out of me," he muttered under his breath.

Alexandra handed him the manuscript, and Thomas felt its weight. Then he examined the front and back covers. Impeccable. The manuscript number was still attached to the spine. He opened it and studied the title in sixteenth-century Portuguese: *Chronicle of King D. John II.* He leafed through the yellow pages until he got to page seventy-six. He looked for the fourth line and gazed at the first words: '*nbo y taliano.*' There were the suspicious spaces between the words. He ran the tip of his finger over the line to feel where it had been tampered with, but the surface was clean. He frowned, surprised, and tried again.

Completely smooth.

He looked more closely, almost not believing his eyes. There was no trace of the alteration. Nothing at all. It was as if it had never existed. He put his hand to his mouth, dumbfounded, as his heart suddenly dropped. He didn't know what to think. He studied the entire page, looking for vestiges of cuts, traces of tears, signs of gluing, differences in the paper, a small imperfection, anything, small as it might be. But he found nothing. The page looked immaculate, genuine. Only the alteration had disappeared. The work of professionals, he thought, almost on the verge of tears. He shook his head, deeply dismayed. The conclusion was inescapable, final. Professional forgers. They had copied the original page and replaced it with another, without leaving any marks, covering any traces of their work, hiding all clues. Professionals.

"Fucking bastards."

Chapter 21

He had stopped hoping for her voice on the other end of the phone, so when Constance did call, the joy in his reply was unmistakable.

"Oh, hi," said Thomas, trying to control himself; he felt surprised and happy but was still aching inside and didn't want to sound relieved. "How are you?"

"I don't know," said Constance. "Dr. Oliveira wants to talk to us this morning."

"This morning? I can't. I have to go to the Tower of Tombo—"

"He said it's urgent. We have to be at Santa Marta Hospital at eleven."

Thomas glanced at his watch. It was nine thirty.

"Why the hurry?"

"I don't know. Yesterday I took Margarida to the hospital for some tests, and he didn't say anything."

"And what was the result of the tests?"

"They said they'd give them to me today."

"Hmm," said Thomas, rubbing his eyes, suddenly feeling tired.

"I think they've found something." Constance could barely disguise her apprehension.

They met at the outpatient clinic an hour and a half later. Constance was wearing a gray tailored skirt and jacket that made her look like an executive. They found themselves in the cloister of the old convent, now a cardiology hospital. Stricken, Constance explained that she'd brought Margarida to the hospital the previous day for a routine test that the doctor had asked for some time ago. The clinician had noticed Margarida's wan complexion and lethargy, which she'd been experiencing ever since the fever began, and wanted to check that everything was okay. Since Margarida's skin wasn't bluish, which would have been an indication that her heart condition was worsening, the doctor didn't feel it was urgent, although he'd insisted on taking blood and urine tests.

They took the elevator up to the pediatric cardiology ward on the third floor and found the doctor at the nurses' station in intensive care. Oliveira waved for them to follow him to his office, which was bright and airy.

"I have Margarida's tests here," he announced once they were seated. He fidgeted and played with a piece of paper. "It's not good news," he said with a heavy voice. "It looks like we might be dealing with leukemia."

The office fell silent as Thomas and Constance tried to absorb the news.

"Leukemia?" said Thomas finally. "But does this have anything to do with her heart?"

"No. It's not a cardiovascular problem. It's a hematological problem. To do with the blood." He held up the lab results and pointed to a number. "Margarida has an excessive number of white blood cells." He pointed at another figure. "This is the hemoglobin level. She has seven grams, when the normal rate is twelve. It's a sign of anemia."

"Leukemia is cancer of the blood," said Constance in a trembling voice, barely managing to suppress her sobs. "It's serious, isn't it?"

"Very serious. To be honest, this kind of leukemia is called acute leukemia, and it's more common in children with Down syndrome."

"But can it be treated?" asked Thomas, feeling panic setting in.

"Yes, of course."

"Then what do we have to do?"

"This problem is outside of my area of specialty. Acute leukemia can only be treated at the Oncology Institute. I know some excellent professionals there. After seeing these results, I took the liberty of consulting a colleague at the institute to discuss what to do next." He locked his eyes on Constance. "Where's Margarida right now?"

"Margarida? At school."

"Okay. Go get her, take her to the Oncology Institute, and admit her immediately."

Thomas and Constance looked at each other in shock. "Right now?"

"Now," insisted the doctor, "immediately." He wrote down a name on a piece of paper. "When you get to the Oncology Institute, ask for Dr. Tulipa. She's looking after everything and will take the case."

"Margarida's going to be okay, isn't she?"

"Like I told you, this isn't my specialty, but she'll receive excellent care," said the doctor, trying to offer words of comfort. "Dr. Tulipa will have to diagnose her, explain everything to you, and present the best solutions."

Déjà vu. Constance sobbed all the way to the school, blowing her nose on a lacy handkerchief. Beside her, firmly clutching the steering wheel, Thomas was silent, overwhelmed with helplessness and dejection. They both realized that it was just the beginning and they weren't sure they'd be able to survive the devastating emotions. They were just two disoriented human beings lost in a labyrinth of worries; parents made desperate by the new trick fate had played on them. Indignation ate at them from the inside.

When they got to the school, Thomas made Constance promise not to shed a tear in front of their daughter. Smiling with lumps in their throats, hearts constricted, they told her they'd have to go to the hospital.

"Am I sick again?" asked Margarida with fear in her eyes.

The trip to the Oncology Institute was painful, with Margarida hollering that she didn't want to go. She soon grew tired, however, and the last leg of the journey was almost in silence, broken only by an occasional groan from Margarida and her mother's attempts to comfort her. Sunk into the backseat of the car, Constance held her daughter in a protective embrace, ensconcing her in a shell of affection.

Margarida was placed under the care of Dr. Tulipa, a sprightly middle-aged woman with thick glasses and gray hair. She led Margarida into what looked like a small operating room, which frightened her parents.

"It's okay, we're not going to operate yet," she said. "I had a look at the results of the blood tests Dr. Oliveira sent me, and I see we're going to have to do a bone-marrow aspiration. We collect some cells from the bone marrow, in her hip, to confirm the diagnosis."

The procedure was carried out with a local anesthetic and in the presence of Thomas and Constance, who kept comforting and encouraging Margarida. When it was over, the bone-marrow samples were placed on glass slides and taken to the lab. The doctor questioned Constance and Thomas about the problems their daughter had been experiencing over the last month, and they described her paleness, fatigue, fevers, and even nosebleeds. Dr. Tulipa didn't go into any detail about what was happening, saying that only the lab results could give them more certainty. Hours later, Tulipa called them into her austere office.

"The results are back," she announced. "Margarida has acute myeloblastic leukemia."

Thomas and Constance stared at the doctor in despair. "I'm sorry, Doctor," blurted out Constance, at her wits' end. "Please tell us what it means in terms we can understand."

The doctor sighed. "I'm sure you know what leukemia is—"

"It's blood cancer."

"That's one way of defining it."

"You said that Margarida has an acute form of leukemia," said Thomas.

"Acute myeloblastic leukemia," she corrected him, "it is relatively common among children with Down syndrome and involves the uncontrolled growth of myeloblasts, which are immature forms of white blood cells." She looked at the test results. "Margarida has two hundred and fifty thousand myeloblasts per cubic millimeter, when she should have a maximum of ten thousand."

"You said this kind of leukemia is dangerous. How dangerous?"

"It can kill."

"In how long?"

"A few days."

Thomas and Constance stared at the doctor, hearing but not wanting to believe their ears.

"A few *days*?"

"Yes."

Constance clapped her hand to her mouth, her eyes watering.

"What can we do?" asked Thomas in utter dismay.

"We're going to start chemotherapy immediately to try and stabilize the situation."

"Will it cure her?"

"It's my duty to explain the reality of your daughter's situation to you. So I'm obliged to tell you that there's a high mortality rate with these cases."

Thomas and Constance looked at each other; this was much worse than they had anticipated. They were both fully aware that their daughter, with the heart problems she'd had since birth, was at the edge of the precipice, but they weren't at all prepared for the possibility of losing her so suddenly. Everything seemed so arbitrary and unfair, their daughter's life subject to a despotic and random game of dice. The possibility of Margarida's death had become surrealistically real, palpable, and threatening.

"How high is the mortality rate?" asked Thomas in a low voice, horrified at his own question and fearing the answer as he had never before feared anything.

"The global survival rate for acute myeloblastic leukemia is somewhere between thirty-five and sixty percent, I'm afraid." She sighed again, depressed by the bad news she was obliged to give. "You have to be strong and be prepared for the worst. You need to know that only one in two survive this kind of leukemia."

Constance and Thomas were devastated. In front of Margarida, however, they put on positive faces, trying to keep her spirits up during the violent treatment she began immediately. The doctors put her through an aggressive course of polychemotherapy, combining several medications with strategies to try to prevent complications due to infections and hemorrhaging. Margarida was given a spinal tap to withdraw fluid for cytological testing, and medications were injected directly into her spinal column. The idea was to completely destroy the cancerous cells in an attempt to force the bone marrow to produce normal cells again.

Soon, Margarida lost all of her hair and grew thinner. The polychemotherapy began to yield results, however. The control exams showed that the number of myeloblasts was dropping dramatically. When it became clear that the situation would soon stabilize, Dr. Tulipa called another meeting with Constance and Thomas.

"I believe Margarida will go into remission in the next week," she announced.

They glanced at each other suspiciously. "What exactly does that mean in this case, Doctor?"

"That the number of myeloblasts will return to normal," she explained. "But in my opinion, the situation will remain unstable and this remission will be temporary. Margarida needs a bone-marrow transplant."

"Is that possible?"

"Yes."

"In Portugal?"

"Yes."

Constance and Thomas glanced at each other again, as if seeking mutual consent, and looked back at the doctor. "So what are we waiting for? Let's do it."

Tulipa took off her glasses and rubbed her eyes with her fingertips. "We have a problem." There was a silence.

"What problem?" Thomas finally whispered.

"Our transplant units are congested. We won't be able to get Margarida operated on for a month."

"So?"

"I don't know if she'll last that long. My colleagues think she will, but I have my doubts."

"You don't think Margarida can wait a month?"

"She can. But it's risky." She put her glasses back on and looked at Thomas. "Do you want to put your daughter's life even more in peril?"

"No. Of course not."

"So there's only one option. Margarida will have to be operated on overseas."

"Let's do it."

"But it's expensive."

"Doesn't the government pay?"

"Yes, usually, but not in this case. Because it's possible to operate in Portugal and because we can't prove the urgency, the government doesn't feel obliged to pay for operations abroad."

"But isn't the urgency proven?"

"In my opinion it is. But not in my colleagues' opinion. Unfortunately, theirs will prevail as far as the government is concerned."

"I'll talk to them."

"You can talk all you want, but you'll be wasting your breath. While you're busy chasing down resources and filing requests, time will be running out. And time is a luxury your daughter doesn't have at the moment."

"Then we'll pay for it ourselves."

"It's expensive."

"How much?"

"I looked into the matter and found a pediatric hospital in London that could operate on Margarida next week. I sent them the genetic references of Margarida's chromosome 6, they ran some tests and found a compatible donor, a miraculous thing in itself. As soon as she goes into remission, which I believe will be in the next week, she'll be fit to be transferred to London and operated on immediately."

"How much will it cost?" Thomas asked quietly.

"The cost of the transplant, plus her hospital stay, should be somewhere in the vicinity of fifty thousand dollars."

Thomas lowered his head, feeling weary and impotent. "I have to go make a phone call."

The turquoise water of the swimming pool glittered under the sun, serene and inviting, a pause in the greenery surrounding Pavilhão, the Lapa Palace Hotel's outdoor restaurant. The sky was bright and welcoming, with the deep indigo characteristic of springtime; the day had dawned so radiant that Nelson Moliarti had chosen this restaurant for the urgent meeting Thomas had requested. Thomas crossed the garden and found the American, immaculately dressed and sporting a tan, sitting at a table under a white sun umbrella, drinking a glass of freshly squeezed orange juice.

"You don't look so good," observed Moliarti, noticing Thomas's pale skin and the rings under his eyes. "Have you been sick?"

"It's my daughter," explained Thomas. He pulled up a chair and stared off into space.

There was a long silence as they watched a tall, dark-skinned girl in large sunglasses and a red bikini walk around the edge of the pool with a towel over her shoulder. She tossed the towel over a deck chair, took off her glasses, and lay down facing the sun, surrendering to the idle pleasure of a worry-free life.

"I need money," Thomas said finally, breaking the silence.

Moliarti took a sip of juice. "How much?"

"Lots."

"When?"

"Now. My daughter needs to have an operation overseas. I need money."

Moliarti sighed. "As you know, we have over half a million dollars to pay you. The check you left on the table at our last meeting. But it seems unwise for you to accept it while you're still telling me you're planning on breaking your contract."

"I know. I have no intention of breaking my contract."

"Half a million dollars, huh? You're going to be rich," he said. "You're going to be able to pay for your daughter's treatment and win your wife back."

Thomas stared at him questioningly. "My wife?"

"You're going to be able to win her back, aren't you? With all this money—"

"How do you know my wife and I are separated?"

Moliarti looked at Thomas in embarrassment. "You told me."

"No I didn't." Thomas's tone of voice was becoming aggressive. "How do you know?"

"Someone must have told me."

"Who? Who told you?"

"Hmm . . . I can't remember. Hey, there's no need to get upset—"

"Don't give me that shit, Nelson. How do you know my wife and I have separated?"

"I don't know. I heard it somewhere."

"Bullshit, Nelson. I'm not leaving until you explain this properly. How do you know?"

"Look, I don't know. It doesn't matter, does it?"

"Nelson. Has the foundation been spying on me?"

"Let's just say we've stayed informed."

"How?"

"It's not important."

"How?" Thomas almost shouted. The people around them turned to stare. Moliarti gestured for Thomas to calm down.

"Tom, take it easy."

"I'm not going to take it easy, damn it! I'm not leaving until you tell me."

Moliarti sighed. Thomas was on the verge of a public meltdown. "Okay, okay. I'll tell you, but you have to make me a promise."

"What promise?"

"That you will not make a scene."

"That depends."

"No, it doesn't depend. I'll only tell you if you do not draw attention to us, and if you do not tell anyone about this conversation."

"Yes. Tell me."

Moliarti sighed again. He took another sip of orange juice, and the waiter came back with Thomas's green tea.

"Ding Gu Da Fang tea," he announced, then disappeared.

"This operation was very important to us," explained Moliarti. "In the course of his research, initially focused on the pre-Cabral discovery of Brazil, Professor Toscano accidentally stumbled upon an unknown document."

"What document?"

"Presumably the one you found."

"Codex 632?"

"Yes."

"The one you people adulterated when you broke in to the National Library?"

"I don't know what you're talking about."

"Yes you do. You rubbed it in my face."

"Do you want to hear the story or not?"

"Go ahead."

"Well . . . so, because of this document, Toscano started looking into the one thing the foundation would never have asked him to investigate. The true origins of Christopher Columbus. We tried to set him back on track, asking him to focus on his research into the discovery of Brazil, but he dug his heels in and continued his study in secret. There was panic in the foundation. We considered the possibility of dismissing him, but that wouldn't have stopped him following through with the investigation. His discovery was too hot. And, besides, there was the problem of the document, since we didn't know what it was or where it was archived. When he died, under strangely providential circumstances in my opinion, we tried to locate it. We went through his papers but only found a handful of incomprehensible ciphers.

"That was when we had the idea to hire you. We needed someone who was Portuguese, a historian, and a cryptanalyst, who could get inside the professor's mind and unravel the secret. It became evident that in reconstructing the entire investigation, you were also going to come to the conclusion that Columbus was not Genoese, and we couldn't risk having the whole situation with Professor Toscano repeat itself. That was when John had an idea. He has some friends with some American oil companies in Angola and asked them if they knew a high-class prostitute who spoke Portuguese well. They introduced him to a stunning young lady, and John hired her on the spot."

Thomas was stupefied. What a fool he'd been.

"Lena."

"Her real name is Emma."

"You bastards!"

"You promised not to get worked up." Moliarti paused, staring at Thomas. "Are you going to make scene?"

Thomas made a Herculean effort to control his fury. He took a deep breath and tried to relax. "No. Go on."

"You must understand that it was very important to the foundation that things didn't start going wrong again. You kept me updated on a regular basis, but how could we be sure you were telling us everything? Emma was our guarantee. She had lived for several years in Angola, where she cavorted with foreign big shots in the oil industry. She knew how to handle herself, and turned clients down when she didn't like them, no matter who they were. We showed her a photo of you, she liked it, and she accepted the job. You should be flattered! We got her tutors so she'd be believable as a student and sent her to Lisbon before we even got in touch with you."

"But I broke it off with her."

"Yes, that threw a wrench in the works," said Moliarti, nodding. "For God's sake, man! It takes balls to give a gorgeous gal like that marching orders! I was impressed. That was some feat! And a big headache for us"—he held out his hands to show how big—"because we lost our most reliable source of information. That was when John had the idea that she should go talk to your wife. He thought that if your wife kicked you out, you might take up with Emma again. As predicted, your wife packed her things and left, and we waited to see if you'd take Emma back."

"Where is she now?"

"We terminated her contract, and I don't know where she is now. It doesn't matter."

Thomas took a deep breath, shocked and sickened by the whole story. "That was my marriage, you assholes! How could you?"

Moliarti lowered his head and resumed filling out the check. "Yeah," he admitted. "It wasn't our finest hour. But what can you do? That's life." He handed the check to Thomas. Typed in blue ink were eight numbers, a five and five zeros. Half a million dollars.

The price of silence.

Chapter 22

LONDON

The neoclassical façade of the majestic British Museum slid past on their left. The black cab drove down Great Russell Street and turned onto Montague. Margarida, an enormous blue ski cap covering her bald head, sat with her nose pressed to the window, steaming up the glass. She gazed at the unfamiliar streets, with their cold gray and white exoticism, but felt there was something welcoming about the city, with its clean spaces, elegant buildings, well-pruned trees carpeting the ground with their leaves, and the people walking down the sidewalks wrapped in cream-colored overcoats and clutching dark umbrellas.

A fine rain was falling when Thomas opened the cab door and gazed at the enormous building in front of him. Russell Square NHS Hospital for Children was a vast complex in a centuries-old four-story building. Margarida got out on her own and Constance took her hand, while Thomas paid the driver and got their suitcases out of the trunk. Inside, a receptionist checked her computer for the reservation they had made from Lisbon. While Constance filled out Margarida's admission form, Thomas signed an Undertaking to Pay form and a check for forty-five thousand dollars, the estimated cost of the treatment.

"If expenses exceed this estimate, you'll have to pay the difference," the receptionist told him very matter-of-factly, as if this was no more than a simple commercial transaction. "Okay?"

"Yes."

"Three days after the treatment is finished you'll receive a final bill, which you'll have twenty-eight days to settle."

Now acting like a hotel receptionist, she gave them directions to the ward and room where Margarida would be staying. They took the elevator up to the second floor and came out in a small foyer, where a sign indicated three different wards. They headed for the Grail Ward, a quiet corridor in the hematology unit. Thomas couldn't help but smile at the name. Whoever drank from the Holy Grail would receive eternal life. What name was more appropriate for a blood-disease unit whose purpose was to offer renewed hope? They found the nurse on duty, and she took them to Margarida's room. There were two beds, one for the patient and the other for a parent, separated by a nightstand with a lamp on it and a vase of purple-petaled flowers.

"What are these, Mommy?" asked Margarida, pointing at the flowers.

"They're violets."

"Tell me the story," begged Margarida, settling onto the bed with an expectant expression. Thomas put down their suitcases and Constance sat next to her daughter.

"Once upon a time there was a beautiful girl called Io. She was so beautiful that the powerful Greek god Zeus fell in love with her. But Zeus's wife, Hera, wasn't at all happy about it, and overcome with jealousy, she asked Zeus why he was paying the girl so much attention. Zeus said it wasn't true and turned Io into a heifer to disguise her. He gave her a field of delicious purple violets to graze on. But Hera was still suspicious and sent a gadfly to torment her. Io became desperate and threw herself into the sea, now known as the Ionian Sea, in her honor. Hera convinced Io to never see Zeus again and, in exchange, turned her back into a girl. The word *violet* comes from Io. These flowers represent innocent love."

"Why?"

"Because Io was innocent. It wasn't her fault that Zeus liked her, was it?"

"No," said Margarida, shaking her head.

The nurse, who had gone to get a form, came back to the room to fill in a questionnaire. She was a middle-aged woman, with her hair pulled back into a bun, and she wore a white-and-blue pinafore. Her name was Margaret, but she asked them to call her Maggie. She leaned against the headboard of Margarida's bed and asked questions about her everyday routine, the food she liked, and her clinical history. She had Margarida hop onto a scale and measured her height. She took her temperature, pulse, blood pressure, and respiration rate.

Thomas and Constance started unpacking. They put toiletries in the bathroom and sat Margarida's favorite redheaded doll on the bed. Constance's clothes were also stowed in the drawers, since she was going to sleep in the other bed for two nights until the day of the operation.

A balding, potbellied man in white scrubs came into the room.

"Hello!" he said, holding out his hand. "I'm Dr. Stephen Penrose, and I'll be operating on your daughter."

They shook hands, and the doctor immediately set about examining Margarida again. He asked more questions about her clinical history and called in the nurse, whom he asked to take Margarida for another bone-marrow aspiration. Maggie took Margarida by the hand, and Constance got up to go with her, but the doctor motioned for her to stay in the room.

"I think this is the best time to clarify any doubts you might have," he said. "I assume you know the details of this surgery."

"Not very well," admitted Thomas.

The doctor sat on Margarida's bed. "What we're going to do is replace the sick bone marrow, removing all of the cells and injecting normal cells, which will produce new marrow. This is an allogeneic transplant, and the normal cells are coming from a compatible donor."

"Who is he?"

"He's just a chap who's going to earn a bit of extra money," the doctor said with a smile. "There are no health implications for him, and he'll have a few more quid to spend at the pub. Your daughter's marrow will be completely destroyed, and she'll receive the new marrow just as someone would receive a blood transfusion. The entire process is incredibly complicated and there are high risks involved. The new marrow will take at least two weeks to develop, and this is the critical period." He adopted a more serious tone of voice. "During these two weeks, Margarida will be very susceptible to hemorrhaging and infections. If she's attacked by bacteria, her body won't be able to produce enough white blood cells to fight off the attack. She's going to be very vulnerable."

Thomas rubbed his forehead, digesting the problem. "But how are you going to stop bacteria from getting into her body?"

"By placing her in isolation in a sterilized room. It's the only thing we can do."

"What if she gets an infection anyway?"

"She won't have any immunity."

"And what does that mean?"

"It means she might not survive."

Thomas and Constance knew that not performing the transplant was even riskier. But it didn't console them. They wished they could put everything off, pretend the problem didn't exist, sweep it under the carpet.

"But the good news," said the doctor, feeling obliged to introduce something positive, "is that after these two critical weeks, her new marrow will begin to produce a large quantity of normal cells, and Margarida will probably be cured of leukemia. Of course she will need a careful follow-up program, but that's something to worry about later."

The prospect of a cure buoyed Thomas and Constance; they felt hope replaced by despair, then hope again, in a hellish sequence, almost all within the blink of an eye, as they were forced to live with contradictory emotions at the same time.

At seven thirty in the morning on the third day, Maggie entered Margarida's room and gave her a sedative. Constance and Thomas had spent the night wide awake, sitting on the other bed staring at their daughter as she slept serenely. The nurse's arrival brought them back to reality. Constance looked at Maggie and almost unconsciously allowed her thoughts to flow, by association, to a death row inmate, being fetched by guards and brought before a firing squad. She had to pinch herself to convince herself that the nurse wasn't taking her daughter away to kill her but to save her. It's to save her, she repeated to herself, seeking comfort in this thought.

It's to save her.

They transferred Margarida onto a gurney and wheeled her down the Grail Ward corridor to the operating room. Margarida was awake but sleepy. "Am I going to dream, Mommy?" she murmured groggily.

"Yes, honey. Pink dreams."

"Pink dreams," she repeated, in an almost singsong voice.

Dr. Penrose, barely recognizable behind his mask and scrub cap, was at the operating room door. "Don't worry," he said, his voice muffled by the mask. "Everything will be fine."

The doors swung open and the gurney disappeared inside, wheeled by Maggie. The doors closed, and Thomas and Constance stood staring at them for a full minute, as if Margarida had been stolen from them. Then they went back to her room and busied themselves packing their suitcases, since Margarida wouldn't be returning there after the operation. They moved slowly, to fill the hours, but time moved even more slowly and they soon found themselves sitting on the bed with their suitcases packed, fretting.

The torture ended two hours later. Penrose appeared in front of them without a mask, his confident smile immediately reassuring them.

"It went well," he announced. "The transplant was successful and there were no complications."

They were back on the roller-coaster; the worry that had reigned just a minute before was replaced by joy.

"Where is she?" asked Constance, repressing an urge to kiss the doctor.

"She's been transferred to an isolation room at the other end of the wing."

"Can we see her?"

Penrose gestured for them to be patient. "Not yet. She's sleeping and it's best to let her be."

"But when will we be able to see her?"

The doctor laughed. "Don't worry, you'll be able to see her this afternoon. If I were you, I'd go out, get some lunch somewhere, and come back at around three. She should be awake by that time, and you can visit her."

Thomas and Constance left the hospital awash with a pleasant feeling of hope, as if they were being carried along on a soft spring breeze. It went well, the doctor had said. Everything had gone well. What wonderful words, so benign, so soothing. They would never have imagined that such a simple sentence could be so powerful. It was as if those three words were magic, capable, all by themselves, of changing reality, of determining a happy ending.

It went well.

They wandered the streets, giggling over the slightest thing. The colors were brighter and the air seemed more pure. They headed down Southampton Row to Holborn Station, where they turned right on New Oxford Street. At Tottenham Court Road and Charing Cross, they crossed the large intersection and lost themselves in the lively confusion of Oxford Street, window-shopping and people watching. They started feeling hungry and headed for Soho, where they had teriyaki in a Japanese restaurant. After a long walk to allow their food to digest, they ended up back at Russell Square shortly before three.

Nurse Maggie told them she was going to take them to see Margarida. Thomas was worried about carrying microbes into the room, but Maggie smiled and reassured him. She had them wash their hands and faces and gave them scrubs, gloves, and masks to put on. "You'll have to keep a distance," she said as she showed them the way.

"But isn't there a risk of bacteria getting in when the door opens?" asked Constance.

"That's not a problem. The air in the room is sterilized and kept at a higher atmospheric pressure than normal, which means when the doors open, the outside air can't get in."

"And how does she eat?"

"With her mouth, of course."

"Isn't there a danger getting an infection from the food?"

"Her meals are also sterilized."

They arrived in the hematology unit's post-op isolation area, and Maggie opened the door. "This is it," she said.

The air was cool and had an antiseptic smell. Propped up with a cushion, Margarida was chattering with a nurse. She looked up and smiled at the sight of her parents. "Hi," she said.

The nurse gestured for them to keep a distance, so Thomas and Constance sat at the end of the bed.

"Gimme kisses," Margarida said, holding her arms out.

"I want to, honey, but the doctor says I can't," said Constance, her voice breaking.

"Why?"

"Because there are some little critters inside me and if I give you a kiss, I might give them to you."

"Really?" said Margarida in surprise. "You've got critters?"

"Yes."

"Yuck!" exclaimed Margarida in disgust.

They sat talking until Maggie returned an hour later and asked them to leave. They arranged a time for their daily visits and said good-bye with lots of waving and kisses blown from fingertips.

Over the next days, Thomas felt his heart leap whenever visiting hour was drawing near. He'd arrive at the hospital early and sit nervously on the sofa in the waiting room, his eyes tuned in to every movement, straining to contain his anxiety. This restlessness, tempered by a sweet trace of something he couldn't put his finger on, only abated when Constance walked through the door, generally ten minutes before the hour. The restlessness was then replaced by a subtle tension, uncomfortable but strangely desired. It had become the high point of his day, the moment he lived for. This was how he followed the recovery of his daughter, who remained expansive and good-humored, even when she had several bouts of fever, which Penrose said was normal. But he couldn't deny that Margarida wasn't the only reason that it had become the best part of the day.

There was Constance.

Their conversations in the waiting room were awkward, full of fits and starts, punctuated by embarrassed silences and subtexts, subtle allusions and ambiguous gestures. By the third day, Thomas found himself planning things to talk about ahead of time. While bathing or gulping down his breakfast, he'd establish a kind of script, taking mental note of topics to cover while they waited to see Margarida. When Constance arrived for their daily visit, he reeled off his list of topics like a student in an oral exam. When he finished one he'd quickly go to the next, and so on. They talked about films, books they'd seen in bookshops on Charing Cross Road, an exhibition at the Tate Gallery, the flowers on sale in Covent Garden, the state of the education system in Portugal, where the country was headed, poems, friends, and stories from their common past. Soon there were no more silences, until the deafening one that descended upon the waiting room that day.

They sat without speaking for a long time, staring at the walls, playing a game of nerves, patience, and wounded self-respect. Neither of them wanted to make the first move, appear weak, swallow pride, heal open wounds, pick up the pieces and rebuild whatever was still salvageable. The visiting hour arrived and they pretended not to have noticed, both sitting on the sofa waiting for the other one to give in. Until one of them realized that someone would have to make a compromise or give a sign. After all, Margarida was waiting for them on the other side of the corridor.

"I can't wait to see Margarida," Constance finally murmured, before getting up.

"Wait, don't go." Thomas held her hand in his, and she stopped, still not looking him in the eye. "Will you ever forgive me?"

Constance remained silent, and looked up at the white, sterile ceiling of the hospital corridor. She sighed, as though the games one plays in love and marriage were, for her, too much to bear. After several seconds of saying nothing, she answered, "Do you think forgiveness is even possible? Given the situation?"

"I don't know," Thomas answered, lowering his eyes. "Is it?"

She bit her lip. "You know, my mom can be a very wise woman when she wants to. She says there are some things in life that can never be forgiven. Ever."

"I see," Thomas managed to mumble.

Constance let go of Thomas's hand and walked toward Margarida's room. Before entering, she stopped, turned around, and finally looked Thomas in the eye. She smiled faintly.

"My mother's opinion isn't necessarily mine."

Thomas spent the next morning walking. He left the hotel with a growing feeling of confidence. Things were clearly coming together, little by little. In spite of her intermittent fevers, Margarida was withstanding the effects of the transplant; and Constance, although still keeping a proud distance, seemed emotionally available. He knew he'd have to move with tact, of course, but he was now convinced that, if he played his cards right, reconciliation was possible.

To keep his mind off his daughter's recovery, he walked down quaint Charing Cross Road, going into one bookshop after another to look at the history sections. He went into Foyles, Waterstone's, and several old-book dealers looking for old texts on the Middle East, fueling his old desire to study Hebrew and Aramaic.

He had prawn curry for lunch at an Indian restaurant near Leicester Square, then returned through Covent Garden, stopping off at the market to buy a bunch of sage at a flower stand; Constance had told him that it represented wishes for health and a long life, highly appropriate for Margarida. He came out in front of the British Museum and, since he still had an hour and a half to kill, decided to take a peek inside.

He went through the main entrance, on Great Russell Street, and headed for the Egyptian art collection, one of the museum's jewels. Wandering through the obelisks and strange statues of Isis and Amon, he only stopped when he came to a dark, shiny slab of stone with three series of symbols etched into its smooth surface. They were messages from long-lost civilizations that had traveled through time until that moment, bringing Thomas, at that exact time and place, news of a world that no longer existed. The Rosetta stone.

He left the museum twenty minutes before visiting hours and was soon at the hematology unit's isolation area, holding the bunch of sage. He approached the nurse on duty and asked to see Margarida. After consulting the computer, she got up and came to the door. "Follow me, please," she said, heading down the corridor. "Dr. Penrose wants to talk to you."

Thomas followed her to Dr. Penrose's office. She was short and took small, quick steps. She stopped, knocked on the door, and opened it.

"Doctor, Mr. Thomas Noronha is here." Thomas smiled when he heard the British pronunciation of his name.

"Come in," came a voice from inside.

The nurse left and Thomas went in, smiling. Penrose stood from behind his desk, a heavy, slow figure, with a serious face and leaden eyes.

"You wanted to talk to me?" Thomas said.

Penrose motioned for him to take a seat on the sofa and sat down beside him with his body tilted forward, as if he was about to stand at any moment, and took a deep breath. "I'm afraid I have bad news."

The dark expression on his face seemed to say everything. Thomas's legs weakened and his heart beat wildly. "My daughter . . ." he stammered.

"I'm sorry to break the news to you, but we've got the worst-case scenario on our hands," said Penrose. "She's picked up some kind of bacteria and is in critical condition."

• • •

With lackluster eyes and a red nose, Constance stood gazing through the window into Margarida's room, sobbing quietly, her hand pressed to her mouth. Thomas hugged her and they stood there looking at their daughter lying in her bed on the other side of the glass. Margarida's head was shiny and bald, and her sleep was restless as she hovered between life and death. Nurses scurried about, and Penrose appeared a little later. After checking on Margarida and giving the nurses new instructions, he went to speak to her terrified parents.

"Will she survive, Doctor?" Constance blurted out.

"We're doing what we can," said Penrose, his expression grave. "But the situation is very serious. Her new marrow still hasn't had time to mature, and she doesn't have any immunity. You'll have to prepare yourselves for the worst."

Thomas and Constance could not leave the window. If she had to die, they decided, it wasn't going to be alone. Her parents would be as close to her as possible. They spent the afternoon and then the entire night glued to the window. A nurse brought them chairs and they sat there in agony, their eyes fixed on their daughter.

Sometime around four in the morning they noticed a sudden flurry of movement and got up from their chairs, concerned. Margarida, who had been tossing and turning in feverish sleep for quite some time, was now motionless, her face serene, and a nurse hurried off to call the doctor on duty. On the other side of the window everything took place without sound, as if Thomas and Constance were watching a silent movie, but a horror movie, so gruesome that they were both trembling with fear. The worst had arrived.

The doctor came quickly, looking groggy, as if he'd just woken up. He bent over Margarida, checked her temperature, pulse, pupils, and a machine she was hooked up to, then talked to the nurses for a few minutes. When he was about to leave, one of the nurses pointed at the window where her parents were, and seemed to be telling him he'd have to break the news. After a slight hesitation, he came out to talk to them.

"I'm Dr. Hackett," he said awkwardly.

Thomas embraced his wife tightly.

"I'm so sorry. . . ."

Thomas's mouth opened and closed without emitting a single sound. Horrified, paralyzed, incapable of speech, so disoriented that he couldn't feel his eyes welling with tears, his knees going weak, and his heart pounding wildly, he saw the expression of compassion in the doctor's eyes and finally understood that it bore brutal news. His worst nightmare had become real; life was no more than a fragile breath, a fleeting instant of light in the eternal darkness of time. His small world had become unbearably poor, and he had lost forever the purity and honesty he so loved in Margarida's innocent face. And in that moment of perplexity, in the split second between the shock of the news and the explosion of suffering, he was surprised to find that instead of outrage at the cruel betrayal of fate, all he felt was a tremendous, awful longing for the little girl he had lost, the deep, painful nostalgia of a father who knows there was never a daughter as beautiful as his.

"Pink dreams, my darling."

Chapter 23

There is no pain greater than that of losing a child. Thomas and Constance were disoriented for months following Margarida's death. They were uninterested in things, alien to life, and gave in to a sick indifference. Shutting themselves off from the world, they sought consolation in each other, revisiting common memories, sharing emotions rescued from oblivion, and in this process of mutual comfort, in which they folded themselves into a cocoon of their own, they grew close. Almost without noticing, as if Thomas's infidelity had now become absurdly irrelevant, a faraway event of which they had only a vague, insignificant memory, they started living together again.

Those were hard times for both of them in their small apartment. Every corner held a memory, every space a story, every object an instant. They spent weeks pacing in front of their daughter's room but didn't dare go inside. They still weren't prepared for it, so they just stared at the door and feared what was behind it. It was as if there was an insurmountable barrier there, the passage to a lost world, a magical place suspended in time, whose spell they were afraid of breaking. They didn't want to face the reality of the deserted room, now a symbol for the daughter they had lost.

When they finally opened the door and came face-to-face with the dolls lying on Margarida's bed, her books lining the shelves, and clothes neatly folded in her drawers, as if everything had just been tidied, they felt like time travelers. Something indefinable hung in the air, a smell, a feeling, an atmosphere, untouched and painfully reminiscent of Margarida's youthful essence. Overwhelmed with emotion, they fled the room and resumed avoiding it. How terrible it was to live like that, heavy with nostalgia and haunted by memories. They suffered in the apartment, and they suffered away from it.

The days followed one another in a directionless flow, existence was hollow, life didn't seem to make any sense.

They gradually became aware that they had to do something, change the course of things, stop the descent into the abyss. One day, sitting on the sofa in silence, sick with depression, considering the dead-end street that circumstances had cast them into, they made a decision. They were going to leave the past behind. But in order to do so they needed a project, a direction, a guiding light, and they quickly realized their salvation consisted of two things.

A new child and a new home.

With the money from the foundation they bought a small house by the sea in Santo Amaro de Oeiras; and they waited for a baby. Oddly, they both discovered they wanted a child just like Margarida, with the joy and generosity which their daughter had displayed in abundance. Their desire for a baby was like the desire to erase a bad dream, as if through it their lost daughter could finally return to her loved ones.

Margarida's death led Thomas to reflect on his professional integrity. He had sold his honor for money to save his daughter's life, but everything that had happened made him feel like he was being punished for the shameful decision he had been obliged to make, as if it were all a severe lesson from God, a test of his honesty, a moral trial that he had failed terribly. This conclusion sent him back to the investigation he had carried out for the foundation. Restless, perturbed by the idea that he had not fulfilled his duties, he thought long and hard. He found himself reading the contract over and over, back to front, going over every clause with a magnifying glass, weighing the words, looking for loopholes, weaknesses. He even went as far as to ask Daniel, a cousin of Constance's and a lawyer, to take a look at the document for him. He swore to himself that if he could get out of his contract, not even the very real fear of what the foundation was capable of would stop him from telling the truth.

He had now convinced himself that his daughter's death had been a punishment for his mistake. But he couldn't burden Constance and their new life with a million-dollar debt. He didn't have the money it would cost to break his silence.

There were two truths he found himself obliged to suppress. One was the objective truth, the ontological truth, the historical truth itself, the truth beyond which everything else was false: the fact that the man who had discovered America was called Colonna, was a Portuguese nobleman of Jewish and Italian extraction, and had conducted a secret mission for King John II of Portugal. This truth had sat in obscurity for five centuries and seemed destined to remain there. The second truth was the moral truth, the subjective truth, the truth of one who only feels comfortable with the truth beyond which everything else is a lie. This was the terrain of ethics, of guiding principles, the values that give form to honesty, integrity, the idea that there is an intrinsic relationship between honesty and integrity. Silencing this moral truth was what hurt him the most. He felt the lie like a knife tearing through everything he believed in, destroying the ethics he had built his life on. What most tormented him was this betrayal of his conscience.

He felt as if he'd prostituted himself. He was miserable, soiled, and indignant. For the first time he became aware that even he was capable of sacrificing the truth for a price. In a way, he identified with the dilemma King John II had been faced with five hundred years before. He imagined the Perfect Prince sitting on the wall of São Jorge Castle, near the olive trees in front of the royal residence, with Lisbon at his feet, mulling over his own choices. There was land to the west and Asia to the east. He would have liked to have had both, but he knew he could only have one. Which should he choose? Which should he sacrifice? He too had found himself at a crossroads and had been forced to make a choice. And he had. Columbus had been his confidentiality agreement, and Asia, his Margarida.

But Thomas wasn't happy with his choice.

King John had only compromised the truth for as long as was necessary to get Asia. His greatest confidant, Rui de Pina, had later taken it upon himself to correct the facts when he thought the truth no longer posed a threat to the survival of Portugal's strategy; and were it not for the intervention of King Manuel, *Chronicle of King D. John II* would have told another story. But Thomas didn't have a Rui de Pina to help him, or someone who could write him another *Codex 632* in which the truth was revealed beneath the deceitful alterations. He felt as if his hands were tied, shackled by fraud, bent under the weight of the condition he had accepted; a lie had won and the truth was defeated.

He didn't know why, but at that instant he recalled the first time he'd had to give in, the first compromise Moliarti had forced him to make, the first time he'd lowered his principles. Sitting on a bench in the cloister at the Jerónimos Monastery, Moliarti had urged him to go to Toscano's house against his will to lie to the widow in order to get the information they needed. It had been a small lie, insignificant in fact, but it was the first step along the path he had taken, the first tilt in the terrain that had quickly become a precipice.

He also remembered a flame that had illuminated him back in the cloister for a few fleeting moments, a cry that had echoed in his conscience—violent, audacious, and tempestuous. It had been an instant of lucidity quickly silenced by the voice of greed.

The Fernando Pessoa poem. It was written on his tomb in the Jerónimos Monastery, etched into stone for eternity. Thomas strained to remember it, and the letters became words and the words became ideas and gained meaning and splendor:

TO BE GREAT, be whole: exclude
Nothing, exaggerate nothing that is you.
Be whole in everything. Put all you are

Into the smallest thing you do.
The whole moon will then gleam in every pool,
Because it rides so high.

He repeated the poem over and over under his breath and felt the lost flame flare up again, at first a faraway flicker, but soon it grew stronger, lighting his heart, leaping up as his voice grew, spreading, setting fire to his soul.

He shouted. "'*Be whole.*' I will. '*Be whole in everything.*' I will. '*Put all you are into the smallest thing you do.*' I will. '*Exclude nothing, exaggerate nothing that is you.*' I won't. '*The whole moon will then gleam in every pool because it rides so high.*' It will."

He had made his decision.

Thomas sat in front of his computer and stared at the empty screen. The first thing that occurred to him was that he needed another name. Perhaps a pseudonym. No, I need someone who will agree to be my Rui de Pina. Hmm . . . but who? A famous historian. No, come to think of it, it can't be a historian. That would be too risky, since the connection could be established too easily. I need someone different, outside of the system, someone who will agree to lend his or her name to the truth I have to reveal. Yes, that's it. But who? Well, I'll work that out later. My first priority now is to figure out how I'm going to tell the story. The contract prohibits me from writing essays and articles, or giving interviews and press conferences. But what if I put it all in a novel? That's not a bad idea, is it? The contract doesn't say anything about novels. I'll always be able to claim it's fiction.

It is fiction. And besides, it won't be published in my name, will it? The author will be someone else. My Rui de Pina. A novelist. I like that: a novelist. Or, come to think of it, why not a journalist? That works. A journalist. They deal with the construction of reality on a daily basis. Hmm . . . The best thing would be a journalist who also writes novels; there are a few around. Maybe I'll be able to convince one of them to write it with me. Anyway, I'll worry about that later.

There's time. For now I'm going to concentrate on what I have to tell, the reality that I'm going to put in a novel, the fiction I'm going to use to tell the truth, to rewrite history. I'll change the characters' names, of course, and I'll only write what I saw, experienced, and discovered. Nothing more. Well . . . perhaps with the exception of an introductory chapter. After all, it all begins with Professor Toscano's death, and I didn't see that, did I? I'll have to use my imagination for that. But I know he died drinking a glass of mango juice in his hotel room in Rio de Janeiro. These are facts. The rest, the way things happened, is a matter of imagination. All I need is a place to start.

This is what Thomas Noronha thought as he sat in his chair gazing at the computer screen as if in a trance, giddy with the sweet possibility of releasing the fury pent up in his soul. He raised his hands and, guided by a redeeming impulse of truth—like a conductor leading his orchestra in a grand symphony—finally set fingers to keyboard and let the melody of his story dance across the screen.

Four.

The old historian couldn't know that he only had four minutes left to live.

Acknowledgments

Christopher Columbus's origins are still shrouded in mystery, tied up in intricate knots that allow us only a hazy glimpse of a highly complex character. The web of secrets seems to have been spun by none other than the great explorer himself, who deliberately and systematically concealed information about his past and left in his wake a long trail of contradictory clues and ambiguous phrases. His reasons for doing so are still not clear and continue to spark intense speculation among historians and laypersons alike.

Making the nebulous features of this man—whose face no one knows—even harder to see is the fact that many documents that might have clarified matters have been lost. This is further aggravated by the fact that most of the texts that have survived are not originals but copies, which may or may not have been adulterated. As if this were not enough, some documents have proven to be skillful falsifications, while there are doubts about the authenticity of many others. For this reason there are few certainties, countless contradictions, and many puzzles surrounding the details of Columbus's life, offering fertile terrain for speculation about who the man who discovered America really was.

I would like to stress that, although inspired by facts and based on authentic documents, which can be found in a number of libraries, this is a work of fiction. The topics covered in this novel come from a wide range of sources, starting with bibliographical ones. The list of works consulted is so extensive and varied that I have not included it here so as not to unnecessarily abuse readers' patience. I shall merely name the most relevant authors on the most controversial aspects of Columbus's origins and life: Luís Albuquerque, Moses Bensabat Amzalak, Enrique Bayerri y Bertomeu, Armando Cortesão, Arthur d'Ávila, Ferreira de Serpa, Jane Frances Almer, Alexandre Gaspar da Naia, Jorge Gomes Fernandes, Vasco Graça Moura, Sarah Leibovici, Luiz Lencastre e Távora, Salvador Madariaga, Mascarenhas Barreto, Ramón Menéndez Pidal, Patrocínio Ribeiro, Pestana Júnior, Alfredo Pinheiro Marques, Luciano Rey Sánchez, Santos Ferreira, Maurizio Tagliattini, Gabriel Verd Martorell, and Simon Wiesenthal.

Many friends have directly or indirectly contributed to this novel, although, naturally, they had nothing to do with the fictional aspects of the narrative. I am indebted to João Paulo Oliveira e Costa, professor of the Age of Discovery at the Universidade Nova de Lisboa; Diogo Pires Aurélio, director of the Biblioteca Nacional de Lisboa; Paola Caroli, director of the Archivio di Stato di Genova; Pedro Corrêa do Lago, president of the Biblioteca Nacional do Rio de Janeiro, and one of the world's most important collectors of original manuscripts; Ambassador António Tanger, who opened the doors of Rio de Janeiro's Palácio de São Clemente for me; António da Graça, father and son, and Paulino Bastos, my guides in Rio de Janeiro; Helena Cordeiro, who provided me with a window on Jerusalem; Rabbi Boaz Pash, the last Kabbalist in Lisbon; Roberto Bachmann, president of the Associação Portuguesa de Estudos Judaicos; Alberto Sismondini, professor of Italian at the Universidade de Coimbra, an expert in Ligurian languages, and an inestimable help with the Genoese dialect; Doris Fabris-Bucheli, my delightful guide through Lapa Palace Hotel, in Lisbon; João Cruz Alves and António Silvestre, gatekeepers of the mysteries of Quinta da Regaleira, in Sintra; Mário Oliveira and Conceição Trigo, cardiologists at Hospital de Santa Marta, in Lisbon;

Miguel Palha, physician and founder of the Associação Portuguesa de Portadores de Trissomia 21, and his Teresa; Dina, Francisco, and Rosa Gomes, who shared their experiences with me; and Rene Alegria, Howard Morhaim, and Alison Entrekin for making possible the American edition of this novel.

But as always, my first reader and most important critic was Florbela, the guiding star that led me through the intricate paths of the narrative.

A Word from the Translator

Three people have been of inestimable help in the preparation of this translation. I would like to thank Judith Yalon for her patient explanations of Jewish and Hebrew language and culture and revision of chapter 14, Daniela Travaglini for her eagle eye and words of wisdom as my first reader, and José Rodrigues dos Santos himself for his willingness and availability to help with anything and everything.

ALISON ENTREKIN